MW01167451

BEULAH'S GRASP
VOIDBRINGER CAMPAIGN BOOK 4

M. ALLEN HALL

For Amelia

Prologue

Madison rushed into the kitchen. Logan was packing up his notebook and dice.

"What happened?" Madison asked, excitement in her voice. "Did you leave Beulah? Are you coming to find us?"

Logan waggled his eyebrows and chuckled. "Oh, no, no, no. Valduin is fully committed right now."

Madison groaned. "You are totally evil, aren't you?"

Logan shrugged. "Maybe. Maybe not. You'll just have to wait and see. It kind of depends on how long it takes for you two to get to me. Tick tock!" He gave her a mischievous grin.

"Amelia! It's our turn! Get down here!" Madison shouted over her shoulder. She sat down at the table and said, "After all that whining about Valduin not wanting to be evil, you certainly seem to be enjoying it."

"That was back when he had a choice," Logan lectured. "Now, his memory has been modified, he's charmed, he's been given a powerful new item, and he's been promised revenge. *Revenge*," he repeated with grim enthusiasm. "He's in this one hundred percent."

Madison narrowed her eyes at her brother and huffed. "Fine. We are still going to find you and get you free of Beulah. Whether you want us to or not. You better finish that history project quick because we are going to need you back here soon." She turned toward the stairs again.

"Amelia! Let's go!"

1

"Adelaide," Rose whispered.

She waited.

"Adelaide," she stated, a bit louder this time. She glanced back and forth between her unconscious friend and the commotion outside. She chewed her lower lip as she considered her options.

Another moment passed.

The commotion grew louder.

"Adelaide Bellamie! It is time to wake up!" she hissed, shaking her friend by the shoulder. She raised her other hand and fired a beam of searing, white energy through the open mouth of the cave. The guiding bolt passed through the ten-foot-tall, spectral guardian that she had summoned to protect the cave. The magical attack slammed into its target, though she had no idea what the thing was. In the dim light radiating from her guardian, Rose could see only a writhing mass of armored plates and skittering legs. The monster let out a screech, an ear-rending cacophony of dissonant tones, as the guardian carved into it again with its shimmering sword.

Adelaide sat up with a jolt. She poured with sweat; her breaths were rushed and ragged. Her eyes locked onto the terror outside the cave, which glowed with the residual energy of Rose's magical attack. Adelaide pushed herself backward, scrambling away from the indistinct horror which was once again rushing toward the cave mouth. She reached the wall at the end of the cave, her back slamming into the cold stone.

"Rose," she whimpered. She could see the outline of her halfling friend between herself and the monster. "Where are we? What is that? What's going on?"

Rose stood up, her back to Adelaide, facing the monster that seemed intent on reaching them. The guardian attacked the creature again, forcing it to retreat, but Rose worried that her magical protector would soon run out of energy.

"We're in a cave. In a desert. I'll explain; just give me a second."

Rose began speaking in Halfling, prayers rushing out of her and into the night. Adelaide could not understand the words, but she watched as Rose raised her hands in front of herself. The prayers grew louder until she was shouting out into the darkness beyond the cave. Her hands burst into flames. Flickering light lit the cave for only a moment before Rose slapped her hands together above her head.

The flames flared brighter. The sound of Rose's hands clapping together was echoed by a terrific explosion outside the cave. Adelaide had to shield her dark-adjusted eyes from the blinding light of a column of fire that filled the area beyond the cave's mouth.

Rose did not flinch. She stood, hands held together above her head, and watched her divine flames rain down on the terrible monstrosity. With another polyphonic screech, the beast skittered away into the darkness.

Adelaide opened her eyes as the sounds of the creature's retreat faded into the night. She could only see Rose's outline, the shadow burned into her retinas by the power of Rose's spell. "Rose?" she whispered. "Are we okay? Are you okay?" She felt Rose slump against the wall next to her. Rose's amulet began to glow with soft, golden light, showing Adelaide the space around them for the first time.

"Yeah. We're okay," the halfling cleric said with an exhausted smile. "How do you feel?"

"Terrible. Terrified. Confused," Adelaide answered. She rubbed the back of her neck. "Where are we? How did we get here? What was that thing? Where's Val?"

"Oh boy. All the questions at once," Rose replied with a weak chuckle. She took a deep breath. "I'm not sure where we are. The magic that I used to get us out of the Ebon Keep would have brought us to our home plane, but we could be anywhere on the plane. We landed in a desert, but that's all I know right now."

"How long was I, uh, gone?" Adelaide asked, her voice falling to a whisper.

Rose patted her hand. "A few hours. Long enough for me to drag you through the desert and find this cave."

Adelaide nodded and stared through the back of Rose's guardian into the dark desert beyond. "What did I miss?" she asked.

"We were in the Ebon Keep. Stela and Tabitha recognized Anise's soul in that one little marble. They attacked us. We killed one of them; Tabitha, I think. Stela escaped with the soul spheres. Then Misery came in. You remember him, right?"

Adelaide nodded along with Rose's story. She remembered all of this. She snarled at the mention of Misery's name. That was as much answer as Rose's question required.

Rose continued, "Misery conjured a river of lava, dividing the room. You rushed him. That's when he killed you. I don't know how he did it. He just said a single word, and you dropped."

"*Toodles*," Adelaide growled. That word had been echoing through her mind ever since. "What happened after I died?"

"Well, we tried to get together so we could escape using the item that Beulah had given us, but Misery kept blocking our magic. I tried to bring you back to life right away, but he blocked that too. I picked you up, told Valduin to use Beulah's item to escape, and then banished us back here. I had no control over where we would land. My magic isn't as strong as the spell Beulah used. We are lucky we didn't land in the water somewhere. When Tabitha banished me, I was in the ocean. I would have drowned if I had been left there."

"Yeah, I remember you getting banished," Adelaide said. "Val told me to just keep hitting Tabitha until you came back. It worked."

"So, that's pretty much it," Rose finished with a shrug. "We landed in the desert. I carried you here, and I brought you back." She narrowed her eyes at her friend. "Now, I have a question. What do you remember from the other side? You were there for a while."

Adelaide sat quietly, staring out of the cave. The sky had a hint of purple in it now, the first sign of the coming dawn. "An endless sea of stars. Above. Below. And through it all, Misery's voice. That one word echoing through the void. I just floated. Then I noticed that some of the stars were moving. One of them was getting closer, but it still seemed forever away. That's when I heard your voice. Your words, your prayer, and *his* one word fighting for my attention. Fighting for my soul. I chose yours, and I woke up in here."

She turned to look at Rose. A weak smile crept across her face. "Thank you."

Rose leaned against Adelaide and hugged the human's arm. "Any time," she said. She settled back against the wall again and furrowed her brow. "Actually, not quite any time. Any time that I've got the diamonds to do it. Which is not now."

"I'm afraid to ask," Adelaide said, "but what about Val? Did he get out of there?"

Rose grimaced. "He used that enchanted glass ball that Beulah gave us. I watched him leave before I brought us back."

"Well, I guess that news is as good as I could expect," Adelaide said. "Alright, what's our plan? Get moving? What was that thing out there?"

"Yes, we need to get moving," Rose agreed. "I don't know what it was, but it looked big and angry. Well, it looked big, and it sounded angry. Let's get out of here before it comes back." She got to her feet, and she helped Adelaide up from where she had been squatting against the wall.

Adelaide groaned and stretched her legs. "Dying is the worst," she moaned.

Rose gave a grim chuckle, but she said nothing. She packed up the few things that she had taken out of her bag the night before. Adelaide turned her pack over with her foot. Before she picked it up, her eyes went wide. Her head whipped around, searching the small cave in a panic.

"Where's my hammer?" she asked, her voice a desperate whine. She already knew the answer.

Rose grimaced. "I'm sorry, Adelaide. I couldn't carry it. Just getting you and your pack was hard enough." She stepped back from Adelaide, expecting an angry outburst.

Rose was surprised, however, when Adelaide merely slumped her shoulders. The human woman scuffed one boot against the hard ground and made no reply. She hefted her pack onto one shoulder, turned toward the lightening sky outside the cave, and walked out into the morning.

The morning air of the desert was cooler than Rose expected. She did not know much about deserts, but, compared to the heat that had been radiating from the sand when they had arrived, the chill morning breeze was a welcome surprise. The wind kicked up into a brief gust. Coarse sand sprayed into the halfling's face, forcing her to close her eyes.

Adelaide took in their surroundings. The cracked earth of the desert spread out from the cliff that held their cave. The horizon was broken by boulders and tall piles of rock worn smooth by eons of blowing sand. Green and purple plants, all tending toward fat and spiky, dotted the terrain. Scraggly, leafless clusters of thorned branches filled in much of the space between the cacti. Everything not made of stone was sharp and hostile in this desolate place.

"Any idea what was attacking us? Did it leave tracks?" Rose asked.

Adelaide inspected the ground outside the cave. Despite the hard, stone surface, she could see the areas where the monstrous creature had been. Many hundreds of sharp feet had chipped away at the dry ground. Its trail headed out of sight away from the cave.

"Which way did it go?" Rose's questions kept coming. She trusted Adelaide's instincts when it came to tracking and understanding monsters. "Do you think it will come back?"

Adelaide shrugged and pointed lazily in the direction of the creature's path. She was gauging the position of the sun now, which was cresting the horizon.

"Do you know where we are?" Rose continued her questions. "Do you know how to get us home?"

Adelaide shook her head. She turned back toward Rose. Her every movement was sluggish. "I don't know any more than you do. I've never been anywhere like this." Even her speech was slower than usual.

"Have you heard of anywhere like this, though?" Rose pushed, her voice brimming with frustration as she tried to get Adelaide to engage.

"I don't know," Adelaide mumbled, looking down at her feet.

"It's a desert, clearly," Rose said. She struggled to keep her voice even. She found herself torn between the urgency of escaping this place and the desire not to compound Adelaide's stress. Rose knew the strain that resurrection placed on the body. "Could this be the Enchanted Dunes? You told me about that place once. How would we get home if we are there?"

Adelaide cocked her head at this suggestion. She looked around again as if seeing the desert for the first time. "If this is the Enchanted Dunes," she murmured in reply, "we are as good as dead."

"What's wrong with you?" Amelia asked. "If you are going to act all dejected like that, I'll go do something else."

"What?" Madison looked offended. "I'm just trying to roleplay the shock of being resurrected. Didn't you do the same after you died? I know Logan did. Logan has been gloomy for like four levels, and you didn't get huffy with him about it."

"Yeah, well, when it's only the two of us, your sulking is really depressing. Don't force me to carry the entire story forward with you along for the ride." Amelia narrowed her eyes at Madison. "Besides, what you saw on the other side wasn't even that bad. Not as bad as Valduin being held prisoner and getting yelled at by Beulah."

"Okay, that's fair," Madison accepted. "Adelaide will cheer up soon. Sound good? Now, how are we going to figure out where we are? And where Valduin is? And how to get to him? I feel like we are in a load of trouble."

"If we assume that we are in the Enchanted Dunes," Amelia said, "then all we need to do is head east until we reach the Sandgate Mountains, right? Then we can try to find Westray or Khal Durum or somewhere else that we know."

"It might not be that easy," Madison said. "The little bit of lore that Adelaide knows about that desert is that you need magic to get across it. Do you have any magic for that? I sure don't."

Amelia flipped through the rulebook to the spells section. After a few minutes of reviewing her options, she grimaced. "Well, I can use Scrying and Sending to try to find Valduin. I'll do that tonight, as long as we don't fight that big centipede thing today. I can use Create Food and Water so we don't have to forage in the desert. Then I can use Commune to confirm where we are. Those are the easy things. Getting us out of here is going to be harder."

She stopped talking as she read some more from the book. Madison said nothing, but she smiled at the sight of her younger sister carefully reading the spell descriptions.

"I take that back. I actually have the perfect spell," Amelia said. She kept reading. "But I don't have the components! Why do the good spells always need *components*?" she whined.

"What's the spell? And what do we need? Maybe I've got something."

"Find the Path. I can figure out *exactly* how to get us back to pretty much any place we have been before," Amelia said. "The problem is that I need 'a set of divinatory tools such as bones, ivory sticks, cards, teeth, or carved runes worth one hundred gold pieces.'"

"Don't you have those tarot cards?" Madison asked, her voice rising in excitement as she remembered the cards that Amelia had used to predict the future back in Mirstone.

Amelia was not caught up in Madison's fervor. "Those are for a different spell. They only cost twenty-five gold pieces," she explained, shaking her head. "We either need to find somewhere to buy some fancier cards, or we need to find our way out of this desert on our own."

2

"Cut that out," Rose admonished her human friend. She grabbed Adelaide's wrist and pulled. Hard. Caught off guard, Adelaide dropped to one knee, coming eye-to-eye with the halfling. "We are going to get out of here. We are going to find Valduin. We are going to free him from Beulah. We are going to get revenge on Misery. We are going to stop the Voidbringer. Got it? You with me?"

"Yeah, sure," Adelaide mumbled. Her eyes fell to the dirt between them.

"That's not good enough," Rose hissed. "I need your head in this. I need you on your game. I can't do this by myself. You want your friend back, right? You want revenge, right? *Are you with me?*" The halfling shouted the question, shaking Adelaide by the shoulders.

Adelaide met Rose's fierce gaze. A smirk tugged at the corner of her mouth. She chuckled mirthlessly. "Oh, yeah. I want revenge," she whispered.

"Good. Don't forget that. Don't for one second forget that. Now, let me figure out where we are and where we need to go." Rose released Adelaide.

The halfling dropped her pack to the ground and rooted around inside. A moment later, she stood up with the vial of holy water that Fulbert had given her during their short stay in Biastal. Rose leaned her shield against her pack as a makeshift shrine to her goddess, Selaia. Careful not to spill the precious liquid inside, she removed the glass stopper from the vial. She dipped a finger into the holy water and replaced the top of the vial, and then she kneeled and closed her eyes. By touch, she traced the rising sun symbol on her shield with the holy water while she prayed in Halfling.

"When the shadow of evil falls over my heart, Selaia will bring the light.

"When the temptation of evil touches my mind, Selaia will give me strength.

"When the corruption of evil poisons my land, Selaia will purify.

"When the power of evil threatens my home, Selaia will be my shield.

"Selaia, guide my footsteps, and my path will ever lead to you.

"Selaia, watch over me, and my soul will forever be yours."

When she finished her prayer, Rose opened her eyes. Adelaide was gone. The desert was gone. She knelt in darkness except for the golden sun shining on her shield. She could feel Selaia in the darkness. With a sigh of relief, she settled back onto her heels, comforted by that looming presence.

"Selaia, we need help. We have lost our way. We have lost our friend." She paused. There was no response. She knew that Selaia was still there, waiting.

"Are we in the desert called the Enchanted Dunes?" Rose asked.

"Yes," came the reply. Selaia spoke in a breathy whisper, but Rose could feel the power behind the voice.

"Is Valduin alive?"

"*Yes.*"

Rose nodded. She had been confident that Valduin had escaped the Ebon Keep safely, but she needed confirmation.

"Is Valduin safe?"

"*No.*" The voice was deeper this time. Rose felt it resonate in her chest. Her face fell. She was not surprised, but she was disheartened by this response.

She blinked. The darkness was gone; the desert had returned. Adelaide stood behind Rose's small shrine, looking at Rose with arms crossed and brow furrowed. She had heard the questions but not the answers.

"This is the Enchanted Dunes," Rose reported as she got to her feet. "Valduin is alive, but he is not safe."

"Like, he's in danger right now? Or generally unsafe? I mean, just being with Beulah would count as not being safe. Right?"

"You heard what I asked. I only get 'yes' or 'no' answers," Rose said with shrug.

"Could you send him a message?" Adelaide asked. "Maybe he can tell us where he is. Or maybe he can come to us somehow?"

"Of course!" Rose replied. She looked toward the horizon, her eyes shifting out of focus. "Valduin, are you still with Beulah? I got Adelaide back. We're in the Enchanted Dunes. I'm not sure how to get back to you."

Rose finished sending the message. Her eyes refocused on Adelaide. She waited.

No reply came.

"No answer," she said, struggling to hide her disappointment. "Maybe he's asleep. Or somewhere that he needs to stay quiet if he is in particular danger right now. We can try again later. Or tomorrow. I'm sure he'll be fine." She did not sound sure. "For now, we know where we are, sort of. If we head east, we are bound to find the Sandgate Mountains eventually. Let's head that way."

Adelaide shrugged. "It's as good a direction as any," she said. She picked up Rose's pack and helped the halfling load up for the trek. "And I definitely want to get away from here before that thing comes back." For a moment, she gazed into the distance in the direction that the monster's tracks led.

"Now you see me; now you don't," Adelaide recited. She set off walking toward the rising sun. Her magic pulled the thin layer of loose dirt into the footprints behind her, erasing all signs of her passage. Rose stayed close behind, and the pair wound their way through the spiked flora of the desert toward the eastern horizon.

For the rest of the morning, the women worked their way east. Once the cave where they had spent the night was out of sight, they found themselves navigating fields dotted with towering piles of broken stone. Another hour passed, and the ground became sandy. Ahead of them, dunes replaced the rock piles.

"This is where we arrived," Rose informed Adelaide. She looked north and south at the line of dunes stretching away from them in both directions. "Or, maybe it's close to where we arrived. We landed on a dune at the border of the sandy desert and the rocky desert. But it could have been any of these."

Adelaide adjusted her pack. She glanced at the sun again, which was still climbing toward the top of the sky. The day had quickly grown hot; Adelaide was thirsty from walking and hungry from the strain of resurrection. She turned in a slow circle, noting the tallest piles of rock behind them, creating an image of the horizon in her mind.

"Let's take a break," she said after a minute of mental mapping. "I need to eat. And we both need to drink before we venture into those dunes. Aren't you hot in that armor?" She looked down at Rose, whose face was bright red. Her hair was dark with sweat. Her crown had slipped down, no longer held in place by the stiff tangle of her bun.

"Wait, what?" Adelaide said in confused surprise, eyeing Rose's new accessory. "When did you get *that*? *Where* did you get that? What's happening around here?"

Rose looked up at Adelaide. She was, in fact, hot, sweaty, tired, and thirsty. She followed Adelaide's gaze to her forehead and reached up to where her circlet usually sat. Her fingers revealed that the magic circlet had changed again. In a rush of excitement, Rose dug into her pack and pulled out the diamond-encrusted hand mirror.

On her head sat an intricate crown of platinum and diamonds. The circlet's neatly braided strands of brilliant metal were now woven together into a wide band around her head. From the band, arcs of platinum formed five short peaks, each topped with a large diamond. Rose smiled and straightened the crown as she inspected it in the mirror.

"It's the circlet," Rose explained, not taking her eyes off her reflection. "It has changed a couple of times before. Remember? Valduin noticed it after I brought him back from the other side. It became more powerful then. I wonder if it is stronger now, too." She continued to inspect the item in the small mirror, holding it up to get different views of the crown. "I wish Valduin was here to tell me if its magic changed again."

Rose stiffened, still holding the mirror up in the air. "Maybe," she whispered. She closed her eyes. "*Selaia, show me our friend Valduin,*" she prayed. When she opened her eyes, they glowed with golden light, as did the mirror in her hand. She brought the mirror down from above her head, and she repeated her plea. "*Show me Valduin, so that I may know how to find him,*" she prayed.

The mirror flashed brighter, but then it went dark.

The glow faded from Rose's eyes. She sighed in disappointment. "It didn't work." The arm holding the mirror flopped to her side. "Maybe I did something wrong."

"Or maybe he resisted the spell. Or maybe he is someplace like the Ebon Keep that blocks people from seeing into it," Adelaide said. She patted Rose on the shoulder. "You can try again later. You'll find him."

Rose nodded. "Not later today, but maybe tomorrow. I've used a lot of magic today already. Besides, even if I could see him, he can't identify the crown from afar. He won't even know I'm watching."

"That was Tor's grandmother's crown, right? I wonder if it looked like this when she had it, or if they only ever knew it as that single, thin band," Adelaide commented, trying to distract her friend from the failed spell.

"We can ask her when we get out of this desert and back to Khal Durum," Rose said, her voice quickening with excitement. "I'd love to see her again. Maybe I'll send her a message when I have some extra magic at the end of the day. Not today, though. We have other things to do first."

Rose dropped her pack on the ground, laid out her bedroll, and placed their empty water skins on it. She held her amulet and said a prayer for nourishment. With a light thump, a pile of food appeared on the bedroll. The waterskins were full to bursting. Adelaide dropped to her knees beside her friend.

"Food!" she roared, diving into the pile and devouring fruit, bread, and meat at a nauseating pace.

Rose giggled and sat down next to the human. "You'll make yourself sick," she teased.

"With everything else going on, I didn't realize how hungry I was," Adelaide mumbled around a mouthful of jerky. "I feel like I haven't eaten for days. Resurrection sure takes it out of you."

"You were only dead for a few hours," Rose said. "I think this is just you." She laughed again.

Adelaide paused in her aggressive feasting to narrow her eyes at Rose, but she made no retort. Instead, she grinned, shrugged, and took a large bite of an apple.

Thirst slaked and hunger sated, Adelaide and Rose set off into the sandy desert. Adelaide kept an eye on the sky to maintain their course as they wound their way between the towering dunes. The sun burned down on them. A dry wind whipped grit up into their faces. The sand under their feet shifted with each step, making the uncomfortable journey even more arduous.

For hours they walked, stumbled, and trudged through the desert. At least, it felt like hours. Despite the creeping fatigue in their legs and backs, the tightening of their skin in the intense sunlight, and the sweat soaking ever deeper into the padding beneath their armor, the sun appeared to be fixed at the top of the sky.

Adelaide stopped. She stretched her back and groaned. She wiped sweat out of her eyes. "How long have we been going?" she asked.

Rose stopped next to her friend. She glanced up at the sun, though only for a moment, as the bright light hurt her eyes. "I don't know. It feels like days."

"I'm sure we've been out here for hours," Adelaide said. "It really should be into the afternoon by now. But the sun is still straight up. I'm not even sure which way is east anymore. I need the sun to move a bit to give me some sense of direction."

Rose grunted, making a sound somewhere between frustration and agreement. "Let me go up this dune. Maybe I'll be able to see something," she said. She let her pack slide off her shoulders. "I wish Valduin was here to make us fly," she mumbled. "For now, I'll just jump." At that last word, she felt the power of her magic ring of jumping wash up her arm and down into her legs. With three terrific bounds, she ascended a tall dune. At the top, she turned in a slow circle, taking in the expanse of the Enchanted Dunes around her.

The sea of sand stretched to the horizon in every direction. There was no sign of the rocky landscape where they had started this journey, nor was there any indication of the mountain range that they hoped to reach to escape the desert.

"See anything?" Adelaide shouted up to the halfling.

"Sand," Rose called back. "Lots and lots of sand," she mumbled to herself. She turned another circle before sliding down the dune.

"Alright, let's keep going. It could be days before we reach the mountains, even if we are going exactly the right way. We might be out here a long time," Adelaide said. She adjusted her pack on her shoulders and trudged forward.

Rose did not follow. "Do you hear that?" she said, her voice a tight whisper. Her head whipped from side to side, checking the dunes around them.

Adelaide stopped, listening intently. She cocked her head at the sound of shifting sand. She turned toward the dune that Rose had climbed.

The dune exploded. Erupting out of the ground was a gargantuan, sand-colored centipede. Adelaide screamed and dove to the ground as the leading end of the monstrous bug barreled toward her.

"Well, that didn't take long," Amelia muttered. Her mouth fell open when the monster's miniature was placed on the table. "Wait, it's *how* big?" she cried.

"It's gargantuan," Madison answered. "So, it's *really* big."

"But look at it!" Amelia continued. "Okay. Okay. What's the plan? You rage and I shoot Guiding Bolts from the back? Not terribly creative, but it will probably work."

"I'm not sure Adelaide is ready for that," Madison said. She pursed her lips, looking thoughtful.

"What?"

"She just died. She isn't ready to risk death again so soon."

"What." Amelia sounded stunned.

"Let's roll Initiative and see how things look," Madison said. "But don't be surprised if Adelaide doesn't dive right into danger."

"We *talked* about this," Amelia growled. "I thought you were in this with me for real."

"We talked about *revenge*," Madison pointed out. "Adelaide wants that. For now, though, she might just want to stay alive."

3

The immense body of the monster, a hundred feet long with hundreds of wriggling legs beneath, flew over Adelaide. Torrents of sand poured from between the armored segments of the beast as it exploded out of the dune and into the air. It slammed into a dune on the other side of the women and turned its head, or at least its leading end, toward them. Its tail end wrapped around the dune, sand still raining down from gaps in its chitinous exoskeleton.

Six triangular flaps spread out like flower petals to reveal the creature's face. In the short moment that Rose had to study the creature, she saw that it had no eyes. The lower half of the face spread apart to reveal rows of jagged teeth. The face retracted slightly before shooting forward and releasing a geyser of foul-smelling mucus, covering Adelaide and Rose in yellow-green goo.

Rose managed to bring her shield up and protect herself from the spray. The smell was rancid, but she ignored it. She grabbed her amulet and prepared to attack the monster.

Adelaide was not so lucky. She looked up from where she had fallen to the ground and took a face full of the horrible, goopy, sticky secretion. She retched twice, her body wracked by waves of nausea. She pulled herself onto her hands and knees as bilious vomit poured from her mouth.

"Rose!" she shouted between heaves. "Help!" Vomit. "I can't—" Vomit. "Stop!" Vomit. A pool of green liquid spread out across the sand beneath her, covering her hands. Her long braid hung next to her face, soaked first with the mucus spray of the monster and now with the contents of Adelaide's stomach.

Rose hesitated. She watched in horror as the bug skittered forward toward the incapacitated human. The monstrosity let out another ear-rending, multi-toned roar, so loud that it shook avalanches of sand down from the surrounding dunes. Rose covered her ears, but she could not pull her eyes away as the creature reared up above Adelaide. The six appendages that wreathed its head snapped together into a single, massive spike.

It looked like it was going to drive that point down into Adelaide's back.

It did not get the chance.

"Banish this foul beast from my sight!" screeched Rose, her voice trembling with terror.

There was a faint *whoosh* as air filled the space evacuated by the gargantuan creature. The bug disappeared.

The desert was silent but for the steady trickles of sand still tumbling from the nearby dunes and Adelaide's heavy breathing. Rose rushed to her friend's side.

"Adelaide! Adelaide! Are you okay? Can you move?"

Adelaide groaned and sat back on her heels. "Yeah, I can move. You got rid of it?"

"Not for long," Rose replied. She pulled on Adelaide's pack, forcing the human to get to her feet. "It'll be back very soon. We need to *go*."

Adelaide's eyes grew wide at the news that the monster was not gone forever. She shook what liquid she could from her hands. Her exposed skin still burned from the creature's foul secretion. "We're running?" she asked. "Do you want me to cover our tracks again?"

"I don't know. I don't know," Rose whined nervously. She looked back and forth between the hole in the dune that the bug had emerged from and the spot where she had banished it from. "But we are running out of time. You used your magic earlier, right? And it still found us. What do we do? How do we get out of here?"

"Like, out of this desert? I have no idea!" Adelaide replied, her voice rising with frustration. "The dunes go on forever. I have no idea which way is east. We haven't seen any other plants or animals since we entered the dunes. And it's been high noon for hours! All I know about this place is that you need to use *magic* to get through it. And we don't have any!"

Rose's mind raced. "How did it find us?" she asked, struggling to keep her voice under control.

"I don't know," Adelaide whimpered in reply.

"Think! How did it find us?"

"I don't *know!*" Adelaide shouted. "I covered our tracks with magic. It shouldn't have been able to follow us." Adelaide's shoulders slumped. She hung her head.

Rose punched Adelaide in the thigh, startling her out of her despondency. "It didn't need tracks! It doesn't have eyes! Did you see?"

"No. *My* eyes were full of bug snot," Adelaide shot back.

"It must be able to feel us walking. Or hear us walking! Quick! Get to the top of that dune!" Rose pointed as she took off, leaping toward a nearby hill of sand.

Adelaide cocked her head. She did not understand Rose's plan, but she trusted her friend. She followed, sprinting to keep up with the bounding halfling. She scrambled up to the top of the dune. Rose was seated in the sand.

"*Sit*," Rose hissed. She grabbed her amulet. "*Selaia, grant us your cloak of silence*," she whispered in Halfling.

The centipede reappeared in the same position in which it had been before Rose had banished it. Moving as if no time had been lost, it drove the spike covering its face into the ground where Adelaide had lain a minute earlier. Sand sprayed up in a geyser around its head as the spike drove several feet into the ground. After the impact, the head pulled up and the collar snapped open again. The beast let out another roar.

At least, that is what the women assumed it did. Within the bubble of silence at the top of their dune, they watched the creature whip its head back and forth, searching. They could imagine the dissonant screams of rage coming from the enormous centipede and the crunching of skittering legs shifting the sand beneath the monster. But they could not hear any of it.

The centipede opened its mouth again. Rose could see sand running down the nearby dunes with the force of its roar. She could see the collar rhythmically opening and contracting, though not completely covering the creature's face. When it roared again, she could see rows of teeth. It had long, jagged teeth that were surprisingly white against the light, sandy brown of the monster's face and the black of its throat. Teeth that looked like they could be used as a sword or a dagger or a piton.

Rose leapt to her feet. She looked down at Adelaide. The human did not take her eyes off the bug; her hands were fixed to the leather straps that held the handaxes on her belt. Her eyes were bloodshot from retching, and her hair still dripped with vomit.

Rose stepped behind Adelaide. She pulled the human's shield off her pack. She undid the straps that held Fiend's Lament in place.

Adelaide looked over her shoulder, her brow furrowed in confusion.

Rose pushed the shield and the weapon into Adelaide's lap. She mouthed, "I'm sorry," through the magical silence.

Adelaide jumped to her feet. She shook her head vigorously.

Rose stepped toward the bug, nodding and wincing apologetically.

Adelaide lunged forward and grabbed Rose by the collar. She shook her head again.

Rose's eyes flashed. The sounds of the centipede rushed across them again as Rose released the silence spell. "We need to kill it. I need its teeth," she said in a rushed whisper.

"*What?*" Adelaide hissed. Too loud. The sounds of the centipede searching the dunes cut off. It reared up and whipped its head, now thirty feet off the ground, in the women's direction. The collar pulled back to reveal its face again.

"Selaia will protect you," Rose said. Adelaide felt a wave of warmth wash over her as Rose invoked her goddess to ward Adelaide against death. "Now, pull yourself together," the halfling said, her voice turning stern. She pulled herself free of Adelaide's grip. "We've got work to do." Rose took off running across the top of the dune, activated her magic ring, and leapt down toward the ground, trying to put some distance between herself and her friend.

Adelaide stood frozen in place. She watched the monstrous bug turn its head slowly, tracking the sounds of Rose's movement across the sand. The creature let out a soft hiss, and its head retracted slightly. Adelaide raised one shaky hand, pointing four fingers toward the monster. The fingernails on the outstretched fingers glowed a bright white and grew into long spikes.

"Go," Adelaide whispered, and the spikes launched from her hand. They streaked through the hot desert air and slammed into the monster's face. Adelaide did not wait to watch. As soon as the magic missiles launched, she turned and sprinted down the back side of the dune, away from the centipede.

Rose reached the low point between the dunes. She turned toward the monster, preparing for another spray of rancid mucus. She watched Adelaide's attack make impact. The creature pivoted toward Adelaide. The collar snapped back into place over its face, and it dove forward into the dune that the women had been hiding on. A moment later, it erupted out the other side, though Rose could not see it. She could only see the spray of sand over the top of the hill and hear Adelaide's surprised scream.

Adelaide had gotten only halfway down the dune when the ground erupted beneath her. Her knees buckled as the armored crown of the centipede emerged between her feet, sending her flying, and screaming, through the air. She slammed into the sand at the base of the dune; it was not as soft as she thought it should be. With the wind knocked out of her, she writhed on the ground, fighting to catch her breath.

"Rose!" she wheezed. "Help!" The centipede reared up over her, blotting out the sun.

"Give me a *break*," Rose muttered. She changed course and ran toward the tail of the centipede, which was still sliding into the near side of the dune. She activated her ring to leap up onto the bug, grabbing onto one of its plates of armor.

"Selaia, destroy this monster!" Rose shouted. She reached one glowing hand between the centipede's segments and sunk her fingers into something soft underneath. She could not see the wave of black, necrotic energy spreading beneath the thick hide, but she knew it was there as the sand-colored armor faded to gray one segment at a time.

The monster released another roar, though at a higher pitch this time. With a grunt, Rose released her grip on the bug and dropped to the ground as its tail disappeared into the sand.

Adelaide scrambled to her feet. The centipede loomed over her. The human did not look up, but instead, she held out one hand to launch another barrage of magic missiles into the creature's exposed abdomen. She turned. She ran.

"Rose!" she screamed as she scrambled away. "Stop it!"

She did not get far. The centipede tracked her footsteps across the sand. In a blur of movement, it lunged forward, driving the chitinous spike that covered its face into Adelaide's back, crushing her into the ground. The wind knocked out of her again, she could not even scream out in pain. Blood dripped from her mouth as she lay gasping on the sand.

Rose had seen the head of the centipede dive out of sight behind the dune. She ran and jumped her way to the top of the mound, her feet slipping against the sand with each step. Reaching the top, she sent a bolt of energy flying from her outstretched finger into the back of the beast's head. She could see Adelaide on the ground. "Over here! Come get some!" Rose screamed at the centipede, hoping to draw its attention away from her struggling friend.

It worked. The centipede, which had opened up its collar again, pivoted toward the sound of Rose's voice. As Rose focused on the bug's head, skittering toward her, it whipped its back end out of the dune and into her side, pushing her toward the approaching mouth. The head lunged toward her, and the flaps that wreathed its head slammed shut, attempting to catch her. She dove, pushed, and twisted away, barely avoiding being trapped inside the creature's head with that awful, rancid mouth.

"Adelaide!" Rose shouted as she fought for her footing and pushed the monster's shielded head away from her. "Where's your fire? Get your head in this!"

Adelaide rolled toward Rose's voice. She saw the monster harrying her friend. It had pulled back its collar again and was rearing up above Rose. Rose, petite to begin with, was minuscule next to the horrific mass of this creature.

Rose, who had healed her from life-threatening wounds countless times.

Rose, who had carried her lifeless body across the planes of existence.

Rose, who had brought her back from the dead, stood defiant in the face of this monstrosity.

"I need you!" the halfling shouted, not taking her eyes off the gaping maw hovering above her. She held a hand up to launch another attack at the monster. The beam of white light flew wide and disappeared into the blue sky above.

Adelaide took a deep breath. She tightened her grip on her battleaxe as she pushed herself to her feet.

She stood up and pulled her shoulders back. She let out a roar.

The desert reverberated with her rage. Rivulets of sand ran down the surrounding dunes, shaken free by the power of her scream.

The centipede adjusted its stance again, turning toward the new source of sound.

Adelaide finished, her lungs empty. She filled them again only to release another furious battle cry and rush toward the bug. She laid into it with Fiend's Lament, carving into the soft spot between two of the segments of the creature's long body. It gave its own screech and dove toward Adelaide.

The six appendages that surrounded its head snapped down on the human. She was engulfed by darkness and sharp pain.

She struggled against them, but she could not break their grip. She felt her weight shift forward as the centipede lifted her off the ground.

One of the appendages folded into the cone in which Adelaide was trapped.

It shoved her down the monster's throat.

"Swallowed *again*?" Madison whined. "Come *on*!"

Amelia winced. "I thought you got advantage on those Dexterity saves. How'd you roll so low?"

"I didn't have advantage because I couldn't see anything. I rolled low because my dice hate me," Madison moaned.

"Are those the same dice you used during the fight with Misery?"

"Yes. They are my favorites."

"Maybe it's time for a new set? Or just give them a break?" Amelia suggested.

"But these glow in the dark!" Madison retorted.

Amelia looked around the room. "It's not dark in here," she said, pointing out the painfully obvious.

Madison glared at her. "Why are we even fighting this thing, anyway? You beat its Tremorsense with your Silence spell—which was awesome, by the way. But then you went and ruined it!"

"I told you, I need its teeth," Amelia explained.

"I thought you were speaking in some sort of code. You meant its *actual* teeth?" Madison raised her eyebrows at her younger sister.

"Yes, its actual teeth. Did you grab any on your way in?" Amelia gave Madison a sly smile.

"No. I did not," Madison answered. She did not sound amused. "*Why* do you need its teeth?"

"I told you the options for the material component to cast Find the Path. One of the options was 'teeth,' but they need to be worth one hundred gold pieces. This big, scary monster's teeth have to be worth a lot, don't you think?"

Madison sat up a little straighter in her chair. "Actually, yes. That's brilliant! Alright, I admit it, you were right. We need to kill this thing. If you wouldn't mind saving Adelaide's life again, she would like very much to help you get us out of this stinking, endless, magical desert."

4

"*Adelaide!*" screamed Rose. She sent another searing beam of white energy burning into the monster's head. Whether it be from the impact of the spell or the volume of her scream, Rose got the bug's attention.

The head swiveled toward her, thirty feet in the air again after the bug had reared up as it swallowed Adelaide. The spike still closed over its face, it dove toward Rose. The halfling managed to sidestep the attack, and the bug slammed its armored head into the sand.

Inside the bug's gullet, Adelaide held her breath. She felt the monster's throat muscles pulling her deeper. The teeth had torn her to ribbons on the way in; acid burned in open wounds all across her body. She focused on keeping her grip on Fiend's Lament with her right hand. With no room to swing the axe, she released a barrage of magic missiles from her left hand instead. Inside the massive beast, she could not tell if she had hurt it. Nothing changed. She was pulled ever deeper.

The monster shuddered. With the front end mere feet from her, Rose could see its face through gaps in the cone. She grabbed onto those gaps as the centipede pulled its head out of the sand next to her.

"I have had *enough!*" she shouted. She held onto two of the appendages that formed the spike. Her eyes glowed with golden energy, as did her hands. The energy turned black as it spread into the bug, and Rose felt the appendages loosen. She wrenched them apart and pulled herself through the gap. She reached for the soft face of the monster, which withered at her touch.

"Give her back," Rose growled. Her hands still glowing, she pulled at the monster's mouth. Its mandibles blackened and shriveled, withering to reveal the black tunnel that had taken Adelaide.

The centipede howled. The dissonant, grating, deafening, multi-toned scream of the bug blasted into Rose's face. She ignored it. The head end of the gargantuan creature whipped from side to side. Rose held on, her hands burning into the monster wherever she touched.

"Give her *back!*" the halfling roared. Her eyes flared again.

The centipede collapsed forward. It slammed into the ground, sending Rose flying out onto the hot sand. The skittering of its many legs stopped. The desert was silent but for the faint hissing of sand trickling out of the centipede's body.

Adelaide felt the impact. She felt the throat muscles around her relax, but she also felt the monster's digestive acid corroding her skin. The pain came on like a wave, stinging heat overwhelming her. Her only focus was cooling that burning pain. The wave crashed over her, and she lost consciousness in that dark, lonely place.

For a moment, Adelaide floated in darkness, thinking of nothing but her body melting.

"Adelaide!" Rose's voice pierced the fog of pain. Adelaide's eyes shot open, glowing softly with pale golden light. The ward that Rose had cast upon her earlier triggered, pulling her back from the brink of death.

Invigorated, Adelaide pushed backward, worming her way toward the monster's mouth. She dared not speak again and risk running out of air, so she could not use her magic. She closed her eyes and pushed with all of her might, trying to escape before the burning acid overwhelmed her.

After a few strong pushes, she felt her feet dangling in open air.

Rose was there. She grabbed Adelaide by the ankles and pulled her out of the centipede's throat. Adelaide crumpled to the ground next to the monster's head. Rose wanted to hug her, but she held back when she saw the state that Adelaide was in. The human was clearly suffering. Before she said anything, Rose used her magic to heal Adelaide's pock-marked skin.

Adelaide let out the breath that she had been holding. The exhale started as a moan, but it faded to a sigh as Rose's magic relieved her pain. "Thanks, Rose," she said, her voice weak with exhaustion. "That was worse than getting swallowed by the troll."

Rose smiled and collapsed next to her friend. She leaned her back against the unmoving monster and closed her eyes, relishing the silence of the desert while she caught her breath.

"So, why do you need this thing's teeth?" Adelaide asked. "It seems like a weird trophy."

Rose hopped back to her feet. "I almost forgot!" she said, giggling with excitement. "I do need its teeth. Can I use one of your little axes for a few minutes?"

"Sure," Adelaide said with a shrug. She held out a handaxe. "But that wasn't really an answer to my question."

"It's for magic," Rose replied. Adelaide did not look satisfied, but she did not ask again. Rose leapt up onto the bug, climbing into the space in front of its mouth. She pulled, pried, and hacked at the sharp teeth that protruded from several parallel ridges within the monster's mouth.

Adelaide listened to Rose's efforts. She thought about helping, but she could not bring herself to get that close to the creature's mouth again. The smell turned her stomach where she sat, twenty feet away. Every minute or two, a white spike of bone would fly out of the conical helmet that shielded the centipede's face.

After an hour of harvesting teeth, Rose turned her focus deeper. She knew nothing of the bug's anatomy, but she was convinced that there would be some organ or substance in its head that she would be able to sell to a potion maker or enchanter somewhere. She had seen what Brizzack had done with the remains of the ettins. She wondered what he might do with this monstrous thing.

For another hour she worked. The bug's physiology did not appear to rely on blood, so the dissection was not messy. She found nothing else in the mouth that she could identify as useful, so she turned her focus to the upper half of its head. There were no eyes, but there were rows of holes lining both sides of the head. With a few swift chops from the handaxe, Rose found the nerves that connected to each of the holes and traced them to a gray, fist-sized knot near the middle of the head. Without hesitation, she removed the soft organ and leapt happily out onto the sand.

"Check this out!" she called. She walked over to her friend and held the slimy, gray object up in front of

Adelaide's face. "I got its brains." She grinned with crazed excitement.

Adelaide opened her eyes to a close-up view of the brain. "What the—" she shouted. "Oh, stop!" She shoved Rose's hand away and turned her head as she vomited again.

"Why would you do that?" Adelaide moaned between heaves, not looking back at Rose.

Rose stepped away from Adelaide. "Oh. Sorry. I thought you'd be excited. Imagine how much we could sell this for! I doubt Brizzack gets many giant desert centipede brains for his potions." She tucked the object into a small cloth bag and hung it on her pack.

"Anyway, are you feeling any better?" Rose asked.

"Yeah, a bit," Adelaide replied. She pulled herself to her feet and, for the first time since the battle, really took in their surroundings. The desert was silent. There was no breeze. The sun remained directly overhead, broiling them. Adelaide surveyed the nearby dunes carefully.

"I have no idea which way we were going," she said with a sigh. "And the sun is still at high noon. That doesn't make *any* sense." She kicked the unmoving body of the centipede. "What now?"

"Well, I think I can use these teeth to perform a ritual that can lead us out of here," Rose said. She looked at the shards scattered across the sand around the monster's head. "Let's find a few good ones," she mumbled. After a minute of searching, she held ten mostly intact teeth, each as long as Adelaide's forearm.

"Alright," Rose said with satisfied finality. "Tomorrow, I should be able to find our way out of this place."

"Tomorrow?" Adelaide whined in dismay. "It's been noon for *hours*. There might never be a tomorrow. And we are almost out of magic for today; pretty soon we'll be out of water too. Then we'll be in serious trouble."

Rose glanced up at the sun, squinting from the brightness. She looked back at Adelaide, blinking several times before she could see her friend through the residual image of the sun. "Well, let's start walking, then!" she said without any of the despair that Adelaide was feeling.

"Which way?" Adelaide asked, getting huffy. "I said I don't know which way is east anymore."

Rose thought for a second. "I guess I could use a little divination warm-up," she said. She knelt next to her bag and bundled the teeth together with a strap of leather. She hung them on her pack next to the bag with the brain, and she pulled out her deck of tarot cards.

Sitting in the shade of the monster's corpse, she shuffled the cards. And shuffled them again. And again. With each cut of the deck, her hands moved faster until they were a blur of slapping and sliding cards.

"If we head to my right," Rose whispered to the cards, "will we be safe?"

She cut the deck. As the halves folded together again, a single card shot out. It landed face-up in front of the halfling. Adelaide bent forward to look over Rose's shoulder at the card. She remembered the last time that Rose had used this magic, the card had shown them the dining hall from the tomb of Galien, something that the maker of the cards could not possibly have known about.

Adelaide gasped. The card was upside down, but she knew what it showed. And who it showed. In a chamber made of black stone stood a red-skinned tiefling with black horns and scraggly silver hair. He wore a red and black robe, the sleeves of which had fallen back from his upraised arms. White lightning arced between his hands.

"Misery," Adelaide hissed. She reached for the card.

Too slowly, however, as Rose snatched the card up and replaced it within the deck. "The Magician," Rose explained, her voice somber, "but in the reversed position. This indicates poor planning. We definitely do not want to go that way." She pointed to her right.

Adelaide growled lightly. She took a deep breath, clearing her head. "Well, then, do you want to ask about another direction? You could try three others, if not more."

"I guess so," Rose replied. She began shuffling the cards again.

A sound interrupted her. From far off over the dunes to Rose's right side came the too-familiar polyphonic screech of a giant desert centipede.

Rose stuffed the cards back into their box and the box into her pack. "This way it is," she said, pointing away from the sound and off to the left from where she had been sitting. She hopped to her feet and shouldered her gear. The halfling took off at a brisk walk. "Can you cover our tracks?" she asked over her shoulder.

"I'm not sure what good it will do," Adelaide replied, "but sure. One last time for today." She channeled her magic to mask their path, and the footprints that they left filled in with sand as they marched away from the dead centipede.

"I think it's moving again," Adelaide mumbled.

"What?" Rose panted. Her hair dripped with sweat. Her skin ached from the prolonged exposure to the sun and blowing sand. Her feet dragged. She no longer left footprints in the sand; her boots had carved two long tracks from her heels to the horizon.

"The sun," Adelaide said. She shielded her eyes with one hand and glanced into the cloudless sky again. "I think it's moving lower. Maybe we're almost out of here."

"That would be nice," Rose replied. She trudged along, staring at the ground, following the sound of Adelaide's footfalls. "I really hate this place."

Adelaide did not respond. She stopped walking.

Three steps later, Rose collided with the back of the tall human's legs. She was not moving fast enough to knock either of them over. Instead, she turned the contact into a hug, closing her eyes and resting her head on Adelaide's hip.

"Are we there yet?" she asked, her voice sleepy, her eyes still closed.

"No," Adelaide moaned. "We are back where we started."

Rose opened her eyes. They had reached the edge of the dunes, and before them lay the rocky wasteland in which their day had started. Instead of dunes, large piles of rocks broke up their view of the horizon. The hard, cracked earth was dotted with cacti and thorny shrubs. The sun was making its way toward the horizon ahead of them with unnatural speed.

"What is happening?" Rose asked. She released Adelaide's leg to look around. The sky behind her was darkening toward purple as she watched. "How long were we out there?"

"I can't be sure," Adelaide said. "But it sure feels like we lost a whole day. Or maybe more. I'm completely wrecked."

"Well, let's find somewhere to sleep, I guess," Rose said with a shrug. She trudged forward, kicking small rocks with each weary step.

"You could *try* not to leave a path directly to where we are sleeping," Adelaide commented with a weak chuckle.

Rose stopped. She closed her eyes and let her head roll back until it rested on top of her pack. She looked like she might fall asleep standing up. "Can you hide our footprints again?" she asked.

"No. I told you, I am out of magic."

"Did you use that pearl I gave you?"

"What—" Adelaide cut herself off. "Oh, that's right!" She strained her shoulder to reach into her pack without taking it off her back. After a moment of struggling with a small pocket, she produced the pearl of power. She closed her eyes and focused on the pearl, rolling it between her thumb and pointer finger.

She gave a half-grin. "Now you see me; now you don't," she recited. The shadows of nearby cacti, grown long as the day faded to evening, curved toward them. "For real this time, that's the last one today."

"Let's check out some of those big piles of rocks," Rose suggested. "Maybe we can find a small cave or crevasse to sleep in."

The women continued forward, and before long they had settled down into a covered recess near the top of a forty-foot-high jumble of broken boulders. Huddling together against the creeping chill of the desert night, they gave in to much-needed sleep.

"Should we have taken turns taking watch?" Madison asked. "This feels like a major oversight."

"Eh, we'll be fine," Amelia said with a dismissive wave of her hand. "We had Pass Without Trace on, and we said we wanted to find something high up and out of sight. And we rolled well to find our little cave."

"*You* rolled well," Madison mumbled. "I'm thinking these dice are cursed." Madison's hand shot up before Amelia could open her mouth. "Don't say a word about what I should do with my dice. Don't touch them. Don't even look at them. They are my favorite, and they will start rolling better soon. There can't be that many more low rolls left in them." Madison glared at the row of dark purple and blue dice in her dice tray.

Amelia smirked, but she heeded Madison's request. "Okay, in the morning, I'll cast Find the Path with those teeth. Then we can get out of this desert! The big question is where we go next. I need an object from the place we want to go."

"From what we know about the geography here, Khal Durum or Westray would make the most sense. Then we can get back to Tarsam or the Virdes or wherever we need to go to find Valduin. How are we going to find him, though? Do you have magic for that?"

Amelia winced at this question. "I can try Scrying again to spy on him. It didn't work last time; I guess he made his saving throw. It's a high-level spell, though, so I don't want to use it a lot. You never know when a giant centipede might appear."

Now it was Madison's turn to wince. "Yeah, that fight was not fun. Good work with the Death Ward. Without diamonds for your resurrection spells, dying now would be *really* bad."

5

Adelaide sat atop the rock pile. The sun peeked over the endless golden dunes to the east. Nothing moved on the desert floor below her. She closed her eyes and let the cool morning breeze caress her sunburned face and arms.

"Adelaide!" Rose called from their sleeping cave within the rocks. "You out there?"

"Yeah," the human called back. She did not move.

"You want breakfast?" Rose asked. She sounded closer now. Adelaide turned toward her voice. "I'm starving," the halfling continued. "I feel like I haven't eaten for days."

"You'd say that even if we had just finished dinner," Adelaide replied with a chuckle. She sighed and opened her eyes. With a faint groan, she got to her feet and dropped down to where Rose stood.

"Yeah, maybe, but this time I mean it." Rose stuck her tongue out at Adelaide. "Also, I need help with these teeth. Come in here."

The pair returned to their small hideout. Rose had the long, pointed teeth of the centipede laid out in a row. She also had Adelaide's shield on the ground next to them.

"I was trying to cast the spell to find our way back to your home, but the teeth didn't quite work. I think they *can* work, but they need to be cleaned up a bit."

Adelaide furrowed her brow. She picked up one of the teeth. It still had blood on it. "Cleaned up? How? Do we need to wash my blood off them?"

Rose picked up another one of the teeth. "Well, yeah, we should start with that. But they need to be more decorative, I think. Picture my cards; they have all sorts of gold scrolling and stuff on them. Things that aren't important to the function, but just make them fancier. These aren't fancy enough to do magic."

Adelaide nodded. "You know what, I think I can help with that." She dug into her pack and found her jeweler's toolkit. She unrolled the tools. "Can I cut them a little shorter?"

"I think that would be okay," Rose said. She pursed her lips as she considered this project. "Do we have any gold or silver or gems that you could decorate them with? That might do the job."

"Yes!" Adelaide said excitedly. She dove back into her pack, and a moment later came up with a small pouch. She inverted the pouch onto her tool roll. Several sparkling shards of red gem tumbled out. "These were in that box that we stole from Azereth. The one that had the fire elemental in it. I would have tried to sell them to the jeweler in Mirstone, but I had forgotten I had them."

Rose picked up one of the pieces of ruby. It had facets cut into one face, but the other sides were rough. "These are perfect!" she said with a smile. "You get started on this, and I'll make us some breakfast. Take this, too." She laid a hand on Adelaide's shoulder as she prayed,

"Selaia, grant her your guidance so we can escape this forsaken place."

Adelaide's pupils dilated in response to Rose's divine magic, her vision clarifying supernaturally. She smiled and set to work on the first tooth, cutting off the broken end, adding decorative carving along its sides, and setting a fragment of ruby into it.

For the rest of the morning, Adelaide worked on the teeth. Rose created food for them, magically producing piles of egg and cheese sandwiches. She spent most of her time eating and granting Adelaide additional guidance to help with her crafting.

"Hey, Valduin, it's Rose. Just checking in. Are you still with Beulah? Are you safe now? I'd love to hear from you! If you can."

Adelaide's hands stopped moving. She looked up from the tooth she was working on and watched Rose stare off into the distance beyond their cave.

After a moment, Rose blinked a few times before returning Adelaide's gaze. "Nothing," she reported. She gave a small, sad sigh.

"You want to try looking in on him?" Adelaide asked, setting down her tools. She chewed her lower lip, her face wracked with worry for their friend.

"Sure," Rose replied, though she did not sound sure. She took the hand mirror out of her pack, holding it while focusing on Valduin. She spoke her plea to Selaia to see Valduin, but once again, the mirror only flashed with golden light before returning to its normal appearance.

Rose shook her head. "I think I'm doing something wrong," she mumbled. She let her head loll back against the wall behind her. "Maybe I'll try again later. Or tomorrow. I need to think about it a bit. How is it going with those teeth?"

Adelaide smiled, holding up a handful of beautifully decorated spikes. "About to finish the sixth one. I've only got one more piece of ruby after this one. Do you think seven will be enough to cast the spell?"

Rose picked up one of the finished teeth. She took a moment to inspect it, to roll it between her palms. She pulled Adelaide's shield in front of her, upside down like a shallow bowl, and tossed the tooth lightly into it. Rose smiled at the satisfying clatter of the tooth tumbling within the shield before coming to rest.

"Actually, I think the five you've got already will work." Rose scooped up the completed teeth. The halfling sat up a bit straighter, closed her eyes, and took a deep, cleansing breath. As she exhaled, she opened her eyes. She rolled the first tooth between her palms, feeling the swirls and whorls that Adelaide had carved, noting the ruby shard with each rotation of the tooth in her hands.

She recited a prayer for safe passage. Her amulet began to glow with its familiar, golden light.

She dropped the first tooth into the shield. Then the second. One at a time, the teeth tumbled around the shield, until all five lay in a jumble at the bottom of its concavity. Rose recited the prayer again.

Adelaide held her breath. She could feel the power radiating off the small cleric like heat from a forge. She smiled, proud of how strong Rose had become in the weeks that they had been traveling.

Rose finished the prayer. The teeth snapped around within the shield, turning so that the ruby on each faced Rose. All five sharp tips pointed in the same direction.

Rose smiled.

"Well, that spell worked, at least." She looked at Adelaide. "Ready to go?"

"Uh, no, actually," Adelaide replied, shaking her head in surprise. "I kind of wanted to finish up these last couple of teeth. Maybe we could sell them. And I haven't gotten to eat anything yet; I've been working my fingers to the bone over here!"

Rose giggled. "Okay, okay! Finish up. I'll pack. It's too hot out there anyway. I will be able to see the path for a whole day, so we can leave at dusk. Sound good?"

In the late afternoon, when the temperature of the sun-scorched desert had started to fall, Rose and Adelaide set off from their hideout. Rose led the way, following the path that Selaia had revealed to her.

"You're sure this is the right way?" Adelaide asked after an hour of travel. The sun was starting to disappear behind the horizon to their left. "This sure seems like we are heading north. I am pretty sure the Sandgate Mountains are to the east."

Rose nodded. "After our experience yesterday, I can't say that I trust the sun to tell us our direction in this place. I know the magic is working. I can see it. Like a path marked on a map, I can see the rubies." She pointed at the ground in front of her feet and slowly raised her arm until she was pointing at the horizon. "A row of glowing red dots from here to Westray."

"Wait, you used my shield for the spell?" Adelaide asked, her voice taking on an edge of concern.

"Yup!" Rose replied, either not hearing or not caring about the change in Adelaide's tone.

"But my shield wasn't made in Westray," Adelaide said. "It was made in Khal Durum."

Rose stopped walking. She looked up at Adelaide, narrowing her eyes and pursing her lips. After a moment, she smiled again, "I totally forgot that. Well, Khal Durum isn't bad, either. We can check in with Tor and maybe sell that bug brain to Enchantress Aloom." She resumed her walk.

Adelaide shrugged. "Yeah, that wouldn't be bad," she agreed. "And once we are there, we will know how to get anywhere else we need to go." She paused and lowered her voice before finishing, "And we can tell Aloom about Taranath. She wasn't far off when she told us to watch out for Valduin."

Rose nodded but said nothing. She strode forward, following the ruby-red dots that she alone could see. The path tracked along the border between the rocky desert and the towering dunes. Rose led on through the fading twilight. They walked well into the night, Adelaide using her magic to cover their footprints until exhaustion forced them to find a hole to crawl into for the night. Rose summoned her ten-foot-tall guardian to protect them while they slept.

For two more days, Adelaide and Rose repeated this process. Rose would find the path to take them to Khal Durum. She would try and fail to use her scrying spell to check in on Valduin. She would send messages to Valduin that went unanswered. She even sent messages to Beulah a few times, but the hag never responded either. As the day cooled down in the afternoon, the women would set off following the red, dotted line toward the horizon.

On the morning after their fifth night sleeping in the desert, Adelaide shook Rose awake.

"We're almost there!" she said, an excited smile on her face. "Come out here, you can see the mountains!"

"No," Rose groaned, turning away from Adelaide and covering her head with her blanket. "Why would you do this?"

"Oh, come on!" Adelaide was not deterred. She scooped Rose up like a toddler and carried her out of the cave in which they had spent the night. "Isn't it beautiful?" On the horizon ahead of them, rising above the dunes of the desert, were the ragged peaks of the Sandgate Mountains. The sun was rising behind those mountains, in the east as Adelaide had expected.

Rose turned away from the bright sun, shielding her eyes by burying her face into the crook of Adelaide's arm. "Make it stop," she moaned. "Let me sleep."

"Fine," Adelaide said. She returned Rose to her spot in the dark cave. "But let's not wait until dusk to head out today. We might reach the mountains tonight. And then it's probably only another day to Khal Durum!"

"Yeah, sure, whatever," Rose mumbled. Before long she was snoring softly again.

Adelaide climbed to the highest point she could find without losing sight of their cave, on top of another of the tall mounds of broken boulders that littered this part of the desert. She spent the rest of the morning perched atop the boulders, staring at those mountain tops. She cleaned her handaxes, especially the one that Rose had used to dissect the centipede, and dreamed about seeing home again.

"We did it!" Madison cheered, patting Amelia on the shoulder. "We're gonna make it out of the desert. You are so amazing with all those cleric spells. I don't know how you keep them all straight." She beamed at her younger sister.

"Yup, I know all the spells," Amelia said without enthusiasm. She sat at the table with her head drooped and her shoulders slumped, staring blankly at her character sheet. "Do you wanna take a break?" She pushed her chair back.

"Whoa, whoa, whoa," Madison said, holding her hands up to stop Amelia from leaving. "What in the world is all this? You just did an amazing job saving us from that giant monster and getting us out of the desert. Why are you moping?"

"I mean, we could have lived in the desert forever," Amelia replied, avoiding Madison's question. "Create Food and Water is only a third-level spell. We can survive anywhere now."

"I don't care about that," Madison said. She narrowed her eyes at Amelia. "I care about what's going on with you. Two days ago you were super excited to keep going and get back to Khal Durum. Now you want to take a break? When we are so close?"

"We'll get there," Amelia mumbled. She stood up and headed for the stairs, "tomorrow."

6

Despite the appearance of the mountains, it took the adventurers two more days to reach the edge of the desert. With each hour of walking, the mountains grew, rising out of the horizon like an unthinkably vast mouth closing on the world.

"Rose, isn't it wonderful?" Adelaide was practically skipping as the land climbed toward the mountain range. The desert flora had given way to plants more familiar to the women, and they now crossed fields of green grass instead of the cracked stone of the desert.

"You're pretty cheerful," Rose mumbled. Her feet dragged. She stared at the grass five feet ahead of her boots, silently counting the red dots and leading them onward toward the dwarven city of Khal Durum.

"I think I've finally recovered. You know, from dying. And we escaped that awful desert. And we are back in the mountains. My mountains! Look! An actual tree!" Adelaide sprinted ahead toward the first tree that they had seen on this leg of their journey. As she ran toward it, the human touched the eagle feathers in her hair and shouted, "I want to *jump*!" She let her pack fall from her shoulders and leapt high into the air, grabbing a branch with both hands. She swung her body to the top of the branch like a gymnast and leapt higher still. When she came to rest, she was hugging a thin bough near the top of the tree. She closed her eyes and basked in the feeling of the cool wind on her face.

"What's your plan?" Rose shouted up at her. "You can't fly. You just gonna drop?"

Adelaide ignored Rose. She took a deep breath, relishing the taste of the mountain air.

Rose trudged along, her head still hanging. As she passed under the tree, Adelaide erupted in a wild scream. Rose lifted her head in time to watch Adelaide slam into the ground feet first. With the sound of bones cracking, she dropped a fist to the ground in a three-point landing to brace herself and stop from tumbling. She looked up at Rose with bloodshot eyes and a crazed grin, her breathing ragged.

"Chill out, will you?" Rose said with a roll of her eyes. She did not break stride; she patted Adelaide on the shoulder and used her magic to heal whatever internal injuries the fall may have caused. "Totally unnecessary," she mumbled. The halfling continued her dreary march past the lone tree.

Adelaide stood up, flexed her legs a few times, and jogged back to grab her pack. By the time she returned to Rose's side, her eyes and breathing had returned to normal.

"What's up with you?" Adelaide asked. "I was just having some fun. Why are you being such a grouch?"

Rose did not reply.

Adelaide put a hand on her friend's shoulder. "Come on, what's up?"

"I'm just tired. Tired of walking. Tired of staring at these red dots. Tired of sleeping in caves." She walked on.

"Well, we'll be able to take a break soon!" Adelaide said, keeping her voice cheerful, hoping to impart some of her happiness to Rose. "One more night in the wild, and then we'll be able to get proper beds in Khal Durum. Have you told Tor that we are coming yet?"

"No. I've been too nervous to use any extra magic while we are still out here in the wild. It's been too quiet these last few days. I can't even remember how long we've been walking."

Adelaide squeezed Rose's shoulder. "We're almost there. Then we'll be able to focus on Valduin. Still no luck seeing or talking to him?"

Rose shook her head. "I don't get it. If he's alive, I should be able to reach him."

"Are you worried he's not alive?"

Rose stopped. Her hair, stiff with a week of sweat and days-old blood, swayed slightly in the breeze coming down from the mountains. Her crown sparkled in the fading sunlight of the late afternoon. She gazed up into Adelaide's eyes, but she said nothing. She sighed, turned back toward the path, and resumed her walk.

Adelaide followed. She did not push the issue.

They walked for another hour until they were well into the forest that filled the valleys of the mountain range, before making camp. For the first time since being separated from Valduin, they had wood for a fire, which Adelaide started. Now at elevation, with summer giving way to early autumn, the night was colder than it had been in the desert. Without a cave to sleep in, Adelaide took the first watch, letting Rose sleep by the smoldering remains of their fire after they had finished dinner.

Rose opened her eyes.

She leapt from her bed. What was once the familiar floor of her bedroom had become the familiar floor of her dreams. The dreams that allowed Halamar, the old elf from Eydon, to visit. She threw open her door and ran toward the main chapel of the temple.

He stood in the central aisle, as Rose had expected. He wore a gray robe, matching Rose's. Rose tried to remember if he had been wearing the same robe during their prior meetings, but, like with most dreams, she struggled to recall such details.

"Hello, Rose," Halamar greeted her. He did not smile.

"Hello, Halamar," Rose said. She stopped in front of the altar. "We did not get to finish your questions last time. Would you like to go first tonight?"

"Yes, I think that would be best. I was wondering if you could give me any more information about the elf that you met."

Rose twisted her mouth as she recalled their short interaction with the elf in the hags' lair in the Mirstone Mire. "Well, he was a full elf, not part-human like my friend Valduin. He was old, not as old as you, but pretty old."

Halamar cocked his head to the side, a half-grin pulling at the corner of his mouth.

Rose noticed the look. "Oh! I'm sorry! I didn't mean to say you were old. Just that you look old. No! I mean..." She trailed away, her face wracked with embarrassment.

"Don't worry," Halamar said with a chuckle. "I am certainly quite old. Go on, please."

"Well, we met him in the lair of a hag. A coven of hags, actually. He only had one foot. I think we decided that the hags had cut off his foot so that they could make something. We freed him from a cage in the hags' lair.

He grabbed the foot bones that the hags had taken and disappeared."

"And he mentioned Eydon," Halamar said, leading Rose on.

Rose nodded. "Yes. He was very upset about the hags having his bones. He said that no one must get access to Eydon and that he would rather die than allow the hags to have the tuning forks. To be honest, he was pretty rude about the whole matter. He didn't even say thank you for rescuing him."

Halamar stiffened; his eyes grew wide. "Did you say tuning forks?"

Rose narrowed her eyes at Halamar. "Yes, why? Are they important?"

Halamar furrowed his brow, his gaze growing distant. He gave a worried sigh. "Tuning forks are used to travel between the planes. If these hags created a tuning fork that targets Eydon, then someone could use it to enter our demiplane. We have defenses for such a circumstance, of course, but it is certainly concerning. These hags, did you find out why they were interested in Eydon?"

Rose shook her head. "Not really. They actually had a lot of different tuning forks. Some looked like feathers or horns. We did kill a couple of the hags. The third got away, though. But, in any event, the tuning forks were probably for the Voidbringer. Oh! Do you know anything about him?"

Halamar stroked his bearded chin. "Voidbringer? A curious name. No, I've not heard of the Voidbringer. It sounds quite ominous, though."

"Yeah, he's this big devil-looking thing. Very evil. We haven't quite sorted out what he's up to, yet," Rose said, her voice falling in disappointment when Halamar had no extra information for her.

"Well, this has been helpful," Halamar said with an air of finality. "I will certainly need to look for an old, but not too old," he winked, "rude elf that has recently visited your home plane in violation of the agreement by which Eydon remains hidden. Did you have any other questions for me?"

"Just one. The last time we talked, you were about to tell me what you saw when you looked into the future and figured out that you should leave the dream anchor behind..." Rose's voice trailed away. She waited for Halamar's explanation.

"Ah, yes, that's true. Well, I saw that I should leave some supplies that a party of young adventurers would find useful. I hope that I did well in that."

Rose nodded, but she did not interrupt.

"And I saw that whoever would acquire the dream anchor would be vitally important to the survival of my people. The one that found the dream anchor would save the lives of the people of Eydon from some future cataclysm. That part was a little fuzzy, to be honest. However, if my visions prove accurate, Rose Fairfoot, you will save my life one day. You could save my city. You could save thousands." He gave a warm smile. He nodded and waved to Rose, and the dream ended.

Rose sat up with a jolt, her heart racing. She had goosebumps all over, not from the cold, but from Halamar's last few words. The words that she had heard in the vision that she received from the Berdakhal.

"You could save thousands."

Rose replayed the vision in her mind. She saw Valduin, dead. She saw Adelaide, dead. She saw herself, dead. All three of these things had already happened. She saw a blue sky crack like glass and fade to gray. A voice told her that she could save thousands.

"What happens next?" she muttered.

"What was that?" Adelaide called from the darkness above. "Did you say, 'Hey, Adelaide, are you ready to sleep so I can take watch?' Because if you did, the answer is definitely yes." Adelaide dropped out of a nearby tree and approached the campfire.

Rose did not smile. She did not laugh. She stared into the softly glowing embers of their fire.

"Hey," Adelaide said, nudging Rose with her knee. "You ready to take watch or what?"

"Yeah, I'm ready," Rose said, snapping out of her reverie. She stood up and grabbed her shield, but she left her chainmail on the ground. She lit up her amulet with magical light and padded off to a tree where she could watch Adelaide without her light keeping the human awake. She sat with her back against the tree. Between reliving her experience below Khal Durum and reviewing the new information from Halamar, her watch passed without any more thought as to what may have happened to Valduin since she last saw him.

"Oh, boy," Amelia said, "I wish Logan had been here for that conversation with Halamar. We probably should have taken some notes."

Madison waved a hand at her sister, dismissing her concern. "It'll be fine. We'll remember all the important stuff. It felt like it was mostly a review, anyway. And him getting information from you."

Amelia paused for a moment, and then she shrugged and nodded. "Yeah, you're right. We'll be fine. And I can always use Sending to talk to Halamar now, too. I had completely forgotten about that whole subplot while we were getting out of the desert."

"So, how are we going to find Valduin? You've been trying to get him with Scrying and with Sending for days now. Do you think he's dead?"

"Well, Rose thinks he's dead," Amelia replied. "But we know that Logan is still playing, so he must be alive. Somewhere. Maybe there's something in the spell descriptions that explains why they aren't working. Maybe I'm using them wrong." She reached for the rulebook. She picked it up and paused, staring at the cover. She pursed her lips and sighed softly.

Madison did not notice the hesitation; she was looking at the spells on her own character sheet. "I love my spells for battle, and Pass Without Trace is *so* helpful, but I really can't help at all with this kind of problem."

When Amelia did not respond, Madison looked up. The rulebook lay on the table in front of Amelia's chair.

Amelia was gone.

7

Rose let Adelaide sleep in. As morning came and the surrounding forest began to lighten, she walked a few short patrols in a loop around their campsite. The undergrowth was not thick, and she made sure to keep Adelaide within sight at all times. When she saw Adelaide sit up and look around, she headed back toward her friend.

"Good morning," she said, her voice level, neither sad nor excited.

"Hey," Adelaide replied as she stretched her arms over her head. "Did you cast the spell yet? Do you think we can make it to the city today?"

Rose shook her head. "No, I haven't. I was waiting for you to wake up. I want to try to find Valduin, and I was saving my energy for that."

Adelaide narrowed her eyes at the halfling. "I'm not exactly sure what you mean," she said, "but don't you want to be sure we can get to Khal Durum? You can try to find Valduin after we get there, can't you?"

Rose's gaze drifted toward the remains of the campfire. She thought for a few moments. "Okay, that's fine," she said in resignation. "One more day probably doesn't make a difference, anyway." She laid Adelaide's shield on the ground and pulled the gemmed teeth from her pack. Repeating the ritual that she now performed every morning, the dotted line appeared on the ground beside her, leading off into the forest.

Rose created their breakfast, and the women packed up camp.

"While I don't mind the sleeping arrangements," Adelaide commented, "I sure am looking forward to a hot meal."

Rose stared into the trees for a moment, trying to estimate how many red dots were left between themselves and their destination. "If we make good time, we'll be having dinner at the Iron Tankard tonight. Then I'll finally get my night in a bed."

Adelaide smiled, and then her eyes lit up. "Have you told Tor that we are coming yet?"

"Not yet. I didn't want to say anything until I was sure we were going to make it."

"Well, do you think she might be able to set up a reception for us? The glorious return of the heroes of Khal Durum!" Adelaide puffed out her chest and pretended to shake hands with imaginary dignitaries.

Rose giggled for the first time in days. "We don't want that. Then we'd have to explain where Valduin is."

Adelaide deflated. "Oh. Yeah, good point. Well, you should tell Tor to visit us at the Iron Tankard anyway."

Rose's gaze became distant. "Tor. It's Rose. We're coming to Khal Durum tonight. Could you tell the guards to let us in? We'll head to the Iron Tankard."

"Rose! It's so great to hear from you! I'm so glad you're safe! Yes, I'll make sure that they let you in tonight without any—" The reply cut off at the limit of the spell's magic.

"We're set," Rose reported.

Adelaide hid her smile when she noticed Rose's.

The women marched on.

The morning passed. Adelaide and Rose walked. The afternoon passed. Adelaide and Rose walked. Darkness fell. Adelaide and Rose walked.

Rose could see those gleaming ruby dots leading her toward the city through the deepest darkness, but the women still used their magic to create glowing torches so they would not trip on anything in the forest as they walked.

Long past sunset, they emerged from the forest to see the road that led south from Westray to the entrance to Khal Durum. Adelaide heaved a relieved sigh. "I was about to ask if we should stop for the night," she said.

"Sorry," Rose replied. "I should have said something. We are close. We should be able to see that cluster of buildings outside the gate soon."

"Great! I am starving. Do you want to jog it out? Get there a little quicker?"

Rose laughed. "Absolutely not. I am wrecked. Unless you want to carry me."

Adelaide kicked a small rock down the road in disappointment. "I don't think I'm up for that right now. Fine, let's just keep walking."

Rose was correct, and before long the women arrived at the oversized door that stood within the entrance to Khal Durum. Despite the late hour, the door was held open a few feet off the ground, as they had seen previously. A few dwarves in armor stood on guard around the gate. They spread out across the entryway, weapons in hand, as the pair approached.

"Hello!" Adelaide called out. "We come in peace. We're friends with, uh, Tor, uh—" her mind raced as she tried to remember Tor's full name.

"Toredrabena Silvermace," Rose spoke up. "She said you would be expecting us. I am Rose Fairfoot, and this is Adelaide Bellamie." She walked with purpose toward the gate.

The guard standing closest to the middle of the entry-way replied, "Welcome back, heroes of Khal Durum." He stepped forward and held a hand out to Rose. The dwarf lowered his voice and said, "I hear you are the one who saved my life. Thank you."

Rose narrowed her eyes at the dwarf, trying to recognize his face in the awkward up-lighting of her glowing amulet. When she noticed the horn hanging from a strap across his chest, she concluded that this must have been the dwarf hit by the boulder when the giants attacked the city. Rose remembered that she had stabilized his injuries and moved him to safety at the beginning of that battle.

"Yes!" Rose said after she put everything together. "That was me. I am so glad you're okay."

"Only because of your bravery and quick thinking." He bowed his head. "Lady Silvermace is expecting you. You may enter." He stepped aside and motioned toward the gate. Rose walked under the door; Adelaide ducked under it. They found themselves within the entry tunnel to the city. The large tunnel arched high over their heads, lit by the steady orange glow of the magic globes set into the walls on either side.

The adventurers passed through the tunnel. They did not even pause on the balcony to take in the majestic evening view of the upper layer of the city. They marched down onto the city streets and headed to the Iron Tankard.

Rose pushed the door open. The dining room was bright, but it was not overly busy at this late hour. Rose took a step toward the bar before being slammed against the wall next to the door.

"You're back! You're safe!" Tor exclaimed. She squeezed Rose.

Rose hugged her back. "Hi, Tor," she wheezed. Tor's hug was too tight for her to say much more.

Tor released the halfling. "You are a mess!" she said, looking Rose up and down. She turned to Adelaide. "Welcome back," she said with a warm smile. She looked past the women and out onto the empty street. "Where have you been? Where is Valduin?" she asked. Her face fell with concern.

"That's a story," Rose said, "for tomorrow. We've been walking for a week. We were lost in the Enchanted Dunes for a while. Valduin is somewhere else. We think he's safe. But we need to sleep." She closed her eyes and placed her forehead on Tor's shoulder to emphasize her exhaustion.

Tor raised her eyebrows, but she said nothing. She patted Rose on the back. With her other hand, she held out a room key to Adelaide. "I already got a room for you both. I'll be back in the morning to hear that story."

Rose shook her armor off and collapsed on the bed. The cool sheets welcomed her, soothing skin that had been burnt by the sun and chaffed raw by days of hard travel in heavy armor. She was asleep before Adelaide had finished washing her face in their private washroom.

Adelaide got herself ready for bed. For the first time since her recent death, she removed her armor. She inspected herself in the washroom mirror.

"Not one, single scar," she muttered in disappointment. "Rose's healing is too good." She sighed.

Adelaide stepped back into the bedroom and looked around. Rose was snoring in one of the two beds. In the handful of minutes since their arrival, the halfling had somehow managed to put something on every surface in the room. The large bedroom, and the attached sitting room, had a messy, lived-in feel already. During her months on the road, Adelaide had never had a suite in a tavern before. She made a mental note to thank Tor the next day.

Adelaide crawled into the other bed and fell into a deep and dreamless sleep.

Adelaide awoke to a knock. She saw that Rose was still asleep. She dragged herself out of bed and padded over to the door.

"Good morning," Adelaide mumbled when she found Tor standing outside the room.

Tor heaved a sigh of relief. "Good morning?" she said with a grin. "How about good evening? I thought you two had died in there!"

"Oh! Sorry. I guess I was more tired than I thought." Adelaide looked over her shoulder. "Rose is still out cold. Do you want her to send you a message when she wakes up? Maybe we can get dinner together?"

Tor glanced past Adelaide into the darkened room. "Yes, that would be good. I need to run out for a few minutes; I've been waiting downstairs since lunch." She chuckled, but she kept her voice low to be sure she did not disturb Rose.

"How close is it to dinnertime now?" Adelaide asked.

Tor shrugged. "Maybe an hour or two away. It doesn't matter. Whenever you are ready, Rose can send me a message."

Adelaide nodded. "Great. I'm gonna make sure she gets cleaned up. We've been through some foul stuff the last few days."

Tor turned to leave. Over her shoulder, she replied with another chuckle, "I could smell it on you both last night. Take your time."

Adelaide let Rose sleep. While she waited, she dumped out her pack and sorted through it. She knew that Valduin had some of their money and magic items, as well as all of their potions. She wanted to see which equipment she still had on her. Especially items that she might be able to sell or trade when they visited Enchantress Aloom at The Eerie later.

She took a proper bath. She closed her eyes and let the hot water grow cool around her. She was in no rush to get out of the tub. She washed her pants and the padding from under her breastplate in the tub and hung them to dry.

"Alright, it's time to get up," Adelaide said to Rose, who still had not moved, once she was dressed in the extra pants and sleeveless shirt that she found at the bottom of her bag. "We've got dinner plans to make." She gave Rose a light shake on the shoulder when the halfling made no reply.

"What?" Rose moaned. She turned away from Adelaide and pulled the sheet over her head. "Leammelone."

Adelaide pulled the sheet off the bed. "Let's go. You need a bath, and we have to meet Tor for dinner. She's been waiting for us all day."

Rose sat up and looked at Adelaide with bleary eyes, their lids drooping. "Why do you keep saying dinner? I need breakfast first."

"Because you slept through breakfast. And lunch. Come on." Adelaide's tone turned stern. "You gotta get moving."

"Alright, alright," Rose said, the fog of sleep lifting from her mind. "I'm going to need a few minutes. It's been a while since I've done this." She slid off the side of the bed and headed toward the bathroom.

Another hour later, Adelaide and a much cleaner Rose were sitting in the dining room of the Iron Tankard when Tor walked through the door. Adelaide, nearly two feet taller than the average guest at the tavern, was easy to spot. Tor joined the adventurers at their table, a wide smile on her face.

"It's so good to—" Tor stopped. She sat, eyes wide, mouth agape, staring at Rose. "How did you do that?" she asked, her voice hushed.

Rose gave Tor a quizzical look until she realized what the dwarf was looking at. She reached up and ran her fingertips across the platinum and diamond crown that she wore on her head.

"Oh, yeah, it got bigger," Rose mumbled.

"How? When?" Tor asked.

"Well," Rose paused as she thought about the question, "I'm not one hundred percent sure. But I think it has something to do with bringing people back from the dead. Since we left Khal Durum, I've had to bring back Adelaide and Valduin. And another guy we met named Greg. Each time, the crown got fancier. And more powerful."

"There was a story," Tor whispered. "I don't know, maybe you would call it a legend, about that crown. My grandmother wore it, as did several other queens of Khal Durum before her. She was the first to be able to use its magic, though. She said that most of its magic was locked away and that it needed to be earned by the crown's bearer. She must have never earned it all." Tor looked from the crown to Rose. "You really are amazing," she concluded with a smile.

Rose looked down at her food. "Thanks," she said with an embarrassed smile.

"Anyway," Adelaide cut in to rescue Rose, "you are not going to believe what we have been up to."

Adelaide and Rose took turns recounting the events of the weeks that had passed since they left Khal Durum to invade Westray. Tor filled them in on the giants' raid of the Platinum Sanctuary and the ensuing activity to solidify the city's defenses. Trade, previously commandeered by King Dunedin while under the control of the warlock Tristan, was returning to normal. A funeral had been held for the dwarves that the adventurers had brought back from the dungeons below the city. Life had returned to normal for the dwarves.

"Are you sure the crown got bigger with each resurrection?" Madison asked. "Because that's pretty cool if that's how it works."

"I'm almost positive. But it's not like we've been checking it every day. Anyway, what's next? We are going to the magic shop, right?"

"That's what we said. We need to see if Aloom will buy those bug teeth or the bug brain you collected. Wait," Madison covered her mouth with her hand as she thought about this statement. "Do bugs have brains? Are you sure that's what you got?"

Amelia shrugged and giggled. "Well, it was a hundred-foot-long centipede in a game of make-believe. It doesn't matter if *real* bugs have brains. I got a 'soft, slimy, fist-sized, gray-white organ' out of the thing's head. I'm calling it a brain."

"Well, whatever it is, it has got to be rare. I hope Aloom can use it and will pay us lots of gold for it. Is there anything we need from her?"

Amelia perked up. "We could get her to identify the crown. Then I'll be able to use the new abilities if there are any."

"Great idea!" Madison said. "Also, do you think she could help us find Valduin somehow?"

Amelia nodded, "Yes! I'll ask her why my spells aren't working to find him. She's bound to have some idea."

8

After dinner, Adelaide and Rose bid Tor goodnight and headed for the Rim Market. The streetlights of the enclosed city had already dimmed for the night, their orange glow highlighting the cavernous space above the buildings. While most of the Rim Market's shops were closed at this late hour, The Eerie's windows shone with inviting light. Enchantress Aloom, who was in the process of arranging a display of dried flowers near the front of the shop, greeted the adventurers as they pushed through the front door.

"Welcome, welcome," Aloom said in her usual, airy voice. She raised her arms as she had the first time they had met her. Her green and blue dress billowed around her when she turned with a flourish to face Adelaide and Rose. Her eyes flashed with recognition, and her smile widened. "Welcome back, adventurers! Staying safe out there?"

Adelaide and Rose smiled politely. Adelaide answered, "To be honest, not usually." She chuckled. "But we made it back all the same. How have you been?"

Aloom glided through the rows of tables toward them, the smile fixed on her face. "All is well here. Now, what can I do for you? Looking for anything in particular?

More potions perhaps? Or just browsing?" She waved an arm to indicate to Rose and Adelaide that the store was at their disposal.

"We have a bunch of things to talk about, actually," Rose said. "We have some things to sell, we could use your assistance with something, and I was wondering if I could ask you a few questions about magic." Rose counted off on her fingers the items on her agenda.

"Well, alright!" Aloom replied, raising her eyebrows in interest at Rose's series of requests. "Let's start with what you might be selling. Then we can talk *magic*." On her final word, her emerald eyes shone with a kaleidoscope of colors and patterns. She turned and moved to an empty table surrounded by chairs near the back of the shop. The chairs slid out at her approach. She sat down, leaning back comfortably, and indicated for the women to sit across from her. "So, what are you looking to sell?"

Adelaide laid out the unadorned centipede teeth on the table. Rose placed the sack containing the brain next to them.

Aloom did not lean forward. She eyed the teeth from her seat. Her irises changed from green to light purple. She raised her eyebrows the smallest fraction. "Interesting," she said, sounding impressed. "Do you know what you have here? Where these came from?"

"We don't know what it's called, but we know what it looks like," Rose explained, "because we killed it."

"You can't be serious," Aloom said with a patronizing giggle.

Adelaide jumped in, "It was a monstrous centipede. At least a hundred feet long. It chased us through the Enchanted Dunes. It did a lot of screaming, which was pretty annoying. We stopped it screaming." She glared at Aloom.

Aloom pursed her lips, returning Adelaide's fierce look. "Well, that does sound like a chylomyria. Very well. What's in the bag?"

Rose leaned forward with excitement, Aloom's disbelief not bothering her the way it bothered Adelaide. "It's brain!" she said with a grin. She released the knot that held the bag closed and pulled the bag down to reveal the contents. The lump of soft matter had dried a bit in the days of walking through the desert but was still clearly the object that Rose had pulled from the head of the dead monster.

Aloom gasped. She leaned forward, her eyes flashing purple again. "Now, this is *extremely* impressive," she said. She stared at the object for a few moments, though she made no move to touch it.

She leaned back again and eyed the adventurers, sizing them up anew. "I must say that you have my attention. Now, what are you looking for?"

Adelaide looked at Rose. She nodded her head to the side to indicate that Rose should speak up about the things she needed.

"Well, the easiest thing, I think, is for you to tell me the magic properties of this crown." She took the crown off her head and placed it on the table. "It has changed recently, and I think it might have different powers now."

"Changed?" Aloom repeated the word. "Magic items do not usually change." Her words trailed off as she picked up the crown and inspected it. Her irises flashed purple again while she looked at all of the different surfaces and details on the crown.

She set the crown back on the table. "That is quite a powerful item. I'm not sure what has changed, but while wearing this crown your magic will be stronger, and its effects harder to resist. Your body will be hardier, and your healing spells more effective for both your friends and yourself. Just being close to you is enough for you to aid your friends in resisting harmful magics. And this crown can pull you back from the brink of death, should you find yourself in a dire situation. Quite powerful indeed." The showmanship was gone from her voice now; she looked at Rose with a degree of respect that the adventurers had not seen before.

Rose replaced the crown on her head. It was a much easier task now that her hair was washed and corralled back into its bun.

"I also had some questions about a particular type of magic," Rose said. "Do you know a spell that allows you to see someone far away?"

Aloom nodded. "Yes. Scrying is not an uncommon magical skill."

Rose nodded back. "Right. Well, I have been trying to scry on our friend Valduin for days. I know he could have resisted the spell once or twice, but every time? Do you know why it might not be working?"

"Well, there are three common reasons that spell will fail. First, as you suspect, is that he is resisting your intrusion. The more times you try without success, the less likely this explanation becomes, especially since you know him so well. Second, he could be on a different plane of existence. That spell only works if you and the target are on the same plane. Third, the target could be using magic, either a spell or an item, that specifically blocks such surveillance."

Adelaide's shoulders slumped. She turned toward Rose and said, "That's what the coven in Mirstone did for David Hancock. I bet that's what Beulah is doing to Valduin."

Aloom jerked forward in her chair. She fixed Adelaide with an intense stare. "Did you say 'Beulah'? Granny Beulah?" she asked, her voice barely more than a whisper.

If Adelaide noticed Aloom's change in demeanor, she did not let on. "Yeah, the old witch in the Virdes Forest. We were doing some work for her recently. We think Valduin is still with her, but we can't find them." With forced nonchalance, she sat back in her chair and took in Aloom's reaction.

Aloom was quiet for a moment, her eyes darting back and forth between Adelaide and Rose. When she spoke, her voice had returned to its usual tone. "And is Beulah Valduin's patron? The source of his magic? I warned you."

"Well, she is now, but she wasn't when you warned us," Rose attempted to clarify the situation. "She actually saved us from his first patron, who we thought was like an old elf or fey guy but turned out to be a big dragon. So, I guess you were right to warn us, but that was a little different situation."

Aloom looked at Rose with wide eyes. "You have been busy," she said before falling silent again.

"Anyway," Rose said, trying to get back on track, "do you know how to get past magic that is blocking your scrying?"

Aloom thought for a moment. "Well, you could always try to guess where they are and scry on the location instead of the person. If you get lucky, you might see him, though that depends a bit on how powerful his

71

warding magic is. Or, if you don't see him somewhere, then you'll know where he isn't. Which might be helpful." She thought for another moment. "As far as overcoming the magical ward, you would need to dispel it first. Which you can't do from afar." She finished with a shake of her head.

Adelaide sat forward and narrowed her eyes at Aloom. "Could you use another item to combine the spells? So you could dispel the ward and use scrying at the same time? Something like an arcane engine?" she asked. She watched for Aloom's reaction to those words.

Aloom gave a haughty chuckle. "Those silly toys that Brixim is always playing with? So he can combine a fire cantrip and an ice cantrip and make hot ice?" She waved a dismissive hand at Adelaide. "I've never heard of one powerful enough to do what you are describing."

Adelaide and Rose exchanged a glance. Rose addressed Aloom, "Well, this has been very helpful. I will try looking for Valduin in particular places. Maybe I'll get lucky. Now, are you interested in buying these things?"

Aloom sighed as she finished laughing. "Yes, back to business. I would like all of this. I will give you five hundred gold pieces for the teeth and one thousand for the brain. How does that sound?"

Adelaide's eyes sprung open. She nodded her head vigorously.

Rose, however, spoke first. "We'll take the five hundred for the teeth. I think I'll hang onto the brain for a little while longer."

Adelaide's head snapped around toward Rose. Rose held up a finger to stop her from saying anything.

Aloom cocked her head to the side, clearly noticing the friends' silent disagreement. "Well, I don't believe you will get a better offer anywhere else, but that is your prerogative. Would you like the five hundred gold pieces now? Or would you like to browse a bit? I do have some more healing potions in stock; I know you bought some of those the last time you were in."

Rose closed the bag around the brain and replaced it on her pack. "What do you think, Adelaide? A potion might be good. Valduin has all of ours."

Adelaide, still stunned by Rose's decision to keep the brain, took a moment to respond. "Uh, you know, we have plenty of healing magic. I think we'll take the coin, thank you."

"As you wish," Aloom said with a nod. She stepped out of sight into the back room.

"What are you doing?" Adelaide hissed once the elf had left the room.

Rose did not reply. She put a finger to her lips and shook her head. She packed the brain back into its sack.

Aloom returned with a jingling sack of coins a minute later. "Best of luck finding your friend. And do keep me in mind if you come across any other powerful creatures. I am always interested in buying such rare components."

The moment the door to The Eerie swung shut behind them, Adelaide erupted, "One thousand gold pieces! And you said no? What were you thinking?"

"I was thinking we would sell it to Brixim," Rose replied. "I think we are going to need his help to find Valduin. And this is our biggest bargaining chip right now."

Adelaide was quiet for a minute while she considered this plan. The women headed toward the Iron Tankard, but they were not in a rush. The hour was late, and the streets of the Circle of Light were empty.

"Okay," Adelaide eventually said. "That makes sense. Does that mean we have to go back to Tarsam? That's a long way away."

"Let me check," Rose said. She stepped to the side of the street and stopped walking. Her eyes went slightly out of focus, and her amulet lit her face with a soft, golden glow. "Seer Brixim, this is Rose Fairfoot. I would like to meet with you. I am in Khal Durum. Could you meet me here?"

Without delay, Brixim's voice erupted inside Rose's head. "Who are you? Why would I meet you in Khal Durum? Are you a dwarf? My shop is in Tarsam! You may make an appointment."

Rose sighed and sent another message. "My friends and I sold you the quasit head recently. I'm a halfling. We are in Khal Durum now. Could you come here?"

"Why would I go there? *You* want to meet with *me*! You may come to my shop. If you make an *appointment*!"

Rose let out a soft growl. Adelaide, who could not hear the gnome's replies, raised an eyebrow but said nothing. Rose sent another message and tried, with only partial success, to keep the frustration out of her voice. "Travel to Tarsam will take us several days. The matter is pressing. If you can travel by magic, it would be faster to meet here."

"I am very *busy*! If you are days away, it would be best to make your appointment *after* arriving in Tarsam."

Rose stomped her foot a few times. "That mean old gnome!" she hissed. She wanted to shout, but she did not want to draw attention to herself. She seethed for a few breaths before shaking her head and looking up at

Adelaide. "It looks like we've got a long walk ahead of us."

Adelaide shrugged. "That's not a big deal. At least it's all roads from here to Tarsam. We can go north to Westray, stop by my parents' place for a night, then take the Sandgate Road east right to the city. Shouldn't take more than ten days. Seven if we are lucky with the weather." She put her hand on Rose's shoulder and got her walking toward the tavern again.

"Seven to ten days," Rose muttered. "It's already been a week since we lost Valduin. I hope he'll be okay until we can find him."

"Did you know that about Scrying?" Madison asked. "The part where you can look in at a location instead of at a person?"

"No," Amelia grumbled. She slumped forward and rested her forehead on the table. She did not say anything else.

Madison picked up the rulebook to read the spell description. "I don't blame you," she said in an attempt to ease Amelia's despondency. "Look at how long this spell description is. That info is in the last two lines. I would have missed it, too." She held the book out to Amelia to show her the spell.

"Yeah, well, Logan wouldn't have," Amelia said, not picking up her head. "I think I'm gonna take a break." She glanced at the open book and pushed herself back from the table.

"Not now!" Madison cried, grabbing Amelia's sleeve. "We have a plan! We know where to go next! Let's keep going for a little while. The sooner we find Valduin, the sooner we'll get Logan back at the table so he can keep track of the inventory and our spells and things."

Amelia pulled her arm away. She looked at the rule-book again, still open in Madison's hand. "I just need a break. We'll go to Tarsam later." She trudged out of the room.

Madison watched her leave, her mouth hanging open in confusion. She closed the rulebook with a frustrated snap and dropped it on the table.

9

Rose and Adelaide sat on the floor between their beds in the suite at the Iron Tankard. Rose held the jeweled hand mirror, turning it over in her hands, looking at it but not really seeing it as she considered her options.

"Where should I try first?" she asked, not looking up from the mirror.

Adelaide was leaning against her bed, her head back, looking at the ceiling. "How about looking inside Beulah's hut? That's the most likely place to find him. And if you can hear them talking, maybe you can get an idea of where the hut is now. We know it can be near Hulte, where we found it first, near Mirstone, where she took us, or near Barnsley, where David Hancock first found her."

"Beulah probably has magic to block scrying," Rose muttered, "but I can try." She held the mirror up in front of her face. She focused on the space in front of the hearth at the end of the hut. The space between the ratty couches. She pictured as many of the pieces of furniture as she could remember. She pictured the raven perched in the rafters.

The mirror glowed with golden light for a moment. The oval mirror clouded over. Rose prayed in Halfling, *"Selaia, show me our friend Valdu—"*

Rose gasped. She felt like the words had been sucked out of her mouth. The glow disappeared. The mirror showed only her reflection.

She sighed and let the mirror fall into her lap. She looked up at Adelaide. "Nope."

"That's okay. Not a surprise, like you had said. How about out in the clearing? Maybe near the creepy chickens?" Adelaide suggested.

Rose held up the mirror again. Again, it began to glow. And again, the glow vanished abruptly.

"This spell has *never* worked," Rose groaned. She raised the mirror as if to smash it on the floor, but she restrained herself. "I can try one more time today before I'm out of energy," Rose said. "What do you think?"

Adelaide sat forward. "Hold on. Let's think about this. Whatever magic she is using probably only covers a certain area. Like the area of the clearing maybe. What if you tried to look down at the clearing from really high up? Higher up than the distance between the hut and the chicken coop in case the ward is a sphere. Can you do that?"

Rose's head hung; her chin rested against her chest. The mirror had slid out of her hand onto the floor at her side. "Probably not," she said without looking up.

"Well, you're going to try," Adelaide said, her voice growing firm. "No more pouting. Pick up that mirror and find our friend. Now."

Rose did not react to the intensity in Adelaide's voice, but she did pick up the mirror. She focused on the shape of the clearing. What the two dead trees that flanked the hut must look like from above. The arrangement of the chicken coop relative to the front of the hut. She even imagined a few of the strange chickens with human eyes languishing in their yard and the raven atop the coop keeping an eye on them.

Rose prayed, "*Selaia, show me the home of the hag Granny Beulah. Show me where Valduin was taken. Show me our friend.*" The mirror glowed. The glow grew brighter, lighting Rose's face in the dim room. The reflective surface of the mirror turned yellow and then white, and then it went dark.

Rose sighed and let the mirror fall into her lap.

"What are you doing?" Adelaide shouted, startling Rose. "It's still glowing! Is it working?"

Rose snatched the mirror back up. Looking into it again, she realized that it had not gone back to being a mundane mirror like it did when the spell failed. The diamonds twinkled with dim light. The mirror was dark because she was looking down from the night sky. Squinting into the small window that the mirror offered, Rose could see the hut, the clearing, the chicken coop, and the diseased forest surrounding it all. Yellow light shone from the front of the hut, illuminating a small area around the building's single door and window.

"I can see it!" Rose whispered, as if talking too loudly might alert Beulah to her presence. "The hut is there, the trees, everything the way we last saw it."

As she watched, a shadow moved across the lit area in front of the hut. Rose jumped; not used to snooping, she was terrified of being caught.

"Someone's moving around inside the hut," she said. The human had leaned forward onto her knees with the excitement of the magic working. She nodded along with Rose's reports but said nothing to distract her.

Rose watched for the next few minutes. Nothing else changed around the hut during that time. The glow faded and the mirror returned only her reflection.

"Not a total failure, I guess," Rose mused. She yawned. "That's enough for tonight. I'll look again in the morning. Maybe I'll get lucky."

"You're leaving so soon?" Tor asked when Rose shared their plan with the dwarf. "You just got here!"

The three women were seated at a table at the Iron Tankard eating breakfast. Rose had sent Tor a message to meet them there.

"I know. I know," Rose said, "but we need to get Valduin back. He's not safe where he is now."

Tor sighed. She stared at her food. Eventually, she nodded. "I understand," she said, "but you had better come back again soon."

"We will. As soon as we can," Rose replied.

"You can give this back to your dad, by the way," Adelaide cut into the conversation. On the table, she placed the golden ear cuff that King Obardean had given her before they had hunted down Kano and Tristan. "It feels like he gave me that thing years ago, but it was only a few weeks," she mused.

Tor picked up the magic jewelry. "I will. And it certainly does. It's amazing how quickly we went back to our usual routines after ridding ourselves of Tristan. I'm not sure if that's a good thing or not. Should we have spent more time grieving? Thinking about how we ended up in that situation? Making sure we are protected against such infiltration in the future?" Her eyes drifted away from Adelaide as she fell silent.

Adelaide shrugged. Rose made no reply. They both knew that those questions were not meant for them to answer. The trio finished their meal in silence.

"Well, we should be heading off. Don't want to leave too late and have to spend an extra night between here and Westray," Adelaide said, speaking a little louder than she wanted to. "Thank you so much for the room, Tor. We really appreciate it."

"It's the least I could do for heroes of Khal Durum. Be safe out there," Tor said, though she addressed Rose more than Adelaide.

Rose stood up and hugged the dwarf. "See you soon."

"This is so much nicer than the desert," Adelaide said. The women had been on the road for a couple of hours, and the sun was nearly at the top of the sky. "I'm not even sweating. Oh! Did you check on Valduin today?"

"Not yet. I figured I'd save my magic until tonight. Just in case."

"Makes sense." Adelaide nodded. "Well, we're on the road again. We'll get to Westray tomorrow, stop by my parents' house, and then it's on to Tarsam!" She did her best to sound enthusiastic.

Rose giggled. "Are you that excited to see Brixim again?"

Adelaide's face fell. "Definitely not. But I *do* want to get Valduin back. Could you please check on him now? You have lots of magic." She gave Rose a plaintive look.

Rose looked around at the surrounding forest. She looked up and down the long road. She shrugged. "Well, sure." She walked to the side of the road, dropped her pack on the ground, and sat down on a tree root. Once again, she took out the mirror and focused on the view of Beulah's hut from the sky.

And she was there, looking down at the hut. It was sunny, and Rose could see a few chickens outside the coop. A breeze wandered through the clearing, kicking up leaves from the forest and blowing them into the open. Rose heard only the wind. She watched intently for the duration of the spell, but she saw nothing notable.

"No Valduin," Rose reported as she put away the mirror and shouldered her pack. "I'll try again tonight."

"Sounds good," Adelaide said. She fell into step alongside Rose. They walked.

And walked.

They stopped in Westray to see Adelaide's parents.

They walked some more.

They stayed in the tavern in the halfling community of Biastal.

They kept walking.

For a week they walked. Each day, Rose checked in on Beulah's clearing. And each day, she was disappointed by what she found. Not once did she see either the witch or her friend.

One rainy afternoon they passed a few farmhouses, the first buildings on the outskirts of Tarsam. Another couple of miles farther, they saw shops and smaller homes along the road. Toward the end of the day, the Crystal Tower peeked over the horizon. They picked up their pace at the sight of the pinnacle of crystal which stood at the center of the city. Soon the entirety of Tarsam lay before them, the square mile of walled metropolis an expanse of gray roofs to match the overcast sky.

"Do we head inside now? Or wait until morning?" Rose asked. "You've spent more time here than me."

Adelaide grimaced. "Valduin and I didn't have much luck when we were here the first time. We got thrown out, remember? Maybe we should wait until tomorrow. People entering the city during the day seem to get less attention from the guards."

"Well, let me see if we can go right to The Lamia's Lair. That would probably be enough of an excuse to get past the guards," Rose said. Her next words were not meant for Adelaide. "Seer Brixim, this is Rose Fairfoot. I would like to make an appointment to see you at your shop tonight. Are you available?"

"*Tonight?*" Brixim's screech pierced Rose's mind. She winced. "You travel for a week or more and you want an appointment on an hour's notice? I am not available."

Rose waited a moment to be sure Brixim had nothing else to say before sending another message. "Could I make an appointment for the morning? I really need to see you soon. It is very important."

"*All* of my business is important," Brixim replied. "Saying yours is *very* important will not win you priority. But yes, I will see you in the morning."

Rose's eyes refocused on Adelaide. "I don't think I like him anymore. Anyway, he'll see us in the morning. Let's stop at the first tavern we see. I don't want to mess with the guards tonight."

Rose knew where she was before she had even opened her eyes. She was back in the dream.

She leapt from her bed and headed for the door, but she stopped herself before she opened it. She looked around her bedroom. It was exactly how she remembered it from the day she left the temple. Her vase with the single pink rose stood on the windowsill. The rose that Valduin had used to make the first magic that Rose had ever seen.

Rose stepped over to the windowsill. She picked up the rose and smelled it. It smelled the way it was supposed to smell, like summer days in her garden. A wave of homesickness washed over her. She stood at the window, holding the rose, not looking at anything as tears clouded her eyes.

She jumped when someone knocked on her bedroom door.

Rose whipped around, surprised by the noise. She stepped to the door and pushed it open. Standing in the corridor was Halamar.

"I was worried you had gotten lost," Halamar said as a stern greeting.

"Oh, I'm sorry! I got a little distracted," Rose said.

"Quite alright. Come." Halamar turned and headed toward the central chapel where they usually met during these dreams.

"Did you find the elf?" Rose asked while she walked behind Halamar. "The rude one?"

He did not answer until they had entered the chapel. He turned to Rose. "I have been asking around. The difficulty with the time difference between my home and yours is that this elf could have been on your plane for days and come back here only hours after he left."

"Yes, of course," Rose said. She furrowed her brow as she attempted to make sense of this statement. "So, you haven't found him yet?"

Halamar shook his head. "Not quite. I have asked for an audience with the council that governs Eydon. They will be able to sort out who it was that left the city. If they listen to me." His voice trailed away on his last sentence. He scratched his cheek, appearing uneasy.

"Why would they not listen to you?"

"Well, there may have been a time when I was part of that council," Halamar replied, still scratching his cheek. "And I may have been part of some decisions that the current council members regret. And I may not have been terribly open to hearing differing opinions back then."

Rose took a moment to absorb this.

"Ah," she said. "You don't think they'll believe you? Or you don't think they'll even give you a chance to talk?"

Halamar shifted his weight from one foot to the other. "What I think now has no impact on their decision," he replied, "but I hope that they grant me an audience. I hope at least one believes me. That's all I need."

"Is there anything else I can do to help?" Rose asked.

Halamar shrugged. "Is there anything else you can tell me that might help me identify the rude elf?"

Rose thought for a moment. She ran through everything she could remember the elf saying. She perked up as she asked, "Did I mention the betrayal comment?"

Halamar narrowed his eyes at the halfling. "I don't think so."

"So, right before the hag came back and attacked us, Valduin asked the elf a bunch of questions. About Eydon and how he got himself stuck in the cage and that sort of thing. The only answer the elf gave was about being betrayed by the one that was supposed to protect him. I'm pretty sure those were the words."

Halamar took a step back from Rose. His mouth fell open. Without a word, he waved his hand.

Rose woke up in the dark.

"Looks like I struck a nerve with that one!" Amelia said, excitement in her voice for the first time in days. "He must know who was doing the betraying."

"But who could it be?" Madison asked. "Could it be a new character? Someone we haven't met yet?"

"I mean, it *could* be," Amelia replied. She held up her notebook to show her last notes to her sister. "I'm not the right one to ask."

Madison saw Amelia's map of the tomb of Galien with a sketch of the Deep Dweller, Gnash. She giggled. "Is that really the last thing you wrote in your notebook?"

Amelia flipped a couple of pages. "I've got some drawings of Rose wearing the circlet in here, too, but that's about it." She looked around the table. "Where's Logan's notebook? He keeps a whole section just for information about the characters we meet and hear about."

"He's been keeping it in his room. On purpose. So we don't see what he's been up to."

"I can't believe he thought that we would go snooping!" Amelia put a hand on her chest to emphasize being offended with dramatic flair.

"You just said you wanted to look through his notebook," Madison pointed out with a smirk.

"Yeah, but that was for a good reason," Amelia countered. "Okay, who have we met that could *possibly* be old enough and powerful enough to have been tasked with protecting Eydon? It would have to be someone that used to be good but now they are evil since the betrayal was a surprise."

Madison's head snapped up to look at Amelia with wide eyes.

Amelia stiffened as the pieces fell into place in her mind.

Together they whispered, "Taranath."

10

Adelaide awoke to a knocking on her door. She pushed herself up on one elbow to look out the window. The sky was beginning to lighten with the coming dawn, but it was certainly too early for her to be awake.

"Adelaide, open up," Rose's voice came through the door.

Adelaide dragged herself out of bed. "What is it?" she groaned as she pulled open the door to her room at the tavern. Standing in the low light of the hallway was Rose, fully armored, with her pack on her back. Adelaide's head and voice cleared as she took in the halfling's demeanor. "What is it?" she repeated, concern written on her face.

Rose slipped through the partially open door into Adelaide's room. "Halamar visited again. And I remembered something. Something that the one-footed elf said."

"What's that?"

"He said that he was betrayed by the one that was supposed to protect them."

"Yeah. I kinda remember that." Adelaide nodded. She closed the door and sat down on the side of the bed.

"Who do we know that has connections to Eydon?" Rose asked.

Adelaide furrowed her brow for a few seconds. She shook her head slowly from side to side, not making the connection.

"Who do we know that was around back when the residents of Eydon were still on this plane? Someone who may have been good eight hundred years ago but certainly seems evil now?"

Adelaide's eyes grew wide. "*Taranath*," she hissed. Her upper lip pulled up into a reflexive snarl as she said the name.

Rose nodded. "I'm not sure what we can do with that information at the moment, but it's an interesting revelation."

Adelaide chewed on the corner of her mouth for a moment while she considered this. "You're probably right," she said, "but it's definitely good information to have. Something tells me we aren't done with that slimy dragon yet."

"Well, I'm not going hunting for a dragon without Valduin. You ready to go see Brixim?"

Adelaide yawned. "Not quite. Isn't it a little early?"

"Brixim said we could come in the morning. It's technically morning. Let's go wake him up," Rose said with a grin.

Adelaide chuckled. "You aren't usually this spiteful. I like it. Let me wash my face first. You want to check on Beulah's hut?"

Rose dropped her pack on the floor. She slumped against the wall opposite the bed. "I guess so," she said as she dug into her pack to get the hand mirror. "It's feeling pretty pointless, honestly. What are the chances

that I happen to be looking when one of them goes outside? I can only watch for ten minutes at a time."

"Just check, will you?" Adelaide urged before heading
to the washroom.

"Fine," Rose mumbled. She held up the mirror, as she
had done three times per day for the past week. Each
time she cast the spell, she pictured the clearing a bit
larger than the last time she had looked at it. Every day,
she moved her vantage a few feet closer to the hut. Rose
assumed that she also moved a few feet closer to whatever magical barrier Beulah maintained around her
home to block this type of intrusion.

The clearing was lit with sunlight, the sun peeking
over the trees to the east. Everything below her looked
as it had every other time she had looked down on it.
She focused on the hut, trying in vain to see through the
thatch roof or to hear some snippet of conversation
between Beulah and Valduin.

A few minutes passed. Rose was on the verge of letting
the magic fade.

The wooden door flew open.

Something left the hut. The more Rose tried to focus
on it, the harder it was to see. There was a smudge, a
shimmer, a ghost crunching through the dry grass of the
clearing. It moved with purpose, marching across the
open space and disappearing into the trees.

Rose looked up at Adelaide, who had returned to the
room and begun packing her gear.

"I think I saw him," she said.

Adelaide spun on her heel to face the halfling. "And?
Is he okay?"

"I couldn't see much. He was like a ghost, but I think
that's just because Beulah is blocking my magic. The

same reason I can't look right at him. But it must have been him. He was leaving the hut and the clearing."

"That's great!" Adelaide beamed. She threw her bag over her shoulder. "Let's go see Brixim. If he can help us find Val now, maybe we can get him while he's away from Beulah. That will make it easier to convince him to leave the witch forever."

Rose got to her feet and followed Adelaide out of the room. "We'll see about that," she muttered.

At Rose's direction, the cook at the tavern prepared the adventurers' breakfast to go, and they headed out. Turning toward Tarsam, they were greeted by the sight of the rising sun shining through the Crystal Tower, which rose high above the rooftops at the center of the city. The women made their way through the city's western gate, alongside farmers with carts of produce headed to the markets. The bleary-eyed city guards that were finishing their night shift greeted many of the farmers. None paid any attention to the adventurers.

"Do you remember how to get to The Lamia's Lair?" Rose asked once they were past the gate.

Adelaide nodded. "Brixim's shop is in the West Market, which should be really close to here. I think if we follow these carts, we'll find the market. Then it will be easy to find the shop."

Before long, they passed into the marketplace, a large city square filled with hundreds of stalls and carts. Adelaide turned to walk along the edge of the square, avoiding the maze.

"Can we walk through the middle?" Rose asked.

Adelaide shrugged. "I guess. It would probably be faster to go around, though."

"I know. It's just so peaceful." Rose had a serene half-smile on her face. Her pace slowed, and she led them into the maze. All around them, shopkeepers were in the process of opening up their stands and laying out goods and produce. They worked in silence. No one called out to the pair as they passed. No one was shouting greetings to other shopkeepers. A few workers looked up at them, surprised at seeing patrons this early. They would smile or nod in greeting before returning to their work.

Near what may have been the center of the maze, Rose stopped. She closed her eyes and listened.

"This isn't—" Adelaide said before Rose cut her off.

"Shush," Rose whispered. "Don't ruin it."

Adelaide did as Rose asked. After watching her friend for a moment, she closed her eyes as well. She listened to the sounds of the market coming to life. Footsteps passing to their left or right. The scrape of a straw broom on the cobblestones. The clank of a chain being released from a cart. The creak of old hinges as a stall door swung open. The thump of crates of fruit being placed onto shelves. Life all around them without a word being spoken.

After a minute, Rose opened her eyes. "Thank you," she said to Adelaide, her voice still hushed. "I needed that."

Adelaide opened her eyes and smiled at her friend. "That was nice. Especially before Brixim starts yelling at us."

"Oh, yeah, Brixim," Rose grumbled. Her face fell. "Let's get to it." She strode forward toward the edge of the square, heading for The Lamia's Lair.

Adelaide tried the doorknob. It did not turn.

She gave the door two firm knocks, and she took a step back.

Rose was looking at the window displays. The pearl-handled dagger sat on its pedestal, in the same place as it had been the first time they had seen this shop. The leather armor that had been displayed next to the dagger was gone. In its place, the mannequin in the window wore a black cloak. Rose could not make out many details on the cloak in the low light, but she noticed a faint silver shimmer across the garment as if a strand of spider's silk ran through the black fabric. In the other window, where the blue and green dress that fluttered without wind had hung, there was now a piece of furniture. An ornate wooden desk with a matching chair. Rose shrugged.

The door creaked open an inch.

From the dark interior of the shop, Brixim's creaky voice rang out, "Do you have an appointment?"

Rose stepped forward. "Good morning, Seer Brixim. Yes, we do. I am Rose Fairfoot, and I sent you a message last night. You said you would see us in the morning."

The gnome's gnarled face appeared from the darkness, though the door remained open a mere inch. Brixim inspected Rose through his floating monocle, saying nothing.

The door slammed shut. Rose could hear the clattering of the chain being released. The door swung open. "Well? Come in!" Brixim croaked.

The women stepped into the musty shop. Aside from the changes in the window displays, the shop appeared the same now as it had when they had hidden here from the city guards. Brixim sat behind the low countertop that wrapped around the store, separating the shoppers from the inventory. Adelaide had to duck beneath bundles of sticks and dried flowers that hung from the ceiling. The shelves and cubbies that lined the walls were full of books, scrolls, and boxes. The shop smelled of leather and incense, though there was a hint of something acrid as well, a smell that both women noticed but neither could identify.

Adelaide closed the door behind them.

Rose stepped toward Brixim. "Good morning. It is nice to see you again. Thank you for meeting with us this morning."

"I'll admit, it is my fault for not specifying," Brixim began, "but to most *civilized* people, the morning starts *after breakfast*." He shifted his glare back and forth between his guests.

Rose took a deep breath, forcing herself to remain polite. "I am very sorry." She tried to sound sincere. "Would it be better if we came back in a little while? We just knew how excited you would be to see what we have to offer. You know, because you were so interested in that quasit head."

Brixim narrowed his eyes at Rose. The monocle remained, hovering within the grip of the wizard's spectral third hand. When he replied, his words came more slowly than before. "Yes, the quasit head. It was *quite* interesting. So, what are you selling today?"

Rose smiled, ignoring Brixim's suspicious tone. She stepped forward and placed the cloth bag on the counter. As she had in Aloom's shop, she released the drawstring and pulled the bag down to show the object.

Brixim did not react to the sight of the small, gray lump. "And what is it that you *think* you have here?" he asked.

"It's the brain of a, uh," Rose faltered, trying to remember the name of the monster. She turned to Adelaide and asked, "What did Aloom call it?" Her back turned to Brixim, she gave her friend a sly wink.

Adelaide picked up on Rose's tone. "Oh! Enchantress Aloom, you mean? Yes, well, when we showed it to her in her shop in Khal Durum—it was a *very* nice shop, by the way—she said that it was the brain of a chylomyria."

Rose grinned at Adelaide's act. She turned back to Brixim, whose mouth had dropped open. "Yes! We didn't know its name when we killed the thing. Ghastly big bug, it was. But Aloom offered one *thousand* gold pieces for it. We said we couldn't possibly take that offer because we *knew* how much you valued the study of such rare monster parts. She didn't think you would know what to do with it, but we told her that you are the absolute *best* when it comes to such studies." She paused to let her words sink in.

Brixim's gaping mouth snapped shut. His eyes flared with anger. "Aloom! That flaky, flimsy, flouncy elf!" His hands shook as he seethed. "Well," he said between breaths. "Well, well, well, well, well." He massaged his temples, muttering in a squeaky language that the adventurers did not understand. After another moment, he heaved a great sigh, and he regained control of himself.

"I do appreciate your, uh, consideration," he said. "I will take it! Did you have a price in mind? Aloom offered you one thousand you said? I could easily beat that."

Rose stepped up to the counter, getting herself as close to Brixim as she could. "We don't want coin," she said, all of the mirth gone from her voice. "We need your help."

Brixim's head cocked to the side in apparent surprise at Rose's change of tone. He narrowed his eyes at the halfling again. "What kind of help do you think I could offer?" he asked with surprising sincerity.

"We need an arcane engine."

"Jumping right into it, then? Okay, let's see how this goes," Madison said, her eyes wide in surprise. She nodded her head slowly. "You got lucky on that Deception check when we talked about Aloom. You think that luck is going to hold out?"

Amelia gave a sly grin. "You know halflings are lucky," she said.

"Halfling Lucky is a very specific game mechanic," Madison replied. "It doesn't mean everything you try will work out for you."

"Well, I've got some more things I can use to persuade him," Amelia huffed. "Remember, this is the *only* idea that we have for finding Valduin. We have to use everything we've got to make it work."

"Well, we probably should have used some magic to get ready for this interaction, then. You think you could cast Guidance or Enhance Ability now?"

Amelia grimaced. "You think Brixim would let me start casting spells in his shop? I doubt it."

"Yeah, you're probably right. Well, my fingers are crossed. I really can't do anything to help at this point. I hope you've got what you need to convince him."

11

Brixim slumped back into his chair. "What do *you* know of such magics?" he hissed, his gaze fixed on Rose.

Rose was not intimidated. "We know they exist. We know they can combine the effects of different spells. And we know that they are the interest of only a few exceptionally talented magical tinkerers."

Brixim said nothing. He stared at Rose, his lips pursed, considering Rose's unexpected request.

Rose continued, "Hemwidick and Hawunzbust had a very nice one. They combined one of my radiant attacks with a fireball spell, I believe. The results were impressive, to say the least."

Brixim sat up straight again. "The Scribblescrabblers! How did those lazy good-for-nothings build an engine that could harness a fireball? And why would they show you?" His voice fell into suspicion again, and he stood up from his chair. Without breaking eye contact with Rose, he took a half step toward the back of the shop.

Rose backtracked, trying to keep Brixim engaged, "We ran into them on the road a short time ago. We were attacked by a group of lizardfolk. It was mostly out of desperation that they brought out the engine. I don't think they would have told us about it otherwise. Especially Hawunzbust. He seemed upset when it broke after we used it."

Brixim grinned. "Ha! I knew they couldn't make something that strong. They stole my plans for a particular type of engine a few months ago. A very powerful one. I knew then that they didn't know enough to use the plans. It sounds like they haven't gotten much further in the interim." He returned to his seat.

"So, you know about arcane engines," he continued. "What is it that you want to do with one?"

"Valduin, the third member of our party, has been abducted," Rose explained with a white lie. "I have tried to locate him, but I believe he is being warded against scrying. I need to be able to see past that ward. Is that something you could do?"

Brixim put his elbows on the counter. He steepled his fingers in front of his mouth, considering the request. After a moment of thought, he answered, "Yes, I believe I could. And you would trade me this brain for the use of the engine?"

Rose smiled. "Yes, if you think that is a fair trade."

Brixim nodded. "Certainly. Stay here. I'll be right back." He hopped down from his chair and strode into the back room.

Adelaide stepped up to Rose and patted her on the shoulder. "Nice work," she commended her friend, keeping her voice low. "That was much easier than I thought it would be."

Rose beamed. "I thought that mentioning the other gnomes might trigger something. Nothing like a little competition to—"

Rose's words were cut off.

The floor vanished beneath them.

The shop disappeared, and they fell, screaming through darkness.

They did not fall for long before they landed on a hard surface. Rose pitched forward into Adelaide's legs, and they ended up in a pile.

"What was that?" Rose moaned, trying to push Adelaide off her.

"*That* is what happens to *spies!*" Brixim's screech cut through the darkness. "You thought you could just walk into my shop and take one of my greatest creations? *Think again!*"

Adelaide pushed herself to her feet. She focused for a moment, and her breastplate lit up with magical light. They were in a basement room of some kind, completely constructed of stone. There was a hole in the ceiling above them, and a chute that must have led up to the floor of the shop, though Adelaide could not see it. There was one wooden door leading out of the chamber; the door was open. Brixim stood within its frame.

"What did you do?" Rose said as she got to her feet. She stepped toward Brixim but found her path blocked by an invisible barrier. "What are you going to do?"

"You can sit down here for a little while and consider your *failure!*" Brixim shouted. "Then, I will banish you from this plane. If you manage to find your way back to your bosses, you can tell those dirty Scribblescrabblers that I will not stand for such insults. They can come and try to take my designs themselves." He slammed the door, vanishing from sight.

"Get back here!" Rose screamed at the door.

"Oh boy," Adelaide muttered. "This was not part of the plan."

"We do not work for them! We met them by accident. We want to stop them! They serve *Misery*. We will kill them all for what they did to us!" Rose roared as she slammed her fists against the barrier. Her eyes and amulet glowed as she sent the magical message to Brixim, wherever he had gone.

Brixim did not reply to the message. A moment later, the door swung open.

The gnome darted to the other side of the barrier. With a wave of his hand, torches flared to life around the chamber. He stared into Rose's eyes. "How do you know Misery?" he asked, his words rushed and his voice hushed.

Rose's intensity did not wane. "We were supposed to make an exchange with him. Things didn't go according to plan. He tried to kill me. He did kill her." She nodded her head toward Adelaide. "We met Hem and Haw on our way to the Ebon Keep. We were ambushed by lizard-folk, the followers of a red dragon named Lady Muriel. We would have all been killed if not for their arcane engine. Now, we've lost our friend. We need him back. Can you help us?"

Brixim listened to Rose's story, never taking his eyes off hers. "How can I know? How can I *know* you are working against them? Against *him*?"

"Because we saved Nyla," Rose said. "We saved your great-granddaughter from the fiends that serve the same master as Misery. They are all working for the Voidbringer. We killed those fiends. And we will kill Misery and the Voidbringer too." Her eyes blazed with fury; she did not look away from Brixim.

Brixim narrowed his eyes as he stared into Rose's.

"What did she wield? When you fought beside her?" he asked.

"A wand that you made," Rose replied without hesitation. "A wand that could throw fireballs."

Brixim stepped back from the barrier. He waved a hand, and the space between them shimmered. "Thank you," he said, the anger gone from his voice. "Thank you for saving her. She told me the story, but I didn't realize that it was you."

He turned away from Rose and walked toward the door.

"Come. This will take some work."

Adelaide and Rose followed Brixim up a narrow spiral staircase. At the top, they found themselves in the back room of The Lamia's Lair. Brixim had a few sets of shelves, all covered in books, boxes, and containers of spell components. Along one wall was a desk with a stool in front of it. In the middle of the room was a larger worktable. Tools, both familiar and alien to the women's eyes, littered both surfaces.

Brixim perched on the stool facing Adelaide and Rose. He took a moment to size them up before speaking. "Tell me again what it is you need to do," he said.

Rose answered, "Valduin, our half-elf friend that was with us the last time we were in your shop, is currently being warded against scrying. We don't know if he is using an item for this, or if someone has cast a spell on him, but either way, I have been unable to find him for a couple of weeks now. We need to get through that barrier. We had the idea that we could dispel the magic, but I can't dispel anything from afar."

Brixim listened, nodding along with Rose's explanation. "Yes, this can be done. I will need to adjust your focus. What do you use to cast the scrying spell?"

Rose produced the diamond-encrusted hand mirror. She handed it to Brixim.

Brixim inspected the mirror. A large, crystal lens on a hinged arm folded down from the top of the desk, moved by an unseen force, and came to rest above the item. Brixim peered through the lens and nodded.

"I can make the adjustments. It will take some time. And supplies. Do you have any loose gems on you?"

Rose thought for a moment. "I don't have anything left but some diamond dust. Would that help?"

Brixim shook his head. "Not for this task, unfortunately." He looked to Adelaide.

Adelaide dug around inside her bag for a moment. When she stood up, she held the jeweled dagger that she had taken from David Hancock's house. She felt a twinge of guilt when she realized that she could have returned it to him before he fled Mirstone. The twinge did not last long. She placed it on the desk. "Would any of this help?" she asked.

He took the dagger and held it under the large lens. "Yes! This will do." He muttered an incantation in what the women assumed was Gnomish. As they watched, the gold of the dagger's handle and scabbard wobbled, as if made of jelly. The gems clattered onto the desktop. Brixim set the dagger aside and sorted through the green and yellow gems.

"How long do you think this will take?" Rose asked. She and Adelaide were still standing in the workshop. Adelaide had to stoop to keep from hitting her head on the ceiling.

"If things go well, a few hours. If they don't..." He let the words hang in the air before shrugging.

Rose laid a hand on Brixim's shoulder and prayed, *"May Selaia guide your hands."*

Brixim grinned. "A long time ago, I had a friend who would use that spell all the time. She wouldn't get out of bed without guidance." He laughed a tittering, fanatical laugh.

Rose had not heard him laugh before, and she found the sound more off-putting than reassuring.

"Thank you," he said. "If you two want to go get lunch or run any errands, go ahead. I'll let you know when it's ready."

"Well, this has been a day," Rose mumbled around a large bite of a sandwich.

"Sure has," Adelaide agreed. They were sitting with their backs against the front of Brixim's shop. They had restocked their food supplies and bought lunch from a vendor in the maze. They were not in any rush, so they took their time wandering through the commotion of the West Market.

They had gone for a walk through the Mosaic District of Tarsam to pass the time. They did their best to avoid the central part of the city, where the city guards had the largest presence. They had done nothing wrong, but they also did not belong here. Adelaide knew that the guards did not take kindly to vagrants.

By the early evening, they had bought themselves more sandwiches from another vendor and returned to The Lamia's Lair. They sat on the sidewalk in front of the shop, saying little, eating dinner, and watching the shopkeepers closing up for the day.

"I am ready to try it," Brixim's voice spoke in Rose's mind. "Come on in." Without delay, the door to the shop swung open behind them.

Adelaide looked up at the sound of the door opening. "Is that for us?" she asked. She sounded nervous.

"Yeah," Rose said. "He just told me he's ready to try it out." She took a deep breath before heading into the shop. "Here we go," she muttered.

Adelaide followed Rose inside. The hinged section of the counter was already up; they walked straight to the back room.

On the worktable lay the mirror. A frame of slim, silver rods now outlined the circular reflective surface. The handle appeared unchanged. The silver rods converged on a point at the top of the mirror, where there was a small gap in the framework. On the table next to the mirror was a pile of green gems taken from the dagger.

Brixim had shifted the stool from the desk to the worktable. He sat with his hands folded in front of him, his forehead resting against them. He looked up as Adelaide and Rose entered the room. Both women noticed the dark circles below his eyes. "Welcome back," he greeted the adventurers, his voice wispy and weary. "Let's see how we did."

Rose stepped forward, not commenting on Brixim's appearance. She picked up the mirror and inspected the changes that he had made. "You work very fast," she commented, "For how complicated these things are supposed to be."

Brixim gave a sly smile. "I had help," he said. "And this space is, shall we say, specifically designed to allow such work to be done quickly."

Rose raised an eyebrow, but she did not probe further on this topic. She had only one thing she needed to know about. "How do we use it?" she asked.

Brixim pointed to the emeralds. "Take a gem."

Rose complied.

"Place it in the space at the top of the engine."

Rose held the stone in the gap where the silver rods came together, making sure that each of the rods was touching the emerald.

"Cast a spell that can remove the magical ward blocking your vision."

Rose concentrated for a moment. *"Selaia, break down the barriers keeping Valduin from me,"* she prayed in Halfling. The gem took on a faint glow, and that glow spread around the frame of the engine until the mirror was wreathed in green light. Rose released the gem. It stayed in place at the top of the frame, held by the magic that she had imbued it with.

Brixim's eyes were wide with excitement. *"Yes,"* he whispered. "That's it. Now, focus on your friend. Look for him. Find him." The old gnome was leaning forward, his wrinkled face a study in anticipation lit by the green glow of the arcane engine.

Rose held the mirror in front of her face, as she had grown accustomed to doing each day when she looked down at Beulah's hut. This time, however, she focused on Valduin. She thought about his floppy hair, his kind eyes, his gently pointed ears. She focused on the feeling of bringing him back from the dead, kneeling on the hard floor of The Tavern in Mirstone, forming a connection that pulled him back from the other side.

The surface of the mirror no longer showed her reflection. It flashed with golden light and faded to dark gray.

There he was. Standing in the rain. It was dark. His cloak flapped against his legs in the wind.

"I see him!" Rose whispered, not wanting Valduin to hear her, though she knew he could not. "Something's weird though," she said. She squinted at the small image. Then she saw the faint purple outline of the broomstick between his legs. "Oh, he's flying. Hovering.

Facing... down?" She rotated the mirror left and right to get a sense of how he was oriented.

She watched. Valduin extended his left hand in front of himself, pointing straight toward the ground below him. With a twitch of his wrist, something appeared to grow out of his palm. A moment later, he held a long, slender stick.

A wand.

This new wand was covered in thorns, and as Valduin held it, his blood dripped from its tip. He shouted words that Rose did not understand over the howl of the wind, and a ray of gray light shot down from the wand toward the ground.

Rose swung the mirror around to change her view. From above Valduin, she watched as the ray hit the ground in the middle of a cluster of tents. A sphere of silent, swirling, black and gray energy spread out until it encompassed the entire campsite.

Rose gasped. She watched as a half-dozen humanoids collapsed within the sphere. She could hear the screams of those that survived the roiling circle of death.

Valduin fell toward the campsite. He landed hard, his boots sinking into the mud.

He flicked the thorned wand from side to side, sending purple sparks of energy into a couple of creatures staggering out of the ramshackle tents. Now that he was closer, Rose could see that the humanoids Valduin was attacking were shorter than he was, with two arms and two legs but with the head and bulging eyes of fish. It was a sahuagin camp.

A screech erupted from across the campsite. A bolt of lightning shot across the area, lighting up the scene and drawing a grunt from Valduin. Valduin dove behind a tent, but not before Rose caught a glimpse of a familiar female figure walking toward him.

"Valduin," Rose whimpered, "run."

"What is it?" Adelaide asked, her voice pressured. She did not want to break Rose's concentration, but she needed to know what was happening.

"He's going after Stela," Rose whispered, not taking her eyes off the mirror. "He's going after the hag all by himself."

"What was that?" Amelia asked, her eyes wide. "What is he doing?"

"Logan!" Madison shouted. "Logan, get down here!"

They heard a door open upstairs. A moment later, Logan walked into the room.

"What? I'm busy," he said, looking annoyed.

"You attacked Stela?" Amelia screamed. "By yourself? What were you *thinking*?"

Logan looked surprised for a moment, and then his shoulders slumped. He replied, "Oh, I didn't know you guys had found me already." He turned and headed back to his room.

"What happened?" Madison shouted after him.

"You'll find out," he replied over his shoulder. "I wouldn't want to spoil it."

"He must have gotten out of there. Right? He would have told us if he died during this fight. Right?" Amelia asked her sister, panic rising in her voice. "He was only acting like he was sad. *Right?*"

Madison glared at Logan's back until he disappeared from view at the top of the stairs. "I'm not sure. I wouldn't put it past him to be trying to trick us. But he definitely would have been sad if he died."

"I'm sure he's just pretending," Amelia said, trying and failing to sound confident. "His Fly spell was still active. He probably escapes now that he knows she's there. Right?"

12

Valduin crouched behind the tent. His hood had fallen back during his run for cover, and Rose had her first glimpse of his face. He looked horrible, his eyes sunken and bloodshot with dark circles beneath them. He looked dirty despite the downpour in which he stood.

Rose could hear Stela screaming something, but she could not understand the words. Valduin, the broomstick still glowing between his legs, kicked up into the air. Ten feet above the tent, he threw three purple eldritch blasts at the approaching hag and dove down behind the cover of the tent once again. He edged toward the side of the tent Stela would be coming around.

Stela did not walk, though. With the light thump of an arcane door closing, she appeared behind Valduin. Arcs of lightning leapt from one outstretched hand, coursing through Valduin. The half-elf's back arched in uncontrollable tetany. His groan crescendoed into a howl. Tendrils of smoke rose from his hair and his cloak. Stela cackled with glee.

Valduin turned, his movements halting and jerky as his body recovered from the second hit of lightning. He shouted out an incantation that Rose neither recognized nor understood. Stela's laughter cut off. Her hand remained outstretched, but it did not track Valduin as he stepped around to the back of the hag.

Stela stood frozen, paralyzed, held in place by Valduin's spell. Her eyes twitched back and forth as she tried in vain to find her assailant.

Valduin caught his breath. He held the thorned wand up and pointed it at the middle of the hag's back. "*To the depths*," he hissed. The three purple sparks appeared, swirling around his hand. Instead of spiraling down the length of the wand, as Rose had seen before, the sparks dove into the wand one at a time, lighting up the creases between its braided strands. The purple lights ran the length of the wand and erupted from the tip. One, two, three, they slammed into Stela's back. Still locked in place, she made no reaction to the impacts. Dark blood trickled from the corner of her mouth.

Stela's arm fell to her side as she shrugged off the effects of Valduin's paralyzing spell. She panted from the pain of his attacks, pausing to spit out blood. Valduin loosed another round of eldritch blasts into her back, spinning her around. Without even catching her balance, the witch lifted a hand and sent a lightning bolt tearing through the half-elf. His hair stood on end; a few ends caught fire from the power of the attack.

Valduin was still on his feet. He gave a wicked smirk as black smoke poured from his hands. He stretched his arms out toward Stela. Stepping away from him, she batted at the smoke as it enveloped her. She opened her mouth to scream only to have the smoke stifle her.

When the smoke cleared, she lay on the ground, unmoving, her green skin drained to gray, withered and cracked. With a flurry of movement, Valduin dropped to one knee and pressed a small glass sphere against the hag. The sphere clouded over.

Valduin gazed at the soul sphere as he got to his feet. He returned it to his pocket and headed for Stela's tent.

Rose followed along, watching through the hand mirror in breathless shock. She watched Valduin go into the tent. She saw him search through a few bags and boxes until he found a cloth sack. She saw a collection of opaque soul spheres in the sack. She saw the bag of platinum coins he pulled from another bag.

Valduin stepped out into the rain once again, and the spell ended. Rose gazed upon her own reflection in horrified silence.

Adelaide waited for Rose to tell her what she had seen. With her right hand, she tugged at the strap that held her handaxe on her belt. The glow from the mirror had faded, but Rose remained transfixed, staring at her reflection.

Rose lowered the mirror, placing it on the table so softly that it did not make a sound. She turned to Adelaide. "He killed her. And he stole her soul."

Adelaide wanted to smile. She wanted to relish this moment of vicarious vengeance, but the look on Rose's face made her hold back. The halfling looked terrified.

"He killed them all," Rose went on. "All of the fish people. With one spell. I've never seen him use it before. But it was *big*."

Adelaide placed her hand lightly on Rose's shoulder. "This is good. We know where he is now. We can find him. We can help him."

Rose's eyes drifted back to the mirror. It lay cocked at an angle on the table; the frame of the arcane engine prevented it from lying flat. She reached out one shaky hand and flipped the mirror face down.

Adelaide turned to Brixim. "Can you get us to Mirstone?" she asked.

Brixim, who had been watching Rose intently, looked up at Adelaide. "What? Mirstone? Now?" he asked. "I don't get a 'Thank you, oh wonderful Seer Brixim, for building us from scratch a marvelous magical engine at a moment's notice'?" He mimicked Rose's voice. "You go straight to, 'Hey, old man, teleport us across the continent so we can find our murderous ally'?" He switched to an imitation of Adelaide's voice.

Rose spoke up, her voice soft and sorrowful. "Valduin is our friend. We could not have saved Nyla without him. And he needs our help. He doesn't look like himself. He isn't acting like himself. I don't know what Beulah did to him, but he needs us. And we can't help him without you." She pulled her eyes away from the mirror to look at Brixim.

The old gnome softened under her gaze. He pursed his lips as he considered their request.

"I can get you to Mirstone," he said, breaking the silence of the cramped workshop. "But how will you find him?"

"He was in the swamp," Rose answered. "He'll go through the town if he's headed back to the Virdes Forest, where Beulah's hut is. I have the magic to find him if we are close to him. Hopefully, we get lucky."

"You could also use the engine to help," Brixim said. "It should be able to extend the range of your other magics as well." He picked up the emeralds that remained on the worktable. "But you've only got enough fuel for three more spells with that engine. If it doesn't break before then, which it might."

"Yes, Hem and Haw said my spell was too big for theirs, and it broke," Rose recounted.

Brixim nodded. "Too much power will break it. This one especially, as I did not have much time to test it for such weaknesses. Well, are you ready? I imagine time is of the essence."

"Yeah, we're ready," Adelaide said. She put a hand on Rose's shoulder.

Rose took the emeralds from Brixim and picked up the mirror. "Thank you, Brixim. We really appreciate the help. I don't know if we've given you enough to pay for all of this."

Brixim gave Rose a warm smile, for the first time looking like the great-grandfather that he was. "Nyla is all you needed to give me." His smile twisted into a smirk as he added, "But giving that brain to me instead of Aloom is a nice touch. I'll be sure to let her know what I make with it." He snickered.

"Now, let's go to Mirstone," he said. He clapped his hands. Without warning, Rose and Adelaide were pulled in toward Brixim, but without moving. Instead, they felt themselves stretched headfirst toward the gnome in a way incompatible with their understanding of their physical bodies. Riding a wave of nausea, the light of the workshop pulled in toward the gnome as well, leaving only darkness around them. The women felt their stomachs flip as they were teleported out of The Lamia's Lair.

Adelaide and Rose collapsed against each other into a puddle. The rain that Rose had seen while watching Valduin continued; the adventurers were immediately soaked.

Brixim stood next to them, grumbling in Gnomish while searching through his pockets. After a moment he produced a short, metal rod. With a flick of his wrist, the rod hummed with energy. He released the rod, which remained aloft within a spectral copy of his hand. Above his head, the rain divided like a river splitting around an island. Protected from the deluge by the magical shield, he brushed water off his sleeves.

"Very well," he said once he was situated within his private bubble. "I believe this should be Mirstone. It has been a while since I have traveled this far east, but I doubt this town has changed all that much."

The adventurers got to their feet and looked around. They were standing in an alley between two wood-paneled buildings. There was a smell of refuse coming from deeper within the alley, even through the downpour. Adelaide stepped to the alley entrance and glanced out. It took her only a moment to recognize the main marketplace of Mirstone; she could see Mr. Surlin's jewelry shop across the plaza. In the evening rain, the market was empty of shoppers and vendors.

"Yeah, this is Mirstone," Adelaide reported back to Rose and Brixim. "We're in the market. I don't see anyone around. What do we have to do next? Head to the swamp?"

"If you both are quite settled, I will be returning home," Brixim said. "I have no interest in traipsing through a *swamp* in any weather, but especially not in these conditions." He wrinkled his nose in disgust.

"That's fine. Thank you so much for getting us this far," Rose said. "Before you go, though, can you tell me how to use this to try to find our friend?" She held up the hand mirror with the arcane engine attached.

Brixim took the item from Rose. With movements too rapid for Rose to track, he removed the spindly engine from the mirror and folded its arms into a rod. He handed it back to Rose and said, "Use this as the focus for casting the spell. With a jewel in it, of course. The larger the jewel, the more the engine will enhance the spell. If you want to use it for scrying again, just reattach it to the mirror."

Rose nodded along with Brixim's instructions. "I'm not sure I'll be able to do that, but hopefully we won't need to," she said. She turned to Adelaide. "Let's head for the swamp. I'll cast the spell when we are closer. I don't want to waste it."

"You got it," Adelaide replied. To Brixim she said, "Thanks for the help."

"You're welcome. Now, I'll need to find somewhere dry so I can get home." He looked around the marketplace. "If anywhere is still open," he muttered.

Rose pointed down the street to the south, away from the market. "If you head that way, and look down the streets to your right, eventually you'll see a sign that says 'The Tavern.' Tell them Rose and Adelaide sent you."

Brixim narrowed his eyes. "A tavern, you say?"

"No. *The* Tavern," Rose said with a smile. "Ask for roots and boots. It's the house delicacy."

Brixim shrugged. "Very well. I guess I'm not really in a rush. And it is dinner time. Be safe!" He gave a small bow and strode out across the market, weaving around puddles while his arcane umbrella hovered above him.

The rain continued. Adelaide and Rose arrived at the remains of the Mirstone carnival grounds. Only a handful of ramshackle constructions still dotted the field, standing and leaning like headstones in the acres of mud and dead grass.

"Wow, this place is creepy," Adelaide said as they picked their way across the soggy field toward the edge of the swamp.

Rose looked around as if noticing where they were for the first time. "Oh, yeah," she mumbled in agreement. Her eyes fell back to the item in her hands. She turned the arcane engine over again, handling the thin rods as if they could break at the slightest touch.

"Are you going to be able to use that without Brixim here?" Adelaide asked.

"I hope so." Rose looked around again. They were approaching the trees now. "Should we try it?"

"Sure." Adelaide lit up her armor so that Rose could see what she was doing.

"Thanks," Rose said. She took one of the emeralds from her pocket and held it to close the gap at the end of the arms of the engine. She focused on Valduin, picturing him the way he had looked when she had watched him destroy the sahuagin camp less than an hour ago. The emerald began to glow. Rose took her hand away, and the gem remained locked in place, fueling the engine.

Rose stared into that green glow, picturing Valduin: eyes sunken and bloodshot, shoulders slumped, blood dripping from that thorned wand in his left hand, slogging through the mud of the swamp. She felt her mind expand, searching for him. Her focus spiraled out from the glowing emerald, though her gaze remained fixed on it. Farther and farther into the swamp it spread, searching for him.

Without warning, the emerald's glow vanished. Rose blinked a few times to clear the green spot that lingered in her vision after staring at the gem for the last minute. When she could focus on the engine again, the emerald was gone.

"That's not the face of someone who suddenly knows how to find a lost friend," Adelaide commented. "It didn't work? Do we need to go get Brixim?"

Rose furrowed her brow. "No, it worked. Almost. I think he might still be protected against this kind of magic. I might need to use a spell to get rid of his protection again and then try to find him. I'm not sure. And I don't know if this thing can handle all of that at once."

"Let's think. He was protected earlier, but you were still able to see him when you looked at Beulah's hut from above, right?"

Rose nodded, but she did not look up from the item she was turning over in her hands. "He looked like a ghost. I could not see him directly, but I could see his effects on the space around him."

"Well, can you target something near him? Like his cloak? Or his armor?"

"I have to be specific," Rose muttered. "It has to be the exact—"

Rose's hands stopped moving. She cocked her head to the side as if some new view of the tool she held had been revealed to her. Without answering Adelaide's questions, she pulled out another emerald and placed it in the gap in the arcane engine.

"Find me the soul sphere containing the soul of the green hag Stela," she whispered to the gem. It glowed again. Rose allowed her consciousness to expand, spiraling out across the swamp, searching for the clouded, magic marble.

And there it was. Rose opened her eyes. Like a green star, the sphere shone in the black night of the swamp. Rose narrowed her eyes, peering into the darkness outside the range of Adelaide's light. The tiny green light was not moving, but it was far away.

"I see it," she said to Adelaide. "Ready to run?"

Adelaide grimaced. "Oof, I guess. Running through this swamp at night? This will be interesting."

Rose lit up her own armor to add to their visibility. "He isn't moving. He's probably still catching his breath after that fight. He'll be able to fly out of there soon. We want to get to him first."

"Oh boy, good point. Here we go," Adelaide said as she tightened the shoulder straps of her pack. The women took off into the swamp, their path lit with shaking light from their bouncing armor. Their boots sloshed through puddles; they leapt over small waterways and scrambled through the underbrush. Rose clutched the arcane engine and focused on that green light, growing ever closer.

"We're gonna get him!" Madison cheered and jumped out of her chair. She grabbed Amelia's shoulders and shook her, unable to contain her excitement.

Amelia pulled away from her sister. "How long has it been since I watched Valduin's fight? I'm sure he used all his spells against Stela, but he only needs to rest for an hour to get them back. I'm *sure* that as soon as he can, he will cast Fly and be gone."

"Well, then we'll track him with your spells and the arcane engine again," Madison replied as she sat back down. "Right?"

Amelia raised an eyebrow at Madison. "How many emeralds do we have left?"

"Oh. One?"

"Yeah. One. And the spell is only supposed to last for ten minutes. I don't know how much extra time the engine is buying us right now, but we already got to extend the range by a *lot*. If we don't catch him now, I think we will be starting over."

Madison's shoulders slumped. "Ugh. Anything else?"

"Since you asked, yeah. In addition to needing more emeralds, we need to be worried that the engine might break. And I'll need to figure out how to reattach it to the mirror."

Madison held her hands up in surrender. "Okay! I get it! We have to get to him now." She scanned her character sheet. "I could cast Expeditious Retreat to speed myself up. I haven't used that one yet."

Amelia chewed on her lower lip as she considered this option. "If you do that, I won't be able to keep up with you, so you won't really know where you are going." She sighed. "But if you don't, we might lose him again."

13

The women ran through the dark swamp, growing more tired, dirty, and frustrated with each passing minute.

"I'm gonna go on ahead," Adelaide panted as Rose stumbled on the landing of another magically enhanced jump.

"Okay," Rose groaned as she got back on her feet. She pointed off into the darkness. "It's still there."

Adelaide took a moment to gauge the direction Rose indicated. She brushed her fingers against her totem, the eagle feathers in her hair, and said to herself, "Time to go!" Her legs, heavy from the sprint through the swamp, felt stronger. The ache in her knees and ankles subsided. The burning in her lungs cleared. She dashed ahead, dodging between trees and tearing through bushes, doing her best to keep the course Rose had indicated.

Rose slowed to a jog. She kept moving toward that glowing emerald ahead of her. Adelaide's light faded from sight as the human sprinted forward.

The light moved.

Only a little at first, as if Valduin was milling about in a small area, maybe the campsite.

The light jumped into the air. About thirty feet up, speeding toward her above the treetops.

"Adelaide, he's flying!" Rose said through a magical message. "Above the trees. He's coming this way. Did you find him yet? We can't let him get away!"

Adelaide's response came in bursts. Rose could imagine the human panting to catch her breath between the phrases. "I'm at... a river... I don't... want to swim."

Rose groaned. She picked up her pace again, sprinting and bounding to intercept the glowing green dot as best she could.

Adelaide stood on the bank of the river, hands on her knees, struggling to catch her breath. She stretched her back, scanning the gray sky above. The rain had slowed to a drizzle, but the clouds made the early evening dark.

A flash of purple caught her eye between the tops of the trees on the far bank.

There he was, a shadow against the clouds, coasting above the treetops on that faint, ethereal broomstick. He was coming toward her.

"Valduin!" Adelaide screamed. "Val! Down here!"

His course did not change. He cleared the last line of trees into the open sky above the river.

"Sorry, bud," Adelaide mumbled. She held up one hand, her thumb tucked against her palm. The nails on her other four fingers shone with white energy as they grew into spikes. She tracked Valduin across the sky to the center of the river.

"Go!" she shouted, releasing the magic missiles toward her friend. The four spikes sprung from her fingers and sped through the air. They spread apart on the way up before accelerating to a single point on Valduin's side.

As Adelaide had hoped, the broomstick disappeared. Valduin fell from the sky, arcing down into the water.

Adelaide ran along the bank but stayed at the water's edge. "Val! Val, get out!" she screamed.

Valduin erupted from the water, thrashing about and gasping for air, but he soon found that the water was not too deep for him to stand. He looked around with wild eyes before seeing Adelaide standing above him.

His eyes locked with hers. His mouth dropped open. His head cocked to the side.

"Adelaide? What? How?" He was still breathless from the shock of the fall. He stood frozen, chest-deep in the river, staring at a friend he knew to be dead.

The green light had dropped in altitude. Somehow, it was below ground level now. Rose did not slow to figure out how this could be. She was happy that Valduin was no longer flying away.

As she ran on, the green light disappeared. She glanced at the magic item she still held in her hand. The glowing emerald was gone.

"I hope she found him," Rose thought. On she ran.

After another minute of running aimlessly forward through the dark swamp, Rose caught sight of the glow of Adelaide's armor. She veered toward it, slowing slightly. Her lungs and legs burned from the run, but she could not stop. She had to get to Adelaide. She had to see if Adelaide had found Valduin.

"Adelaide!" she called out as she crashed through the bushes onto the bank of the river. "Where is he?"

"He's right here," Adelaide called back. She waved Rose over to where Valduin sat with his back against a tree.

"Rose? You too? You're here? You're real?" Valduin asked, awe in his voice. He pushed off the tree and crawled forward to greet the halfling with a hug.

Rose did not accept the hug. She stopped a few feet short of Valduin, her eyes narrowed, her hands on her hips. "Where have you been? Why didn't you come looking for us? Why didn't you respond to any of my messages?" She looked the half-elf up and down. "And why do you look so awful?"

Valduin sat back on his heels. His shoulders slumped. He stared at the ground between Rose's feet, unable or unwilling to meet her gaze. He did not reply.

"Well? I'm waiting. Here we are, in the middle of the swamp again. No one left alive but the three of us. We need some answers."

Valduin winced. He sat in silence.

Adelaide took a step back from both Valduin and Rose. "It's Val, Rose," she said, lowering her voice to try to calm her friend down. "We found him. What are you worried about?"

"What am I worried about?" Rose hissed back, turning toward Adelaide with fire in her eyes. "I've been sending him messages almost every day for the last two weeks. I *know* he's been hearing them. And not *once* did he respond. Why?"

She paused for a second before shouting the question, "*Why?*"

Valduin winced again. He took a deep breath. "She said I might hear your voice. She said it was normal for that to happen after a friend dies. She said to ignore it. I *had* to ignore it," he said, his voice barely audible over the steady pitter-patter of the rain on the surface of the river next to them.

Rose stepped forward. She grabbed Valduin's chin and turned his face up toward her own. Her eyes flashed with golden light as she said, "Tell the truth."

Valduin felt the power of Rose's magic weighing on his mind. He had felt this magic before, used by Fulbert during their interrogation in Biastal. He knew that Rose would know if he resisted its effects. He let the magic take hold in his head. His eyes glistened with tears as he looked up at Rose and said, "I have nothing to hide from you."

Rose, feeling that Valduin had given into the zone of truth, let herself relax a fraction. Then the questions came. "Where have you been?"

"With Beulah," Valduin replied, "and doing things for her."

"Could you hear my messages?"

"Yes."

"And why didn't you respond?"

"She told me not to. I couldn't disobey. I still can't."

"Why?"

"Her magic. Like what Tristan did to King Dunedin. If she says to do or not do something, I *have* to listen."

Rose turned to Adelaide. "What do you think?"

Adelaide remained focused on Valduin. "Why didn't you come looking for us?"

Valduin shifted his attention to the human. "Because you were dead. I watched Misery kill you."

"I was dead. Rose wasn't. She got me out of there. Why didn't you come looking for her?"

"Because I saw her die in the Ebon Keep too." His gaze turned back to Rose.

"I didn't die," Rose said in shocked confusion. "Misery certainly tried. But I picked up Adelaide and told you to leave. After you used that glass ball to plane shift out of there, I banished us back here as well."

Valduin's eye twitched. His breathing sped up. "I saw you die," he said, his voice soft. His eye twitched again.

"And I saw you tell me to leave." He squeezed his eyes closed and rubbed his temples. "I thought you both were dead. I knew you both were dead because I watched it happen."

Adelaide put her hand on Rose's shoulder. "It was Beulah. All along it was Beulah. Let's get out of here. We'll have plenty of time to talk."

Rose did not pull away. She pursed her lips as she appraised the half-elf's story. After a moment, she sighed and let her shoulders relax. "Yeah, let's get moving," she agreed. "Should we go back to The Tavern for tonight? I'd love to see how Greg is doing."

"No!" Valduin interjected, his head snapping up. "We need to head north. I... we have work to do."

Rose took a step away from Valduin again, back on her guard. "What do you mean? Who has work to do? What kind of work?"

Valduin held up his hands in a show of surrender. "I told you that I have been doing things for Beulah. Well, it is not just for her. It is for me too. And it was for you both. After I came back from the Ebon Keep, she promised me revenge. She said I could get my revenge on Misery for killing you. And that we would go after the Voidbringer after Misery. She said we would stop the monster from whatever his plans might be."

"And you believed her?" Rose spat back at him. "You still believe her after seeing us alive?"

Valduin's eye twitched again.

"I know where his house is," he said. "He has a castle on this plane, too. Beulah told me where it is. We know he is not there right now. This is the first step of our revenge."

"What's your plan?" Adelaide asked. Rose's attitude still had her on edge, but a hint of excitement crept into her voice with the mention of revenge against Misery. "Are you going to burn the place down?"

Valduin shook his head. His mouth twisted into a grin. "*We* are going to rob it."

The adventurers zipped along above the treetops, each with their own purple broomstick between their legs. To keep from being a blazing beacon in the night sky, Adelaide quenched the light on her armor. Valduin led the way, and Rose created a dim light on Valduin's pack. She and Adelaide focused on following that light through the darkness.

They flew for an hour, touched down near the edge of the swamp so that Valduin could recast the flying spell, and then they flew some more. Heading north, they stayed east of the road connecting Mirstone and Verasea, between the road and the ocean. When Valduin's spell ran out for the second time, they stopped to make camp.

"What a day," Adelaide groaned as she stretched out next to their campfire. "I never want to go back to that swamp again," she added through a yawn.

"At least you did not get dumped in a river," Valduin said with a chuckle.

"Oh, yeah, sorry about that." Adelaide winced. "It was the only way I could think of to get your attention."

"I do not mind," Valduin said with a dismissive wave of his hand. "I am glad you did it. I am glad you found me."

Rose, who had been silent since they had taken off from the riverbank, spoke up from the other side of the fire. "That's right. We found you. You didn't even try to find us. Why did Beulah lie to you about us dying? How do you feel about her lying to you like that?"

Valduin gazed through the flames at the halfling. He did not reply right away.

His eye twitched.

"I still do not even know if she was lying," he replied. "Everything around then is fuzzy. I think *I* might have told *her* that you died. Then, she wanted me to focus on the task at hand, so she recommended I ignore anything you might say. She said that people with human ancestry sometimes hear the voices of the dead, but they are not real. It is an inherited weakness of humans. Which is why I never replied to your messages." He finished with a shrug. "I am sorry about that, by the way."

"And what is your plan now?" Rose repeated one of her questions.

"I plan to go to Misery's castle, break in, and take anything that I can find that might help us stop him and the Voidbringer," Valduin replied with conviction. "This is our chance to get ahead of them."

Rose watched with an unusual intensity as he talked. When he finished, the three adventurers sat in silence for a few minutes, listening to the crackle of the fire and the nocturnal chirps of insects all around them.

Rose did not say anything. She turned away from the fire, lay down on her bedroll, and pulled her blanket up to her chin.

Adelaide yawned.

Valduin spoke up, "I can take watch. You two look exhausted."

"You don't look like a bunch of roses, yourself," Adelaide shot back through another yawn. She lay down and covered her head with her blanket. "But wake me when you get tired," she mumbled.

"You got it. Goodnight, Adelaide."

Valduin slunk away into the darkness once he was certain the women were asleep. He took a piece of silver jewelry with a single onyx stone hanging from it and affixed it to his ear.

"Stela is dead. I got the souls. Adelaide and Rose found me. I convinced them to come with me to Misery's castle. Any orders?"

Beulah's voice filled his mind as she replied, "I never doubted you. Get the book and leave them behind. They will only hold you back. That's why they died, and you didn't."

Valduin's eye twitched.

"You are totally evil now!" Amelia shouted at her brother. "I *knew* it. I *knew* you weren't following the rules when you were in the Zone of Truth."

"Hey!" Logan exclaimed. "That's not fair! That spell blocks me from *knowingly* telling a lie. I *knew* you were dead. I still know you were dead. I followed the rules. You needed to pick better questions."

Amelia glared at Logan, seething, but said nothing.

Madison spoke up, though she was eyeing Amelia to be sure she did not trigger another outburst. "How can you know we were dead while seeing that we are very much alive right now?"

Logan grinned. "That's the fun part of this situation. Valduin's brain is doing all sorts of gymnastics to try to justify those two facts. We'll have to wait and see what happens as he tries to work that out."

Madison did not return Logan's grin. "If you say so," she replied. Trying to break the tension between her siblings, she said, "Anyway. We are back together, and it's time to level up! I get a new second-level spell, and I know *just* the one. You guys getting anything good?" She passed the rulebook to Logan.

He flipped through a few pages. "Well, at level twelve I get to bump up some ability scores, which is always helpful. And a new invocation. Decisions, decisions. What about you, Amelia?"

He looked up at his younger sister's seat at the table.

She was gone.

14

Adelaide awoke to the sound of Valduin cooking breakfast. She sat up with a start when she realized that the sun had already risen.

"You didn't wake me up?" she asked in a tone of mixed surprise and curiosity. "You looked so tired last night. Did you not sleep at all?"

Valduin glanced up at her from his work over the fire. He still looked exhausted, his eyes sunken and bloodshot and his mouth hanging open a fraction. He smiled at Adelaide, nonetheless. "Oh, yeah, I was feeling okay, so I took watch the whole night. You two have been through a lot recently. You needed a rest."

"I'm not sure we've been through worse than you," Adelaide said. She wrapped up her bedroll and reattached it to her pack. "I definitely want to hear what you've been up to, but that can wait until Rose wakes up."

"You want to fill me in on your travels, instead?" Valduin asked as he tipped the frying pan out onto two plates. He handed one to Adelaide and continued, "How in the world did you find me?"

Adelaide eyed the pile of food on her plate. "Hold on. Where did you get this food? You carry eggs everywhere these days?"

Valduin chuckled. "Well, kind of." He patted his pack, which Adelaide noticed for the first time was different than the one he usually carried. "Beulah gave me a new bag. This one makes carrying fragile items a little easier. Among other things, I have eggs for breakfast every day."

"Oh, well, that's pretty nice, I guess," Adelaide said with a sidelong glance at the bag. She took a cautious first bite of the food.

"So, what have you two been up to? And how did you find me?" Valduin repeated his questions.

"Where to start? We were together at the Ebon Keep. We almost made that exchange for Beulah when Stela and Tabitha freaked out and attacked us."

"Yeah, I was there for that."

"And then Misery showed up, and he recognized us. He killed me. He tried to kill Rose, but she was too tough for him."

Valduin's eye twitched.

Adelaide noticed. She paused for a moment, giving Valduin a chance to speak up.

He could not hold her gaze. He looked down at his plate and took another bite.

Adelaide continued, "Rose told you to escape, and you did. She carried me back to this plane. We dropped into the Enchanted Dunes. She resurrected me. Then we started walking." She paused to take another bite, though her eyes were locked onto Valduin's, watching for another twitch.

"We stopped by Khal Durum and Westray. We went to Tarsam and talked to Brixim. He helped us find you, and then we came to Mirstone. We caught up with you in the swamp, and you know the rest," Adelaide concluded, keeping the story vague.

Valduin nodded along with each point of Adelaide's recounting. "How did Brixim help you find me?" he asked, narrowing his eyes at her.

"He didn't say," Rose's voice cut in before Adelaide could answer, surprising both Valduin and Adelaide. They looked toward the halfling, who was sitting up on her bedroll. "We told him we needed to find you. He went into the back room of his shop for a little while, and, when he came back, he said you were near Mirstone. He brought us to Mirstone, and we found you in the swamp."

Valduin finished chewing a bite while he digested this answer. Eventually, he shrugged and said, "He *was* a strange little gnome. Well, I'm glad to have you here. We have quite the task ahead of us."

"Please elaborate," Rose said, her voice icy. "I was wondering what you were planning, and what role you see us playing in that plan. I also wouldn't mind hearing what else you have been up to recently."

If Valduin noticed her tone, he did not show it. He dumped the last of the food in the skillet onto another plate and handed it to Rose. "Right, of course. Well, after you two died in the Ebon Keep—"

"I didn't die," Rose cut him off.

Valduin's eye twitched again.

Both women saw it this time. Neither said anything.

"Right. After I escaped the Ebon Keep, I was back in Beulah's hut. I told Beulah everything that happened. She told me that she could help me get revenge. Revenge on Stela, on Misery, on Taranath, on the Voidbringer. All the revenge I could ever want." He paused, his gaze drifting to the crackling fire.

After a moment, he blinked his eyes and looked at Rose again. "So, we got to work. I had to collect a few things to get ready first, but last night we started with Stela. And everything went according to plan. Now, we head to Misery's castle, Gloomtide Tower. There is a cloak there that Beulah knows to be an extremely powerful magic item. She said that she saw it in his museum in the tower, back when they were friends. Or at least friendly. I am supposed to go in and steal the cloak and anything else that looks useful while he is still at the Ebon Keep."

Adelaide was grinning and nodding along with Valduin's story.

Rose was not.

"Again, I am struck by the thought that Beulah could do these things for herself," Rose said. "If she is so powerful, wouldn't it be easier for her to attack these people without you?"

"Apparently, it has something to do with 'plausible deniability,'" Valduin said, making quotation marks in the air with his fingers. "It is like when she sent us after the green hags the first time. It would look very bad for her to get caught attacking these other powerful and well-known magic users. She does not want to attract attention from other equally powerful parties in her social circle." He finished with a shrug.

Rose pursed her lips. "And what will you do after we steal this cloak? When you've had your revenge?"

"Stealing the cloak is not the revenge," Valduin said with a mirthless laugh. "It is what we do with it later. *Then* we get our revenge."

The party spent the rest of the day trekking through the forest north of the Mirstone Mire. They were still a couple of days of travel from the next big city, Verasea. There was not much development here, and the adventurers did not see a building or another person for the entire day.

They did not talk much. Rose spent most of the walk brooding over what was going on with Valduin. She felt that he was somehow different, changed since their trip to the Ebon Keep. There was something strange about his attitude toward Beulah and their current mission. And there was that eye twitch. Her heart skipped a beat every time she saw it. She knew it meant something, but she had yet to put her finger on what that something might be.

While his twitch made her uneasy, Adelaide was not bothered by Valduin's demeanor. The possibility of revenge had eclipsed all other concerns. She spent the day concocting schemes to exact her revenge on Misery, each one more gruesome than the last.

By midafternoon, the smell of salt water overwhelmed the residual stink of the mire's mud. The party arrived at the rocky cliffside overlooking the Aegean Expanse. A few small waves lapped on the rocks below. Beyond the surf, though, the surface of the ocean stretched to the horizon as still as a sheet of glass.

Rose stood at the edge of the cliff, mesmerized by the sight. The calm ocean mirrored the blue sky. Clouds floated through the deep, mimicking their twins in the heavens. Rose's head swam as she searched for the horizon, only to find the blue ocean and the blue sky merging seamlessly into a single azure curve at the edge of her vision.

"It's beautiful," Rose whispered.

Hearing Rose's words, Adelaide glanced over her shoulder to see that the halfling had fallen behind. Adelaide turned to look at the ocean the way that Rose was looking at it. She smiled. "It really is, isn't it?"

"Have you seen it before?" Rose asked. She tore her eyes away from the water and moved to catch up with her friends. "I thought you were from the mountains."

"No, I haven't," Adelaide replied, still looking out over the ocean. "I'm just used to walking right past this kind of thing. You know? Staying focused on the task at hand."

Rose stepped up on a rock next to Adelaide so that they were shoulder-to-shoulder. She gazed at the water again. "Sometimes you need to stop and smell the roses," she said with a wry smile.

Adelaide turned toward the halfling, put her nose in Rose's hair, and gave an enthusiastic sniff. She jerked her head back, coughing and gagging dramatically. "That's the last time I smell Rose on purpose," she wheezed as she pretended to choke.

"Very funny," Rose said, leaping off the rock and onto Adelaide's back. The human caught the halfling without even a step to steady herself. "I took a bath like two days ago! Or was it a week ago? Well, either way, this is as good as it gets."

Rose turned her attention to Valduin, who had not stopped walking. "Hey, Valdoozie, how much farther?"

"Maybe by nightfall? Beulah said it is less than two days out from Mirstone, so I'm hoping we can find it tonight and start doing some reconnaissance," Valduin called over his shoulder.

"Carry me," Rose said to Adelaide. The halfling laid her head on top of the human's as she clung to Adelaide's pack.

"Not a chance," Adelaide said with a laugh. She stopped walking and shook her pack around until Rose let go and dropped to the ground.

"Fine. Be like that," Rose said as she stomped past Adelaide.

Adelaide rolled her eyes. She jogged to catch up with her friends.

The three adventurers marched forward.

Dusk came and went. The party marched on, now guided by the dim glow from Adelaide's armor and Rose's amulet. They followed the top of the cliff northward. The surf crashed on the rocks below them, though the sound had been receding as the cliff climbed higher above the water.

"It's getting late," Adelaide said, breaking the silence through which they had walked for the last couple of hours. "We should probably sleep. It could still be hours away."

"Yeah," Rose agreed with a jaw-cracking yawn. "I'm wrecked. Let's make camp."

Valduin pursed his lips, scanning the darkness around them one last time, hoping for some sign of their target. "Okay, yes, fine," he conceded. "We can stop. We would not be able to do anything tonight, anyway."

"Let's at least back away from the cliff a bit to make camp," Adelaide suggested. "I like the sound of the water, but I don't like the idea of sleepwalking off the edge."

"You do not sleepwalk," Valduin said with a chuckle.

"Yes, I do," Adelaide replied. "Sometimes."

"We have been traveling together for *months* and I have never seen you sleepwalk," Valduin retorted. "Not once."

"Have you been watching me sleep every night? You some kind of creeper?" Adelaide asked, narrowing her eyes with feigned suspicion.

"No! I mean, not *every* night. I watch you when I take watch at night, though. But I am not *watching* you. Just in general, when I take watch. When I am awake, and you are asleep, I would notice if you were walking around!" He was blushing with frustration as he stumbled through his response. He did not wait for Adelaide's next question. He stormed off into the darkness, away from the cliff as Adelaide had asked.

Adelaide grinned and followed the half-elf. Rose was close behind, yawning again.

"Well, since you like watching her sleep, you can take first watch," the halfling called out to Valduin's back. "My eyes are useless in the dark. And I need sleep."

Valduin shouted over his shoulder, "I never said I *liked* watching anyone sleep!"

"Will you keep it down?" Adelaide scolded Valduin, her tone serious but her expression playful. "You'll wake up every monster between here and Verasea." She marched past Valduin, who had stopped and turned to gape at the human.

Rose patted Valduin on the hand as she walked past him. "What's for dinner? Got any potatoes in that fancy bag of yours?"

Valduin made no response. He closed his mouth, hung his head, and fell in line behind Rose. Before long, they made camp by a small stream that meandered through the fields along the coastline.

"We're still looking for the tower. Had to stop for the night. Could it be hidden somehow? Could we have missed it?"

"You don't need to stop. Leave them behind; the clock is ticking," Beulah hissed at Valduin. "Of course, it might be hidden. Use your brain. Find it!"

Valduin tucked the earring back into his pack. He paced the perimeter he had been walking around their campsite. The sun was almost up; he would need to wake his companions soon.

He could pretend to sleep for a few minutes if needed.

"Why aren't you sleeping? What did she do to you?" Madison asked.

"It's one of my new abilities. I'll still need to sleep to regain my hit points if we get into a fight, but I can skip long rests without any real penalties now," Logan explained.

"Oh, so *that's* why you look terrible," Amelia commented. "I was wondering why you kept emphasizing the dark circles under your eyes and things."

Logan gave his younger sister a thumbs up. "You got it. It works well for me since I get my spells back after a short rest. As long as we aren't fighting, I could go forever without sleeping."

"Okay, that is pretty sweet," Amelia said, nodding her head. "I know I gave you a hard time about choosing Warlock early on, but I'm starting to see how that class can be cool."

"All the classes *can* be cool," Logan said. He picked up the rulebook and waved it at Amelia. "Haven't you read this? There are so many classes and subclasses I want to try, so many characters I want to play!"

Amelia recoiled at the sight of the thick book. She looked down at her hands.

Logan did not notice, but Madison did.

Madison narrowed her eyes at Amelia. "You okay?"

"Just a little tired," Amelia mumbled. She pushed herself back from the table. "I'm gonna take a break."

15

Adelaide shook Rose awake. The sun had risen, birds chirped somewhere nearby, and the creek babbled beside their campsite.

"Come on, sleepyhead," Adelaide murmured. "Let's get moving."

Rose stretched and yawned before snapping to attention. She made a quick scan of the campsite, looking for Valduin.

She snatched Adelaide's wrist and pulled her in close. "Is he sleeping?" she whispered before Adelaide could protest being grabbed. Rose narrowed her eyes at the lump under the blanket on the other side of the smoldering campfire.

"What? Uh, I think so," Adelaide whispered back, picking up on Rose's tension. "What's wrong?" She crouched next to the halfling.

"Stay here." Rose slid out of her bedroll. Too nervous to stand up and risk making undue noise, she crawled around the fire, toward Valduin. She took hold of his pack, turning it toward herself with painstaking care so as not to make a sound. The bag was light, too light for what Rose knew must be inside of it. One of the side pockets was open. She reached inside.

It was empty.

Rose chewed on her lower lip, fighting to keep her breathing quiet, looking back and forth between the bag and Valduin.

Her heart pounded in her chest.

She reached for the clasps that held the flap closed over the main compartment.

"Do you need something?" Valduin asked. His voice was clear and firm. It was not the voice of a person who had been awoken by someone sneaking a look at their personal belongings.

"I was just looking for the eggs," Rose replied in a hurry. She winced, hoping that Valduin would not notice. "You said you had more eggs. I was going to make breakfast for you." She sat back on her heels and let the pack lean back against Valduin's legs.

Valduin did not open his eyes. "Reach into the side pocket and think about eggs. The bag will let you find them. It always gives you what you are looking for." He pulled his blanket up over his shoulders. "Let me know if you need any help."

Rose got to her feet. She reached into the pocket again. This time, her hand returned with a large, brown chicken egg. "Nope, I've got it figured out. I'll let you know when it's ready." She tried to sound cheerful.

She doubted that he believed it.

The adventurers resumed their journey northward, looking for Misery's castle. They did not talk. Only their crunching footsteps and the crashing of waves far below the cliffside broke the tense silence amongst the party.

Early in the afternoon, Adelaide stopped short, staring into the distance ahead of them. "What is that?" she asked no one in particular.

Rose, who had been hanging her head and staring at the ground in front of her feet, ran into the back of Adelaide's legs. She wrapped her arms around Adelaide to keep from falling over. She steadied herself and looked ahead. "What's what?"

"That." Adelaide pointed up the coastline again. Far off near the horizon, still a few miles away, a monstrous, spindly structure crouched on the edge of the cliff.

It took Rose a moment to process everything before it became clear what they were looking at. Her eyes grew wide as she put the pieces together. "Is that a boat? A ship?"

Valduin, who had been walking at the back of the group with his attention focused on the rocks of the shoreline below, caught up to the women. He looked ahead and groaned. "Yes. That is a highdock. Which means we missed it." He kicked a few pebbles off the cliff. "I cannot believe we missed it." He looked down at the water and then back to the south along the way they had come. "Maybe because it was dark? Maybe it is hidden?" he mumbled his questions.

"And what is a highdock?" Rose followed up. She looked from Valduin to Adelaide.

Adelaide shrugged. "Beats me. I'm a mountain girl, remember? It sounds like a dock for a ship, but just really high. How am I doing, Val?"

"You got it," Valduin said over his shoulder. He had already reversed course and begun heading south. Adelaide and Rose jogged to catch up with him as he continued to explain, "The city of Verasea is up on the cliff. They bring the ships up to the city to unload and load, rather than carrying the cargo up from and down to the water. I cannot tell you if it is more efficient, but it is certainly more impressive. The important thing is that if we can see Verasea, we missed Gloomtide Tower." He groaned with frustration.

Rose fell in line behind Valduin. She said nothing.

Adelaide clapped Valduin on the shoulder. "Don't worry about it, Val. We'll find it."

Valduin shook his head in disappointment. He did not respond.

Adelaide continued, "Let's think about it. How would you hide an entire tower? How about that spell that Veneranda used to hide us from the roc? Would that work?"

Valduin stopped shaking his head. He looked at Adelaide, though he appeared not to be focused on her. After a moment, he nodded. "Yes," he said, "Maybe not the exact same spell, but there must be some kind of illusion magic that could hide an entire tower. Beulah said that it was not very big."

Rose winced at the casual mention of the hag's name. She stayed quiet.

Valduin continued, "So, if we try to find some illusion magic somewhere around here, then we should be able to find it!" He grinned as the plan formed in his head.

"I can do that," Rose said, though her voice did not carry Valduin's enthusiasm, "but that spell only lasts ten minutes. We've been walking for hours. I'd need to cast it so many times; I wouldn't be able to do anything else today. And we still might miss it."

Valduin turned to look at Rose, still grinning. In Abyssal, he grumbled, *None may hide.* His eyes flashed with purple light, which receded until only his irises remained a vibrant purple. "I can do it now, too, and it does not use any of my energy."

Rose looked up at Valduin, staring at his glowing eyes for an extra moment. He had changed so much in the few weeks they had been apart. He was thinner. More haggard. The purple glow accentuated the wrinkles at the corners of his eyes. Had those always been there? Rose was not sure, but seeing them made her sad. She said nothing. Once Valduin turned southward, she again fell in line behind him, hanging her head.

For hours they walked. Every few minutes, Valduin repeated his incantation, continuously scanning the cliffside for the glow of magic that might indicate the presence of a hidden castle. The sunset. The sky grew dark; it was another moonless night. Adelaide and Rose lit the path with their magic, but they allowed Valduin to travel a little way ahead of them to continue his scan for their target.

Near midnight, the women caught up with their friend. Valduin had stopped walking; he stood on the edge of the cliff, staring to the south.

"What's up?" Adelaide asked in a hushed voice when she arrived at Valduin's side. "You see something?"

"I think so." He pointed off into the darkness. "There's a big space right there that is glowing with illusion magic. This must be it."

"Okay, so, now we know where it probably *is*," Adelaide said in an attempt to lead Valduin to an explanation. He did not take the bait, so Adelaide continued, "Now what? Do we just need to walk past the barrier, and we'll be able to see what we are looking at?"

Valduin grimaced. "I don't know. With this kind of magic in the past, as soon as we knew it was magic, we could see through it. Remember that crater in the Virdes Crossway when we met Venez? This seems different, stronger maybe? I'm not sure." He looked back and forth between Adelaide and Rose.

Rose spoke up first. "I could try to turn it off. Dispel it."

Valduin's eyes lit up. "You can do that?"

"Sometimes," Rose said. "How far away is it? I need to be kind of close."

Valduin glanced down the coastline. "Still a little ways off. It's big. Do you need to be able to see it, too?"

"Nope. Once we are close to it, point me in the right direction."

"Great!" Valduin said. He turned away from Rose, cast his spell to allow him to see the magic again, and led the way toward it.

Rose and Adelaide stayed close. Adelaide had taken Fiend's Lament off her pack. She held it in one hand by the end of the handle and let the enchanted blade swing by her side as she walked, slicing through the tall grass that lined the cliffside.

After another half an hour of walking, Valduin stopped again. "Here it is," he said, gesturing straight off the cliff toward the ocean. "A sparkling cube of magic that comes right up to the edge of the cliff here." He had a self-satisfied smile on his face.

"Okay, let's try it," Rose said, taking her amulet, still glowing with her light spell, in her hands. She looked in the direction that Valduin had indicated. In Halfling, she prayed, "*Selaia, reveal that which is hidden. Remove this veil of illusion, that we may further your will to spread love through the world.*"

Her eyes flashed with golden light, even brighter than that coming off her amulet. She flinched, and the light cut off. Nothing else changed.

Rose pursed her lips. "It must be some strong magic," she mumbled.

"You cannot do it?" Valduin asked. His shoulders slumped.

"Oh, I'm gonna do it," Rose said. She took a deep breath. "Guide me," she said to Valduin, her voice stern, determination writ upon her face.

Valduin noticed the change. He stepped behind Rose and laid a hand on her shoulder. Rose felt Valduin's magic wash over her like a wave of goosebumps. She did not like the feeling, but she did feel the clarity of focus granted by the magical guidance.

She spoke again in Halfling, *"Selaia, reveal this foul structure to us, that we may find the tools of our vengeance."*

Again, her eyes flashed with golden light. And again, the light vanished.

No castle could be seen.

Rose snarled. She let out a low, menacing growl.

"Is it too strong?" Valduin asked.

"No," Rose hissed. "Count to ten and then guide me again." She placed her amulet against her forehead and prayed, *"Selaia, grant me your wisdom. Allow me to see that which is obscured, to find that which is hidden, to know that which is obfuscated."* She opened her eyes and focused on the empty space off the cliff.

"I'm ready," she muttered. Valduin placed his hand on her shoulder again to bestow his arcane guidance.

Rose held her hands up in the direction of the illusion. No longer worried about discretion, she roared in Halfling, *"Show yourself!"* Her eyes flashed. In a blink, the castle appeared. The magic which had been conceal-ing it was annulled across its entirety in an instant.

Rose lowered her arms, staring up at the foreboding structure. The party stood in front of a fifteen-foot-high wall of dark stone. Not as black as the Ebon Keep, but dark enough to get the message across that this was an evil place. The wall was thirty feet wide before it turned out toward the sea, the only contact between the castle and the land on which the adventurers stood. No door or gate could be seen in the wall.

Adelaide stepped back a few paces, staring up at the buildings showing over the wall. A windowless tower of the same dark stone rose close behind the wall to a pointed top about thirty feet high. Farther behind the wall was a taller, wider tower. Adelaide could not guess its height with what little she could see from this angle below the wall. Like the closer tower, the larger one rose to a steep point without a window to be seen.

Adelaide's inspection of the castle did not last long, as a new arrival drew her attention. A figure stepped up to the edge of the wall, obstructing her view of the far tower. Clad in dark, heavy armor with a full helmet, the figure looked down at the adventurers. The helmet struck Adelaide as odd, but she did not take the time to figure out why.

"Guys, guys!" she hissed at Valduin and Rose. She still had her weapon in her hands; her knuckles were white as she gripped the axe's handle and stared up at the silent observer approaching the edge of the wall. "Look out!"

"Well, this isn't great," Madison mumbled. "Maybe we should have tried being sneaky for this part."

"Yeah, well, someone just *had* to shout out their incantations when they were casting spells at the evil wizard's tower. Who could have seen this coming?" Logan said, rolling his eyes.

"Rose was *frustrated*," Amelia growled at her siblings. "I'm sorry that I'm the only one of us with useful spells right now. I'm just playing the game." She glared at Logan.

"And you are doing a great job," Madison said, using the softest voice she could manage without sounding patronizing. "No one is upset with you. That was great that you were able to dispel the illusion at all. If Misery cast the spell, you know that it will be hard to overcome."

"Well, you can act frustrated without shouting," Logan continued, not picking up on the tension at the table. "Just be frustrated and say you growl or hiss or something. Don't shout."

Madison elbowed Logan in the ribs, but it was too late.

"Fine! You don't want me to mess up your game? I quit!" She stormed out of the room as she burst into tears.

Logan looked to Madison. "What's wrong with her?" he asked.

Madison punched him in the shoulder. "Have you not been paying attention at all? She's been acting weird for days now. Did you not notice that every time she needs to look in the rulebook, she gets tears in her eyes? Or that she keeps leaving the table without saying anything?"

Logan rubbed his shoulder as he considered Madison's questions. "Oh," he finally said. "I guess you're right. Well, still, what's wrong with her? Is she afraid of the rulebook all of a sudden? It's not that big, and she only needs a little bit of it to play a cleric."

Madison ran her fingers through her hair and groaned. "You really are clueless. You know what? Don't worry about it, just let me deal with it. I'll talk to her soon. I'll figure it out."

16

Valduin and Rose picked up on the panic in Adelaide's voice. In tandem, they stepped away from the wall so that they could see its top. They looked up as an armored figure leapt down from the wall and landed with a metallic clatter mere feet in front of them.

Closer now, and lit by the glow of Rose's amulet, Adelaide could see why the helmet looked strange. The face was completely covered without holes or slits for the eyes. Neither was there a visor covering such openings. It was a solid sheet of metal.

The metal did not appear to impede the creature's vision, however, as it lashed out at Rose with a long pike, slashing across her shoulder.

Rose cried out in pain, reflexively grabbing toward the haft of the weapon. She did not have a chance to touch it. The armored figure whipped the weapon back and unleashed another attack. With Rose staggering from the first hit, this time the pike whizzed past her before again being snapped back to the hands of the attacker.

"What's the plan?" Rose asked Valduin, her voice breathless and frantic from the shock and pain of the unexpected attack. She grabbed her amulet and held out a hand toward the armored figure. *"Hold it right there!"* she shouted.

She cocked her head to the side, confused by the sensation of the creature resisting the spell. It was less that it had overcome the power of her magic, but more like the spell could not affect it. "I don't like this," Rose mumbled, glancing back and forth between their armored assailant and her friends.

"We should run," Valduin answered Rose's question. "We won't be able to get in like this." In a cloud of mist, he vanished from his position next to Rose. Reappearing behind Adelaide, he raised his left hand to point at the creature.

With Valduin's hand extended past her shoulder and lit by her glowing armor, Adelaide saw for the first time the length of braided, thorned tendrils around the half-elf's wrist. When he held his hand out, the band came alive and slithered across his palm and out between his thumb and forefinger. It stretched out into a crooked wand. The wand left a trail of bleeding punctures where its thorns tore through Valduin's skin, though he did not appear to notice.

"To the depths," he muttered, summoning three purple sparks around his bleeding hand. The sparks dove into the wand, sped down its length, and leapt from the tip to blast across the darkness and into the chest of the armored creature. It took a half-step back to brace itself from the assault, but it regained its footing a moment later. It turned its covered face toward Adelaide and Valduin, distracted from Rose for the time being.

"Yes, definitely run," Valduin whispered in Adelaide's ear. He turned his back on the castle and took off into the darkness away from the cliffside.

Adelaide glanced over her shoulder at Valduin's re-treat. "Don't disappear," she hissed at him. She turned back toward the figure standing next to Rose.

"Rose, it's time to go," she said, her voice strained. She broke into a sprint directly at the creature. Raising the handle of Fiend's Lament and slamming it into the armored figure, she cross-checked it away from Rose. It slammed against the wall, its head snapping back against the stone with a resonant clang. Adelaide closed the gap and feinted an attack at its torso. As its hands came up to shield itself, she spun low, hooked the blade of the axe behind its knee, and swept its legs out from under it. It clattered to the ground with a heavy thud.

Satisfied that the creature would at least be slowed by its position, Adelaide turned toward Valduin. In the same way that he had escaped the range of their attack-er, Adelaide vanished in a cloud of mist, reappearing in the darkness in the direction that Valduin had fled.

"See ya," Rose muttered to the armored figure as it pulled itself to its feet. She turned and leapt away into the night, following the light of Adelaide's armor.

Rose ran through the high grass toward the scattered trees they had seen in the meadows that lined the high coastline. Purple eldritch blasts and white magic mis-siles fired by her friends flew over her head as she fled the armored guard. Despite the onslaught, she could hear the steady advance of the creature's clanking steps behind her.

Focused on nothing but running, she soon caught up with Valduin and Adelaide.

"What do we do?" she asked between gasping breaths. "Do we kill it? Can we kill it?"

"Adelaide, can you cover our tracks?" Valduin asked after loosing another barrage of purple sparks toward the oncoming suit of armor. "I don't want to get stuck fighting this one and a bunch more show up."

Adelaide nodded. "We just need to get out of sight first," she explained.

"I can handle that," Valduin said. He stopped running and raised the wand high over his head. With a rapid sweeping motion, he whipped the wand through the air, pointing out a swath of ground between the adventurers and the oncoming creature.

It was difficult for Adelaide to see what was happening in the low light, but at first she thought that the tall grass had turned into a bed of snakes. The snakes were not snakes, however, but rather thick, thorn-covered vines. The vines twisted over each other as they grew, rapidly building up into a ten-foot-high, living wall that spread out into the darkness in both directions.

"Let's do it," Valduin said. "I don't know how long that will hold it. But we have cover for a moment."

"Now you see me; now you don't," Adelaide recited. The light from her armor dimmed further as the darkness of the moonless night swirled around them. "Let's get out of here," she whispered.

"You got it," Valduin whispered back. He led the way into the darkness. He veered to the left, changing their course from what the armored guard had last seen, but he kept the wall of thorns between them and their pursuer.

A few minutes of running later, Valduin stopped at a small stand of gnarled, leafless trees. He turned back toward the castle and squinted into the night.

"You see anything?" Adelaide asked. "Is it still coming?"

"No, I think we are okay. Let's make camp here. In the morning, we can look around a bit to see how we are going to get in there."

"No fire, I'm assuming?" Rose asked. She dropped her pack against a tree and collapsed next to it.

"I mean, if you want to get caught, sure," Valduin said, his voice dripping with derision. "I would prefer they did not know we are here."

"Whoa! Chill out," Rose said, her hands raised in surrender. "I was just making sure I understood the master plan. Weirder things have happened recently."

Valduin dropped his bag at the base of another tree. "Sorry," he said. He sounded like he meant it. "I am a little on edge with how close that was. Beulah was pretty clear that she wanted this to be a stealth operation. We have already been seen by the guard. Not a good start."

"Well, if things go well tomorrow, it won't matter, right?" Adelaide said. "We get in and get out without being seen, and it won't matter that the guard saw us. Right?"

Valduin grimaced. "We can hope," he replied.

"It's fine," Rose mumbled as she crawled onto her bedroll. "You're fine. We're fine. Everything is fine. We're all tired. Can you make it through first watch, Valduin? This night is too dark for me to be of any use. Wake me when the sky starts to lighten. Sound good?"

"You got it," Valduin replied as he pulled a small loaf of bread out of his pack. "Tomorrow is going to be interesting. Get ready."

"We found it. Will investigate defenses tomorrow. Plan to make entry tomorrow night. Adelaide is on board. Rose isn't sure."

"She doesn't need to be sure," Beulah's response slithered into Valduin's mind. "You be sure. Get the book. The cloak, if you can. But I need the book."

Valduin crept back toward the stand of trees to finish his watch. He kept his eyes toward the cliffside, his ears trained for the clanking of heavy armor in the darkness.

When the sky began to lighten with the coming dawn, he shook Rose awake. He would need to sleep this night, for the first time in weeks, if he was to be in top condition for their task today. He tucked his pack under his bedroll as a pillow. Sleep came quickly when he shut his eyes, the deep, dreamless sleep of a man without conscience or regret.

Rose sat with her back against a tree. She listened to the birds greeting the day. Their songs used to fill her with happiness. Now they were a reminder of the carefree life she used to have. One where she was not hunted by gargantuan centipedes in a magical desert. Where she was not tasked with running errands for a witch. Where she did not have to keep watch over her friends so that they would not be murdered in their sleep.

Listening to the birds singing, she felt tears building in her eyes. She blinked them away, focusing on the task at hand. She could not shake the strange feeling that the armored guard had given her when it had ignored her attempt to hold it in place. The feeling that this creature was somehow beyond such magic. Superior to it.

She did not like that idea one bit.

She looked at her friends, trying to change the subject in her mind. Adelaide slept as she usually did, blanket kicked off, limbs sprawled out off her bedroll, mouth hanging open. Even now, the image made Rose smile.

Valduin looked like he might actually be asleep this time. He had clearly lain awake the last night when he caught Rose snooping in his pack. But he looked more relaxed tonight. His breathing was slower, deeper. He looked like he had not slept since they last saw him. For a moment, Rose wondered what was different about tonight, but there was no answer for her here, and she could not ask him directly.

Not yet, at least. Not until he was free of Beulah.

Rose tapped Adelaide on the shoulder. "Your turn," she whispered.

Adelaide wiped the drool off her face as she sat up. "Yeah, okay," she mumbled. She squinted into the bright morning sunlight. She looked around at the campsite. "Is he asleep for real this time?" she asked, keeping her voice low.

"I think so. I don't know how, but Beulah did something to him. I'm sure that's why he hasn't been sleeping. I don't like it. It isn't natural."

"Yeah, well, we'll deal with that later. You gonna go back to sleep?"

"Maybe for just a few minutes," Rose said. She lay down on her bedroll, turned her back toward the sun, and covered her head with her blanket.

Adelaide smiled. "Just a few minutes," she repeated to herself. "Right."

The human stood up, stretched, and began to pace the perimeter of the stand of dead trees while her friends slept.

She spent the quiet minutes of her watch reliving the brief fight from the previous night. She saw the covered face of the guard. She heard the clang of the guard's helmet hitting the stone wall. It had sounded empty. She could think of a couple of explanations for this observation. She did not like the possibilities that these thoughts opened up for what they would face within the castle.

The sun was well on its way to the top of the sky by the time Valduin and Rose woke up. Adelaide had not rushed them. She wanted everyone in top form for their job today.

"Misty step is so amazing!" Madison said to Logan. "It's only a bonus action? I can get anywhere I want now."

"For sure. That's why I took it so early," Logan agreed, nodding his head. "Also, awesome job getting that thing away from Rose so she could escape. I love you pushing people around during fights. Like when you kicked the stone giant off the cliff. Such a cool image."

Madison grinned. "Yeah, it makes my fighting a little more interesting than the same two whacks every turn. Remember when I launched that assassin into your wall of fire? That's teamwork." They high-fived across the table.

"Are you two done?" Amelia asked, glaring at her siblings.

"What? What's wrong with you?" Logan asked, returning Amelia's glare.

Madison jumped in to stop Logan from making Amelia upset again. "Yeah, we're done. What's up?" She turned herself in her chair to give all of her attention to her younger sister.

"What's our plan here? We have demonstrated time and again that we can't pick locks. We aren't sneaky unless you use your spells, and we don't want to use them all up just to get into the castle. Rose doesn't trust Valduin right now. And that fight with the guard was pretty discouraging. You guys were pummeling it with spell attacks, and I don't think we even got it down to half of its hit points," Amelia counted off their challenges on her fingers.

Madison's face fell as she listened to the list. "Well, those are all very good points, Amelia," she replied, "and I'm sure we can figure them all out. For being sneaky, I can cover us for up to three hours. And a fourth if I use that Pearl of Power you gave me. That's a lot of time for a mission like this."

"Plus, Beulah gave Valduin some other tools to help with this quest," Logan said. "I can handle a few locks."

"And when is Valduin going to share those things?" Amelia asked.

"When they become important," Logan replied.

Amelia glared at her brother. "He should probably start sharing some of this info," she said. "The more he hides, the harder it is going to be to earn Rose's trust back."

"Valduin's eye twitches," Logan said with a mischievous smile.

17

"You look a lot better, Val," Adelaide said. The adventurers had finished breakfast and packed up their gear. "You should try sleeping every night. You'll probably be less cranky."

"I have not been cranky," Valduin shot back as he shouldered his pack. "We are planning something quite dangerous. We all have been feeling that stress."

"We don't have time for arguing. What's your plan?" Rose asked. She had her hands on her hips as she looked up at Valduin.

"Well, we need to do some reconnaissance. I did not see a way through the wall last night, though we did not have much time to investigate it. We need to see if there is a way into the tower that we could access without being seen by the guard. And we need to see if there are more guards like the one we fought last night."

"How do you plan to perform this reconnaissance?" Rose asked, her demeanor unaffected by Valduin's description of his plan. "Are you going to fly around the castle? That might be a little obvious. And from what I can remember, you can't be invisible and fly at the same time."

"Very good point," Valduin conceded. He smiled, held up his right hand with a flourish, and snapped his fingers. Without warning, a raven appeared on Valduin's shoulder. The large, black bird cocked its head to point one beady eye down at the halfling.

Rose stumbled backward, colliding with a tree that saved her from tumbling over. She raised a hand toward the raven and shouted, "What's *that* doing here?"

"Stop!" Valduin exclaimed, turning the shoulder with the raven away from Rose and holding up his hands to shield the bird. "This is my familiar! This one is *mine*, not Beulah's." He stepped back from Rose, who still had one hand outstretched toward the raven.

Rose remained leaning against the tree. She glared at the bird, and then Valduin, and then the bird again. "It looks like hers," she hissed.

"Yes, well, how often are you able to tell birds apart? They all pretty much look the same to me," Valduin said. He continued to back away from Rose. "Please do not attack him!" he pleaded.

Rose lowered her hand. "Fine. So, that's your whole plan? Have him fly around the castle while you look through his eyes?"

Valduin shrugged. "Sure, it does not sound very impressive when you say it like that. He will do the flying for us, and we will stay safely hidden until we know which way we need to go. Then, if we need to fly in or climb the wall or whatever else we decide, we can do it under cover of night."

Rose narrowed her eyes at the half-elf as she considered his plan. "And what if the castle is invisible again?"

Valduin blinked. "Oh. I had not considered that. I guess you would need to make it visible once more. We will need you to be a little more discreet this time."

Rose straightened her pack on her back and began the walk toward the cliff. "Well, then, we've got a plan. Let's do it."

The adventurers retraced their steps from the previous night, though, on account of Adelaide's magic, there were no tracks to follow. The first thing they saw as they approached the cliff was the taller black tower, straight and windowless, peeking out over the high grass. They slowed their movement, continuously searching the space around them for signs of surveillance. There was not much terrain in the field that bordered the cliffside to hide their approach, but they capitalized on the sparse trees and boulders for cover as best they could as they made their way toward the castle.

The party stopped at a cluster of trees fifty or sixty feet from the wall and hunkered down. Adelaide gave Rose a pained look. "What are we going to do about your armor?" she whispered.

"What do you mean?" Rose asked, putting a hand on her chainmail shirt. "We don't need to *do* anything about it."

"But it's so loud," Adelaide continued. "It's going to make sneaking into the castle so hard. Do you think you could take it off? Just for this one task?"

Rose's mouth fell open in shock. "And just let the guard stab me to death? That one last night managed to hurt me even with the armor on! What would happen if I didn't have it to protect me?"

"Shush!" Valduin hissed. "Do you want to fight that thing again already? Keep your voices down. And Adelaide's right. If you take off that armor, it will be much easier to sneak around. It might save some of Adelaide's magic too."

Rose pursed her lips. She took a few deep breaths as she looked back and forth between her friends. After a minute, she let her pack slide to the ground. "Fine. Give me a hand," she muttered.

With Adelaide's help, Rose quickly doffed the chainmail. The armor, which had lost its shine over the last few months, lay in a pile at Rose's feet. "Now what?" she asked. "Do I leave it here and hope we can swing by on our way out of the castle? Because I am guessing we will be leaving in a hurry."

"Put it in my bag," Valduin said. He dropped his pack next to the pile. "I'm going to send Blackie out. Shake me if you need me." He sat with his back against a tree and closed his eyes. The raven took off from his shoulder, flapped up into the air above the cliff, and coasted out over the ocean to circle behind Gloomtide Tower.

"Did he say that the bird's name is 'Blackie'?" Adelaide asked. She put her forehead in her hand and shook her head in dismay.

"I'm afraid so," Rose said. She dropped her chainmail shirt into the main compartment of Valduin's bag. It vanished into the darkness within. To her surprise, the bag did not feel any heavier. She added the rest of the suit of armor, and yet the bag still felt no heavier. She reached into the bag and fished around with her arm; the pocket was empty.

Rose glanced at Valduin, who was sitting still and silent. "Hey, Valduin," she said, testing that he was truly within the bird's senses. "Valduin, what's this?" she asked, a little louder, still testing him. He made no movement to indicate that he could hear her.

In a hurry to not get caught, Rose reached as far into the bag as she could. She found nothing. She checked the side pockets. They, too, were empty as far as she could tell. She turned the bag upside down. Nothing fell out.

"He said if I ask for eggs, I'd find eggs. How do I get stuff out of here if I don't know what I'm looking for?" she asked Adelaide.

Adelaide, picking up on what Rose was doing, knelt next to the halfling to inspect the bag. She took a turn searching through the pockets, but she also found nothing. She shook the bag; it made no sound to indicate that it was full of chainmail or anything else. "I don't know," she said, glancing at Valduin to make sure he was still out of touch, "but that's not a big deal right now. We can ask him later. Let's just focus on the mission." She handed the bag back to Rose.

Rose did not reply. She stared at the bag. She knew there was something important that Valduin was not telling them. Maybe many important somethings. And she thought that she could find the answers in the bag. If only she could see what it held.

"Alright, here's what's going on," Valduin said.

Rose jumped back and dropped his bag in a panic like a child caught playing with something they know they should not have.

Valduin did not appear to notice. His eyes remained closed as he continued, "The castle is built on a promontory off the cliff. The wall extends all the way around the outcropping, but I do not see any gates or doors through the wall. We will have to go over it. Just behind the wall near where we were last night is a small tower, let us call that the guard tower. It has a door to give

161

access to the top of the wall and another door to enter from the courtyard below."

He paused, eyes still closed, taking in everything that he could through the raven's eyes.

"Okay, we could go over the wall from here," Adelaide mumbled to Rose. She glanced toward the castle again, making sure no one had noticed them. There was no movement there. "But that feels like it will be the most protected part of the castle. Maybe we'd have better luck if we approach from the cliffs on the sides or back of the castle."

Rose nodded but said nothing. She sat and waited for Valduin to continue.

"Alright, there is not much in the courtyard. There are a few small structures built at the base of the wall, maybe the guards' quarters? There are three guards on top of the wall, one on either side and one on the front section. They all look like the one we fought yesterday, suits of armor with no faces." He paused again.

"I don't like those guys one bit," Adelaide said. "The way he dropped from the top of the wall. The way he took the hits from our attacks but kept chasing us. The way he did not make a single sound, not even a grunt, that whole fight. Creepy."

"Yeah, creepy," Rose agreed. Her eyes crept back to Valduin's bag.

"Now for the main attraction," Valduin continued. "The big tower sits at the tip of the promontory. The tower rises out of a short, rectangular building with a flat roof. The exterior wall attaches to this building. On one side, the walkway on top of the wall ends at a door on the large tower. On the other side, the walkway connects to the flat roof of the short building. There is another door into the large tower from the rooftop."

He paused for a moment. He wrinkled his nose. "No windows. There is a double door into the tower from the courtyard. That is probably the main entrance." He fell silent again.

"If I had to pick now, I'd say we go for the door from the wall into the big tower," Adelaide said. "That one is probably for the guards. Maybe it won't be as well protected because the guards are always close by."

Rose chewed on her lower lip. "We need more information," she muttered. She reached out to shake Valduin's knee, but she hesitated when he spoke up again.

"Oh! There is a window. Near the top, on the back. It is small. Shall we see what is in there?" He had a small smile on his face as he stopped talking again, presumably waiting for the raven to get close to the window.

With a start, he jerked forward, his eyes flying open.

"Come on!" he whined, slapping one hand against the ground beside him.

"Quiet!" Adelaide hissed at him. "What happened?"

"It ate Blackie," Valduin moaned. He slumped back against the tree in dejection.

"*What* ate Blackie?" Adelaide asked. She glanced between the trees at the castle again. Still no movement.

"The tower. Or the window. I am not sure. He flew up to the window and perched on the ledge to take a look inside. Before I could see anything, the window snapped shut. Not the glass in the window. The hole in the stone wall where the window was placed closed like a mouth. I did not have time to get Blackie to safety. He is gone. Again." Valduin hung his head, closed his eyes, and breathed a heavy sigh.

Rose patted his leg. "It's okay. Do you have enough incense to get him back?"

Valduin shook his head, not looking up.

"Well, we'll make sure to find you some soon. I know you like having your familiar with you, even if you don't know what to name them," Rose continued.

Valduin looked up, his brow furrowed in confusion. "What?"

Rose ignored the question. "Anyway, what do you think about getting into the castle?"

Valduin pursed his lips, his eyes drifting toward the dark stone wall. "If we fly, we can skip the short tower and the courtyard. I say we head to the door that opens up onto the rooftop."

"What about the other door, from the walkway on the wall? If that's for the guards, it might not be as difficult to open," Adelaide said, defending her choice.

"True, but it might not go where we need to go if it is only for the guards. The rooftop had a few chairs and tables like a patio. If that area is for Misery, then the door on that side probably leads to someplace more important to him," Valduin countered.

Adelaide did not argue, but her pursed lips showed that she was not convinced.

Rose interjected, "We need more information. I can help with that. What is it that we are looking for in there?" she asked Valduin. "You said a cloak? That's it? Only a cloak? Nothing else? What does it look like?" She propped her shield up against a tree while she waited for Valduin's reply.

She did not notice Valduin's eye twitch.

"Yes, it is a magic cloak that is supposed to shimmer with all of the colors of the rainbow. It is extremely powerful, allowing you to protect yourself with a sort of wall of light. Beulah did not give any other details, other than that she saw it one time when she visited the tower. She did not say what its powers are; she only said that it would be useful for our revenge."

"Okay, that will do, I guess," Rose said. She finished setting up her shrine to Selaia by lighting a candle in front of the shield. She dipped her finger into the holy water that Fulbert had given her and traced the rising sun on the shield as she prayed, "*When the shadow of evil falls over my heart, Selaia will bring the light.*

"*When the temptation of evil touches my mind, Selaia will give me strength.*

"*When the corruption of evil poisons my land, Selaia will purify.*

"*When the power of evil threatens my home, Selaia will be my shield.*

"*Selaia, guide my footsteps, and my path will ever lead to you.*

"*Selaia, watch over me, and my soul will forever be yours.*"

She felt her mind expand as she completed the ritual. She opened her eyes. All of the light around her was gone as if that one candle was the only source of light in the entire universe. She felt Selaia's presence looming in the darkness.

"We need to get into this castle. We need to take something, a cloak of many colors, from Misery so that we can stop his evil deeds. Is there a way into the castle that we have not seen yet?" Rose asked her first question aloud.

"Yes, child," came the answer, Selaia's voice emanating from all sides at once. The voice was soft but immense, resonating in Rose's chest.

"Is the entrance that we have not yet found better than the ones we can see for the task at hand?"

The voice hesitated. "Perhaps. Each path presents challenges."

Rose paused. She considered what question to ask last. This question she spoke in Halfling so that he would not understand it.

"Can I trust Valduin?"

The voice did not hesitate.

"No."

"What?" Madison screeched.

"I told you!" Amelia shouted. She jumped to her feet, knocking her chair over. She ignored it. Pointing an accusatory finger at her brother, she continued to shout, "He's evil!"

"I am *not* evil!" Logan shouted back. "I'm playing the game! Valduin is brainwashed; you need to *fix him!*"

"It would help if you gave us *something* to work with," Amelia huffed. "Maybe tell us how to get into your bag. Or tell us what you are really after here." She crossed her arms, standing beside the table and glaring at her brother.

Logan's mouth fell open; he gave a dramatic gasp of shock. "I will not *cheat,*" he said. "You had a chance to look at the bag without me seeing. You couldn't figure it out. You had a chance while I was sleeping to look at it. You didn't. You have had plenty of times to do insight checks, but you haven't done any. Don't act like this is all on me. You've been playing this game long enough. You should know what you need to do. Do you need to read the book again to refresh yourself on the rules?"

Amelia's hands dropped to her side. She stared at Logan for a few seconds, saying nothing.

She stormed out of the room.

"Way to go," Madison said to Logan once she heard the bedroom door slam. "That's exactly what she needs."

18

The candle flickered out as the spell ended, leaving Rose in darkness until she blinked her eyes. The world around her returned. Adelaide and Valduin sat nearby, watching her, but Rose kept her eyes fixed on the shield. She did not want to look at Valduin.

"What did she say?" Adelaide asked. "Which way do we go?"

"There are other entrances. Or at least one other that we haven't seen yet. I think we should take a look at the cliffs below the tower before we rush into this. There might be an entrance to the basement or something that isn't guarded as closely." Rose kept her gaze locked on Adelaide as she answered. When she finished speaking, she forced herself to look at Valduin.

"Maybe when we fly in tonight," Rose said to the half-elf, "we can take a minute to look around down there. What do you think?"

Valduin grimaced. "I cannot make us fly forever. I would not want to use up all of my magic just so we can look for a door that might not even exist. We should use one of the entrances that we can see."

"Agreed. We're gonna need all of our energy when we get inside," Adelaide said. "We should go for the door on the rooftop terrace. That's our best bet."

Rose shrugged and turned away from them. She focused on packing up her shrine and avoiding catching Valduin's eye.

Adelaide peered through the sparse branches above them. "We've got a while to wait. You sure you want to do this in the dark? Rose and I see much better during the day."

Valduin nodded. "We should definitely do it after dark. There is no other way we can get to that door without one of those guards seeing us. They were not moving or patrolling or anything. They were just standing in their places. I think we will be okay to hide here, even though we are close to them."

"Fine," Adelaide conceded. She settled back against a tree trunk. "You can take first watch, Val. I'm taking a nap."

Rose leaned against her pack. She let her eyes close, but she knew there was no way she was letting Valduin be the only one awake. Not anymore.

The day dragged on. Adelaide napped. Valduin kept an eye on the castle. Rose rested, though she would not let herself sleep.

Afternoon became evening. Valduin produced a loaf of bread from his bag. Rose waited until Adelaide had started eating before she took her first bite.

"Anything happening over there?" Adelaide asked while they ate.

"Absolutely nothing," Valduin replied. "I have not heard so much as a single footstep from one of those armored guards. I know there were three of them up on the wall earlier. From what we saw last night, I thought we should have been able to hear them moving around from here. At least a little clank or scrape."

"That is not very encouraging," Adelaide said. "Do you think we need to go down the coast a bit before we approach the castle? Or do you think we can fly out from here?"

"I'd vote for moving away from here first," Rose said. "If we are not positive that the guards have moved, I would not want to risk them seeing us before the mission is even underway. We need to be as sneaky as we can be right from the start."

"I agree," said Valduin with a nod.

"All right," Adelaide said as she pushed herself to her feet. She leaned on the tree while she stretched out her legs. "Let's head out. It will be dark soon."

The party made their way back from one cluster of trees to the next until they were out of sight of the castle. Looping around to the south, they approached the cliffside once more. Valduin led the way, his vision unimpeded by the gathering darkness.

Nervous about being spotted, Adelaide and Rose did not use their magic to light their way. They instead relied on the faint light from the waxing crescent moon above them to keep Valduin in sight. They followed him through the darkness, trusting the path he chose.

The women heard the coastline before they saw the drop-off, the steady crashing of waves against the rocks over a hundred feet below them. Reaching the cliff, they looked out across the Aegean Expanse once again. The moon and its reflection shone back at them, like the drowsy eyes of a giant lying on its side. A breeze blew up from the water, bringing the salt smell of the ocean with it.

Rose stepped to the edge of the cliff. She closed her eyes. The cool breeze made her shirt flap behind her. She had not been out of her armor in weeks. Goosebumps covered her bare forearms.

She breathed in the smell of the ocean. She savored it, held it in, the freedom of it, the life of it.

For a moment, she let herself forget what they were here for. What they were doing. What they had done. What they still needed to do. She filled herself with the wild breath of the ocean, and she was lost in it.

She let her eyes open. The giant stared back at her, its drooping lids reminding her that sleep would not be coming any time soon. Not while Valduin's mind remained ensnared by the hag.

She took another breath.

"Shall we?" Valduin asked. While Rose had stared out over the water, he had been focused on the castle, the towers a black silhouette against the night sky. Not a single light shone from the dark stone structure.

"Yeah," Adelaide answered. She put a hand on Rose's shoulder. "You ready?"

Rose nodded.

"Good. Stay close," Valduin said. *"On the wings of my master,"* he recited in Abyssal. The dim purple glow of ethereal broomsticks appeared under each of the adventurers. Valduin did not hesitate; he leapt from the cliff.

"Here we go," Adelaide said, a wild grin on her face. "I love this part." She dove after Valduin. She let herself fall for a second. The ocean breeze gathered into a gale to batter her. Her long braid waved behind her; the eagle feathers on her headband whipped at the side of her face. She fought the urge to call out, to shout, to scream with untethered joy.

The second passed.

She took control of her descent and angled northward, following the speeding half-elf along the cliff's face.

Rose watched her friends become shadows racing across the surface of the water. She took one last breath of the cool ocean air before diving after them.

"Selaia, watch over me."

"Go for the balcony next to the big tower, right?" Adelaide asked, glancing back and forth between Rose and Valduin. The three adventurers hovered over the calm water below Gloomtide Tower. The steady glow from the purple broomsticks between their legs cast their faces in ominous shadows.

"Are you sure we can't check out these cliffs first?" Rose asked. "There are other entrances that we haven't seen yet. We should at least try to find them. They might be easier to get through. We know that there are guards up on the wall."

"No. We do not have the time. I cannot make us fly forever, and your eyes are useless in the dark anyway," Valduin shot back. "We made a plan. We approach from the back, get onto the terrace, and get through the door we saw. Follow me."

He flew close to the cliff face and ascended through the light mist of the waves crashing into the rock. In the darkness, Rose could not see the look on Adelaide's face. She wanted to say something about Valduin, but she did not get a chance. Adelaide chased Valduin toward the tower.

"Follow me, he says," Rose grumbled. "We'll see about that." She flew forward and higher to catch up to her friends.

The promontory was made up of a series of ridges, the stone protruding, breaking, and folding back on itself in waves around the base of the castle. In the scant moon-light, Rose could not tell what lay in the shadows of the rocky crevasses, but she was sure that a cave or door could have easily been hidden there. One that led into a lower level of the castle. One that the faceless guards were not watching from their posts atop the wall.

"*Each path presents challenges.*"

Rose could hear Selaia's voice in her mind. She shook her head, trying to clear her doubts and suspicions. "Focus," she admonished herself. "Be patient. Watch him."

She caught up with Valduin and Adelaide beside the castle. They hovered next to the dark stone wall. The wall was without doors, gates, or windows on this side as well. The large tower loomed over them. Valduin poked his head over the top of the wall for a moment.

He ducked back down and looked at the women.

"Those guards, they have not moved. Or at least there are still three guards, one on each of the other walls. They all look the same to me. I cannot tell if they are just wearing the same armor or if these are the same three guards I saw earlier. The terrace is right above us here," Valduin reported. "We are only twenty or thirty feet away from that door."

"How much longer can we fly like this?" Rose asked. "You keep saying that we can't do it forever."

"Not much longer," Valduin whispered. "We go for the door. I can unlock it if it is locked." From one of the small side pockets of his bag, he produced a thin metal tube as long as a finger. He spun it in his fingers; it glinted in the sparse moonlight.

"What if it's trapped?" Rose asked.

"Yeah, great point," Adelaide said. She turned to Valduin. "What if it's trapped?"

Valduin did not reply at first. He hovered up and peeked over the top of the wall again as he considered this question. Returning to the party, he said, "I don't know. I can look for traps once we are close, but that will take time. I could try to disarm a mundane trap. Magical traps might be an issue." He twisted his mouth and chewed on his lower lip.

Rose gave an exasperated, and exaggerated, sigh. "You can still detect magic, right? You tell me if there is magic on the door. If there is, we assume it's a trap, and I'll take care of it. Then you can get the door open."

Valduin, either ignoring or not noticing Rose's attitude, nodded. "Great. Let's go now before my flying spell ends and we all fall to our deaths." He ascended toward the terrace once again.

"Now you see me; now you don't," Adelaide said, hurrying to cast her stealth spell before Valduin was within sight of the armored guards. They became nothing more than shadows in the darkness, humanoid voids absent of even the sparse light of the crescent moon.

The party crested the wall and flew to the door, taking advantage of their last few moments of flight so as not to set foot on the stone terrace. The three guards remained at their posts, motionless, each watching the castle's surroundings in a different direction. None looked toward the adventurers.

They touched down in front of the door, which was made of blood-red wood carved with intricate, flowering vines. The flowers, menacing, spiked blooms with petals that lay open like the jaws of a bear trap, shifted at their approach. The vines bent toward them, bringing the dozens of tiny mouths closer, though they remained an image carved into the surface of the door.

Rose whispered to Valduin, "You don't even need to check. I know a trap when I see one." She held her amulet up toward the door. "*Selaia, protect our passage. Rid this door of its foul magic.*" The amulet pulsed with pale golden light. Adelaide leapt to Rose's side and spread herself as wide as she could to block the flash of light from the view of the three guards.

The carved flowers snapped shut, their spiked petals intertwining into a hundred snarling mouths. They stopped moving, stopped trembling, stopped seething, stopped writhing. The door was reduced to mundane wood carved with a threatening image of vines and flower buds.

Valduin pointed the metal tube at the black, iron door handle and the matching keyhole above it. With the middle finger of his other hand, he flicked the tube. The tube rang; a single tone, clear and cold, sprung from the tiny instrument. The door responded with a clunk as the lock disengaged.

Another sound rang out over the ever-present sound of the surf far below them. The sound of metal scraping against stone.

Adelaide and Rose spun around at the sound.

All three guards, their faces obscured by the solid face guards of their helmets, had turned toward them.

"Open it! Open it!" Adelaide hissed to Valduin. She swung Fiend's Lament off her pack, readying herself for the coming onslaught of animated armor.

Valduin looked from the handle to the flowers carved into the wood of the door. "Here we go," he muttered. He grabbed the handle and turned it down. Without a sound, the handle turned. The door swung inward.

The nearest guard ran toward them, its heavy armor clanging and clanking as it moved from the walkway on the southern wall onto the far side of the terrace. It brought its spear up over its shoulder in one hand like a javelin.

"In! In!" Adelaide shouted. She grabbed Rose with one hand and Valduin with the other and dove through the door.

The party tumbled to the floor in the darkness of the interior of the tower. From her place at the top of the pile, Adelaide kicked the door closed behind them. The guard's spear sunk into the wood with a heavy *thunk*.

Unable to see in the darkness, Adelaide pushed herself to her knees and felt for a knob that might lock the door.

She found none; there was only a handle on this side of the door.

She spun around and sat with her back against the door, bracing her feet against her companions in preparation for the guard to burst through. She held the door handle above her head with both hands so that she might fight its turning.

She braced.

She waited.

"Well, we're in," Logan said. He did not sound excited.

"Yeah, and they know we're here!" Madison lamented. She had her elbows on the table and her face in her hands. "This is our first heist mission, and we got seen before we even opened a single door! We are terrible at this."

"Yeah, awesome job with the Chime of Opening," Amelia said. She rolled her eyes. "You probably should have known it would make a loud noise."

"It doesn't say it makes a loud noise!" Logan shouted. He waved the item card at Amelia. "It only says 'a clear tone.'"

"Well, we could have cast Silence around them so they wouldn't have heard us," Amelia continued. "I could have covered one and you could have covered another. Or we could have used a diversion on the other side of the castle. We could have done lots of things, but *you* wanted to rush in and go for the door to the tower."

Logan opened his mouth to argue when Madison elbowed him in the ribs. He whipped his head around toward her, but the fire in Madison's eyes stopped him before he said a word. He looked at Amelia again, who was staring with empty eyes at the map of the tower on the table.

Logan sat back in his chair. "You're right, I forced us to go for the door," he conceded. "And I can't tell you why, but it's not because of me. It's Valduin. He has reasons that he hasn't shared and that he can't share. Yet. Remember? You have to fix him."

19

No attack came. No shoulder or foot slammed the door at her back. No hand attempted to turn the handle against her resistance.

A moment at a time, Adelaide let herself relax. Her hands fell to her sides. Her breathing slowed.

The darkness of the tower closed in on her. She opened her eyes as wide as she could, painfully wide, trying to see something, anything, in the space around her. She could hear her friends' anxious breathing. She felt them shifting beneath her feet. Beyond that, she could sense nothing.

"You two okay?" she whispered into the darkness.

Before Valduin or Rose could respond, a flare of light blinded Adelaide. All three adventurers covered their eyes, groaning in surprise. Adelaide's body tensed up again. She waited for the pain of an attack or a trap. Again, none came.

Adelaide peeked between her fingers. Valduin and Rose lay at her feet, their faces covered. As her eyes adjusted to the new brightness inside the tower, she let her hands fall from her face.

"Whoa. We made it," she muttered. She nudged her friends. "Take a look," she said.

Valduin sat up, blinking against the light of the lamp on the table next to him. He squinted and looked around.

Rose did the same, keeping one hand on her forehead to shield her eyes. "Is this what you were expecting?" she asked Valduin.

"I guess so. Maybe. I had not really thought about what it would look like in here," he replied. He got to his feet and surveyed the room.

They were in a study or library. Bookshelves lined most of the walls of the circular room. There was an arched doorway to their left. Across the room from the doorway, a desk stood in front of a section of bare stone wall. In between the doorway and the desk was a collection of sofas and reading chairs upholstered in a variety of floral patterns. Each seat was accompanied by a side table with a lamp. Every lamp in the room was blazing with yellow flames.

"It looks so," Rose paused as she took in the decor, "*nice*. Not all sinister like the Ebon Keep was. These sofas look like they belong to Enchantress Aloom, not Misery."

"I agree," Valduin replied. He stepped toward the doorway. "I found the stairs," he said over his shoulder to the women. "Up and down. Which way do you think we need to go?"

"This is your quest," Adelaide replied. She remained seated on the floor with her back against the door through which they had entered. "Where do *you* think we need to go? What else did Beulah tell you?"

Valduin turned toward Adelaide. "She told me the cloak would probably be where he gets dressed," he said. "Probably in his bedroom, which I'm guessing is at the top."

His eye twitched.

"So, I'd guess we have to go up," he concluded. "How long are you going to sit there, anyway?" he asked Adelaide.

Adelaide inspected Valduin with narrowed eyes. She had seen the twitch, but she did not know what to make of it. She pushed herself to her feet, though she continued to lean against the closed door to the terrace.

"I'm just making sure no one comes barging through here," she answered. "We *were* being chased by one of those suits of armor. I'm trying to play it safe as we break into the evil wizard's tower."

"Fair," Valduin conceded with a nod and a shrug. "Shall we ascend?"

"Wait. We are skipping this room? Don't you want to check this place out? What if what you need is right here?" Rose asked. She was standing in front of a bookcase near the door they had come through. Her head was cocked to the side as she tried to read the writing on the books' spines. At least the ones that had writing in a language she could read. "These books look mighty old," she said, trying to tempt the half-elf.

Valduin shook his head. "What have we learned about sneaking into the homes of powerful magic users? We only touch what we absolutely have to." He paused, and his eyes flared with purple light. He scanned the room. "As expected, everything in here is magic. From the lamps to the rug to the bare stone wall." He pointed past the desk. *"Everything."*

"Fine," Rose conceded. "Well, which way do we go? Up or down?"

"Up," Valduin said. He turned back toward the archway. "See, even the stairs are magical." He led the way up the steps. Rose and Adelaide followed close behind.

The staircase ascended for ten steps to a landing, and from the landing, there were ten more steps back to the main part of the tower.

"I don't remember seeing this staircase sticking out of the side of the tower," Rose commented when the party paused on the landing. "Shouldn't this have been obvious? I feel like the tower was perfectly circular."

Valduin shrugged. "The tower is magic. The staircase is magic, too. It probably is not very hard to hide this structure from the outside. Anyway, it does not matter to our mission. Focus." He proceeded up the rest of the stairs and passed through another arched doorway, much like the doorway in the study.

In fact, it was exactly like the doorway in the study.

It was the doorway in the study.

They were back in the study.

Valduin looked around in surprise. "That is not right," he muttered.

Adelaide stepped through the doorway and stopped at Valduin's side. She groaned.

Rose sighed. "I can't say I'm surprised. Of course, it wouldn't be that easy."

"Maybe if we go one at a time?" Valduin mused. He stepped onto the stairs heading up once again.

Adelaide lunged forward and grabbed the back of Valduin's bag. "Are you joking?" she asked. "We are *not* splitting up in here."

Valduin shook himself free of Adelaide's grip. "I'll only go to that landing," he said, pointing up into the darkness, "and take a look."

Adelaide pursed her lips, but she did not argue. She stepped to the side so that she could look down the other set of stairs.

Valduin walked up to the landing. He turned the corner.

He looked up at Adelaide.

He stepped back around to look down the steps he had come up.

He looked down at Adelaide.

He groaned and rejoined his companions.

"Nope," he said with a sigh.

"What if we go down?" Rose asked.

"Won't we just come back here again?" Adelaide asked.

"Only one way to find out," Rose answered. She walked down to the landing below them. She leaned around the corner to look down the second half of the flight of stairs. The stairs descended into darkness. She leaned back and hissed at Valduin, "It's dark. It's different. Get down here and tell me what you see."

Valduin skipped down the stairs to Rose's side. He stepped to the other side of the landing to look down into the darkness. The stairs ended in a white marble floor. He descended one step at a time, each step revealing more of the room at the bottom of the stairs. There was another arched doorway here that let out into what Valduin assumed was a foyer, as it had only a few narrow tables along the walls and a large, lightless chandelier hanging from the high ceiling.

He would have taken a moment to marvel at that ceiling, as it was much too high for there to be a study at the top of this short flight of stairs, but he did not have time. His focus was drawn to the ornate door at the other end of the room, about fifty feet away. The door was flanked by two faceless suits of armor, suits of armor whose clanking footsteps echoed through the foyer as they came toward him.

Valduin raced back up the stairs to the landing. He turned the corner and slammed into Rose, his knee hitting her in the chest and knocking her onto the stairs behind her.

"Watch it!" she cried. She struggled to push Valduin away as he stepped over her and up the stairs.

"More guards," Valduin hissed at her. "Down there!" He reached the top of the stairs and spun around, his left hand extended toward the landing below.

Rose looked up from where she lay on the stairs to watch the thorned wand unravel from his wrist. It crawled down his palm and grew out between his fingers until it reached its full length. Two drops of Valduin's blood fell from the tip of the wand and splattered on the last wooden stair.

Rose did not stand up. She scrambled up the stairs, pulling herself up with her hands until she flopped onto the floor next to Valduin. She sat up, grabbed her amulet, and extended her hand toward the landing as well.

Adelaide leapt over Rose, down to the second step. She pivoted and braced herself against the wall, Fiend's Lament held high in her right hand, waiting for a target to come around the corner.

The clanking footsteps grew faster, louder, closer.

They waited.

The footsteps stopped.

They waited.

Nothing happened. No more sounds came from the bottom of the stairs. After a minute, Valduin released the wand, which slithered back and coiled around his wrist. Adelaide lowered her battleaxe. Rose let her amulet fall against her chest. A twinge of pain reminded her that she was not wearing armor.

She rubbed her sternum where the amulet had fallen. "What have we gotten ourselves into?" she muttered. She did not expect an answer.

"What now?" Adelaide asked. She stood between the door through which they had entered the study and the archway leading to the staircase. She looked back and forth between the two entrances to the circular room. The hand with Fiend's Lament rested at her side; her other fingers tugged at the strap that held her handaxe to her belt. "I don't like this one bit. We've been seen twice. Why haven't they come in here to get us?"

Rose shrugged. "Beats me," she said.

"I am not sure either," Valduin said. He chewed on the corner of his mouth as he peered down the stairs toward the foyer. "But I do not like it. It feels like they know that once we are in here, we are handled, controlled, neutralized, no longer a threat. Which means there is something in here worse than them." He shivered.

"We need to get the stairs working," Adelaide said. She looked around at the area near the archway that led to the stairs. "What about this? Is this magic? It looks like it might be connected to the stairs." She pointed to the wall next to the archway.

Valduin and Rose joined her. Embedded in the dark stone wall was a palm-sized square of smoother, lighter stone. An oval track was carved into the stone, and the track held seven spheres of varying colors. On one side of the oval, the track straightened and ran through a smaller circle that was cut into the stone.

"*None may hide*," Valduin recited. His eyes flared purple again. "It is indeed magic," he reported. "Transmutation magic. It could be the control for the stairs. Maybe it can change them so they work. I see no hints of

184

abjuration or evocation, so it should be safe to touch." He held up a hand toward the square.

"It should be safe," Adelaide repeated as she stepped back from the wall. "Well, let's not bunch up and make it easy on them." She returned to the exterior door, the only part of the room that she felt safe touching.

Valduin laid a single finger on the corner of the stone square.

Nothing happened.

He moved the finger up and touched one of the colored spheres.

Nothing happened.

He pushed the sphere. All seven spheres rolled along the track together.

He ran his finger along the smaller circle cut into the stone. Without a sound and without resistance, the circle turned. This broke the oval, holding two of the spheres in a separate segment of track. He rotated the circle halfway around, lining up the track again. The spheres had switched places.

"Okay, okay, okay," Valduin muttered. "Nothing bad happened, right?" He glanced over his shoulder.

Rose and Adelaide both looked around as well.

"Seems fine," Rose reported.

"Good." Valduin turned back to the colored spheres. "Now we need the code. Seven spheres. Seven colors. We can flip any two adjacent spheres by moving them around the track and turning the small wheel. What order should they go in?"

Adelaide, still leaning against the other door, asked, "What colors are there?"

"Is that pink? Then dark purple, maybe violet. Cerulean or cobalt maybe. Dark blue, possibly midnight blue or Prussian blue. Yellow, but maybe gold or even ochre. Orange. Chartreuse," Valduin called out the color of each sphere in the order that they sat in the track.

Adelaide shook her head. "What?"

Valduin ignored her response. "Maybe it has to be alphabetical by color. But in which language? Hey, Rose, how do you say chartreuse in Infernal?"

Rose was holding her head in her hand. She looked up at Valduin and shook her head. "What are you talking about?" she hissed, frustration boiling over. "Chartreuse? Are you serious? The colors of the spheres, Adelaide, are red, violet, blue, indigo, yellow, orange, and green."

Valduin squinted at the colors. "How can you be sure that is indigo? It could be a dark ultramarine."

"Trust me," Rose replied.

"Very well," Valduin said with a shrug. He flipped the small wheel, transferring the spheres from one position to another, sliding the line of spheres around the oval track after each flip. After a moment, he stepped back. "There we go. Blue, green, indigo, orange, red, violet, and yellow." He looked around again. He stepped through the archway and peered up the stairs.

"I don't hear anything," he said. "Let me check."

He bounded up the stairs. He turned the corner at the landing. He came running up the other side of the staircase, back into the study.

He grunted in disappointment and returned to the square on the wall. "Alphabetical in a different language maybe? I wish we had a hint somewhere."

"How about color order?" Rose asked.

"Color order?" Valduin turned to her. "What's that?"

"You know, like the order of the colors of a rainbow. The colors as the ancient celestial Ro Ygbiv created them at the beginning of time. Didn't you learn about that at your fancy elf school?"

Valduin blinked. "Oh, actually, now that you mention it, that name does ring a bell." He turned back to the puzzle. "Red first, correct?"

Rose giggled. "Red, orange, yellow, green, blue, indigo, and violet," she recited the color order. "Just as Ro Ygbiv set them out."

Valduin pushed the spheres and spun the wheel until the order matched what Rose had said. With the last flip, the spheres flashed with light, each sphere in its own color. Valduin stepped back with a smile.

"Let's try this one more time," he said as he headed toward the stairs.

Madison and Logan laughed.

"Ro Ygbiv! That was amazing," Madison said. She patted her sister on the shoulder.

"Yeah, Amelia, that was perfect," Logan conceded. He set the puzzle on the table. "Although, in my defense, these colors are definitely not regular old red and blue and green."

"Why do you have to make everything so complicated?" Amelia asked Logan, though she was smiling. "It's just a plastic toy. It isn't going to have *chartreuse* balls in it."

"I thought that was a pretty good description of that green," Logan mumbled. He poked the puzzle with one finger. "It is sort of a sickly, violent shade of green."

"Anyway," Madison said, "what's next? Up the stairs, right? Looking for a cloak?"

"You got it," Logan replied.

"You really think Misery keeps a super powerful magic item in his closet with his socks and underwear?" Amelia asked. She narrowed her eyes at her brother.

"You really think he wears underwear?" Logan countered.

"Come on! That's gross!" Madison cried, covering her ears. "Don't make me think about that!"

Amelia was not deterred. "We both know that is ridiculous. What is Valduin really looking for? What does he expect to find in Misery's bedroom?" She pointed an accusatory finger at her brother.

Logan shrugged, a mischievous smile creeping across his face. "We'll see."

20

Valduin climbed the stairs up to the landing. He looked down at the light spilling through the archway behind Adelaide and Rose. He stepped to the other side of the landing so that he could look up.

The stairs ascended into darkness.

"I think we did it," Valduin whispered, leaning back around the wall that divided the landing. He waved for Adelaide and Rose to join him.

"Go take a look," Adelaide whispered back as the women cautiously climbed toward him.

Valduin crept up the steps. The darkness did not impede his vision. Halfway up the flight, he was able to see past the top step and across the floor of the next level of the tower. He peered through a forest of square trees that rose to become chairs and tables.

He paused.

He watched.

He waited.

Nothing moved in that dark, silent forest. He continued to climb, now seeing the entirety of the dining room. Or possibly the banquet hall, for several curved tables filled this floor, each with a dozen chairs. The tables were curved to form a circle within the larger circle of the tower's wall. An aisle passed between the tables, leading from the stairs straight across the room to the far wall. Tapestries hung edge-to-edge like deep-pile wallpaper on either side of the room. The only uncovered areas were the archway to the staircase and the segment of curved wall at the opposite end of the central aisle.

Valduin stood at the top of the stairs, taking in the sight of the dining room. A crystal chandelier hung in the center of the chamber; tiers upon tiers of unlit candles waited at attention for the next dinner party. Without turning around, he waved for his companions to join him. He continued to take in the splendor of the dining room, with its domed ceiling, much higher than the ceiling had been in the study. The tapestries were more in line with his expectations of Misery. While it was still much brighter than the Ebon Keep, scenes of dragons battling over charred landscapes and stylized representations of tentacled horrors adorned the walls of this chamber.

Valduin shivered.

He looked around. Adelaide and Rose had not joined him.

He pointed a finger down the stairs and whispered a message to Adelaide, "You okay?"

"Yeah. You okay? Is it safe to come up?" Adelaide whispered back.

"Oh, sorry," Valduin said into the darkness of the stairwell. "I forgot that you would not be able to see me. Come on up."

Adelaide and Rose joined him, guiding themselves by putting their hands on the steps in front of them. They reached the landing and stood up.

"You think I could make some light?" Rose whispered. She could hear Adelaide and Valduin near her, but she could see nothing.

"Yes, I think it is fine," Valduin replied. "There is nothing moving in here."

Rose's amulet lit up the area between the stairs and the dining room. In the soft glow, Rose could see the first few chairs at the nearest ends of the tables. She squinted in vain into the darkness beyond. "Dining room?" she asked.

"Looks like it," Valduin confirmed. "The cloak would not be in here. I say we keep moving up. Do not go in. Okay?"

"Yeah, okay," Adelaide agreed. "Same as before. Go ahead." She lifted a hand to gesture toward the stairs leading higher into the tower.

Valduin climbed, each step a quiet tap on the stone stairs. Without Adelaide and Rose nearby, the oppressive silence of the tower enveloped him. The sound of his breathing filled the stairwell. He held his breath. He turned the corner at the landing and continued to climb, spending an extra second on each step so that he could place his foot on the next one without a sound. The next archway stood in the darkness at the top of this short flight. He continued holding his breath; his heartbeat pounded in his ears.

He reached the point where he was at eye level with the next floor. A hallway stretched out from the archway. It ended in the bare, dark stone of the tower's exterior wall. There were doors leading to the left and right at several points down the straight passage. To Valduin's eye, it looked like the hallway one would find upstairs in a tavern, with guest rooms on either side.

The doors that Valduin could see were closed. Nothing moved within the hallway.

Valduin exhaled.

He took a few deep breaths to soothe his lungs, aching from the minute without air.

He stepped onto the landing. The hallway waited in front of him, dark and silent. He pointed a finger through the floor and sent a message to Adelaide to join him. The women's footsteps echoed up from behind. He winced at how loud they were.

"What do you see?" Rose whispered. She stood next to Valduin, the light from her amulet illuminating only the first few feet of the hallway. The whisper might as well have been a shout through a megaphone in this silent space.

"A hallway. Closed doors on either side. Looks like they could be guest rooms. Or something. There are more stairs up. I think we keep going."

"Lead the way," Adelaide said.

Valduin continued upward, the silence weighing on him again as he climbed higher.

The next floor held an art gallery. The center of the room was empty of furnishings or decorations. Pictures hung around the walls of the circular room, four on either side, with a gap in the middle at the far side of the tower. Eight paintings of eight landscapes, each alien in its own way. Whether it was the pools of air in one, a forest of lightning in the next, or a river of stone in another, each painting was twisted enough from Valduin's experience that he had to study them for a few moments to process what he was seeing.

Nothing moved within the gallery, so Valduin called the women up. When Rose's glowing amulet shed its dim light into the chamber, Valduin noticed a glinting from the floor at the center of the room. A golden circle had been laid into the stone floor and surrounded by golden runes. Valduin's mind raced as he tried to place the memory of such a circle of runes. He could not remember where he had seen this arrangement before.

Rose peered into the darkness. "What's this one?" she asked.

"Art gallery," Valduin whispered back. "Weird paintings. Some kind of circle, probably magic, on the floor. I wish I could go closer, but I do not think we should."

"Agreed," Adelaide said. "I think we've gotten lucky too many times already. Let's get to the top and then get out of here."

Rose nodded. "I'm okay with that plan. After you." She indicated toward the next flight of stairs with an open hand.

Valduin sighed. "Off I go," he mumbled, and he left the women at the entrance to the gallery. He crept up the steps.

"What do you think we're looking for?" Rose whispered to Adelaide once Valduin had disappeared around the corner on the landing.

Adelaide looked down at the halfling. In the light of Rose's amulet, the confused creases between Adelaide's eyebrows were deep and dark. "What?" she asked, louder than Rose would have liked.

"Shush!" Rose hissed. She grabbed Adelaide's wrist and pulled the tall human down to her height. "What do you think we're looking for? Do you really think Misery would keep a powerful magic cloak in his closet? We should be looking for a vault or some kind of display room or something. Not a bedroom."

Adelaide's face relaxed from confused to pensive. She stood up straight and looked up the stairs to where Valduin had disappeared.

"I hadn't thought about it," she answered. "Maybe Beulah gave him more information than he gave us. Maybe she told him that is where it would be."

"Or maybe she told him that he was here to get something different. And the cloak is a diversion."

"A diversion for the two of us?" Adelaide looked confused again. "Why would he do that?"

"Because he's here working for *her*. We are just along for the ride. He is hiding something. He's been acting weird. He never acknowledged that we survived the Ebon Keep on our own. Something here isn't right."

Adelaide took a moment to digest this idea. "Well, do you think—"

Valduin's voice in her head stopped her question. "This is it. The stairs stop at a door. Come on up."

"Coming," she replied through the magic of the spell. To Rose, she asked, "Do you have that spell prepared that lets you can find an object nearby?" She took the first step, but she did not rush up toward their friend.

Rose nodded. "I was saving my energy because I was expecting a fight," she whispered. She climbed a few steps. "Let's see what's up here. Then I'll use it." She led the way up the stairs to the top floor of the tower.

Valduin stood in front of a door. Like the door at the bottom of the tower, this one was carved with flowering vines. When Valduin had stepped onto the landing at the top of the stairs, the vines had begun to writhe, the flowers opening toward him, though they could not reach past the plane of the door. While he waited for Adelaide and Rose to join him, more flowers appeared on more vines, each bloom lined with thorny teeth. More flowers on more vines, all moving, swaying, intertwining, reaching, twisting, yearning for him. The silence at the top of the tower was ringing in his ears, but in his mind, he could hear those tiny mouths snapping at him through the wood of the door.

He took a step back.

He waited for his companions, his gaze fixed on the swirling, slithering, undulating vines.

Rose's light approached, but Valduin kept his eyes on the door.

"What we got?" Adelaide asked as the women arrived on the landing. "Oh, another one of these? Rose, can you turn it off?"

Rose stepped past Valduin, though all he could see was those tiny floral mouths opening and closing, the vines clambering over each other to reach him, ignoring Rose.

He took another step back.

Rose held up her amulet. "*Selaia, protect our passage. Rid this door of its foul magic,*" she recited. The amulet flashed. The vines stopped moving. The flowers snapped shut. Rose stepped back.

"You're up," she whispered to Valduin.

From behind her, Valduin held out his arm. A floating, spectral copy of his hand appeared and drifted to the handle of the door. The handle did not turn.

"Locked," Valduin murmured. He reached into his bag and grabbed the chime of opening. He pointed the hollow tube at the door.

"Wait," Adelaide hissed. She looked down the stairs behind them. "What about the noise? Do we need to do anything to block it?"

Valduin did not lower the chime. "They know we are here," he said. "Why they are not coming in to find us, I do not know. But I would rather not waste any time or energy." Without waiting for a response from Adelaide, he flicked the tube. Compared to the sound the tube had emitted outside on the terrace, in the open air with the sea breeze in the background, this was a monotone detonation. The chime reverberated within the enclosed landing, making all three adventurers wince and glance over their shoulders. After the chime's sound had faded, they all could hear its echoes, a lingering note haunting the stairwell, fighting against the buzz of the tower's silence.

Clunk.

The lock disengaged.

Click.

Valduin's mage hand turned the handle.

Creak.

The door swung inward.

The adventurers stood at the entrance to the bedroom. A chandelier of twisted, black metal hung from the ceiling. No candles were set on the chandelier. Instead, a ball of flame hovered at the center of the structure like fire caught within a mangled cage. The flames lit the space well enough for Rose and Adelaide to take in all of the details as clearly as Valduin could.

There was no bed in this room, only a large, straight-backed chair of reflective, black stone that sat like a throne facing a fireplace. To their right, a waist-high chest of drawers of a similar black stone stretched fifteen feet long, matching the curve of the tower wall. At either end of the dresser loomed double-doored armoires almost ten feet tall. Sitting on top of the dresser was an assortment of small boxes and dishes, as well as a leather book on a stand.

"This is more what I was expecting," Rose said. "This looks like a room at the Ebon Keep."

Valduin did not respond to Rose's comments. "Stay here. I'm going to look around a minute," he said. His voice was hushed, breathless with excitement. He stepped toward the dresser and said, *"None may hide."* His eyes glowed with purple light as he scanned the room for traces of magic.

He stalked toward the dresser. His eyes scanned the room to the left and right, but his feet maintained their course. He stopped in front of the book. Its brown, leather cover looked old, its corners worn down, its pages yellowed. He inspected the sides of the book. There were no words written on it, only an image of a moth pressed into the cover. A leather cord held it closed. He stood on tiptoes and leaned forward to look at the back of the stand. There was a dome of glistening energy around the book, but he could see no other tricks or traps. He stood back.

"Rose, I need you," he hissed, not looking away from the book. He pointed at it. "I need you to dispel this bubble."

Rose narrowed her eyes at Valduin's back as she walked toward him. "I thought we were here for a cloak? Don't you want to check the closets?" she asked, nodding her head toward the nearer armoire. "That isn't a cloak." She stopped a few feet behind the half-elf.

"I know. I know," Valduin replied, "but look at this book! Think of what magic it might contain. Or what abilities it might bestow. We'll get the cloak next." His glowing purple eyes darted back and forth between Rose and the book. "I can see a dome of magic over it. I need you to dispel that so I can get it."

"It looks creepy to me," Rose said, stepping up next to her friend. "It's got a skull on the cover! That usually means something is dangerous."

Valduin cocked his head as he looked at the image on the book. "Oh, it does look like a skull. I thought it was a moth. In any event, it *has* to be powerful. Maybe Beulah can help us use it safely. *Please* dispel the protection so I can get it. I *need* it."

Rose stared up at Valduin's eyes, glowing with Beulah's magic, sunken with days of sleep deprivation, and wild with excitement at the sight of this book. Sadness gripped her heart.

She held a hand out toward the book. *"Selaia, clear this magic from our path. Let us retrieve this book and the knowledge it contains."* Her amulet flashed. A dome of matching golden light flashed around the book on its stand.

"It worked!" Valduin said, nearly squealing with delight. He snatched the book with both hands, hugging it to his chest.

Rose watched him. She took a breath, bracing herself for her next action. With one hand, she held her amulet. The other she placed on Valduin's side.

Valduin looked down at her hand. "What are you doing?" he asked.

"Fixing you," she replied.

Before she could cast her spell, however, a grinding, rumbling sound filled the chamber. Valduin stepped away from Rose and spun toward the sound. Rose, her hand still outstretched, swung her arm toward the source of the noise.

The wall opposite the entrance was moving. It was sliding up. At first, there was only darkness. Inch by inch, the light from the burning chandelier lit the space behind the wall.

They saw two thick, gleaming, armored legs with greaves so broad that no feet could be seen.

The legs stretched up, longer than any humanoid's legs, before they met a metallic body, wider than the three adventurers standing side-by-side.

Inch by inch, the body was revealed, flanked by metallic arms that ended in monstrous fists as big as anvils.

Between two mountainous shoulders sat a domed metallic head. There were no eyes, no ears, no mouth. The head was a smooth helmet of silver plates with golden runes etched along the seams. The more the adventurers looked, the more golden runes they saw, lining every joint and every plate of armor.

The wall stopped. Silence fell.

Valduin inched toward the stairs, his gaze fixed on the twelve-foot-tall construct across the room from him.

A red crystal blazed to life atop the domed head of the construct.

Rose, her outstretched hand trembling, hissed at Valduin, "Check the closets! We need the cloak!"

The construct took a step forward, out from its hole in the wall.

The stone tower shook.

"Forget the cloak," Valduin said. "We gotta go!"

"Well, ya gone done it now," Madison groaned. "Look at this thing!" She held the miniature that represented the monstrous metal creature.

"I wish you still had Tog's Chasing Hammer," Logan said. "With its extra damage against constructs, it would have been perfect for this guy."

"Don't remind me," Madison replied. "Why do you think it woke up? Didn't you dispel the trap?"

"I dispelled one trap," Amelia said. "There could have been multiple. If someone wasn't so *grabby*," she glared at her brother, "maybe we could have identified any others and dispelled them, too."

"That book is the number one priority for Valduin. There, now you know it. There is a cloak somewhere, and it would be cool if we could find it, but Beulah really wants this book," Logan said. "What were you going to cast on me, by the way?"

Amelia stuck her tongue out at him. "Wouldn't *you* like to know, Mr. Secret Secretface. You'll find out when I'm good and ready."

Logan smirked. "We'll see about that."

Amelia narrowed her eyes. "What's that supposed to mean?"

Logan gave a playful shrug. He mimicked his sister's voice and said, "You'll find out when I'm good and ready."

21

The machine took another step forward.

The tower shook.

A beam of golden light shot from Rose's hand. In a flash, it crossed the room, headed for the construct's broad chest. When the guiding bolt was a few feet away, it vanished in a flash of red light.

The machine stepped.

The tower shook.

"Rose!" Adelaide screamed from the doorway. "Run!" She stepped backward toward the stairs, her eyes darting back and forth between her friend and the monster headed toward her. Adelaide raised her own trembling hand, and the nails on three fingers grew into luminous, white spikes. She launched the magic missiles across the circular bedroom.

One, two, three, the glowing white spikes vanished in flashes of red before they reached the construct.

The machine stepped.

The tower shook.

Valduin was already halfway down the first flight of steps. Adelaide beckoned Rose with a frantic wave.

Rose ran. As she approached the doorway, she activated her ring of jumping, the warmth flowing from her hand, through her body, and into her legs. She leapt through the door and arced into the stairwell. She flew past Valduin and landed on the first landing, staggering into the wall with the extra momentum of descending eight feet of stairs.

Adelaide came stumbling down the steps behind them. She grabbed Valduin by the collar as she ran, pushing him forward past the landing.

The tower shook.

"Can it fit in the stairs?" Valduin gasped. "Are we safe?"

"Definitely not safe," Adelaide panted back. "Keep running."

The party rushed down to the next floor.

Valduin froze at the archway. There it was, gleaming silver and gold and lit by the glowing red gem on its head, standing on the other side of the gold circle at the center of the art gallery. The far wall stood open. The open space between the paintings on the right and left sides of the gallery was now a gaping darkness identical to the space the construct had stepped out of in the bedroom.

"It's here!" he screamed. He staggered back, eyes wide in terror. He raised one shaking hand to throw three purple sparks of energy at the colossus.

With three tiny flashes of red light, the sparks vanished before they reached the monster.

The machine stepped.

The tower shook.

Adelaide and Rose glanced into the art gallery. The circular chamber was lit with the faint red glow from the crystal atop the machine. The women looked for only the moment it took to note the presence of the construct.

Rose leapt down to the next landing. Adelaide pushed Valduin onto the stairs.

"Keep moving!" Adelaide shouted, her voice wild with panic.

They descended the next flight and arrived at the next archway.

The tower shook.

The metal mountain was halfway down the hallway of guest rooms. Its shoulders scraped the walls on either side of the hall. Its colossal fists hung at its sides.

The machine stepped.

The tower shook.

The adventurers did not pause. They ran. Down to the landing. Down to the next archway.

The machine was in the dining room, in the aisle between the tables.

Run. Leap. Run. Stumble. Run.

The machine was in the study, somehow having crossed the room without disturbing the furniture. Closing in on the archway. There was no room to get to the exit without passing next to the construct.

"Keep going!" Rose shouted. She leapt to the next landing. Valduin and Adelaide followed, scampering down the stairs, holding onto the smooth stone walls for balance.

They arrived at the entrance to the foyer. There was no machine. Instead, the room was filled, wall to wall, shoulder to shoulder, with faceless armored guards. A hundred or more standing at attention in the dark, quiet chamber.

The adventurers stood in the archway, staring at the army. The army stared back.

The tower shook.

"Nope," Adelaide said. "Nope, nope, nope." She again grabbed her friends by the collars of their shirts. "Down! Keep going down!" She pulled them toward the stairs.

Down to the landing they raced. Down to the next floor. They burst through the archway and skidded to a stop, nearly colliding with the monstrous construct.

One arm swung forward and slammed into Adelaide. The human flew backward and landed on the stairs with a grunt.

The other arm swung out and slapped Rose to the side, sending the unarmored halfling tumbling into the corner of the chamber.

Rose came to rest with her back against a wall. She looked at Valduin staring up at the mountain of metal, with its featureless face and fearsome fists. She saw his hands shaking. In the red glow from the top of the machine, she could see a single tear escape his eye and roll down his sunken cheek.

She watched him reach into a side pocket of his bag. He withdrew a small glass sphere. The same sort of sphere that Beulah had given them before their journey to the Ebon Keep. The sort of sphere that would cast a spell when broken. The sort of sphere that could teleport the holder away from danger.

"Valduin!" Rose screamed. "What are you doing?"

Valduin turned toward her. His eye twitched. "I'm sorry," he said, "but you're already dead."

He crushed the sphere in his hand, wincing as the shards of glass lacerated his palm.

The fragments flashed with red light and fell from Valduin's hand, tinkling on the floor.

Valduin remained, standing in front of the machine as it brought its fists up together.

"Oh no," he mumbled. He stepped back and raised his arms over his head as if he could block the coming blow.

Rose pushed against the wall behind her to get to her feet. She strafed to her left to get out of the corner while keeping her distance from the machine. She took a moment to survey the room as she moved behind a glowing blue pillar.

The chamber was filled with these pillars, nearly a dozen of them, arranged in a horseshoe around the archway to the stairs. As she moved behind the first pillar, she noticed an object floating inside. A black crown or circlet that appeared to be made up of braided, thorned vines.

She glanced at the pillar to her left. Hanging in the air, as if draped over an invisible mannequin, was a dark cloak. As Rose moved, an iridescent shimmer spread across the garment.

She paused next to the cloak. She raised a hand toward the machine and shouted out, *"Selaia, banish this monster from my sight!"*

The red gem on the top of the machine flashed. It remained in its place, looming over Valduin, a high-pitched whine building in volume from somewhere inside its tremendous form.

In a cloud of mist, Adelaide appeared in the center of the room, which Rose had decided must be the tower's museum. Weapon in hand, she charged at the back of the construct. She swung the axe into it, but even the keen blade of Fiend's Lament scraped lamely across the plates of the machine's armor.

The whine coming from inside the construct built to a steady, ear-ringing squeal. With shocking speed, it brought its fists down on the ground in front of it. The squeal turned into an eruption as a shockwave of thunderous energy burst from the monster. The explosive wave smashed Valduin into the stairs, the same spot Adelaide had landed a moment earlier. Adelaide was blasted backward, and she slammed into one of the pillars of blue light at the back of the room.

Valduin leapt to his feet and ran for cover behind the first pillar to his right, across the room from Rose. Wand in hand, he launched three more purple sparks at the machine. Each vanished in a flash of red before it could reach the monster. He slammed his fist against the pillar in frustration.

When he glanced at the pillar, he froze. Hanging in the air, slowly rotating, was a necklace. A gold chain with a large pendant. The pendant was made up of three overlapping gold rings; each ring contained a flat gemstone of a different color. A single, silver thread wrapped around the pendant, crossing and connecting each of the gemstones. He remembered this necklace. This was the necklace that his mother kept locked up in the secret safe in her closet. The necklace he was never supposed to tell anyone about. The necklace that she had been wearing on the day she had taken him to the Inner Plane of Light. The necklace that she had been wearing when she died.

Rose did not notice Valduin's distraction. Her focus was already divided between the cloak in the column next to her and the robot that was turning to face the room. She tried to reach through the blue column to grab the cloak, but the wall of light might as well have been made of iron. She glanced back at the monster, and her eye was drawn to the red, glowing crystal on its head. The same shade of red that flashed each time they cast a spell at the construct.

"Adelaide!" she shouted. "Hit the gem. That's blocking our magic!"

She held a hand against the blue column. *"Selaia, remove this magic from my path. Allow me to take this item to better do your will."* Her amulet flashed with golden light. The column of blue flickered, but it did not disappear.

Adelaide pushed herself to her feet. For the first time, she took in the room. She saw Valduin and Rose focused on the columns that they each stood next to. She looked over her shoulder at the column she had crashed into. A shiver ran down her spine.

Hanging in the air, as if waiting to be grasped, was Tog's Chasing Hammer.

Adelaide put a hand out toward it, but she only stubbed her fingers against the magical barrier of blue light. She spun back toward the machine, eyes wide with rage. She pulled one of her handaxes from her belt and slung it at the red crystal atop the construct's domed head. The blade slammed into the crystal, bouncing to the side. The red light flickered for a moment, but it did not go out.

Adelaide gave another longing glance at the hammer behind her, and then she ran toward Rose. She knew that the halfling, not wearing her armor, would be an easy target for their monstrous foe.

The construct seemed to have realized the same thing, and it took a step toward Rose where she hid behind the pillar containing the cloak. As it moved, it pulled back a fist. It arrived at the front of the pillar. The red light of the crystal flared brighter. The fist swung forward. The blue column disappeared, and the fist caught the cloak a moment before it slammed into Rose, smashing her against the stone wall. Rose screamed and fell to the ground, blood dripping from her nose and mouth.

The machine pivoted. It swung the fist to the side and caught Adelaide before she could reach Rose.

Adelaide raised her shield but could not stop the momentum of the machine's arm. It slammed into her, throwing her across the room, where she landed at the foot of another blue column. The cloak flew off the arm and fluttered to the ground next to Adelaide.

"Adelaide!" hissed Valduin from his hiding spot behind the column that contained the necklace. "How did you get the cloak out?" He could not see what had happened on the other side of the room with the bulk of the construct blocking his view.

"The thing," Adelaide muttered in a daze. She pointed at the crystal. "The red light. It turned the shield off. We gotta break the crystal. So we can hurt it," she said between panting breaths.

"Not yet," Valduin said. "I need this first." He stepped out from behind the pillar and shouted at the machine, "Hey! Hey, you! Leave that little one alone. Pick on someone your own size!" He held his hands up above his head and beckoned the machine toward him.

Rose clutched the stone wall as she dragged herself to her feet again. She looked at the red crystal, high above her head. She pulled her mace off her belt.

"Gonna have to jump for it," she muttered to activate the magic in her ring. She leapt up and back, planted her feet on the wall behind her, and sprung higher, toward the glowing crystal. She raised her mace above her head as she flew, preparing to smash the crystal.

When she got close, however, the crystal flashed. She felt like she weighed a thousand pounds as she entered the machine's anti-magic field. No longer carried by the magic of the ring, she slammed face-first into the construct's wide, smooth chest. She fell to the ground, landing on her back once again.

"Rose!" Adelaide screamed. "Get out of there!" She got to her feet, stepping sideways toward the handaxe that lay on the ground while hurling her other one at the crystal. This one flew high, missing the target. Adelaide snarled and picked up the first axe she had thrown, preparing herself for another shot at the crystal.

"Stop it!" Valduin shouted at Adelaide. "I need it to open this pillar!"

Adelaide turned her face toward Valduin, still snarling. "If we save Rose, *she* can open the pillar. Get your priorities straight," she growled. She turned back toward the machine.

The machine, unmoved by Valduin's challenge, centered itself over Rose. It raised its arms over its head. It leaned over the halfling.

Slam.

Slam.

It pummeled the tiny cleric with punches that shook the foundations of the tower. When it stood back up, Rose lay on the ground, unmoving.

"Rose!" Adelaide screamed. "No!"

"Over here!" Valduin shouted over Adelaide's screams, unaware of or unconcerned with Rose's plight. "Come get me!" He hurled a dagger at the construct; the weapon bounced off its metallic armor with a pitiful clatter.

"What are you doing?" Adelaide shouted at Valduin. "We need to help her!" She disappeared in a cloud of mist, reappearing beside Rose's unconscious form. She patted her pockets in a frantic rush before realizing that Valduin still had all of their healing potions. She kicked the blue, glowing column in front of her as she remembered passing on the opportunity to buy more from Aloom.

"Valduin, I need you!" she shouted.

"And I need this," he muttered. He did not care if Adelaide could hear him or not. The machine was walking toward him now. He knew what he needed to do.

"The real Valduin comes out," Madison said, her face grim. "You got your book, and you were going to leave us behind. What's your plan to get out now, sneaky boy?" She poked her brother in the ribs. Hard.

"Ow!" Logan recoiled from the poke, squeezing his arm down to cover his flank. "I'm still working on that, but I need this necklace more than anything now. I might even risk breaking Beulah's Geas spell to get it."

"Ah-ha!" Amelia cried. "You *are* charmed. I *knew* it. Well, I can fix that." She sat back in her chair, a satisfied smile on her face.

"You got it. I'm not going to lie though, as long as Valduin is charmed, I'm going to play it that way. He'll do whatever it takes to get this book back to Beulah. Even leave you both behind. Maybe even fight you."

"Whoa, whoa, whoa," Madison said, holding her hands up to cut Logan off. She smirked and said, "You don't want to be trying that. I guarantee it won't work out for you."

Logan shrugged. "Well, Rose is already unconscious, and you are pretty hurt. I've got a couple of big spells up my sleeve. You haven't seen everything Beulah gave me yet."

"We're gonna have to circle back on that," Madison said. She turned to Amelia. "About you being unconscious. I thought your crown could bring you back from making death saves. Why don't you use that?"

"Because you are so close to me," Amelia explained. "You have healing magic. Valduin has potions if he will let us use them. I can only use the crown in that way once per day. I figure I'll save it for a time when I really need it. This battle is not even close to over. We literally haven't dealt a single point of damage to this thing."

22

Valduin waited behind the blue column. He watched the behemoth approach through the arcane glow. His hands rested against the column's smooth surface, ready to grab the necklace as soon as the machine's anti-magic field suppressed the barrier.

The moment came, and he did not wait. The machine stepped up to the column, and the light vanished. The necklace hung in the air, now bathed in red light instead of blue.

Valduin snatched it; there was no resistance. He jammed the necklace into the pocket of his cloak and dashed toward the back of the museum before the construct had a chance to swing at him. Once he reached the next blue column, in which floated a small silver cage, he vanished in a cloud of mist, reappearing at Adelaide's side, standing above the unconscious Rose.

"We gotta go," he panted. "We can't fight this thing."

"Go where?" Adelaide hissed. "Up to the army in front of the door? This thing is on every floor, remember? And look at Rose!" Adelaide dropped to one knee next to the halfling. She concentrated for a moment, her hands glowing with dark green energy, and she placed them on Rose's caved-in chest.

The green light spread out, seeping through Rose's shirt. Her ribcage snapped up to its normal shape, pushing Adelaide's hands back as it reformed. Rose sucked in a long breath and opened her eyes. Her face was still bruised and bloody, but she was alive.

Adelaide helped Rose to her feet. The machine was turning toward them.

"Thanks," Rose muttered. "What's the plan?"

The machine stepped.

The tower shook.

"We need a way out," Valduin said. He held up his wand over his head, and then he swept it in a wide arc to mark a line on the floor between themselves and the construct. The stone floor appeared to crack along that line, and thorned vines grew up from the cracks. The vines snaked around each other, weaving a wall of thorns that split the museum in half.

"*Selaia, heal me*," Rose said, speaking into her amulet. Despite the brevity of the prayer, the amulet glowed brighter than any of them had ever seen. The light crept up the chain that the amulet hung from and poured down over Rose's body. After a second, the entirety of the halfling was glowing with brilliant glowing light. Another second later, the light faded. Rose's bruises were gone. Her black eyes had cleared. Her hair and clothing were still stained red and brown, but the steady streams of blood from her nose and ears had stopped flowing. Rose tilted her neck back and forth to crack it, and then she sighed.

"Much better. Okay, Selaia told me there were other entrances to the tower, but we haven't seen any. There has to be one down here," Rose said. She peered through the dim blue light of the chamber. "Is that a doorway over there?" she asked, pointing to a dark corner of the room, outside of the horseshoe of display columns.

Valduin was staring with building anxiety at his wall of thorns, wand still raised. He glanced in the direction Rose indicated. "Yes!" he said when he saw the archway. There was no door, only a passage out of the dark corner of the museum. "Let's go!"

Adelaide stood with her back to her friends. She had her hand against the column of blue light that held Tog's Chasing Hammer. "Rose, I know we don't have much time, but can you open this?"

The tower shook.

The wall of thorns writhed.

Rose winced when she saw what Adelaide had found. "I don't have much energy left," she admitted. "I think we need to go."

Adelaide's hand on the column clenched into a fist. Her shoulders heaved as she seethed with anger.

The machine stepped.

The tower shook.

The whirring whine that Rose had heard earlier was building in volume again.

The wall of thorns melted away as the robot stepped into it, the red glow of the crystal pushing the vines back from the oncoming construct.

With a battle cry to answer the building shriek of the machine, Adelaide whipped around and hurled her handaxe at the crystal. It connected with the pulsing, red light. The crystal cracked. The red glow vanished.

The whine built to a crescendo. The machine raised its fists over its head.

Rose held up her hand toward the machine, but before she could begin to cast a spell, the fists slammed down on the floor.

The tower shook.

The shockwave hit all three of them, blasting them against the back wall of the museum.

Rose groaned and rolled over. She looked down the wall. Adelaide was slumped in a heap in the far corner, near the exit. Valduin, closer to Rose, pushed himself to his feet. He looked over at Adelaide and then up at the machine.

"Heal her!" Rose shouted as she struggled to get up. "You have the potions!"

Valduin pointed his wand at the construct. Black smoke poured from the hand that held the wand. *"Death comes for all,"* he recited. The smoke swirled out from his hand and enveloped the machine before dissipating. The machine made no sound, no indication of pain or injury.

Valduin staggered backward toward the back door, his wand still raised, his hand trembling.

"Banish this monster from my sight!" Rose screeched. Her hand was held out toward the construct, but her eyes were burning holes into Valduin.

The machine disappeared.

"What are you doing?" Rose screeched again. She got to her feet, wavered, and steadied herself with a hand on the wall. She staggered past Valduin to Adelaide's side.

Valduin looked from the spot where the machine had vanished to the halfling. He said nothing. He turned and ran past Adelaide and out the back door.

Rose gasped. She gave chase, sprinting toward the exit. Arriving at the archway, she glanced down at Adelaide's broken body. "Hang in there," she muttered.

She looked through the archway. At the edge of the blue glow of the museum's display columns, she could see Valduin moving through a stone tunnel.

"Hold it right there!" she screamed.

Valduin froze in the middle of his run, one knee bent, one hand on the rough stone wall of the tunnel.

The monster returned, appearing in the same place from which it had disappeared a few seconds earlier, its fists still planted on the floor from its last thunderous attack. It righted itself and scanned the room for the adventurers.

The machine stepped toward the archway.

The tower shook.

Rose grabbed Adelaide by the collar and dragged her into the tunnel toward Valduin.

"I need you," she whispered to the human.

Adelaide's eyes snapped open, glowing with golden light. She groaned.

"It's not over," Rose said to her friend. "Get up." She walked toward Valduin. The half-elf stood in the tunnel, frozen.

Adelaide sat against the wall as she caught her breath. She looked toward Rose and saw Valduin, though she did not understand why her friend was not moving.

The tower shook.

Her head whipped around to look up the tunnel toward the museum. The machine's metallic body, gleaming even in the low light of the museum, filled the entirety of the archway. With two mighty swings of its fists, it smashed through the ceiling of the tunnel, splitting it open. It pushed its way into the gap, tearing the stone apart to pursue the adventurers.

Adelaide skittered away from the monster, crab-walking instead of taking the time to get up. She bumped into Valduin's frozen leg. "Val! Move! We gotta go!" she urged her friend.

Valduin made no reply.

Rose ducked under the half-elf's outstretched arm to get in front of him. She looked up into his face. His eyes met hers.

"I know we have a lot to talk about," she said, her voice soft despite her anger. "I know this isn't you." She reached up and put her hands on Valduin's chest. *"When the power of evil threatens my home, Selaia will be my shield. Selaia, there is evil in this man; root it out. Break the chains that bind his mind. Free him that he may do the work of good."* Her amulet flashed. She dropped her hands to her sides.

"Be free," she said.

Valduin collapsed. He held his face in his hands.

The tunnel shook as the construct continued its assault. It had dug almost ten feet into the passageway.

"I am so sorry," Valduin sobbed. "I had to. I could not stop myself."

"Get up," Rose said. Her voice was stern. "Help us now. Save us."

Valduin sniffled. He sat on the ground.

"That's enough of that," Adelaide said. She grabbed Valduin under the arms from behind and hauled him to his feet. "We can cry later. For now, let's just get out of here." She gave him a shove away from the machine and followed him, staggering down the passage.

Rose reached up to light Adelaide's armor so they both could see where they were going. The trio rushed farther away from the museum and the monstrous construct that was demolishing the tower's foundation in pursuit.

After a few twists and turns, the tunnel ended at a wooden door. From the inside, the door looked well-made but plain. Rose guessed the other side would be carved with vines covered in flowers with tiny mouths.

"If there's a trap, I can't dispel it," Rose said. "I have almost no magic left."

"I'll take care of it," Adelaide said. She pulled herself past Valduin and charged forward. She let out a roar and laid her shoulder into the center of the door. It splintered outwards, half of it swinging open on its hinges and the other half tumbling off the cliff on the other side of the entryway. Adelaide stumbled toward the cliff but caught herself on a rock before she could follow the door down to the water below.

The cool sea breeze buffeted them. They could hear the construct burrowing toward them, clangs and crunches echoing out of the tunnel. "Can we fly?" Rose asked.

"Yes," Valduin said. He laid a hand on the shoulder of each of his companions. *On the wings of my master,*" he recited. The purple broomsticks appeared. Adelaide and Rose did not hesitate; they leapt from the ledge and turned south, back the way they had come.

Valduin looked back into the tunnel behind him. He could make out the glint of metal armor through the billowing dust of crushed stone. He looked at the women's backs as they flew away.

He took off, following his friends away from Gloomtide Tower.

The cracking of rock faded behind them. The adventurers flew on, level with the cliff they had walked the last few days.

"I can't believe we made it out," Adelaide said. Her eyes glowed green as she spent the last of her energy healing herself from the shockwave that had knocked her out. She sighed and stretched her neck from side to side. "Not one hundred percent, but that's a good bit better."

"What's the plan?" Rose asked Valduin. "I broke one hold that Beulah had on you, but there might be more."

"There are definitely more," Valduin replied. "I feel it every time I look at you. I still remember you dying in the Ebon Keep."

"I can work on that later," Rose said. "For now we need to get somewhere that Beulah can't find us. Any ideas?"

"I am not sure there is any place that she cannot find us," Valduin muttered, though Rose could not hear him over the rush of air as they flew south.

As if she had heard him say these words, Beulah's voice filled Valduin's mind. "Did you get the book? I see you leaving the tower with the dead ones. You were supposed to return to me alone. Explain yourself."

Valduin took a deep breath. He exhaled. He answered, "We left without the book. If they died, they are alive now." His eye twitched. "They are my family. I will not leave them. You cannot make me."

All three adventurers screamed out in pain as Beulah's laughter pierced their minds. Adelaide's eyes fluttered, but she clung to consciousness. Rose shook off the psychic intrusion. Valduin gritted his teeth and focused on keeping them in the air, maintaining his concentration on the flying spell.

"Very well," Beulah's voice returned, cold and emotionless. "I'll be coming for my things, the souls and the wand. Don't go far."

The broomsticks disappeared.

The adventurers plummeted.

One hundred screaming feet they fell until they crashed into the shallow water lapping at the base of the cliff.

The night was quiet again, the only sound was the gentle crashing of the waves on the rocks.

In the faint glow of the crescent moon, a flash of brilliant white light enveloped the halfling lying broken in the shallow water. The flash subsided, but the platinum and diamond crown upon her head continued to glow.

Rose opened her eyes.

Everything hurt. She could taste blood in her mouth. A few teeth wiggled when she touched them with her tongue. Her left arm hung at her side; her shoulder was dislocated, if not broken. Her ribs were definitely broken.

With her right arm, which hurt a fraction less than the left, she pulled herself to her feet. The water was only knee-deep between the large rocks.

She leapt up on a large rock using the magic of her ring of jumping, and she let out a scream as the landing jarred her fractured body.

Hunched over in pain, panting, she scanned the water for her friends. Adelaide had landed close to her, and Rose spotted the human floating at the base of a nearby boulder. It took Rose an extra moment to find Valduin, whose limp body floated twenty feet out into the open water.

Rose took her amulet in her hands and prayed, *"Selaia, if I've ever needed your help, this is the time."* A swarm of tiny specks of golden light poured out of the amulet, swarming around Rose at first and then spreading out and heading toward her friends. The motes disappeared as they soaked into Adelaide and Valduin's wounds, straightening bones and knitting together muscles and tendons and ligaments.

Adelaide sat up in the shallow water. She groaned and rubbed her neck. "Rose," she moaned. "Rose, where are you?" She did not look around.

"I'm right here," Rose called down from the stone she had climbed onto, "but I gotta go get Valduin."

The half-elf was awake, but he was floundering, splashing about and coughing up seawater.

"Valduin!" Rose shouted as she waded out toward him. "Valduin, you're okay! We're okay!" She swam the last few feet and took him by the shoulders while she treaded water. "Hey! Put your feet down!" she said as she shook him.

Valduin did as he was told. He stopped coughing and spluttering. He whipped his head around, scanning the water. He looked up into the sky.

"It's dark," he moaned. "It's gone."

"What's gone?" Rose asked. She held Valduin's shoulder to stay afloat. He stood in the chest-deep water. He made no attempt to wade to shore.

"My magic. It's gone. Again." He held a hand up toward the cliff above them.

To the depths," he said in Abyssal. Nothing happened.

To the depths," he said in Sylvan. Nothing happened.

"To the depths!" he screamed in Common. Nothing happened.

He started crying.

"Come on," Rose said. "Let's get you dried off and cleaned up. You're gonna be fine. I'm sure of it."

She did not sound sure.

"And *that* is why I saved the crown," Amelia said. "We would have been toast without it."

"I can't believe I lost my powers *again*," Logan groaned. "You guys get to level up, and I get nothing!" He folded his arms on the table and hid his face in them.

"We'll figure it out," Madison said. She patted her brother on the back. "Either we make things better with Beulah, or we'll find you another patron. There have got to be more options than her and Taranath."

Logan did not lift his head. "There aren't really that many," he muttered. "And we don't have contact with any other super powerful beings right now, so I'm gonna say it doesn't look good."

"Okay, you go ahead and sulk," Madison said. She gave Logan a final slap on the back. He winced. "Amelia and I need to level up. I can't believe we made it to thirteen!" She pulled the rulebook out from under Logan's arms.

"Do you know what you get, Amelia?" Madison asked.

Amelia looked at the rulebook in Madison's hands. She pursed her lips and sighed. "Seventh-level spells," she replied. "I don't know about anything else."

Madison snapped the book closed and turned toward her sister. "Okay, you," she said, raising a finger to point at Amelia. "You've been acting all weird about this book for a while now. Logan is already sulking. I can't play with both of you like this. What's wrong with you?"

Amelia shrugged. "Nothing," she said. She hung her head, not meeting Madison's gaze.

"Absolutely not," Madison replied. "You are a better actor than that. Tell me what happened."

Amelia sighed again. She looked from Madison to Logan and back. "Can we talk later? I want to take a little break." She pushed herself back from the table.

Madison tracked Amelia's gaze to Logan, who still had his face buried in his arms. "Sure. Later," she said to her sister, "but I'm gonna hold you to it."

23

The adventurers perched on the slick boulders at the base of the cliff. The wind off the ocean was as cold as the pale light shining down from the crescent moon. Salt water sprayed up at them with each wave. Water dripped from their hair and rinsed blood from their clothes. Rose had healed their gravest injuries; only a few aches and pains lingered from the evening's escapades.

Valduin sat with his legs pulled up to his chest, forehead on his knees, crying.

Rose sat with her back against his, balancing with him atop the wet stone.

Adelaide lay on her back on another rock. She had her eyes closed.

"You dead?" Rose called out over the crash of the surf.

"No," Adelaide called back. "You think we're safe here? I want to fall asleep."

"Absolutely not," Rose said. "You want to fall in and drown? I don't have any diamonds to bring you back right now. No dying allowed."

Adelaide lifted her head and stuck her tongue out at Rose without opening her eyes. She rested her head back on the stone again.

"What's the plan, then?" the human asked. "This cliff is pretty high, and we can't fly anymore."

Rose felt Valduin's shoulders heave as his sobbing intensified.

She elbowed him in the flank. "That's enough of that," she said. "I'd *make* you stop crying if I had any magic left, but with all of the not-dying we've been doing, I'm spent."

Valduin's sobs subsided. He lifted his head and stared at the dark water spreading out in front of him, his gaze empty and cold.

"We'll have to climb," Rose answered Adelaide's question. She craned her neck to look up to the top of the cliff. She grimaced. "We've got rope, right?"

"Yeah, I've still got some rope," Adelaide said. "But not much. I'm a decent climber, but I can't carry you guys." Her voice trailed away. She pursed her lips and narrowed her eyes, lost in thought. "Actually, maybe I can. Tomorrow. How about we find a dry spot to sleep? Tomorrow this climb will be much easier."

"I'm okay with sleeping," Rose said. "I am totally wrecked. It's probably safer down here anyway, as long as we get off these rocks. If we go up, and those guards find us, we're toast."

"Agreed," Adelaide said. She pushed herself to her feet, being careful to stay perched atop her private boulder. She scanned the base of the seaside cliff. There was no beach; the waves crashed on the rocks in the shallows and lapped against the bottom of the cliff's face. Every surface was dark and slick with water and algae.

"I don't see any good spots here," she reported. "Let's go, you two. We move until we find a safe spot to sleep. We keep moving until morning if we have to." She took two quick steps and skipped to another rock.

"Come on, Valduin," Rose said. She stood up and grabbed him under the arms. She pulled at him until he got to his feet.

He said nothing. He leapt to the boulder where Adelaide had lain, wobbled for a moment, and then jumped to the one where the human now stood. Rose followed suit, using her ring of jumping to assist her leaps from one stone to the next.

The party worked their way south along the base of the cliff. The horizon was lightening with the coming dawn by the time they found a recess in the stone big enough for them to fit in together. They did not set a watch. They piled into the small cave, and Adelaide and Rose were asleep in moments.

Valduin lay on the cold, wet stone with his eyes open. He did not cry. He stared into the darkness, his chest heavy with disappointment. He thought about leaving, about sneaking out of the cave and wandering away.

He blinked a long, slow blink.

Without magic, he could not help Adelaide and Rose combat Misery or Taranath or the Voidbringer. He could not free them from Beulah's curse.

He blinked again. Closing his eyes felt so nice.

He could not even get himself out from under this cliff.

If he could not get away, he might as well close his eyes again.

He slept.

Valduin stood in a windowless room of dark stone. A sarcophagus sat in front of him, waiting. It might have been a table, or a platform, or a chest, for Valduin could not make out any details other than its shape. However, he knew it was a sarcophagus.

"Slimy Taranath. Taranath has no power here!"

Valduin spun around. That hissing, slurping voice echoed through the chamber. He watched Rose send beams of golden light up at the whirling mass of eyes and tentacles. He watched Adelaide throw her handaxes, each one bouncing off Gnash, the deep-dweller, and clattering to the floor.

He held up his hand.

"To the depths," he hissed, remembering the last time he met this monster.

Nothing happened.

He shouted for Adelaide and Rose.

They did not respond.

Like he was sitting in the audience at a gladiator battle, he watched his friends fight for their lives.

Adelaide ran to pick up her weapons. She grabbed the axes and turned back toward the horror above her.

Gnash unfurled a tentacle to release a purple bubble, no bigger than an apple, in Adelaide's direction. A second tentacle pointed at Rose; a burning red bubble spun toward her.

The purple bubble hit Adelaide in the head and popped. Adelaide's face went slack. Her arms flopped to her sides.

Rose raised her shield, but it did not protect her. The bubble popped against it and burst into flames that poured over the shield and engulfed the halfling.

Rose screamed and fell forward.

Valduin screamed and staggered backward.

Adelaide was silent, staring up at Gnash.

Gnash burbled and giggled. It dropped toward Adelaide with a strange, halting motion that Valduin could not comprehend. The ball of tentacles would roll through the air, and then the space around it would stretch and twist, and it would jump a few feet farther ahead. The jump was not like when Rose jumped, where she traveled between two points on the ground by passing through the air. Gnash traveled between two points in the air by passing through somewhere else. It never quite disappeared, but it blurred for a moment while it leapt through space.

Gnash rolled and hopped through reality until it fell on Adelaide. It grabbed her, absorbed her, superimposed itself upon her.

She did not scream.

She was gone.

Gnash jumped-rolled-teleported onto Rose.

She disappeared into Gnash's swirling, writhing body.

"*One more for me!*" it babbled with glee. A dozen eyes opened between the tentacles, all looking at Valduin.

He took another step away, holding his hands up in front of his face.

Gnash swirled toward him. Cold and wet and wriggling it enveloped Valduin.

A different voice pierced the panic that roiled in his mind.

"I'm coming."

Beulah's voice.

Blackness and silence.

Rose sat with her back against the wall of their cave. She watched Valduin wince and shake his head and mumble in his sleep. She swept his hair back from his forehead.

"We should get going," Adelaide said. She stepped back into the mouth of the cave, blocking out the light of the rising sun. "He's still asleep?"

"Yes," Rose replied, keeping her voice low. "He needs to sleep, but I think he's having a nightmare. He's been going on like this since I woke up."

Adelaide crouched down next to Rose. She took Valduin's hand. "He's sweating like crazy. Let's get him up. I really want to put some miles between us and that castle. Besides, he doesn't look very restful, anyway."

"Definitely not," Rose agreed. She shook Valduin's shoulder. "Valduin, time to go."

Valduin sat up with a start. His dripping-wet hair flopped into his face. His left hand shot out in front of him as if aiming his wand.

Adelaide and Rose pulled away from him as he jumped up, pushing their backs against the stone wall. "Whoa, whoa, whoa!" Rose said, holding her hands up to reassure her friend. "It's just us! You were having a nightmare. You're okay. We're safe. Everything is fine."

Valduin's breathing slowed. He turned his left hand to look at his wrist. Visible under the sleeve of his cloak was a band of woven, thorn-covered sticks. Red and brown dots covered the inside of the cloak's cuff, drops of blood, new and old, that had dripped from those thorns.

"Everything is definitely not fine," Valduin said. "And we are not safe." He met Rose's gaze, his eyelids slack with exhaustion.

"Did she do something?" Adelaide asked. "Did she say something to you?"

He nodded. "In a nightmare. She made me relive every fight we've ever had. Only this time, you two died. Every time."

Valduin's eye twitched.

"Gnash killed you."

His eye twitched again.

"Azereth killed you."

Twitch.

"The stone giant blacksmith killed you."

Twitch.

"Kano killed you."

Twitch.

"Stop," Adelaide said. She put a hand on Valduin's shoulder. "We get it."

"No, this is important," Valduin said. He put his hands on the sides of his head as if trying to squeeze the memory out of his brain. "It went right up to Misery killing you, but that one felt real. It matches what is in my head now. You both died there."

He looked up at Adelaide. His eye twitched. "Did you die?"

"Well, yeah, I did," Adelaide conceded, "but Rose didn't. She survived and told you to leave. She got me out of there. She brought me back to life."

"Could Beulah have changed your memories?" Rose asked.

Valduin shrugged. "Probably. She is very powerful."

"Well, let's fix them," Rose said. Her hand dove into her pack. She rooted around in the bag, pulling out all manner of items that had drifted to the bottom during their weeks of travel. A minute later, she sat back with an old, leather pouch in her hand. She untied the knotted cord that pinched the pouch closed and pulled open the top with one finger. The diamond dust inside glittered in the early morning sunlight that filled the cave.

"Adelaide, you found this dust on the body of Tor's grandmother in the dungeon below Khal Durum. We guessed it was for some sort of holy magic, though I did not know what back then. I've got it figured out now," Rose said. To Valduin, she commanded, "Lie down."

Valduin did not ask questions. He rested his head back down on his pack.

Rose prayed, *"When the shadow of evil falls over my heart, Selaia will bring the light."*

As she prayed, she dipped one finger into the diamond dust and tapped it onto Valduin.

"When the temptation of evil touches my mind, Selaia will give me strength."

Dip. Tap.

"When the corruption of evil poisons my land, Selaia will purify."

Dip. Tap.

"When the power of evil threatens my home, Selaia will be my shield."

Her fingerprints glittered across his forehead, cheeks, chin, neck, chest, and shoulders.

"Selaia, guide my footsteps, and my path will ever lead to you."

The glittering fingerprints glowed with golden light.

"Selaia, watch over me, and my soul will forever be yours."

The light flared brighter. Adelaide squinted and turned her face away. Rose did not; she reached out and tapped Valduin on the forehead one last time.

The light faded. Valduin opened his eyes. He looked up at Rose.

He smiled.

"You toughed it out. Misery tried, but he could not bring you down."

Rose smiled back.

"Thank you," he said. He looked to Adelaide. "For everything."

"Nice work!" Logan said. "That's Modify Memory and Geas taken care of. I guess all that's left is whatever that curse was the first time we met her. The one that lets her see us and talk to us and hurt us from far away." He patted Amelia on the shoulder as he walked toward the kitchen. "I'm making popcorn. Back in a minute."

The moment Logan stepped out of the room, Madison spun toward Amelia. "Okay, what's going on?"

"What? Nothing," Amelia said. She could not hold eye contact with her sister. She stared down at her lap.

"Again with the terrible acting. For how well you play Rose, I would expect you'd be better at lying," Madison said. She chuckled, trying to break through Amelia's hesitancy. "Come on. What's wrong?"

Amelia heaved a heavy sigh. Without looking up, she replied, "Well, I was at school..." her voice trailed away.

Madison waited.

"...and I brought the book of monsters to read," Amelia continued. "You know, like Logan used to do."

"Before he had them all memorized," Madison said. They both rolled their eyes. Amelia gave a weak half-smile.

"Well, I was reading it at recess, and these two boys started making fun of me. They were calling me a nerd and stuff. And then they took the book and threw it in the dumpster behind the school." Amelia had tears in her eyes. "And every day on the bus they make fun of me now."

Madison's shoulders tensed, and her eyes grew wide. "Who did it?" she asked, her voice stressed, on the edge of bursting into a shout.

Amelia put her hands up to calm Madison. "You can't do anything!" she said. "They'll just make fun of me more."

Madison seethed, taking deep breaths through her nose, her shoulders heaving. She did not know what to do with her hands; they moved from making fists to squeezing the sides of her chair to pushing her hair out of her face. "What are you going to do about it?" she asked Amelia. "If you can't fix it, I'll fix them for you."

Amelia slumped back in her chair. "I figure they'll get bored of it eventually. You can only call someone a nerd so many times, right? It'll stop being funny soon, right?" She stared into her lap again.

"Who wants popcorn?" Logan shouted. His voice was brimming with excitement as he burst out of the kitchen, oblivious to the mood in the room. "And what's the plan to climb this cliff?"

24

"Okay, what was the big secret?" Rose asked Adelaide. "How are you going to carry us up this wall?"

The adventurers stood at the base of the cliff, small waves lapping against the rocks around them. The sea beyond was as still and quiet as it had been the first time they had seen it, a mirror of the blue sky above.

Adelaide grinned. "Remember that potion that Brizzack made for us? The one with the ettin's pitunary in it?"

"Pituitary," Valduin corrected her.

"Right, petunia-tary. Well, I've been thinking about that for a while, and I think I've sorted out how to do that magic myself. I don't think it will last very long, but I should be able to get us pretty far up the cliff if the climbing goes well." She inspected the cliff face, mapping out the cracks, crevices, and prominences that she could use on her way up. She handed her coil of rope to Rose. "Hold onto this for me."

"I'll help where I can," Rose said. She took the rope and put her hand on Adelaide's. "*Selaia, grant her the strength of the bull, that she may take us safely away from this place.*"

The warmth of Rose's magic washed over Adelaide. She felt her legs and arms swell with power. Her pack felt lighter; her step felt easier. She picked Rose up and plopped the halfling on her shoulders. Even with her armor back on, Rose felt like nothing more than a rag doll.

"I *like* this spell," Adelaide said. She flexed her arms. "Alright, now, watch this." She closed her eyes, focusing on the feeling that the potion had given her. She touched the eagle feathers in her hair, channeling her connection to nature.

She grew. Like a coiled snake reaching upward, she stretched toward the sky. Rose rode her shoulders higher. She grabbed the leather headband to keep it from falling off. A moment later, she was peering down from over ten feet in the air.

"Amazing!" Rose cried from her perch. "Valduin, climb on! Quick!"

Valduin did as he was told and grabbed onto Adelaide's pack. Adelaide reached up the cliffside and grabbed a rock jutting out fifteen feet above the ground. She tested it with a tug, and when it felt secure, she hauled the party up onto the wall. She jammed her foot into a crack in the stone and pushed higher still.

With her magically enhanced size and strength, one hundred feet of the rock wall flew past. She paused twice to cast her spell again, making sure that she did not return to her normal size before they reached the top.

The edge of the cliff came into view. Rose pointed out handholds above as Adelaide continued to climb. Valduin clung to her pack, his legs looped through the shoulder straps on either side. He buried his face into the side of the bag.

"Hey, Valduin, whatcha doing back there?" Adelaide muttered over her shoulder. "You could help out, too, you know."

"I have no magic. I have no powers. I can't do anything to help," he called back. He did not take his eyes off the bag in front of his face.

"Well, not with that attitude!" Rose shouted. "You could at least keep an eye out to make sure no one is following us or watching us or anything. Your eyes still work fine in the daylight."

"Nope. I cannot," he said.

"Are you afraid of heights?" Rose asked, her voice playful. She was grinning, though neither of her friends could see it. "You leapt off a mountain in Eydon! You have flown over swamps and forests and oceans and cliffs! You are better than this!"

"All of those times, I could fly. Remember last night when we fell on those rocks? That did not feel good, did it? Adelaide, please keep climbing. Just get us onto solid ground again."

"I need that book. Go back to the tower, and you'll get your magic back. Bring me the book, and you'll keep your magic," Beulah's voice slipped into Valduin's mind.

"No!" he screamed.

Adelaide flinched, her fingers slipping from a crevice that she was reaching for.

Valduin continued shouting into the air, "You tricked me! You lied to me. You changed my memories. You—" His words cut off with a scream. He squeezed Adelaide's pack with all four extremities, tensing with the pain in his head.

The pain passed. He stayed up, clinging to the enlarged backpack almost a hundred feet in the air. "Go," he said between panting breaths, his voice weak. "Get to the top."

Adelaide reached for the crevice again. She dug her fingers in and heaved, pulling the party another few feet closer to the finish.

"The good one. You want to stop the Voidbringer? I am your only hope. There's no one else that will help. Get me the book," Beulah spoke to Rose, her voice a hoarse whisper echoing through Rose's mind. The feeling gave her chills.

She did not respond. Instead, she said to Adelaide, "Hold on to this." She thrust the end of the coil of rope in front of Adelaide's face.

Adelaide did not understand what Rose's plan was, but she did as she was told. She leaned forward and took the rope between her teeth, biting down on it.

"I'm gonna jump," Rose said. When she said that last word, the wave of power pulsed out of her magic ring. She stood up on Adelaide's shoulders. She placed one foot on top of Adelaide's head and leapt toward the top of the cliff. With the help of the ring, she soared over the lip, rolling to a stop on the flat ground above.

As she landed, Beulah's laughter filled her mind, overwhelming her, making her head feel like it would burst. She clutched her temples and staggered to her feet. The world spun around her, but she steeled herself. She knew what would happen when Beulah hurt Adelaide, and she could not risk losing both of her friends. She spotted a tree fifteen feet from where she had landed. She sprinted for it.

"You want your revenge? Misery killed you. And laughed while he did it. I can help you get revenge. I need the book. Get it." Stern and cold, Beulah's voice filled Adelaide's mind. After hearing her friends' screams, she knew what came next. She dug her feet into the cracks of the rock wall as best she could. She leaned against the cliff, clutching the crevice above her head with one hand. With her other hand, she took the rope and flopped it over her shoulder.

"Val! Hold this! And me! Tight!"

"I can't!" he cried.

"Do it!" she roared, panic taking over.

The laughter came, a whirlwind inside her head. She gritted her teeth, closed her eyes, and pressed her forehead against the cold stone as the noise built to a crescendo of agony.

She screamed.

The pain was too much for her to bear.

Valduin felt the shift before he understood what was happening. The straps that he had hooked his feet into grew tight around his knees. The fabric pressed against his face pulled down and away from him. His weight shifted; he felt like he would fall backward at the slightest push.

He pulled his head out of Adelaide's pack. She had told him to grab a rope. It dangled over his shoulder. Her head, which had been high above him, was shrinking. As was the rest of her. Adelaide moaned in pain from Beulah's psychic attack, the pain distracting her from maintaining her spell. Her feet no longer reached the footholds she had made, leaving the pair of adventurers dangling by the one hand that remained clamped onto the crevice above.

Without taking his legs out from the bag's straps, Valduin locked his ankles in front of Adelaide. He squeezed her tight and lunged for the rope. He fell backward, pulling Adelaide away from the wall. He grabbed the rope as Adelaide flopped over him, still stunned by the aftereffects of Beulah's mental intrusion.

Valduin screamed as he caught Adelaide's weight and slid down the rope, the rough material tearing the skin from his palms. He held on, gritting his teeth to suppress another cry, squeezing his legs as hard as he could to keep Adelaide from falling.

The pair hung in the air. The cool morning breeze coming off the ocean set them swaying. Valduin's hands were on fire. His shoulders ached from the strain of hanging from the rope. His legs were cramping with the effort of keeping Adelaide aloft.

"You guys okay?" Rose shouted from the top of the cliff. Valduin craned his neck, squinting up into the bright sunlight, but he could not see her.

"Not really!" he shouted back. "Adelaide is small again!"

A groan came from the weight below him.

"Who you calling small?" Adelaide moaned. She twisted in an attempt to look up at Valduin.

"Don't move!" Valduin screeched.

"I'm gonna need to get closer to the wall," Adelaide said. "Can you swing me over there?"

"No! I can't move, or I'll drop you."

"Then what's your plan?" Adelaide asked.

She did not sound worried or anxious or stressed or scared, all of the things that Valduin was feeling. This caught Valduin off guard. His head cleared, as did the shrill in his voice. "Oh, uh, I am not sure yet."

"Aren't your arms getting tired? How long do you plan to wait before making a plan?" Adelaide asked. She sounded like she was smiling, though Valduin could not bring himself to look down to check.

"I do not know! What do you think we should do?"

"I think you should swing me over to the wall. I will climb up by myself and then haul you up with the rope."

"I can't hold on for that long!" Valduin whined.

"You don't need to," Adelaide replied. She reached behind Valduin's leg to grab the rope. She had a few feet of rope dangling below her to work with, so she looped it and tied a knot. "Here is a foothold. All you need to do is stand here and not fall for three minutes. Can you manage that?"

"Oh. I think so."

"Good. Now," She grabbed the loop of rope with both her hands. "Drop me."

"What?"

"Drop me. Release me. Let me fall."

"Are you sure?"

"Ugh, yes!"

Valduin slid his ankles an inch apart. His exhausted legs flopped to the side, and Adelaide plunged out from under him. She fell only a foot before the loop that she was holding ran out of slack. With a jerk that nearly made Valduin lose his grip, Adelaide's momentum set the rope swinging like a long pendulum. She kicked her legs to swing them from the wall, and she twisted her body around as they swung back toward it. She released the rope with one hand to grab a narrow crack, arresting their movement.

"Great!" she said. "You can use the foothold now. I'll have you out of here in no time."

Valduin did as he was told. He wrapped the rope around one of his tired legs a few times, and he allowed himself to slide down to the loop at the end of the rope. Adelaide, no longer burdened by carrying the rest of the party, ascended the last fifteen feet of the cliff without an issue. A minute later, Valduin flopped onto the grass as Adelaide and Rose pulled him to safety.

"I am never flying, climbing, or jumping anywhere high ever again," he muttered as he nestled his face into the grass. "I am never leaving the sweet, sweet ground for any reason."

"We have got to do something about her jumping into our heads like that," Adelaide said.

The adventurers were headed south. It had not taken long for them to find the main road that would bring them to Mirstone.

"Do you think you can fix it?" Valduin asked Rose. "Like you fixed the other things she did to me?"

Rose chewed the inside of her lip as she considered this challenge. "I'm not sure. I might be able to use the spell that fixed your memories. The only problem is that one is expensive, and I am all out of diamond dust. I'm out of diamonds too, while we're on the subject. We haven't found much good loot recently."

"Well, I got this cloak," Adelaide said. She pulled the crumpled garment from her pack. She shook it out, and the dark fabric glimmered and gleamed in the bright sunlight. Rainbows scintillated across its surface. "Val, can you tell me what it does?"

As soon as the words left her lips, she winced.

"Nope," Valduin said before Adelaide could take the question back. He hung his head. "Not anymore."

"Sorry," she said. She did not know what else to say.

"What about the book?" Rose asked. "Do you know what's in it? Did Beulah tell you?"

Valduin swung his pack off his shoulder so that he could reach into it.

He did not reach in, however. He paused.

"Nope, no idea what was in that book," he said, more loudly than he needed to for his friends to hear him. "It's really too bad that we couldn't get it. I'm sure that would have gotten us out of this trouble with Beulah."

He put his bag on his back again.

Rose and Adelaide made eye contact and nodded in understanding.

Rose glanced at the cloak and shook her head in disappointment.

"Beulah, we got the cloak!" Adelaide called out to their surroundings. She looked around for a moment. When nothing happened, she shrugged.

Refocusing on her friends, she said, "Well, in any case, the big question is whether I put this cloak on or not." She swirled it around her back and then back around in front of herself, not letting it touch her shoulders.

"You should," Valduin said. "I have been telling you to cover your arms up for a while."

"Oh! Good point," Adelaide said. She gave Valduin a sidelong glance. "I definitely do *not* want it then. You should wear it. Maybe it will keep you safe until we figure out how to get your magic back." She tossed the cloak at Valduin.

The cloak hit him in the chest. He let it slide to the ground. "I am not putting that on. What if it is cursed or something? I doubt I could use it, anyway. I cannot do anything anymore." He turned and walked away from the women with his shoulders slumped and his head hung.

"Wow, Logan, you're really playing this up," Madison said. She did not sound impressed. "You know, it's gonna get super boring if you keep acting all sad like that."

"For real. Just multi-class into fighter or rogue or some other non-magical class so you can level up with us," Amelia said. "Besides, you can still use the cloak even if you don't have your own spells. It *must* be cool if Misery had it in his museum."

Logan shrugged. "We've talked about this. Valduin's character flaw is his desire to use magic at all costs. That's why he took the pact with Beulah when she offered it."

"Fine," Madison said. "Well, what do we do next? We got the cloak and book from Misery. Beulah wants that book real bad. We could give it to her and get your magic back. Isn't that what she offered?"

"At this point, I don't trust her to follow through on that," Logan said. "She might just take the book and kill us. No, we should keep the book, and ourselves, far away from her."

"Then what are we doing?" Amelia whined. "We are out of quests, and we still need to do something about the Voidbringer! Do we go talk to Brixim again? We are close to the Mossy Hills. Should we go home and visit Halfred?"

"I think we need to follow up on the necklace," Logan said. He held up the index card he had received when he picked the necklace up in the basement of Gloomtide Tower. "This is our only lead on my backstory. Since we have nothing else pressing, we should figure out why Misery had it."

25

"Welcome to The Tavern!" a chorus of voices shouted as Adelaide pushed through the door. A round of laughter followed the greeting, and the room settled back to a low din of discordant conversations.

"Welcome back!" called Shea from across the room. She moved toward them, a tray of food on her shoulder. Rose smelled stew. She closed her eyes and breathed in the heavy aromas of The Tavern. Most of it was familiar, but there was a spice mixed in that she did not recognize.

"Sit anywhere you like," Shea continued. "I'll let Greg know you're here."

The party dropped into their preferred booth at the foot of the stairs. Valduin rested his head against the high back of the bench and closed his eyes. Adelaide scanned the room for familiar faces. Rose stared at the steaming bowls that Shea had delivered to a nearby table. She sniffed again, trying to place that new smell. It had an edge to it that she could not quite identify.

"Welcome to The Tavern," Greg said. He appeared beside their booth with a tray of mugs. He placed one in front of each of the adventurers, stood back up, and smiled at them. "Ready for dinner? And will you be staying the night?"

"All business now, huh, Greg?" Adelaide ribbed the half-orc.

Greg blushed. "Well, you know," he mumbled, his voice trailing away. He looked down at his feet.

"I'm just teasing!" Adelaide said. "Yes, we need food. And yes, we'll spend the night. Business going good?"

Greg waved at the dining room behind him. "We are full for dinner almost every night. And we have people staying most nights. I've bought furniture for the rest of the rooms upstairs, and I'm probably going to have to hire another helper. Shea has been running like crazy."

"You could pay me double," Shea shouted as she swooped past Greg with a tray of empty bowls. Cheers rose from a couple of the tables. Shea chuckled as she headed to the kitchen.

Greg rolled his eyes, but he did not stop smiling.

"Oh! Did you meet our friend Brixim?" Rose asked. "We told him to come here a couple of days ago."

"Oh, we met him," Greg said, raising his eyebrows. "Interesting friend you've got there. You have him to thank for tonight's dinner."

"I don't like the sound of that one bit," Adelaide said. "What do you mean?"

"You'll see," Greg replied. "He had a few comments on the food. He seemed to like the roots and boots, but he thought that the menu needed a little more spice. So, I'm trying something he gave me. Let me know what you think. Back in a minute." He returned to the kitchen.

"Alright, bub," Rose said. She elbowed Valduin in the ribs. "Let's talk."

He winced, his arm snapping down to shield his flank, and opened his eyes. "What?" he moaned.

Rose continued, "Where are we headed next? We have no more leads on Misery or the Voidbringer. They could be anywhere, and they are probably someplace we can't even get to right now. Taranath is still out there, but he's a bad guy too. Beulah is probably in her hut, and she is watching us and hurting us and sending messages to torment us. What do we know? What have we found?" She looked back and forth between her companions as she reviewed their situation.

Adelaide pulled her pack into her lap and rustled through it. "We've used up all of my gems and fancy daggers and things," she said. "We still have all of those tuning forks, right? The ones that the coven made?"

Rose nodded. "Yup. I've got those. I actually have an idea about how to use them, too. I've been thinking about how it felt when Beulah sent us through to the Inner Plane of Shadow. I think I could do that, too."

"Well, that's cool," Adelaide said, her eyes gleaming. She lowered her voice. "Want to try it?"

"Whoa, whoa, whoa," Valduin said, holding his hands up. "Absolutely not. We do not know what planes those tuning forks lead to, and, even if we did, planes are *big*. What if we plane shift and get dumped into an ocean or a volcano or something? We would not even know how to get home!"

"Well, I could always banish us back," Rose pointed out.

"Does that bring us right back to where we left from?" Valduin asked, his tone implying that he already knew the answer.

Rose's smile faded. "Oh. No, definitely not. When that hag banished me, I dropped into an ocean and almost drowned. And when I banished myself and Adelaide, we ended up in the desert." She shrugged. "Well, I can use them if we ever need to. What do you have, then?" she asked Valduin. "Any leads on what we should do next? Anything else cool in that magic backpack?"

Valduin did not answer. He sat back as Greg deposited bowls of stew in front of them.

Rose leaned over her steaming bowl and breathed in the scent, relishing the warm, exotic aroma that she had noticed earlier. It tingled in her nose. Her mouth watered. She tasted the broth. It was salty and savory, with an ephemeral flash of spice as she swallowed it. It was amazing. Before their host walked away, she asked, "Greg, what is it? What is the spice? This is so good!"

Greg grinned. "That's a house secret," he said, in a way that made Rose think he had been coached in how to say this line.

Rose grabbed the edge of Greg's apron before he could turn away. Greg looked down at her. Her eyes flashed. "Brixim, it's Rose," she said as she sent a magical message to the gnome. "We are at The Tavern. What did you give Greg? This stew is out of this world."

Greg's mouth fell open when he realized what Rose was doing. He glanced at Adelaide. "She can do that?"

Adelaide nodded. "Oh yeah. You can't hide from Rose Fairfoot."

Greg swallowed hard. He did not try to pull his apron out of Rose's grasp.

"Interesting choice of words," Brixim replied into Rose's mind, his voice playful in a way that Rose had not heard before. "I gave Greg a pepper plant, of sorts. Native to the Fire Plane. It packs quite a punch."

Rose released Greg. She sat back and smiled. "You better take good care of that plant, Greg," she said. "Because I will be coming back for more of this stew. Or anything else you make with it."

"He said that people would say that," Greg replied, smiling again. "I'll grab your keys in a few minutes. Let me know what else you need. There's no charge for the food or the rooms. You three have already given me more than I could have ever dreamed of."

The adventurers sat in a circle on the floor of one of their rooms upstairs at The Tavern.

"How do we know if Beulah is watching us?" Adelaide asked.

"If we could see invisible things, we could see the sensor that the spell creates," Rose said. "I'm sure if I tried to look at her, she would be able to see it."

"Well, how were you able to block Rose from watching you?" Adelaide asked, looking at Valduin. "She tried for days before Brixim helped us find you."

"That was Beulah's magic," he replied. "She would cast a few spells on me whenever I went out on errands. Not that she told me what they were, but I guess one of them blocked scrying."

"Can you do that, too?" Adelaide asked, turning to Rose.

Rose winced. "No, sorry."

"We will just need to be careful about what we talk about," Valduin said. "She can't be watching us *all* the time, but if we act like she is, we should stay safe."

"Well, alright. What's our next move?" Adelaide asked.

"I need to find out how Misery got this," Valduin answered. He held up the necklace that he had taken from the museum.

"Where did that come from?" Rose asked. "I haven't seen it before." She reached for the necklace.

Valduin's hand pulled the necklace back before Rose could grab it. He held it to his chest and took a breath to settle himself. "This is what we have to figure out next." His gaze was fixed on the necklace, which he held in his open hand with a reverence that Rose had not seen from him before.

Rose and Adelaide exchanged glances, both confused by Valduin's behavior. Rose repeated her question, "Where did that come from?"

"This was hanging in the museum beneath Gloomtide Tower," Valduin answered without looking up from the necklace. "This was the item I pulled from the pillar after you got the cloak."

"And you know what it does?" Adelaide asked.

"No."

"Then how do you know that it's important?" Rose followed up, impatience straining her voice.

"Because this is my mother's necklace. Was my mother's necklace," Valduin said, his voice faltering. He blinked back tears.

Adelaide and Rose said nothing. They let Valduin collect himself.

After a moment, he wiped his eyes and continued, "I had seen this necklace on my mother before, from time to time when she was going out or coming home late at night. I knew she kept it in a safe in her closet. She never talked about it. One time I asked my father about it, and he just stopped talking and left the room. She was wearing it on the day that she took me to the Inner Plane of Light. The day that I met Taranath. The day that she died."

Valduin sat, staring at the necklace.

The women waited.

"How did Misery get this?" Valduin continued. "We have already decided that Taranath was *not* my savior that day. I do not know what his involvement was in my mother's death, or what his motivation was, but I know Taranath is partly responsible. Was Misery there too? Or did he acquire the necklace later? Are Misery and Taranath connected? They are both working for the Voidbringer now. Has this been going on ever since then?" Valduin's voice was rising with each question, anxiety taking hold.

Rose responded, her voice low and soothing, "We don't know those answers. We can't know them. I agree with you, though, that this is worth investigating. You said your mom was part of some secret organization in Alomere, right? We should go there. Maybe they will be able to give us information about Misery. Maybe they know about the Voidbringer."

Valduin sniffled. "I do not know anything about that group. How to find them, what they are called, what their goals are or were." He counted off on his fingers the gaps in his knowledge. "As I said, my mother was secretive, and my father covered for her, though he did not seem an enthusiastic participant."

"He must have known *something*," Adelaide said. "We'll have to start with him. Alright you two, time for bed. Valduin, tomorrow, you're going home."

"What you're saying," Madison said, "is that this entire campaign has been built in the holes in the backstory that you wrote. Why did you have to make it so complicated? Look at me. I worked in a shop until I wanted to go get rich. Easy. Simple. No mysteries, no super powerful enemies." She sighed.

"I was just trying to make things interesting," Logan explained. "I had to explain how Valduin had access to a warlock patron. I didn't think it would blow up like this."

"Well, we know what we are doing next. That's good," Amelia said. "What are we going to do about Valduin? How are you going to defend yourself? And Beulah? Is she going to keep pestering us?"

Logan flipped through his notebook to the inventory page. "Madison, I gave Adelaide my crossbow back in Khal Durum, right? I'll take that back. I have a decent Dexterity score still, so I can use it."

"Yeah, of course," Madison said. She sat up straight as she had a realization. "Wait. Did I pick up my handaxes? I was throwing them at that robot thing. Do you remember?"

Logan flipped forward to the page that held his notes on the battle under Gloomtide Tower. "You threw one, picked it up, threw the other," he muttered as he scanned through his notes. They were illegible to his sisters. "Then you threw the first again and broke the crystal. Finally, the shockwave knocked you out, and Rose dragged you into the hallway." He winced and looked up at Madison. "You left both of them there. Sorry. You're down to Fiend's Lament only." He scooted his chair away from his sister, preparing to dodge the coming outburst.

Madison chuckled. "That's what I get for you taking such good notes," she said with surprising levity. "We'll buy some more before we leave Mirstone. I need more rope anyway, and we probably need to stock up on food."

Logan sighed in relief. "Sounds good. On to Alomere."

26

Valduin stood on a road of hard, packed dirt. Trees lined both sides of the road. He was in a forest. The sky was dark with clouds.

It was silent but for his own breathing. He heard no singing birds, no droning or chirping insects, no scurrying animals. He took a step; in the silence, the crunch of his boot on the dirt was loud enough to hurt his ears.

The faint smell of wood smoke hung in the air. Valduin smiled. He must be close to their camp if he could smell the campfire. He took another step.

This step brought him to the edge of a crater, a hundred feet wide and a hundred feet deep.

He glanced over his shoulder. The road, surrounded by forest, stretched to the horizon. He looked into the crater.

"Where did this come from?" he wondered aloud.

The smell of smoke was stronger now. And beneath that smell was the tang of something else, something acrid, sinister, dangerous, evil.

Screams split the still air, bringing a torrent of wind with them. Valduin staggered, almost falling into the crater. When he regained his balance, he spun toward the source of the howling gale.

A gargantuan red dragon dropped down through the treetops onto the road, its wings kicking up the winds that buffeted Valduin. It let out a roar, loud enough to make Valduin clutch the sides of his head and squeeze his eyes closed. The roar ended; the screams continued.

Adelaide and Rose stood in the center of the road, staring up at the dragon, frozen in place and screaming in terror. Valduin opened his mouth to shout for them, but he was too late. The dragon lunged forward.

They disappeared into its mouth. It did not even chew.

The dragon, its head still lowered, blinked. Its large eyes—the sclerae yellow with icterus and the irises the blazing red of hot iron—locked onto Valduin. The force of that gaze was too much. He stumbled backward and fell into the crater.

He fell, watching the crater entrance shrinking above him.

He fell, wondering when he would hit the bottom.

He fell, letting the darkness swallow him.

"I'm coming."

Blackness and silence.

Adelaide walked through the empty lower floor of The Tavern. The hour was early; she had not heard a floorboard creak or a door squeak since she had woken up.

Greg was asleep in the kitchen, his head resting on his folded arms on the small table. Adelaide did not wake him. She put a kettle of water on the stove, placed a couple of logs in among the lingering embers from the previous night, and returned to the dining room to sit down.

She reached for one of her handaxes, intent on cleaning it to pass the time until her water boiled. The loop on her belt was empty. She checked the other side, and she found that loop equally devoid of weathered wood and sharpened steel.

She closed her eyes and groaned. Her father had made those handaxes. They were meant to be sold in the shop, but when she saw them, she begged to keep them. Growing up, she had carried them all over the mountains that surrounded Westray. They had cut kindling and firewood. They had brought down rabbits and deer. They had protected her from goblins and bugbears. They had lopped tentacles off an otherworldly monster in the tomb of a long-dead elf.

Something creaked from the upper floor of The Tavern. Always on her guard, she shifted to a chair that let her face the staircase. Slow, heavy footsteps descended the steps.

Valduin looked awful. His hair was a damp, tangled mess. His eyes were sunken and bloodshot. At the bottom of the steps, he leaned on the banister like he was worried his legs might betray him at any moment. He stopped and scanned the room before heading toward Adelaide, moving from booth to chair, keeping a hand out to support himself for the entire journey across the dining room.

"What happened to you?" Adelaide asked, keeping her voice down so as not to wake Greg in the next room. "Did you stay up all night?"

Valduin collapsed into the seat next to Adelaide. He groaned. "More bad dreams," he replied.

"Beulah?" Adelaide asked, lowering her voice further.

Valduin nodded.

"What are we going to do about this?"

Valduin shrugged. "Ignore it. She will get bored of tormenting me eventually."

"I doubt it," Adelaide said. "She gave you that back-pack. That little thing that opens doors. That crazy wand. Don't you think she's going to want her stuff back?"

At the mention of the wand, Valduin winced. With his right hand, he covered the wrist with the thorny bracelet, touching it enough to know that it was there without digging the thorns into his skin. "We will see. For now, there is nothing to do about it. We have a goal. We should focus on that."

Adelaide leapt from the table as the kettle in the kitchen began to whistle. She snatched it off the stove.

Greg looked up with an inquisitive groan.

"Sorry, Greg," Adelaide said. "I was making tea. I didn't want to wake you up."

The half-orc slurped the drool from the corner of his mouth and wiped his cheek. "No problem. I need to start making breakfast, anyway."

"Do you sleep in here every night?" Adelaide asked as she took a moment to synthesize the scene before her.

"What? Oh, no. Well, actually, yeah. Most nights."

"I thought that the tavern keeper usually had their own bedroom or apartment close to their tavern."

"There is a small room attached to the back," Greg said with a nod, "but I gave that to Shea. She works as hard as I do."

"That's fine, but you need to take care of yourself," Adelaide said, shaking a finger at Greg. "You'll burn out if you don't. Promise me that you'll set aside one room upstairs for you to sleep in. Then, when you've got some more money, you can build another apartment out back."

"That's a good idea," Greg mumbled. He put his head back down on the table.

"Promise!" Adelaide hissed, in a tone that was more aggressive than she intended.

Greg's head snapped up. "Promise!" he replied, surprised at the sudden shift in Adelaide's demeanor.

"Good," Adelaide said with a smile. She pulled a few mugs down from a shelf. "Where's the tea?"

"How far is it to Alomere?" Rose asked around a mouthful of egg sandwich. The party had departed The Tavern early with breakfast to go. They had stopped by a general store on the south side of town to stock up for the journey. Adelaide acquired more rope and two gleaming handaxes to fill the loops on her belt. Valduin refilled the quiver of crossbow bolts that Adelaide had returned to him. Rose bought all of the bread and cheese and dried sausage that the small shop had to offer. They left town heading south along the road that would take them to Alomere.

"I am not sure," Valduin answered. "I have not made this journey before. I would say at least two days. Maybe three. We need to cross the Virdes Delta and pass through the town of Triroad first."

"Anything we need to worry about between here and there?" Adelaide asked. "I don't like the sound of going through the Virdes on this trip. That's a little too close to someone's hut."

Valduin shrugged. "I said that I have not made this journey before. I only know the places that were named on the map that my mother had. The Virdes Delta is outside the Virdes Forest, I believe. Beulah really does not like leaving the forest. Her coming to collect us when we were in the Sandgate Mountains was the first time she had left the Virdes in over a century. On this plane at least."

"She told you that?" Rose asked, narrowing her eyes and glancing up at Valduin. "What else did she tell you? Any info we could use?"

Valduin stroked his chin, his eyes unfocused as he replayed his conversations with Beulah in his head. After a minute, he shrugged. "I cannot be sure. She did not talk a lot, other than to tell me things to do. If something comes up, I will be sure to mention it."

"Be sure," Adelaide repeated, her tone as threatening as one can be without enumerating the bodily harms that would result from disobedience.

The adventurers walked along the road of packed dirt and gravel. The day passed. Rose handed out food from her pack, eating as much herself as her friends did together. Adelaide kept a keen eye on their surroundings, her head swiveling to the left and right in continuous motion. Valduin sulked, his eyes fixed on the road fifteen feet ahead of them. The sky was overcast. The air was still.

A few hours of travel brought them to the first bridge. It was not large. Neither was the stream that it crossed. Nonetheless, crossing that bridge brought the party out of the rolling hills and open meadows that filled the space between the Aegean Expanse and the Virdes Forest and into the flat, marshy Virdes Delta. The bridge had no railing or handhold, no roof or covering. It was a simple bridge, with an arched deck and an ankle-high ledge along either side. It was, however, beautifully made. Its deck of well-planed boards neither creaked nor shifted underfoot. Not a nail or screw could be seen; the boards were connected with seamless joints. The road crossed that first bridge and then a second, identical bridge, and then it passed through a cluster of wooden buildings built up against the road.

Adelaide's uninterrupted scanning of their surroundings continued as she checked windows and alleys while they passed through the cluster of buildings. Valduin did not react to the change in scenery; his eyes remained fixed on the ground ahead of him. Rose wandered closer to the side of the road to inspect one of the buildings. The façade struck her as strange. The wooden planks that made up the front of the building went from side to side, instead of up and down as she was used to seeing. The one-story building was made up of five panels of these horizontal planks. When she was close enough to touch the building, she noticed that the panels bowed outward by several inches, giving the building a squat, squished appearance.

"Hey, guys," she whispered over her shoulder, not wanting to disturb the silence of the village, if this was a village, "do these buildings look strange to you? Why are the walls curved like this?" She ran a hand along the smooth, unpainted wood of the building in front of her, verifying by touch that it was, in fact, curved.

Adelaide checked another alley on the far side of the street before looking in Rose's direction. For the first time, she looked at the buildings themselves, rather than looking between, around, and through them for threats. "Yeah, they look a little weird," she replied, her voice hushed. "I don't know why they would build them like this. Val, any ideas?"

Hearing his name, Valduin jumped. He looked around with wide eyes as if realizing for the first time that their surroundings had changed. "What?" he said, much louder than either woman liked.

"Shush!" Rose hissed. Valduin looked toward her. She gestured at the building next to her and asked her question again, "Why are these walls curvy like this?"

Valduin shrugged, "I do not know. I told you, I have not been here before. It must be some regional style or something. Is there anyone here?" He peered through the window above Rose's head.

"I don't think so," Adelaide answered. "It's dead quiet. No wind today; I would have heard if someone was moving around. I haven't seen anything move, either. Let's just keep going."

Rose rejoined her friends, and they made their way out of town on their journey south. She glanced over her shoulder, still curious about the architecture of the buildings.

Standing in the middle of the road, at the far side of the town, was a small figure, a child, perhaps. Rose turned the rest of the way around and waved.

The person, or creature, or shape, disappeared. It did not run away. It did not fly away. From Rose's vantage, it appeared to shrivel up, to shrink away to nothing.

"Did either of you see that?" she asked over her shoulder. She took a step back toward where the figure had been.

When neither of her friends answered, she looked over her shoulder again. Valduin and Adelaide continued their trek, walking away from the village and Rose.

Rose sighed, turned around, and jogged to catch up with Valduin and Adelaide. The party passed over another bridge, its perfectly planed planks arching over another babbling branch of the Virdes Delta.

For hours the party continued across the delta, crossing bridge after bridge. The flat, open marshlands in between the bridges were an unbroken sea of tall, green grass, unmoving in the still air.

Toward evening, they passed through another small cluster of buildings. These were built in the same style as the cluster they had encountered on first entering the delta, with bowing, wooden walls and cold, dark, empty windows.

"This place is creepy," Rose whispered. "Where is everyone? They don't look abandoned or in disrepair. Just empty."

Adelaide nodded after checking the space between two of the buildings. She looked to the other side of the street to scan the windows and rooflines for prying eyes.

"Agreed. It's like they are hiding from us," she whispered back. "What's that?" she cried as she caught sight of movement at the corner where two buildings met. She pulled a handaxe from her belt and sprinted to get a line of sight into the alleyway.

Rose leapt in front of Valduin, her shield held high to defend both of them. She waited for Adelaide's report.

"Never mind," Adelaide called once she had reached the corner and looked down the alley. "I think it was a mouse. At least there's *something* that lives around here." She replaced the weapon on her belt as she headed back to her friends.

"You don't need to protect me," Valduin mumbled to Rose, making sure that Adelaide could not hear him.

"Yes, I do," Rose whispered back. She winked at Valduin. "Just until we get your magic back. Then you can protect me."

"Yeah. I imagine I will be dead at the hands of a random goblin or something before that happens." Valduin hung his head and kept walking.

"How's that new axe feel?" Rose asked Adelaide once they had gotten back together. "It's really shiny."

Adelaide grimaced. "It feels heavy. And it's definitely too shiny. I'll have to work on that."

"Anyway, there's something else that's been bothering me," Rose said once they had resumed their walk. "Where do they get the wood for these buildings? Or the bridges? I haven't seen one tree since we crossed that first bridge."

Adelaide cocked her head. "Huh," she said. "That's a great question. I have no idea." She chewed the inside of her lower lip as she considered possible explanations and implications of Rose's observation.

"Should we sleep here? Maybe in one of these buildings?" Valduin asked, oblivious to the women's discussion.

"Definitely not," Adelaide answered. "Let's put a few miles between us and this place before we make camp. It's not dark yet, anyway."

"I'm pretty tired," he said. "I'm happy to stop early and sleep first while it's light enough for one of you to keep watch."

Adelaide and Rose exchanged a glance.

"Okay," Rose conceded. "How about getting out of sight of the town first?"

Valduin trudged along with his head hanging. "Sure," he mumbled.

The party continued out of the town, back into the grassy marshlands of the delta.

"Alright," Madison said. "What's with these buildings? The curved walls seem important. The fact that they are made of wood seems important. Why? And where is everyone?"

"We should have gone inside one," Logan said. "Explored a little bit. Maybe looted a little bit."

"Is Valduin still evil?" Amelia asked with a sly smile. "He wants to do some breaking and entering? And burglary? And robbery? And thievery? And stealery?"

"Yeah, that last one isn't a word," Logan said with a chuckle, "and I'm not sure about the second-to-last one either."

"They are now," Amelia replied. "I just invented them, book boy. Write those down, and save them for later." She stuck her tongue out at her brother.

Logan rolled his eyes.

"Anyway," Madison said, "I feel like we aren't going to make it out of this place without figuring out what's going on with the buildings. For now, we make camp, sleep, and hope Val doesn't have another nightmare. If he gets another point of Exhaustion, our travel is going to get really slow."

"Is there a way one of you could protect me? Amelia, does Rose have any spells that might block Beulah?" Logan asked.

Amelia pursed her lips. She looked at the rulebook, sitting on the table in front of Logan. "I don't know," she said, her voice somber. "How about you find out and let me know?" She stood up from the table and wandered out of the room.

27

The grasslands to either side of the road were soft and muddy, and without a tree to be seen, the party set up their camp on the side of the road.

"I can't even start a fire," Adelaide complained, "unless we want to burn one of these bridges. They've got enough of them around here." They had crossed dozens over the course of the day, all of identical construction.

To Adelaide's surprise, her flippant comment was answered by a squeak of shock from the tall grass beside their camp. All three adventurers spun toward the sound. Adelaide swung her battleaxe off her pack, Valduin lifted his crossbow, and Rose snatched up her amulet into her hand.

"Who's there?" Adelaide called out into the gathering darkness. She used her light spell to set Fiend's Lament glowing and stepped to the edge of the grass. "Show yourself, or I'll burn every bridge from here to Triroad."

A gasp answered her this time. "You can't!" squealed a small voice.

"Then come out here," Adelaide growled. "I don't like people sneaking around."

The grass rustled. A small figure appeared at the edge of the light shed by Adelaide's weapon. "Don't hurt me," the figure said. "I was just curious." The figure stepped forward into the light. It was a human child, maybe seven or eight years old and about as tall as Rose.

"We won't hurt you," Rose said, though she was looking at Adelaide more than the child.

Adelaide relaxed. She let her axe slide through her hands so that she was holding it below the gleaming head. She stepped back to where Rose and Valduin were and sat down on her bedroll.

"Come. Have a seat," Rose said. She sat down on her bedroll and patted the space beside her, beckoning the child to sit. "Are you hungry?" Rose held out a three-day-old egg sandwich. Valduin grimaced, but the girl's eyes went wide. "Here, have some. What's your name?"

"I'm Nix," the child said. She stepped forward and snatched the sandwich, but she did not sit. She held the sandwich in both hands and nibbled at it, taking quick looks around at the adventurers between bites. With the child standing closer to Adelaide's light, Rose saw a girl with dirty, stringy, brown hair that hung to her shoulders. She wore leather pants with patched knees and a long-sleeved shirt that might have been white once but was now stained yellow and brown by use. Over that she had a leather vest with a variety of tools stuck in loops and pockets across the chest. She was dressed like a carpenter, though Rose could not imagine someone so young doing that type of work. As Rose inspected her, Nix finished the sandwich.

"You have a lot of tools," Rose commented, trying to keep Nix comfortable. "Are those all yours? I've never seen someone so young using tools like that."

Nix beamed. "Sure are!" She ran her fingers across the loops of leather that held a row of chisels on her chest. "We always keep our tools with us."

"What do you need tools for?" Rose asked.

"To build the bridges, of course," Nix replied. "Sometimes to fix the bridges. Or change the bridges. But mostly to build the bridges. We're the bridge builders."

"Well, the bridges are beautiful," Valduin said. "You must be very good carpenters."

Nix took another step closer, a wide, proud grin on her face. Bits of egg clung to the corners of her mouth. She swept her greasy hair out of her eyes with the back of one grimy hand.

"Were you the person I saw back in the town near the first bridge we crossed?" Rose asked. "Have you been watching us since then?"

Nix's smile faltered. "Yes, that was me. Don't be mad!"

"Don't you see travelers all the time?" Valduin asked. "This is the main overland travel and trade route between Alomere and Verasea. Why were you curious about us?"

"We were curious about something, too," Adelaide jumped in after Valduin. "Where do you get the wood for the bridges? There aren't any trees around here."

Nix glanced over her shoulder before answering. Her smile was gone. She whispered, "The Gnarled brings the trees." She shivered as she spoke those words. She looked at Valduin. "And The Gnarled warned us about you. The Gnarled has never done that before. That's why I was curious. But you seem nice. I don't know why The Gnarled would say that."

"Who is The Gnarled?" Adelaide asked. "And where are the other bridge builders?"

A whisper of wind rustled the grass. Nix stiffened. She let out a small squeak.

"What's wrong?" Rose asked, sensing the change in Nix's demeanor. "We aren't going to hurt you. Do you want some more food?"

Nix did not reply. She turned and ran. Her footsteps did not fade away. Once she left the glow of Adelaide's axe, they cut off, as if she had stopped running once she had reached the darkness. Or as if she had taken flight. Or as if she had been snatched away by some magic or other.

Adelaide leapt to her feet at the girl's sudden movement. "Nix? Nix?" she called out to the field of high grass. There was no response.

"That was weird," she said. The marsh was still and quiet again. She returned to her seat. "I'm more confused now than I was before we met her."

"I am too tired to be confused," Valduin mumbled through a yawn. "Wake me up for my watch, but I need to sleep now."

"You got it," Adelaide replied.

"What if she is still watching us?" Rose asked.

"She's a little girl," Adelaide said. "I'm not worried about her. And if the rest of her people have been warned to stay away from us, then we are safe, right? This is the best possible scenario for this leg of the journey. You sleep, too, Rose. I'll wake you up in a bit."

"What do you think, Valduin?" Rose asked, not sounding convinced by Adelaide's logic.

Valduin did not reply. He was already asleep.

Valduin stood in a forest. It could have been any forest, but he knew that it was the Virdes Forest. A particularly dreary and depressing part of the Virdes Forest. Dead leaves lined the forest floor. His breath hung in the icy air. A frigid breeze blew through the trees, their stiff branches scratching against each other. More brown leaves fell around him.

Valduin pulled his cloak tighter around his shoulders, shivering against the wind. It did not make him feel any warmer.

"Adelaide! Rose!" he shouted.

He surveyed the forest. Most of the trees were blackened, twisted, and leafless. Diseased by their proximity to Beulah's clearing, to Beulah's hut, to Beulah's corrosive power.

He looked over his right shoulder. There were two trees, stunted but still green, standing behind him. One of the blackened ones was visible behind them.

"Rose?"

He scanned around until he was looking over his left shoulder. The two trees were still there.

The blackened tree was between them now.

Valduin turned to face that tree. He took a step backward, away from it.

Something creaked behind him.

He spun around and found his nose mere inches from another of the blackened trees. He staggered backward again.

He slammed into something. Something tall. Something unmoving. Not expecting the blow, he fell to the side.

He looked up from the ground at another blackened tree.

"Stop," he whimpered. "Please stop." He was crying now. He scuttled away from those two trees through the drifts of dead leaves. This time his head made contact first.

He collapsed, holding the top of his head in pain. When he wiped the tears from his eyes and looked up, a wall of blackened tree trunks had encircled him. One huge, twisted tree leaned over the top of the wall, blotting out the scant light coming from the overcast sky. Through the darkness, Valduin could see the shadow of a face in the tree's bark.

"Adelaide!" he cried out. He knew it did not matter. He closed his eyes.

The trees creaked as they bent toward him, and in those creaks, Valduin heard her voice.

"I'm coming."

Blackness.

And Silence.

Valduin woke up drenched in sweat, shivering. He sat up with a jolt and looked around. The hour was early, and the overcast sky was the dark gray of wet stone. The unbroken clouds hung like a ceiling over the marshland, compressing it, containing it, constraining it. He felt their oppressive weight squeezing him. The still air of the marsh made the sensation of suffocation worse. There was no breeze to move that stale air; the grasses around him stood in silent reverie like mourners at a funeral.

"Hey, you're awake," Rose said, her voice hushed. "More bad dreams?"

Valduin turned toward his friend. Adelaide lay nearby, sprawled out on her bedroll, legs and arms poking out from under her blanket on all sides.

Valduin shrugged, paused, and then he nodded. He hugged his knees, and his gaze returned to the horizon while he considered the string of threats Beulah had sent him.

Rose tiptoed over. She put her arms around the half-elf's shoulders and squeezed him tight. "You're gonna be okay," she said. She sat down next to him. "We're gonna fix it."

"I am not sure how," Valduin muttered. "She can get in my head whenever she wants to. She sends me nightmares when I am asleep. She sends me threats when I am awake. How can we stop her? We are not strong enough. Especially now, when I have no magic. I'm worse than useless."

Rose patted his knee. "We will work on the magic. That's why we are going to your home, right? To figure out what your mom was doing, and to see if there is some way to get magic like she had? Then we will probably have to go visit Beulah."

Rose's suggestion startled Valduin, and his head snapped around toward her. "No!" he cried.

"*Shush!*" Rose said, slapping Valduin's shoulder and looking toward Adelaide. "She's sleeping," she hissed. Rose stared at Adelaide for a few seconds to make sure that she was not going to wake up, and then she continued, "Listen. There is no end to this if we don't go talk to Beulah. We can't let her push us around for the rest of our lives. First of all, we did the three tasks that we agreed to, so there is no reason why she should be bothering me or Adelaide. Right?"

Valduin thought about this for a moment, his eyes fixed on the horizon again. He shrugged and nodded again. "Yes, I think that is right."

"Good. Second, what does she still want with you, anyway? She took away your magic already. Why would she keep bothering you?"

Valduin held up his left hand. He pulled back the sleeve of his cloak to reveal the band of thorns that he still wore. "This is what she wants. This is her wand. And I do not mean that it is a wand that she had; it is *her* wand. She let me use it when I was going to find Stela because she thought I might need its power. She was right. She might also want the magic haversack, or the door opener, or anything else that she gave me over the last few weeks."

"Well, let's give it back, then. You can't use it anymore, right? And we can get you a regular backpack. These are easy problems to fix. We go back to her hut, give her the stuff, and tell her to leave us alone. We don't get upset because that's what she wants. She wants you to be angry, to do something that you'll regret. We just talk to her very cool and composed and tell her that we are done with her." Rose leaned back on her elbows and smiled, content with her plan.

"You really think that will work?" Valduin asked, not hiding his reservations.

Rose nodded. "I'm sure of it."

Valduin stared at the band around his arm. He flexed his wrist and winced as the thorns drew fresh blood. "I do want to be rid of this," he muttered.

Rose sat forward with a start. "What's that?" she asked, her voice even lower than before. She pointed to the high grass.

Valduin looked to where Rose was pointing. A few stalks of grass rustled. Then a few more. Something was moving through the marsh, approaching them. Valduin's hand crept toward the crossbow that lay on top of his pack. Before he could grab it, however, a small, brown mouse poked its head out from the grass ten feet from them.

The mouse froze, half in the grass and half out. It stared up at the two adventurers. It appeared to think for a moment, as much as a mouse might think, before scampering across the road and diving into the grass on the other side. The marsh was still once again.

"Are we really going to go right back to Beulah? I feel like we should focus on finding a way to break her connection to us. She doesn't like leaving the forest. We might be safe staying away from her," Logan said.

"Sure, fine," Amelia replied, her words dripping with sarcasm. "Why don't you take that wand off your wrist, then? I'll tell Beulah where it is, and we can leave it on the side of the road. What could possibly go wrong with that?"

Logan groaned. "I told you that I can't take it off. It's cursed."

"Then why didn't it come off after I used Remove Curse on you to break the Geas? That spell says that 'all curses affecting one creature or object end.' It should have broken that curse, too," Amelia pointed out.

"Because the curse on the wand specifies that you need to cast Greater Restoration at a really high level to break it. We already talked about that," Logan replied.

"I just wanted to prove the point that we won't be able to fix this on our own. It will take too much time and be too expensive. We need to figure out how to stop the Voidbringer! We are getting toward the final tier of the game, and we don't even know how to find the big bad guy!" Amelia threw her arms up in exasperation. "We need to go to Beulah and give her whatever she wants to have her release these curses. Then we can focus on the rest of the story."

Logan was quiet. He turned to Madison. "What do you think?"

"Amelia is right," Madison said without hesitation. "We need to confront Beulah without fighting her. We need to nip this in the butt."

"*Bud*," Logan corrected.

"I said what I said," Madison replied.

28

Bridge.

Marsh.

Bridge.

Marsh.

Bridge.

Marsh.

The party continued their voyage south through the Virdes Delta. The road serpentined every few hundred feet, lining itself up to cross the next waterway. The bridges, all of identical workmanship and impeccable repair, carried the adventurers toward Alomere.

The party approached the largest bridge that they had seen so far. It arched twenty feet above ground level to cross a river nearly two hundred feet wide.

"This must be the main branch of the Virdes River," Valduin commented as they hiked up the bridge. "It's as wide as the river we saw below Eydon."

"It's still weird how deserted this place is," Adelaide said. "We haven't seen a single traveler in either direction. And the only local we've met is Nix."

"Well, their gnarly dude said to stay away from us," Rose said. She huffed, "I don't like having a bad reputation."

As if in reply to her comment, a small squeak came from behind them. Rose spun around to see a brown mouse pacing along the ankle-high ledge on the side of the bridge, ten feet away. It froze when Rose turned.

Rose narrowed her eyes at the mouse. "Is that the mouse we saw this morning at our campsite?" she asked Valduin out of the corner of her mouth, not wanting to startle the animal further.

"How should I know?" Valduin replied. "It looks like a mouse. They all look the same to me."

Adelaide turned to look at the mouse. "I can ask," she said. She ran her fingers through her hair, touching her fingertips to the eagle feather totem that hung from her headband. She focused on the mouse as she spoke, "Have you been following us?"

The mouse squeaked again and scurried backward, not taking its eyes off Adelaide.

"I'm not mad!" Adelaide called to it, stepping forward. "Just talk to me."

The mouse turned and ran back toward the north side of the bridge.

Adelaide took off in pursuit. "Wait!" she called.

"This is interesting," Valduin commented to Rose. They watched their friend chase the mouse.

In the open track of the bridge, Adelaide made up ground on the mouse. Before the mouse reached the end, Adelaide dove for it. She landed hard on the edge of the bridge with the mouse in her outstretched hand, sliding on her flank for a couple of feet, and then she tipped over onto the bank of the river below.

"We should see if she is okay," Rose said with a giggle. Neither of the adventurers moved.

"I am sure she is fine," Valduin said, a grin tugging at the corner of his mouth. "Hey, Adelaide!" he shouted. "You get it?"

"Kinda!" Adelaide shouted back. "Look what I found!" She trudged up the bank and back onto the road, dragging a small, dirty child by the collar behind her.

Rose gasped. Valduin raised an eyebrow.

"Nix?" Rose asked, though she knew the answer. "Were you a mouse? Is that how you followed us without us noticing?"

Nix, now deposited on her feet in front of Valduin and Rose, stared at the wooden deck of the bridge. She gave a weak nod.

"Well, that is very interesting," Valduin commented. "Can all of the bridge builders do that? Do you all have magic?"

Nix shook her head. "Some others can. But not everyone."

"What else can you do?" Valduin asked.

Nix lifted her head to look at Rose. "What's your favorite color flower?" she asked.

"Uh, pink, actually," Rose replied, surprised by the question. "Why?"

Nix raised her right hand with a flourish, and a single green stem grew up between her thumb and pointer finger. As they watched, a flower bud grew at the end of the stem. The bud bloomed into a pink rose.

Nix held it out to Rose. Rose took the flower with a faint, awed smile. "It's just like the ones I grew at home," she mumbled.

Nix did not appear affected by Rose's reply. "I can fix things too," she continued. "That's why I'm such a good bridge builder."

"That is incredible," Rose said. She tied the rose to the shoulder strap of her pack. "Where are the rest of the bridge builders? Where is your family? Aren't they missing you?"

Nix lifted her chin in the air as she answered, "The bridge builders are my family. They are all in Southtown like The Gnarled told them. I am a bridge builder. I have my tools. I am doing my job, tending to the bridges as The Gnarled requires."

"I would ask you to show us the way, but there is only one way to Southtown, correct?" Valduin asked.

Nix nodded. She pointed south across the large bridge, along the solitary road through the delta.

"In that case, I will instead offer to hire you as a guide for the remainder of our journey through the Virdes Delta," Valduin said. He tried to sound cheerful, but something about Nix's responses had put him off. "Ten gold to take us safely to Southtown. Would you walk with us?"

Nix chewed the corner of her thumbnail, her eyes darting from one adventurer to the next. "The Gnarled warned us," she mumbled.

"Who is this gnarly guy, anyway?" Adelaide asked, both perturbed by the implication that someone should be afraid of them and proud that they were gaining a reputation. "And how does he know anything about us?"

Nix squeaked, quite like a mouse, at Adelaide's question. "*The Gnarled,*" she snarled at the human. "The Gnarled is not a *guy*. The Gnarled is our benefactor, our protector, our patron. The Gnarled brings trees. The Gnarled brings travelers. The Gnarled brings food. The Gnarled brings water. The Gnarled brings shelter. The Gnarled brings work. The Gnarled brings life." Her voice changed as she spoke; the words were rhythmic, almost a chant.

Adelaide and Valduin exchanged similar, wide-eyed looks.

"Okay," Rose said, holding up her open palms both to stop Nix's recitation and to indicate that she meant Nix no harm. "That is very interesting. We would love to hear more about The Gnarled as we walk. We can eat while we walk, too, if you like. Won't you walk with us?"

Nix glanced once more at each of the adventurers before nodding. "Sure, I can walk a bit. I need to head south anyway. More bridges to mend. Always bridges to mend. Bridges to mend. Bridges to mend." Her voice trailed away to a mumble as she took off at a brisk walk across the large bridge, not waiting for the party.

"She's scaring me," Adelaide whispered to Valduin.

He nodded in agreement, his eyes still wide as he stared at Nix's back. "Is this a cult? Are the bridge builders the cult of The Gnarled?"

"Only one way to find out," Rose said. She jogged ahead to catch up with Nix, who had stopped walking at the apex of the arched bridge.

"Everything okay?" Rose asked when she reached Nix's side.

Nix nodded, her eyes focused on the road off in the distance. "You will see," she said, her voice sweet and innocent again. "I told you The Gnarled brings the trees."

Rose followed Nix's gaze. She gasped.

From the top of the bridge, she could see out over miles of the flat Virdes Delta. The branches of the Virdes River, large and small, snaked their way from right to left through lush, green marshes, headed toward the ocean. The brown dirt road cut across those snakes, with its multitude of perfect wooden bridges navigating the creeks, streams, and rivers. Steely-gray clouds hung over the landscape like the too-low ceiling of an expansive, windowless basement. None of these features was a surprise.

The surprise was the trees. About a mile to the south of the bridge, the road entered a small forest, a perfect square of large trees. Rose would have thought that they had been planted there, in their neat rows on either side of the road, if not for Nix's rather confusing exaltation of The Gnarled.

Nix was beaming. "Come, maybe you can meet The Gnarled and learn of The Gnarled's blessings." She skipped ahead, leading the way down the south side of the bridge toward the road. And the trees.

Valduin and Adelaide stopped at Rose's side, taking in the scenery.

"This isn't right," Adelaide whispered. "Those trees should definitely not be there like that."

"I figured out that much myself," Rose hissed back. "But that's the way we have to go. Nix isn't scared. Maybe we'll meet The Gnarled. Then we can find out why he's bad-talking us to these people."

Valduin shivered at the sight of the trees. His nightmare from the night before flashed through his mind. Saying nothing, he fell in line behind Adelaide and Rose as they followed Nix.

The party walked with their young guide toward the looming forest. The air was hot and still, the clouds overhead only made the humidity more stifling. The tall grass on either side of the road stood at attention, like thousands upon thousands of spectators watching the parade of the young bridge builder and the three adventurers. The only sound was their crunching footsteps; even the droning insects had paused in reverence for the procession.

Valduin walked with his head down, but Adelaide and Rose studied the forest as they approached. Like bristles on a brush, the trees stood in neat rows. The varieties of the trees varied, some were evergreen, and others were deciduous, but they were all familiar to the adventurers from their time within the Virdes Forest.

"I don't think these trees grew like this here," Rose whispered, trying not to let Nix hear her. "They are in perfect rows. And look at the roots," she pointed to the nearest tree. "It's like they were dropped on top of the marsh grass."

Adelaide looked, and she nodded her agreement. There were five rows of trees on either side of the road, standing with thirty-foot gaps between them, and the rows marched forward into darkness below the canopy. Each tree was at least thirty feet tall; some were much taller. Adelaide took in the spaces between the trees, filled only with more of the waist-high marsh grass that they had been passing since they crossed the first bridge of the delta.

The party reached the edge of the geometric cluster. They hesitated.

Nix had not. She was skipping along ahead of them, looking even smaller now that she was flanked by the towering trees.

When she was thirty or forty feet ahead of the adventurers, she realized that they were no longer behind her. She stopped and turned, a wild smile on her face. She beckoned them forward.

She waited, her grin unfaltering.

"I don't think I like her anymore," Adelaide whispered. "She's creepy."

"I'm usually all for creepy," Rose replied, "but this time, I agree. We need to get out of here before we get drafted into her weird cult."

"If there is a cult," Valduin added. "It might just be her. Little, cute, deranged her." He turned his body as if to look behind them, and he pulled his crossbow from the side of his pack to his hand while Nix could not see it. "We need to be careful."

"Yeah," Adelaide agreed. She resumed her walk, crossing into the shadows of the grove. While she moved, she patted the handle of Fiend's Lament, taking reassurance from its presence. She did not remove it from her pack. She did not want to scare Nix. Not yet, at least.

Rose and Valduin followed, and the party reconvened with Nix as they traversed the improbable forest.

"Nix," Rose said, struggling to keep the anxiety out of her voice, "What does The Gnarled look like? I want to be sure we know The Gnarled when we see, uh, The Gnarled. So we can be properly polite."

Nix waved a hand at the forest. "The Gnarled looks like a bridge before it is made into a bridge." She giggled at her joke.

No one else laughed.

"The Gnarled is a tree," the young girl continued. "An old tree, all bent and crooked and leafless and black and beautiful and bountiful and benevolent and wise and violent and helpful and watchful and loyal and vengeful and merciless and generous..." Nix droned on and on, her eyes glazed over, her pace slowing as she regaled the innumerable qualities of The Gnarled.

Adelaide and Rose exchanged another nervous glance.

Valduin's stomach flipped. His heart raced. Cold sweat dripped from his brow. Leafless. Black. Crooked. He knew what The Gnarled looked like.

The sound of tree branches rustling in the wind swept through the forest.

Valduin felt no wind.

The sound came again, from their right. Nix stopped. The adventurers did as well.

Valduin looked up. The trees and their branches were as still as statues.

The rustling repeated, louder now. Angrier.

Valduin looked toward the source, off to his right. The grass between the rows of trees stood at attention, unbothered by gust or gale.

The adventurers jumped as Nix shouted, "I'm sorry!" with terror in her voice. "I was doing my job! They didn't seem dangerous!" She was stepping backward, away from the rustling sound, her hands held up in surrender.

The ground shook. Adelaide and Rose stepped toward each other while scanning the forest. They both spotted movement from the right side of the road, fifty feet ahead of them, but they could not process what they were seeing.

It was strange.

It was unnatural.

It was impossible.

Valduin, however, saw what he expected to see: a blackened, gnarled tree, fifty feet tall, walking on feet made of knotted masses of twisted roots. Monstrous hands steadied the monstrous body against nearby trees, which appeared to brace themselves against The Gnarled's weight. A monstrous face resolved from the rough, chipped bark of The Gnarled's monstrous trunk.

It opened its mouth, a dark, rotten, gaping hollow, and more of the whistling, scratching, rustling noise blew forth from it.

Nix burst into tears. *"Forgive me,"* she screamed, her voice raspy. "I am a good builder. The Gnarled brings trees. I build bridges. The Gnarled brings travelers. I mend bridges," she chanted in desperation. She backed away from The Gnarled.

The Gnarled spoke, this time in words. Words foreign to Adelaide and Rose, but familiar as Sylvan to Valduin. *"Which one?"* it rumbled, its voice resonating through the trees around them.

"Which one has the wand?"

Valduin took a step back. He raised the crossbow in trembling hands.

"Beulah needs her wand."

"Initiative!" screamed Madison. *"Oh man look at that thing it's so huge what are we gonna do?"* Her chair toppled backward as she leapt to her feet at the sight of The Gnarled's figurine. The gargantuan tree towered over their miniatures.

"Wait. Wait," Logan said, sitting up straight. He counted the other, smaller trees that were now arranged around them.

"Wow," Amelia said. "That's a lot of terrain. We could have just imagined we were in a forest. I can't even see my mini now."

"This is bad," Logan mumbled. "This is really bad."

"Care to elaborate?" Madison asked after she had picked up her chair and sat back down at the table. "There's only one bad guy. You can stay away from it and let us do the work. We'll be fine."

"Amelia," Logan said, his voice rising in panic. "You have the monster book, right? Where is it? I need it!"

"I think I left it at school," she muttered, avoiding eye contact with her brother.

"Come on!" Logan shouted. He threw his head back in frustration. "I think treants can awaken other trees to make more treants!" He swept his hand over the battle map, now covered in tree figurines. "This entire forest might be an *army*."

"Oh," Madison said, her voice tiny, her confidence gone. "That would be bad."

"And I'd be able to tell you if *someone* hadn't left the book at school," he finished, glaring at Amelia.

Amelia pushed back from the table, closed her notebook, and left the room. She did not say a word.

"Where are you going?" Logan called after her. "We need to fight this battle!"

"Way to go," Madison muttered. "Just sit here. Actually, no. Make some popcorn. This might take a minute." She followed her sister upstairs while Logan sat agape, clueless as to what he had done wrong.

29

"Hey, Amelia," Madison said. She stood in the doorway to the girls' room. Amelia lay on her bed, staring at the ceiling. Her hands were folded on her stomach. She did not reply.

Madison walked in and sat down on her own bed, across the room from Amelia's. "They haven't stopped, have they?" she asked.

Amelia pursed her lips, opened them as if to answer, but then stopped herself. She closed her mouth again. Her eyes stayed fixed on the ceiling. She remained silent.

Madison sighed. "So, what are we going to do about it?"

"*We* aren't going to do anything about it. It's none of your business."

"If it means you acting like this, it sure is my business. We have a forest of angry trees to fight, a little cultist girl to protect, and a warlock with no powers. I need you on your game."

Amelia let her head fall to the side so that she was looking at her sister. "Why do you take this so seriously? It's just a game."

Madison's mouth fell open. "Just a game?" she cried. "*Just* a *game*? You take that back right now. This is our *thing*, and you know it."

Amelia blinked a long, slow blink. She turned back to stare at the ceiling. "Yeah, I know. I just wish those boys at school wouldn't keep making fun of me over it."

"Alright, let's talk about that," Madison said. She sat forward on the edge of her bed, putting her elbows on her knees. "What's your plan to deal with those boys? Waiting it out clearly hasn't worked."

Amelia shrugged. "There's nothing I *can* do."

"Don't talk like that!" Madison erupted. "What would Rose say? What did Rose *just* say to Valduin about Beulah picking on him?"

Amelia didn't reply.

"Do I need to get Logan up here with his notebook to remind you? Because I'm sure he wrote it down."

Try as she might, Amelia could not help but grin at this. "For the love of Selaia, please don't," she said.

"Well, then? What did Rose tell Valduin to do?"

"She said to go and talk to Beulah. To not get angry or upset. To tell her that he was done with her," Amelia recounted.

"Exactly," Madison said, clapping her hands for emphasis. "I'm Rose now, and I'm telling *you* that you need to do the same. You go to those boys, and you tell them that you are done with this nonsense. You tell them that they have no business teasing you or bullying you. You don't get angry. You tell them that you are done with it. Then you walk away."

"What if they get mad?" Amelia asked. "What if they push me or something?"

"Did Rose tell Valduin to go to Beulah by himself?"

"No," Amelia said. "She said that we would do it together."

"Exactly. Rose wants Valduin to be safe. And we want you to be safe. I will stand behind you if you want. You know Logan would, too. If you'd rather do it without us, you do it at school, with an adult nearby."

"And that's it?" Amelia sounded skeptical. "Just tell them to stop? And you think they'll stop?"

"Probably not," Madison conceded. "Which is why you are going to tell Mom, Dad, and the school counselor, too."

Amelia's head whipped around toward her sister. "Are you serious? They are only teasing me. It isn't that big a deal."

"Where's the book of monsters?" Madison asked, her focus unflagging.

"In the dumpster," Amelia mumbled. "Gone now."

"That's right. They stole your book. That's *illegal*. You have to tell the counselor. She is the only one that can fix that. Telling Mom and Dad is good too. They'll help. You can't do this alone."

Amelia lay on her bed, considering everything Madison had said.

Madison waited.

"You'll come with me?" Amelia asked after a minute of silence.

"Absolutely," Madison said. "I'm bigger than any boy in your grade, anyway. I'd love for them to try something while I'm watching."

Amelia smirked. "You're sounding more like Adelaide than Rose now."

Madison stood up. She held her arms up and flexed her muscles. "I feel more like Adelaide than Rose. I need more sleeveless shirts."

Amelia laughed. She got to her feet and threw her arms around her sister. "Thanks," she said.

Madison hugged her back. "We'll get it sorted out. But first, I'm gonna go Paul Bunyan on the gnarly dude. I am sick and tired of hearing about bridges."

Nix stumbled backward with her hands raised above her head. "Forgive me!" she screamed. "I am a good bridge builder. I build the bridges. I mend the bridges."

Valduin pulled the trigger, loosing the crossbow bolt at The Gnarled. The shot hit the monstrous tree, chipping away a bit of bark from the trunk, though the tree made no indication of injury. "Kill it!" Valduin screeched as he backed away, reloading the crossbow. "Beulah sent it!"

Adelaide grinned. "Finally," she mumbled as she swung Fiend's Lament into her hands. She sprinted toward the towering tree that stood in the middle of the road. "You're next!" she roared, tagging the tree with her magical hunter's mark. She slammed her battleaxe into the tree's rootball feet, hacking twisted tendrils off to fall squirming on the ground.

The Gnarled did not acknowledge Adelaide's attack. It opened the rotting hollow that it used for a mouth and spoke in that rustling, windy language again. It pointed long, gnarled limbs at Nix and Valduin as it spoke.

Rose watched The Gnarled. Seeing that it was targeting them with something, she took up her amulet and prayed, "*Selaia, grant us your aid. Protect us from this evil, that we may continue your work.*" She also pointed at Nix and Valduin, sending Selaia's divine aid to them, bolstering their strength for the coming battle. She turned to face The Gnarled again, still holding her amulet, her mind racing as she considered her options for attacks.

Those options were put on the back burner when a crash and a weak scream sounded behind her. Rose spun back around to see that a tall oak tree had wrenched its roots from the soft ground of the marsh and stepped onto the road. It swung a large bough down in front of itself and swept the tiny form of Nix out of its way. With a terrible crashing of branches, Nix tumbled to the ground and went silent.

"Nix!" Rose screamed. "No!" She took a step toward the girl, but a flurry of activity on the other side of the road drew her attention.

Two more trees, one maple and one that might have been some sort of pine, stepped forward and swung at Valduin. The trees pummeled the half-elf with their branches, the repeated attacks battering him this way and that. He stayed on his feet, but when Rose could see him again, he was holding his side and spitting out blood.

"Valduin!" Rose shouted. "Get out of there!"

Valduin looked up at the trees, each of which was staring back with an angry face formed from bark and boughs. He pointed his crossbow at one and then the other. Considering the size of the crossbow bolt and the size of his assailants, he changed his mind. He ran, dodging through the newly formed legs of the maple tree, and looped around to the far side of Rose. He crouched down, trying to hide behind the halfling.

"What do we do?" Rose asked. She held her amulet in one hand and pointed her other hand first at one tree and then the next, unsure about which one to target or how to attack them.

"Get rid of The Gnarled," Valduin replied. "I think if The Gnarled is gone, the other trees will stop attacking."

"I'll try," Rose mumbled. She spun on her heel, turning away from the three trees that had attacked them to face down the road toward the larger, angrier, gnarlier treant that Adelaide was attacking. The human was howling with rage as she hacked off the blackened tree's rooty toes.

This caught The Gnarled's attention, and the evil tree slammed a thick branch down on top of Adelaide. A blow that would have crushed Valduin was merely an inconvenience to Adelaide, as it knocked her off balance and interrupted her flurry of attacks. She caught herself, her rage blocking the pain of this walloping, and prepared for another round.

"*Selaia, banish this monster from my sight!*" Rose screamed.

The Gnarled paused in its attack on Adelaide. It squeezed its bark eyelids closed. Its form shimmered for a moment, but the shimmer passed. It opened its eyes and focused on Adelaide again.

"Oh boy," Rose muttered. "What next?"

Valduin did not get a chance to answer. With a crash of small branches breaking, the oak tree that had knocked Nix out slammed down on the back of Valduin's shoulders.

"Rose," Valduin whimpered. He turned to face the oak tree. He raised the crossbow. "Help—"

The oak tree slammed him again, flattening him onto the ground.

Rose watched the maple tree step forward, snatch Valduin's body with a hand that had a dozen branches for fingers, and step over Rose to carry the half-elf toward The Gnarled.

"Valduin! No!" Rose screamed. She raised a hand toward the maple tree, but she did not get a chance to cast a spell before the pine tree slapped her in the side, knocking her to her knees. The second hit came before she could get to her feet.

Rose, on hands and knees, took a deep breath. She pushed herself back until she was sitting on her heels. Two large, menacing trees loomed above her, readying their next round of attacks. A third was carrying the unconscious body of her friend toward The Gnarled, which was even larger and more menacing than the trees around her. Adelaide was preparing to go for the big tree's ankle with her magic axe.

"Adelaide!" shouted Rose. "Adelaide, it's got Valduin. Don't let it get to The Gnarled!"

Adelaide spun, her eyes wide with rage. She stopped her attack and held her axe across her body instead. She charged toward the maple tree that carried Valduin, her roar echoing through the grove. With each step, she grew a foot taller. By the time she reached the tree holding Valduin, she had reached her fully enlarged height of almost twelve feet. Now eight feet long, Fiend's Lament glistened even in the low light of The Gnarled's manufactured forest.

The maple tree's stride faltered with this unexpected challenge from the human. The Gnarled stepped forward and attacked Adelaide from behind, slamming into her back. Adelaide did not turn around; she did not even flinch. Her gaze burned holes into the tree that held Valduin, her shoulders heaving with each breath. A low growl rumbled in her throat.

"Selaia, if ever we've needed your help, now's the time," Rose prayed. *"Send me your assistance. Send me your blessing. Send me your champion."*

Rose's amulet glowed, and so did the rising sun emblem on her shield. She could feel the warmth on her arm as the glow from the shield intensified. Halfred had told her that the shield could be used as a focus, but she had never lost her amulet, so she had never thought that she would need it. Now, however, the shield was doing the work. The glow of the emblem became brighter and brighter, the light spreading and turning the entire surface of the shield into a sheet of golden light. Rose pointed the shield toward The Gnarled, unsure of what was coming.

As if the shield had become the end of a golden, glowing tunnel, a head emerged from the light. It was a serpent's head, glistening with gray scales to match the robe Rose used to wear. Its eyes glowed with golden light, and a plume of golden feathers adorned its head. It slithered out of Rose's shield, all ten or twelve feet of it, and opened its wings. Large, feathered wings, gold fading to red at the tips. It took in the scene around it, then it looked at Rose.

Rose staggered back, terrified by the giant serpent.

"Disciple of Selaia," Rose heard the celestial say, though the couatl's mouth did not move. *"How may I be of service?"*

Rose collected herself. She took a deep breath.

"We need to get out of here," Rose answered out loud. "Me, the girl," she pointed at Nix, "and those two," she indicated Adelaide and Valduin.

"Do you have the strength to hold on?" the couatl asked.

"Yes, for now," Rose replied. The couatl lowered its head. Rose grimaced, gulped, and then leapt onto its back. She wrapped her arms around its neck, which was warmer than she expected given its scaled appearance.

"Please hold on," it said. With a flap of its wings, it dove between the two trees that were threatening Rose. It scooped up the small body of Nix in its mouth, flapped its wings again, and tore upwards through the canopy. With the incredible speed of the couatl, Rose slid backward along the neck until her legs caught at the front of its wing joints. She dug her fingers in as best she could.

"Can you heal her?" Rose asked. "She's dying."

"As you wish," Rose heard in her head. Rose could see a warm glow come from the serpent's mouth, bathing Nix in golden light. Nix opened her eyes.

The girl screamed. She writhed in the serpent's mouth for a moment, but then her eyes went wide. She stopped moving, though she still looked terrified to Rose.

"We need to help the other two," Rose shouted. "How can we help them?"

"Trees, sentient or not, do not like fire," the couatl said. *"Let us bring them fire."* It rolled into a steep dive, though Rose guessed that they had soared beyond the battlefield by now. The couatl crashed through the upper boughs until it snagged a large branch with its tail. The tail wrapped around the branch, allowing the head, with Rose atop it, to hang below the canopy. They looked down on the fight.

Adelaide, still enlarged, was surrounded by trees. The maple tree was holding Valduin out toward The Gnarled, over Adelaide's head. But not far over. Adelaide took a step forward, put her foot on the tree's trunk, and leapt up toward her friend's limp body. She grabbed the branch that served as the arm for the twelve-fingered hand that held Valduin. With a one-handed swipe of Fiend's Lament, she removed the hand from the tree.

"Adelaide!" Rose screamed from her perch. "I've got Nix. Let's go!"

Adelaide looked up to see Rose sitting on the back of the gray and gold couatl. "That's new," she mumbled. She touched the eagle feathers in her hair and said, "Time to go." She felt herself returning to her normal size, but her legs gained new power. She threw Valduin over her shoulder and took off, dodging swinging branches and boughs from the swarm of animated trees around her. She broke from the cluster and headed south along the road as fast as she could magically manage.

The Gnarled turned, howling in its raspy, breezy language. More trees began to move, the forest was coming alive and collapsing toward the speeding Adelaide.

Rose held her arms out as she shouted through the forest, "*Selaia, bring your righteous flames down upon thy enemies!*" Her hands burst into flames. She slapped them together above her head, and an eruption of flames engulfed The Gnarled. Its dry, blackened branches crackled and popped in the heat of the flame strike. Its howl turned from anger to pain. It stepped forward, out of the column of fire, smoke rising from every twig and branch.

"Don't hurt The Gnarled!" Nix shouted.

Adelaide ran on, pausing only long enough to heal Valduin so that he would not die from his wounds. She continued running toward the southern edge of the forest.

Rose kept her arms outstretched. They burst into flames once more. She shouted, "Again!" and slammed her hands together. The Gnarled was shrouded with fire again, howling and screeching and popping and smoking. Again he stepped forward.

"Stop!" Nix pleaded. "Don't! The Gnarled brings the trees!"

"Again!" Rose screeched, ignoring the girl. She slapped her hands together. The flames raged around the old tree. Burning branches dropped behind it as it stalked forward.

"Would you like to continue your assault?" the couatl asked. *"Or shall we make our escape?"*

"Fly low," Rose instructed through gritted teeth. "Keep it in view."

"As you wish." The serpent released its hold on the tree branch and swooped down toward the road.

Over her shoulder, Rose sent a searing guiding bolt toward The Gnarled, blasting a gaping, glowing wound into its trunk.

"Stop," cried Nix, her voice softer now, tears running down her face. "The Gnarled brings life."

Rose lowered her hand. She still seethed with anger, but the sadness in Nix's voice had broken through her rage. "That thing just tried to bring you death," she said.

Nix did not reply. She was bawling as The Gnarled and its army faded into the distance.

"Shall I fix her?" Rose heard the couatl say in her head. *"It seems her mind has been corrupted by this monster."*

"Yes," Rose replied, her voice steely as she watched Nix cry. Her anger at The Gnarled left her unmoved by the child's sadness.

The golden glow came again from within the couatl's mouth.

Nix stopped crying, but only for a moment. She looked around with wide eyes, and then she burst into tears again.

"Amelia, that was amazing!" Madison said. "Again! Again!" she mimicked Rose's repeated attacks on The Gnarled, complete with explosive sound effects for the Flame Strike spell.

Amelia smiled. "I can't believe it's still alive," she said. "I used my two fifth-level and my sixth-level spells on those attacks, and it took double fire damage. That thing must have crazy hit points."

"Well, it had those Legendary Resistances," Logan pointed out. "Which is how it resisted your Banishment spell at the beginning of the battle. I think you two could have killed it if you didn't have to worry about me and Nix getting killed. And if I could have used Blight? Oh, man." He sighed. "I really don't like being useless."

"We've got a plan for that," Madison said. She patted Logan on the shoulder. "We go to Alomere, figure out what kind of magic your mom had, and then we get that magic for you. Easy."

"Yeah, we'll see," Logan mumbled. "Maybe we can leave Valduin with his dad, and I'll play as Nix. At least she can do magic."

"What *are* we going to do with Nix?" Amelia asked. "I think the couatl un-culted her, which is good, but it means we can't leave her with the other bridge builders, right?"

"Definitely not," Madison agreed. "We'll take her with us. At least she can start fires with Druidcraft. That will save Adelaide some work rubbing sticks together or however she's been doing it for the whole campaign."

30

The crackling of The Gnarled's burning branches faded behind Adelaide.

She ran.

The crashing of trees tearing through each other, like the crashing of a felled tree that never stops falling, roared behind her.

She ran.

The snapping of roots coming to life and pulling free of the marshy soil chased her. New trees stepped onto the road and swiped at her as she sped past.

She ran.

Valduin held on to her shoulders, trying to keep himself stable without slowing her down. He could not have kept up with her magically enhanced escape, so he did what he could not to impede it. He wished he could have at least thrown a few eldritch blasts at the army of trees, if not some of his more powerful magics, but all he could do at the moment was hang on.

The pair emerged from the improbable forest. Adelaide ran.

"Want a lift?"

Adelaide's head jerked up toward Rose's voice, surprised by its sudden proximity. The gray and gold, winged serpent glided ten feet above Adelaide's head, its tail moving back and forth as if it was slithering across the surface of the air rather than flying with its wings. Even though she knew this creature was friendly to Rose, its undulations made Adelaide shiver.

"Maybe just take Val," Adelaide panted. "I can run for a bit longer."

"*This I can do*," Adelaide heard in her head. She made eye contact with the celestial snake. Those golden eyes, despite their serpentine slits for pupils, were reassuring in a way she could not comprehend. She trusted the couatl.

Adelaide slowed to a stop and put Valduin down. The couatl dropped to the ground beside them. The half-elf staggered when his feet hit the ground, his legs wobbling. The couatl whipped its tail around to support him.

"Could I ride on your back now, too?" Nix asked, her voice small, her tone apologetic. "I promise I won't do anything bad." Her cheeks were stained with tears, rivers of clean skin through the layer of dirt that covered most of the girl.

The couatl released her from its mouth. Nix looked from Adelaide to Valduin to Rose to the feathered snake. "Thank you," she said, her voice low.

The distant crashing of trees paused. A rock the size of a horse cart smashed into the road ten feet behind the party, took an odd bounce to the side, and came to rest on the edge of the tall marsh grass.

"No time for that," Adelaide said. She grabbed Nix under her arms and tossed her onto the couatl's neck in front of Rose. "Escape now. Thanks later." She took off at a sprint, her speed unfettered by the exhaustion that was creeping into her body.

The couatl used its tail to lift Valduin onto its back behind Rose. It flapped its wings and shot into the air, slithering away from the onrushing army of trees. Another rock bounced down the road as they climbed into the sky.

"You feeling okay?" Rose asked Valduin as the half-elf leaned forward and rested his head on the back of Rose's shoulders.

"No," he groaned.

Rose summoned the swarm of golden lights from her amulet and sent them coursing into Valduin. Valduin sat up straight and stretched his neck from side to side.

"Much better," he said. He glanced down toward the road. His eyes went wide for a moment, and then he clenched them closed. He collapsed forward, hugging the sides of the couatl's body with both arms. "Maybe not so high?" he whimpered.

"Oh, okay," Rose replied. To the couatl, she shouted through the rushing air, "Could we stay a little lower now? In case Adelaide needs support?"

"*Of course,*" the couatl replied into Rose's mind. It changed course, drifting lower as it continued to race forward. In the air, it was faster than Adelaide, and a few seconds later the couatl and its cargo were coasting along ten feet above the human's head.

They ran and flew for half an hour. Every ten minutes or so Adelaide would pause to recast her spell that granted her extra speed. She was sweating, panting, and groaning with the strain of the constant sprint. When she had run out of magic to aid her retreat, she collapsed in the middle of the road.

The couatl circled above and landed beside the human. Once its passengers had disembarked, it shot straight up into the sky like a scaled rocket. It circled the party from a thousand feet up for a few moments and then returned to them.

"I believe the treants have abandoned their pursuit," the couatl said to Rose. *"I would advise against staying overlong, but you should be able to take a short rest now."*

"Thank you so much for your help," Rose said. She thought about petting the snake, but then she thought that such a gesture might be offensive to so powerful a creature as this. Instead, she clasped her amulet in her hands and inclined her head in a small bow.

"I can remain for a few minutes longer," the couatl said. *"Do you require anything else? Otherwise, I can fly a patrol above you until I must go."*

Rose looked at the rest of her party. Adelaide had gotten up, though she was still winded. Valduin sat hugging his legs with his forehead on his knees. He looked exhausted, but he was no longer dying. Nix appeared sad but healthy.

"I think that would be perfect," Rose said. "And please tell Selaia that we appreciate your assistance."

The couatl's face did not change, but Rose could hear its smile when it said, *"You can tell her yourself. She is always listening."* It rose into the air again and flew circles around the party, its gray body nearly invisible against the cloudy sky.

Rose turned to her friends. "Ready to walk? Or do you need an actual break?"

"If we can keep it to walking, I should be okay," Adelaide said. She pushed herself to her feet. "Let's go, Val," she said. She grabbed Valduin under the arms and hauled him to his feet. He did not help, but he did not fight her either. Adelaide strode forward along the road. As she passed Nix, she patted the girl on the shoulder.

"Come on, you," she said. "I guess you're coming with us."

"Will we reach Southtown today?" Valduin asked. He eyed the darkening clouds above them. They had been walking for a few hours since the battle with The Gnarled, and there had not been any indication that the treants were still following them.

"We could," Nix said. "It would be very late, though."

"I think we should sleep before we get there," Rose said. "I used a lot of my energy in that fight. If anyone in Southtown gives us trouble, I won't be much help."

"I'm out of magic too," Adelaide said. "We should sleep sooner rather than later. Nix, do you know a good place to sleep where we won't be easy to find?"

Nix shrugged. "The grasses are the same in every direction. There really isn't much here but grass, mud, and streams. And the bridges." She shuddered as she spoke this last word. "All these bridges," she muttered.

"Could we sleep under a bridge?" Valduin asked.

Nix shook her head. "Not really. Maybe we could have slept under the big bridge; there is enough of a bank underneath it. On most of the bridges, there wouldn't be enough space."

"What if we wade upstream from a bridge?" Adelaide suggested. "It's mighty hard to track someone through running water like that. We head east until we are out of sight of the bridge, and then we make camp on the bank. No light or fire, just sleep."

Nix considered this for a moment, and then she gave a thoughtful nod. "I think that could work," she said.

At the next crossing, the party dropped from the side of the wooden bridge into the stream below, sinking a couple of inches into its muddy bottom. They trudged upstream and around a couple of bends to be sure they would be out of sight from the road, and they made camp along the bank.

"Let me use your cloak for a minute," Rose said to Valduin.

"For what?" he asked, making no move to take it off.

"For dinner," Rose replied.

"What?" Valduin took a step away from Rose.

"I can create food for us," Rose said with a sigh, "but I need a place to put it. Just put your cloak on the ground so the food doesn't get muddy."

"Oh," Valduin said. "Okay, sure." He took off his cloak, which was approaching a condition that might be considered tattered, and laid it out on the ground.

With a quick prayer, Rose filled the cloak with piles of fresh bread and vegetables. The adventurers dug in, this simple meal filling their bellies like a celebratory feast. Nix nibbled at a roll, holding it in both hands, while crouched on the edge of the stream.

Rose sat next to the girl. "You don't need to be sad," she said.

Nix did not look up. She stared into the water. "It was all a trick. The Gnarled was a bad guy the whole time. And I helped him. I almost got us all killed."

"It isn't your fault. You were brainwashed. You're right that it was a trick, but it's not your fault for falling for it. We've fixed that now. You're free."

"I should have known," Nix continued. "I knew it was a tree. And it brought us trees. And we cut those trees down. What kind of creature brings its own kind to be slaughtered?"

"An evil one," Rose answered with confidence. "No doubt about that."

"What do I do now? I can't go back. I can't see The Gnarled again."

"Where are your parents?" Rose asked.

Nix shrugged. "I never knew them. All I've ever known are the bridge builders." She clenched her small hands into fists. "Do you think they stole me? Or hurt my parents?"

Rose paused before answering. "I don't know," she said, "and I don't think you'll ever know for sure. You will not return to the bridge builders. We will take you someplace safe. Of that, I *am* sure." She put her arm around Nix's shoulders.

Nix pulled her eyes away from the water to look at Rose. She was not crying, though her cheeks were still streaked with her tears from earlier. She gave a weak smile, leaned her head against Rose, and closed her eyes.

"Now we've got to protect Valduin *and* Nix?" Adelaide moaned. "What can she even do? Other than get knocked unconscious?"

"Hey! That's not nice. She's a druid, and she just got to level three! She can turn into some animals, and she has a few nice spells," Amelia said as she read over Nix's character sheet. "She might actually be a decent support character if we can keep her out of harm's way."

"And remember," Logan spoke up, "that when Valduin quits the adventuring life to move into his dad's basement in Alomere, I'll play as her. At least a druid is a real magic user. No more patrons and pact magic for me."

"Don't be silly," Amelia said, waving a hand to dismiss Logan's concerns. "We are going to get Valduin all sorted out."

"And how are we going to do that?" Logan asked. He counted off on his fingers, "I have no magic. We have no other patrons that could give me my magic back. We have an evil hag haunting me. We've been through this. Even if we get Beulah to leave us alone, this character is toast."

"Maybe she'll leave us alone now," Madison suggested. "We did just escape the assassin she sent. Almost killed it, too, I'd guess. Rose was *on fire* during that battle." She waggled her eyebrows at her sister to emphasize the pun. Logan rolled his eyes. "Maybe we are done with her already!" Madison concluded.

Logan did not sound convinced when he replied, "Yeah, we'll see."

31

Valduin fell.

He fell through clear sky.

He fell through smoke and mist.

He fell through darkness.

He fell for so long that he lost the feeling of falling. He floated in space while winds whipped past him. He could turn into the winds, or he could hide his face from them. They came nonetheless.

The winds whispered in his ear. Then they spoke. Then they screamed. Words that he did not understand. Wild, wheezing, whistling words wailed and wavered around him.

The wind brought sand to sting his eyes. It brought embers to burn him. It brought shards of glass to tear his skin.

The wind brought the ground, wide and flat and absolute, rushing toward him.

"I'm coming."

The ground came, and it brought blackness and silence.

Adelaide watched the horizon lighten with the coming dawn. It had not rained, yet, but the clouds were still there, a gray blanket smothering the Virdes Delta. Adelaide shook Rose awake.

"Hey, let's get moving," she said. "I want to get out of this place today."

"Yeah, okay." Rose groaned, "You got it." She sat up and looked around. "When did he do that?" She pointed at Valduin, who lay with his legs in the stream up to his knees.

"Maybe an hour ago?" Adelaide replied. "He was really restless all night. He wriggled himself down to the water. I would have moved him back, but I didn't want to interrupt his sleep, so I just kept an eye on him. He's been so tired recently."

"That's fair," Rose agreed. "Nix still here?"

"Yup." Adelaide pointed to the tall grass at the top of the bank, where the young girl was curled up in a ball among the reeds.

"Good. I thought she might run off in the night."

"It crossed my mind too. You get her," Adelaide said. "I'll wake up Val. Then we get moving."

Rose packed up her bedroll, strapped it to her pack, and climbed the bank to rouse Nix.

Adelaide shook Valduin's shoulder. "Time to go."

Valduin sat up with a start and scuttled back from the water. He hung his head and moaned.

"How do you feel?" Adelaide asked. "Because you look terrible."

"Terrible," he agreed. "More nightmares. More of Beulah's voice. I feel like I did not sleep at all."

"Well, we need to get moving anyway," Adelaide said. "I don't want gnarly boy catching up with us. And we still need to figure out a way past the bridge builders. I doubt they will be happy to see us."

"Yes, okay," Valduin muttered. He pushed himself to his feet, wavered for a moment on the slope of the stream's bank, and then he pulled his pack onto his back. With his head drooping, he stepped back into the stream and began the slog toward the bridge, not looking back or waiting for the rest of the party.

Adelaide watched him walk away for a moment before turning toward Rose and Nix. "Ready?"

"Let's go," Rose said. She led the way into the water, with Nix close behind. Adelaide brought up the rear, and they quickly overtook Valduin.

"You're not moving so good," Adelaide commented after Rose and Nix sloshed past the half-elf. "What's wrong? Other than the usual?"

"I do not know," Valduin muttered. "I just feel extra tired. I really have not been sleeping well."

"Well, we aren't going to get anywhere with you dragging like this," Adelaide said. She chewed the inside of her cheek while she thought. "Maybe Rose can do something to pick you up a bit."

When they reached the bridge and climbed back up to the road, Adelaide asked, "Rose, Val is moving pretty slow. Could you do anything to make him less tired?"

Rose stepped in front of Valduin. "Bend down," she commanded. Valduin did as he was told. Rose looked closely at his eyes, pulling up the lids to inspect his bloodshot sclerae. She felt the sides of his neck and looked in his mouth.

"I could help you if I had more diamond dust," she said, her voice pensive as she considered her options. Her eyes widened with realization, and she said, "Or I could get my friend to help. I think the couatl could make you feel better. Then we could fly for a bit too! How's that sound?"

Valduin winced. "As long as we stay low. I really do not like heights."

Rose brought her shield around in front of herself. With a quick prayer, the shield glowed with golden light, and the couatl slithered out like the shield was a hole into another realm. It turned on itself, coiling up in the middle of the road, and raised its head to look at Rose.

"*Hello again, Disciple of Selaia. How may I be of service?*"

Rose smiled and bowed to the feathered serpent. "Do you have the magic to make my friend feel better? He has not been sleeping well."

The serpent stretched toward Valduin. It inspected him with its glowing, golden eyes. "*I can help you,*" Valduin heard in his head. "*Will you accept it?*"

"Yes. Please," he replied.

The serpent pressed its snout against Valduin's forehead. Valduin closed his eyes.

A wave of warmth spread over him, starting at the point of contact with the couatl. He sighed with relief as the exhaustion was washed away. He smiled and opened his eyes. "Thank you."

The couatl dipped its head in a nod. It turned back to Rose. "*Anything else?*"

"Well, since you're here, could you carry us for a while? You are so much faster flying than we are walking."

The snake looked from one to the next of them as it considered the question. "*I might not be quite as fast with all four of you, but I can carry you for a short time.*" It stretched out along the ground so that the party could climb on.

"We can fly, but with all four of us, it might not be as fast as yesterday," Rose reported to the group. "Let's go. Maybe we can get past Southtown like this."

"I would like very much not to see anyone there," Nix said. "Oh! And this might help." In a blur, she spun in a circle, shrinking to the ground as she whirled. A moment later, returned to her mouse form, she climbed up Rose's leg and tucked herself into a pocket of Rose's pack. Her little mouse face peeked out under Rose's arm.

Rose patted the mouse on the head before climbing aboard the large snake.

The party positioned themselves on the couatl's back, and the celestial serpent took to the air. Honoring Valduin's request, it stayed only fifty or so feet above the ground. Southward they sped, passing over bridge and marsh and road and stream.

At the terrific speed that the couatl could maintain, Southtown came into view less than half an hour after they had taken off. The couatl gave the town a wide berth, swinging east over the marshes, before returning to its course following the main road out of the Virdes Delta. It flew for the remainder of the hour that Rose could keep it on the material plane. As its time grew short, it set the party down on the road.

"Thanks!" Rose shouted as the couatl flapped its wings and rocketed upward into the overcast sky.

"*I am always available*," came the reply, though it did not look back. It plunged into a dark cloud and disappeared.

Valduin, Adelaide, and Rose resumed their walk southward. Nix leapt from the pocket of Rose's pack, stretching back into her human form before her feet touched the ground. She shook her mass of tangled, scraggly hair out of her face and smiled at Rose.

"Will anyone miss you?" Rose asked. She glanced back up the road toward the bridge builders' Southtown.

"I doubt it," Nix replied. "And if they ask, I'm sure The Gnarled will say some hateful thing or other. I am free. This is better."

"Well, on to Alomere," Adelaide said. "Val, are you feeling good enough to walk? I can carry you if you need me to." She smirked at him.

"I am feeling much better now. No carrying will be required."

She shrugged. "Consider it a standing offer. How much farther do you think? It's still pretty early. We've got a full day of travel ahead."

Valduin thought for a moment. "If we push it, we could probably get there tonight. Triroad should be close, and then it's only a half day's journey farther."

Rose sighed in relief. "Thank goodness. Let's push it. I am getting tired of sleeping on the ground without a campfire. These nights are getting cold."

The party moved along, ever onward to Alomere. The marshes were gone, and the road once again passed over rolling hills dotted with farmsteads. Around midday, they reached the town of Triroad, at the junction with the Seawalk Road that headed west toward Tarsam. They did not pause to take in the sights. They walked straight through the town and kept moving south.

As they left Triroad, two things changed. First, the storm that had been brewing for two days arrived. A steady downpour began and quickly soaked the travelers. Second, the lead wagons of the caravan from the mountains passed them. Throughout the afternoon, the rain poured down and the wagons rumbled past. No one from the caravan paid the adventurers any mind; the rain had forced most people into the cover of their wagons and carts.

Notably missing from the caravan was any sign of the ettins that they had heard about back in Tarsam. Adelaide wanted to ask about them, but in the downpour, no one seemed interested in fielding any questions.

The party pushed on through the storm. The caravan wound down the road for over a mile, cart after cart splashing along in single file. The afternoon passed. Night came early during the storm; Adelaide and Rose used their magic to light their way on the road. As the darkness deepened, the storm strengthened. The wind drove the rain into their faces as if it was trying to keep them from reaching their destination. Thunder rumbled in the distance.

Torchlight appeared in the darkness ahead. Squinting through the rain, the adventurers could see more lights strung out on either side of the road. The walls of Alomere. The gate stood open; the two large doors were swung out to flank the entrance. Torches mounted on the inside of the doors glowed steadily despite the rain, not even flickering with the blasts of wind.

"Follow my lead," Valduin said as they approached. Adelaide, Rose, and Nix fell in line behind him without an argument. Valduin stepped through the gate and paused under the cover of the arching city wall. He stood with his empty hands visible in front of him.

"It's a wild night to travel," a voice spoke from the shadows of the wall.

"We have been on the road for several days," Valduin replied. He waited.

"And what brings you to our fair city? You missed the caravan by twelve hours," the voice continued.

"This is my home. I have been abroad for a few years. My name is Valduin Yesfiel. My father is Eamon Yesfiel, and my mother was Thalia of the House of Alomeen." He let the last few words hang in the air.

The figure stepped forward from the shadows. He was a young man, taller than Valduin, with ears indicating some amount of elven heritage. He was dressed in dark red leather armor. He held a spear in one hand, but he did not brandish it. Closer now, he inspected Valduin through narrowed eyes.

"The House of Alomeen? I do not remember anyone named Thalia."

"She passed nearly two decades ago." Valduin returned the guard's invasive look. "Before you were born, I would guess."

The guard stood up straighter. "Close," he replied, his voice lowered. He stepped back into the shadows. "Welcome home, Valduin Yesfiel, of the House of Alomeen."

"Wait a second. Wait a second," Madison said, holding up her hand to cut Logan off. "Did you just say she passed nearly two *decades* ago?"

Logan furrowed his brow in confusion. "Well, yeah. Because that's when it happened."

Madison grinned and chuckled. "And did you not say that the whole incident with Taranath killing your mom happened when you were eighteen years old?"

"I said I was nineteen. Which you would know if you took any notes. What's your point?"

"So, does that mean that Valduin is almost *forty years old*?" Madison burst out laughing. Amelia giggled.

Logan pursed his lips. "Yeah, so what? We said we were playing as adults because we didn't want a childish campaign."

"Yeah, adults," Madison said between bouts of laughter. "Not grandparents!" The girls continued laughing.

"I can't believe we never talked about this. Well then, how old is Adelaide? I thought you were in your thirties at least," Logan huffed, crossing his arms.

"Uh, no! Adelaide is twenty-six."

"Okay, fine." Logan turned to Amelia. "How old is Rose?"

"I was thinking twenty-two," Amelia replied.

Madison redoubled her laughter, leaning out of her chair to put her head against Amelia's shoulder.

"Really, it isn't *that* funny," Logan muttered.

"Yes it is!" wheezed Madison. "Can you just cut one decade out of it and be closer to our ages? Otherwise, everything we've done for the last 13 levels is a little weird."

Logan sighed. "Fine, we can adjust what I said to the guard to be one decade instead of two. And we'll say I didn't call him out for being really young. Satisfied?" He tried to change the subject without waiting for an answer. "Amelia, awesome work with the couatl, by the way. It's a free casting of Greater Restoration every time you summon it, and summoning it doesn't cost anything. That's actually a pretty awesome loophole."

"Thanks," Amelia said. "I *really* wanted to cast Fire Storm during that battle, but with you and Nix getting clobbered, we needed to escape. I had been looking through the rulebook to figure out how all the seventh-level cleric spells work, and I found that couatl. It's pretty awesome, isn't it?"

32

Valduin led the way through the streets of Alomere with his hood up against the rain, glancing over his shoulder at each turn to make sure his friends were still with him. Oil lamps did their best to push back the night, but against the wind and rain, they could light little more than a few feet of the paved street around each lamppost. Buildings loomed over them. Most were dark or had only a single window aglow at this late hour. Adelaide and Rose took in as much as they could as they walked through the city, but this was not a sightseeing tour. They hurried along behind Valduin, making sure not to lose sight of the dark-cloaked figure in the night.

The wind drove stinging rain in Valduin's face. An image of his last nightmare, the wind blowing shards of glass, flashed in his mind. He checked over his shoulder again, looking past the other members of the party this time. He saw no one else in the street. He pushed forward with his head down; his feet knew the way home, even if this was his first time returning in three years.

Turn after turn, angled street after angled street, Valduin weaved through Alomere. To the women, the city did not make any sense. No street was straight for more than a hundred feet. The intersections were built at odd angles. They joined and divided like a maze with no interest in efficiency or transparency. Beside buildings of all manner of sizes and shapes, they walked past parks and plazas, along arcades and gardens. The city would certainly have been a sight to behold if they could have seen farther than twenty feet through the storm.

At last, Valduin turned up a walkway that led to a door. The door was set into a building that Adelaide would have described as somewhere between a mansion and a palace. For the expanse of the façade, with four stories' worth of windows, there was little space to either side. To the left was another home of similar construction; to the right, a tower stretched into the darkness overhead.

Valduin hesitated. Under the lee of the house, he pulled back his hood and pushed his wet hair, which was becoming ever more bedraggled over the course of their ongoing adventures, out of his face. He glanced back at Adelaide.

In the light of the lamp that hung next to the door, Valduin looked younger, scared and innocent in a way that Adelaide had not seen before. Maybe the angle of the light made his cheeks look less sunken. Maybe the rain had washed away the grime that had been accumulating around his hairline. Maybe being back in his hometown had brought back a twinkle to his eye that the adventuring life had extinguished. Whatever it was, Adelaide could feel his reluctance to knock on the door and face his father.

Adelaide stepped forward. She put one hand on Valduin's shoulder. With the other, she knocked three times on the door. "Welcome home," she said.

The door opened sooner than Adelaide expected. She had been planning on stepping back behind Valduin, but she spun and found herself looking into the eyes of a tall, human man, taller even than Valduin. He had graying hair and a full, well-trimmed, salt-and-pepper beard. He wore a button-down dress shirt with dark pants and shiny shoes. His hands were clasped behind his back.

"Can I help you, young lady?" he asked Adelaide.

Adelaide said nothing. She nodded toward Valduin and did what she had hoped to do a moment before. She stepped behind her friend and gave him a nudge toward the door.

"Well, can I—" the man stopped in the middle of his question. "Valduin?" he asked, his voice quavering, incredulous. Without waiting for Valduin to reply, he stepped out into the rain and threw his arms around his son's shoulders.

"Well, what have you been up to? And what brings you home in the middle of the night?" Eamon Yesfiel asked.

After a quick round of introductions, the party had taken off their saturated outer layers. The four adventurers were drying and warming themselves in front of the fireplace. Valduin had found an old shirt in his bedroom for Nix. The girl had curled up on a couch and fallen asleep with her head in Rose's lap. Rose, Adelaide, Valduin, and Eamon were drinking tea, each with their own lounge chair or sofa in the sitting room off the foyer of the grand home. Eamon was unfazed by the dripping mess that followed the adventurers through his home, focused as he was on his son's return.

A crystal chandelier hung in the middle of the sitting room, though its many candles were dark. The room was instead lit by the warm glow of a handful of oil lamps and the crackling fire in the hearth. Bookshelves lined the walls of the room, displaying as many decorative trinkets and baubles as they did books. A portrait of the three members of the Yesfiel family hung above the fireplace; Valduin appeared to be a young teenager when it had been painted. Rose noticed a familiar necklace hanging around his mother's neck.

Valduin glanced at Adelaide and Rose before answering, "We have been up to, uh, quite a bit." He paused, unsure of where to start or how much to share. The silence was filled with the howling of the wind outside. Somewhere in the house, a shutter banged against a window.

"We have been working on a few things," Valduin said.

He hesitated again and looked to Adelaide and Rose for help. Neither offered any.

"A few things," Eamon repeated, his tone thoughtful as if somewhere in those words was hidden the answer to his questions.

"Well, there has been a lot going on," Valduin said, his voice straining. He dragged his bag onto his lap, leaving a damp, dark streak up the side of the armchair as he did. He reached into the bag and pulled out his mother's necklace. "I found this." He held the necklace by the chain; the pendant rotated slowly in the air, the firelight glinting off the flat gems that filled the three circles.

Eamon's mouth fell open. He placed his teacup back into its saucer without taking his eyes off the necklace, his shaking hand rattling the porcelain and slopping tea onto the table. If he noticed, he did not care. He reached for the necklace.

Valduin handed it over. Eamon sat back in his chair, his eyes glistening as they remained fixed on the pendant.

"Where?" he asked. His voice was as shaky as his hands.

"In an evil wizard's trophy room," Valduin answered.

Eamon looked up. "Evil wizard? What *have* you been up to?"

"Remember that day when I came home alone?"

Eamon's voice fell to a whisper. "I'll never forget it."

"I told you someone had saved me?"

Eamon nodded.

"It seems that there was more to it. I did not tell you everything. That creature's name was Taranath. He gave me magic that day. I did not use it until a few months ago, to save myself and Adelaide from a sticky situation. Things have gotten sort of, uh, complicated since then. Taranath came back; it turned out he is actually an ancient, evil dragon who subsequently tried to kill us; I started working for an evil hag who has more recently tried to kill us; we have hunted and killed a few other evil hags who *also* tried to kill us; we broke into an evil wizard's tower to steal some things because *he* tried to kill us; just yesterday we got attacked by an evil *tree* that tried to kill us and Nix." The words came pouring out of Valduin, rushing out of his mouth like the water of the Virdes rushed off the cliff at the edge of Eydon.

"Everywhere we turn people are trying to kill us. Everyone we meet turns out to be evil. And now I think the wizard and the dragon may *both* have been involved that day that Mother died, and it may or may not be related to the fact that both of them, and some evil gnomes and an evil hobgoblin and a devil—obviously evil, but dead now—are all working for *another* devil that calls itself the Voidbringer—also obviously evil—that wants to end the Astral Peace and maybe destroy part or all of the multiverse." He leaned forward, the words coming faster.

"It all gets a little fuzzy at the end there. We don't really know who wants what or why or how they plan to get it but they are all evil and I had magic and then I lost it and then I got it back and now I lost it again and I cannot help fight the evil people without magic so here we are. I know Mother could do magic and was part of some kind of magic army or guard or defense force, and I need to find them and find out how to get my magic back so we can save the world!"

He sat back in his chair, panting.

The wind howled. The shutter banged.

Eamon stared at Valduin.

For an entire minute, no one said anything.

The shutter banged again.

"That is," Eamon replied, "quite a bit." He paused. His eyes returned to the necklace in his hands.

Sheets of rain pelted the windows of the study.

"I suppose there is no harm in you knowing what I know," he continued after a moment. "I certainly wasn't told everything. Your mother could do magic, as you know. Most of the members of the House of Alomeen can. It is in their blood, since before they settled in Alomere."

"Do you know where they were from before this?" Valduin cut in. "I always thought we were from Eydon, the lost city in the Virdes. Which we found, by the way."

Eamon cocked his head and nodded in approving surprise. "Well, that's a bit more, now, isn't it? No, they were not originally from Eydon, though I think a few of them might have lived there. They came from a city on the Inner Plane of Light. I don't know if anyone can remember the name now. But the children of the House of Alomeen have always been children of the fey."

Valduin shivered. Azereth had called him that. Venez had too.

"Well, back to your mother. She was part of the Circle of the Silver Thread." With one finger he traced the silver thread that connected the three rings of the pendant. "This is a group that has been around for a long time. I know a little about their goals, but I was never privy to much about their activities. They actually did have some connection to Eydon, I believe, at some point before the city was lost. They had charged themselves with protecting this plane from the creatures of the outer planes. Very high-level, noble, hero stuff." His tone had turned bitter, but he continued.

"The Astral Peace was a big success for them, but it wasn't enough. Apparently, the Astral Peace is maintained by the honor system, if you can believe the celestials would have agreed to that. There is no magical barrier to stop the fiends from leaving their bubbles or from coming right into this room. The Circle of the Silver Thread sought to rectify that oversight. They wanted to lock the boundaries of the planes, preventing planar travel of any kind."

"Well, with what we've seen and heard," Valduin said, "it is no surprise that someone attacked them. The Astral Peace is a touchy subject with extraplanar beings."

The shutter banged.

Eamon's head turned upward at the noise. He gave the kind of grunt that one makes to acknowledge that there is a task that needs to be done but cannot be completed until a later time. He looked back at Valduin. He nodded grimly. "That is one way to put it. In any event, as you got older, she intended to help you unlock your magic. That is why she took you to the Inner Plane of Light that day. She needed something from there to open your inner connection to that place. Or something."

"The flower," Valduin recalled.

Eamon shrugged. "Whatever it was, that's—"

He did not finish his sentence. He was cut off by another bang, this one much closer. He spun in his chair to face the foyer, where the howl of the storm had intensified.

Adelaide jumped to her feet and stepped out of the room. The front door had blown open and slammed against the wall. Rain and wind blew in from outside. She grabbed the door and closed it, locking the deadbolt and shaking the handle to make sure it would stay closed. A whisper of wind rustled in the foyer.

The blow felt like being punched by air. There was no mass behind the hit, only a sudden application of force to the back of her head, slamming her face into the door. She spun on her heel, grabbing her nose, which was pouring blood. There was nothing behind her.

Her hair whipped in her face as the wind kicked up again. She leaned against the door to close it, but it did not budge. It was already closed. The wind was in the house.

The wind intensified, growing to a steady, swirling gale, blowing a stack of letters off a long table near the front door. A vase tipped off a pedestal and shattered on the floor. The wind grabbed her face and smashed her head back against the door. She smelled something strange, acrid and sour, and it burned her throat. The room spun around her. She turned her head left and right, trying to wriggle out of the wind's grasp. Before she could free herself, another blow came, this time hitting her in the stomach. The invisible force released her, and she doubled over, coughing and leaning against the door.

Adelaide fought for breath, stumbling toward the sitting room, reaching out for the wall to steady herself. "Help," she wheezed, her voice inaudible over the growing gale within the house. Droplets of blood dripped through her fingers and splattered on the wood floor. "Help!"

"Uh, what?" Madison stared in disbelief as a battle map of the Yesfiel mansion was set up on the table. "What hit me? Why am I poisoned? What is happening?"

"The wind hit you? It might be some sort of conjuration spell. Or maybe an illusion? Or an assassin with invisibility somehow? Assassins use poison." Logan said though he did not sound confident. "I'm not sure, but this has to be Beulah. I don't like that you didn't see anything. And I don't like that there are no miniatures on the map other than ours."

"Oh! Oh!" Amelia cried, sitting up straight. "I remember this! We fought this when we did the introduction adventure in the box set. Right when we first got the game. There was an invisible thing on one of the missions we had to do!"

Logan pursed his lips. "Yeah, that was an invisible stalker. That would explain the invisible part, but I'm pretty sure they don't have poison. And they are not very strong. This thing hurt Adelaide *bad*."

"Well, whatever it is," Madison cut in, "we don't stand a chance against it. *I* can't see invisible things. Can either of you?"

Amelia slouched back into her chair. "Oh. No, I can't," she said.

Madison turned to her brother, waiting for his answer.

"Well, no, obviously I can't either," he replied, sounding annoyed. "That requires *magic*, and I don't have any, remember? You can still hit it, though, if you can figure out where it is. Your attacks will just be at disadvantage."

"How am I going to figure out where it is, book boy?"

Logan stared at the empty squares on the battle map. "I'll be the bait," he said after a moment. "It will hit me, then you figure out where it hit me from, and then you hit it." He gave a weak shrug and waited for his sister's approval.

Madison returned the shrug. "As long as Rose can keep you alive long enough, it might work."

33

The door to the sitting room blasted open, slamming against the wall and rattling picture frames around the room.

Valduin leapt to his feet. Rose turned in her seat on the sofa, putting one hand on Nix's shoulder and trying not to let the sleeping girl fall off her lap. She had to squint against the gust of wind that swirled into the room. Papers blew off the side tables, and a decorative, crystal plate fell from one of the bookshelves and shattered on the floor.

"What is the meaning of this?" roared Eamon. He pushed himself out of his chair.

"We're in trouble!" wheezed Adelaide. She stumbled through the doorway and leaned against a high-backed chair. Bracing herself, she doubled over and vomited on the floor.

Rose did not even have time to get to her feet before the wind that was whipping around her coalesced into a fist. The attack slammed her back against the arm of the sofa, jarring Nix awake.

"What? What happened?" Nix mumbled as she looked around the room with sleepy eyes.

Valduin took one step toward Adelaide. Before he could take another, a burst of wind impacted the side of his head, sending him tumbling onto a chair. When he regained his composure, he found his face inches from Fiend's Lament, still strapped to Adelaide's bag where she had left it on the floor. He pulled the weapon free of its straps, stood up, and leapt over the chair to reach Adelaide's side. He thrust the axe into her hands and said, "Pull yourself together. I need you."

Adelaide righted herself and looked at Valduin. She swayed. His face shifted in and out of focus, the poison still warping her senses. She took a deep breath and let out a roar that shook the room. Another vase rattled its way off a shelf and onto the floor.

Valduin winced, taking a half-step back from her. She lifted a foot and kicked the chair she had been leaning on, sending it sliding across the room. Now with enough space to swing her axe, her wild eyes scanned the maelstrom that swirled within the sitting room. She waited for a target to materialize from the storm.

Rose got to her feet. She pulled her shield up from her pack. To Nix, she whispered, "Hide. Stay safe." In a blink, the girl, still lying on the sofa, shrunk down into her mouse form and tucked herself beneath a pillow.

Rose looked around the room. "Where is it?" she shouted to Valduin and Adelaide.

"It's invisible!" they shouted back in unison.

Rose growled. She scanned the room again as she took her amulet in her hand. "*Selaia, protect us from evil in all of its forms,*" she prayed. The amulet glowed. Bouncing out of the rising sun on Rose's neck came a stream of tiny, glowing bunnies hopping through the air. The stream spiraled around Rose and spread through the room, filling the space with an army of guardian spirits.

Adelaide and Valduin winced as the wave of protective rodents washed over them, remembering their vicious bites from their battle in the dungeon below Khal Durum. They let out simultaneous sighs of relief as the bunnies ignored the adventurers on their hopping paths to the far corners of the sitting room.

Eamon's eyes were wide with terror and confusion at the unexpected flurry of action. The wind whipped past him, though he could not figure out how there could be wind inside his home. He backed away from the halfling and the swarm of flying, glowing, snarling rabbits that she had created. The little girl had disappeared as well, though, for all he could tell, she had turned into one of these spectral animals that was hopping past him. He backed into a bookcase, knocking an entire shelf of leather-bound tomes to the floor at his feet. He did not look down.

"Valduin, what is this? What's happening?" he shouted over the howling wind.

"Just stay—" Valduin began before being cut off by an invisible force slamming into his throat. His hands shot to his neck. He fought to breathe, but each breath only worsened the burning pain as foul poison filled his lungs. He coughed and gagged and sputtered, doubling over while holding his throat. The wind whipped around and smashed down on the back of his head. His vision went from blurry to black for a second. The world spun under his feet, but he kept his balance, leaning against the sofa.

Adelaide, her blood-boiling rage giving her the focus to ignore the poison, did not step forward to help Valduin keep his balance. She did not step forward to hold back his hair as he vomited on the floor. She did not step forward to heal his wounds with her magic.

She stepped forward to swing her enchanted battleaxe through the cloud of swarming golden bunnies. When Valduin had been hit, the bunnies had descended on the space in front of him, nibbling and gnawing at the invisible attacker. Adelaide made a rapid decision about the attacker's most likely shape and size, and she laid into that space with Fiend's Lament.

She felt the axe make contact. The wind screamed around her. She swung again, and again she felt the edge of the axe sink into their assailant. When she pulled the weapon back, blood the color of blueberry jam dripped from the blade.

Adelaide let out another battle cry and swung the axe again. This time, however, the blade passed straight through the space in front of Valduin and lodged itself into the back of the sofa. Adelaide grunted as she dislodged the axe from the furniture. She snarled and looked around the room for her quarry.

Rose leapt up onto the couch and put her hands on Valduin's back. "Keep it together," she whispered to him, and the wave of warm, healing energy spread out through his body. He was still nauseated, but his breathing eased as the feeling that his vocal cords had been shattered passed.

"Valduin!" Eamon shouted. "What do we do?" He was edging his way along the back wall toward the door, slipping and sliding over the books that had fallen around him.

Valduin stood up, away from the sofa he was leaning on, and turned toward his father. Again, he did not get a chance to answer. This time, his mouth fell open as he watched Eamon lift off the floor. The older man reached for his neck, trying to pry the formless fingers away from it. He grimaced and thrashed his head from side to side. Before Valduin could collect himself enough to shout out, Eamon's body slammed backward into the bookshelf. He collapsed in the heap of books and shattered shelves on the floor.

"Father!" Valduin screamed. As he leapt over the sofa to get to Eamon, another invisible fist materialized in front of his face. His head snapped back, blood spouting from his nose, and he collapsed onto the floor. On hands and knees, he dragged himself between the chairs to his father's side. He pulled a vial of shimmering liquid from the leather holder than hung on his belt and poured it into Eamon's mouth. Eamon groaned and rolled over, clutching his neck again, as the healing potion took effect.

"We need to get you out of here," Valduin muttered. His head swam, the assassin's poison still eating away at his senses.

Adelaide vaulted the sofa and pushed her way toward Valduin and Eamon, her weapon at the ready. She scoured the room for a sign of the stalker, waiting to unleash her attack.

After Rose and then Valduin and then Adelaide had climbed onto and over the sofa, Nix emerged from under the cushion and scampered up to the safety of Rose's shoulder. Rose glanced at the mouse to make sure it was not going to fall, and then she also moved toward the cluster of people at the back wall. Her hand shone with radiant energy as she joined Adelaide in waiting for a sign of their attacker.

Eamon got himself up onto his hands and knees before retching again, the vomit covering the wrecked bookcase beneath him. "Valduin," he moaned between heaves. "What's happening?"

Valduin opened his mouth to answer. Before he could get a word out, he felt the wind swirl around him, and out of that wind, a force smashed into the back of his head. He collapsed, facedown, next to his father.

Eamon screamed. The wind screamed. Adelaide screamed and swung her axe into the space above Valduin. She made contact, and a gout of blue blood sprayed over Eamon and Valduin. Rose released her spell, the bolt of golden light searing through the same space that Adelaide had attacked, but the spell did not connect.

Adelaide pulled her weapon back, but she noticed that Rose's golden bunnies had spread out again. She did not waste any time; she knelt and laid a hand on Valduin. "No dying today," she muttered, and her hand pulsed with dark green energy. Valduin's eyes shot open.

Nix made her move. Four tiny feet leapt from Rose's shoulder, and two child-size feet landed on the ground. She was seething with anger to match Adelaide's. She raised her open hands out wide. Her hair crackled with energy, floating up off her shoulders as if she were floating underwater. "Leave us *alone*," she screeched. She clapped her hands together.

The sound was deafening. Rose felt the force of the clap pushing her backward, but she held her ground. Their attacker, however, did not, and a bookcase next to the window shattered as an invisible body slammed into it. A collection of vases and urns crashed to the ground.

Rose's ears were ringing. Her head was aching, but she had something to aim at. She raised a glowing hand and fired another guiding bolt at the destroyed bookcase. This time, the magical attack slammed into the stalker, searing a radiant, golden target onto its chest as it howled in pain.

That golden glow flew right back in her face. The stalker slammed into Rose with two mighty fists, battering the halfling against the wall. Rose kept her feet and resisted the creature's poisonous gas.

Nix glared up at the glow that showed her where the creature was standing. She took a deep breath, and then she blew out through pursed lips like she was blowing out a candle. The air sparkled as if Nix had blown a handful of glitter into the stalker's face. Despite the whirlwind within the sitting room, the glitter drifted down and settled across every nearby surface, including the stalker itself.

Highlighted in shining specks of light, the adventurers could see the stalker for the first time. It was bigger than Adelaide, though its body was fuzzy at the edges, blending in with the storm on which it rode. Its face was twisted in anger, its eyes wide with pain and rage.

Adelaide spun away from Valduin and Eamon and slashed Fiend's Lament through the creature. Her howls of fury matched the stalker's howls of pain as the axe sunk into its torso. Adelaide made no attempt to remove the weapon. She was content to hold it in place as Rose approached.

Rose stepped up to the creature. "I could send you away, send you home," Rose said, her voice calm, barely audible above the howling wind. "I could spare you, ask you to run away, convince you to leave." She raised a hand toward the stalker's chest. "But Beulah would send you right back, wouldn't she? Sometimes, you need to set an example."

Her hand touched the stalker's glitter-strewn chest. The specks of light that Nix had sprayed over it turned black as Rose's spell rotted the stalker's invisible flesh. The wind kicked up again, swirling around the stalker, as wounds opened up across its body, dumping blue blood on the floor.

The wind stopped.

Rose's ears rang with the sudden silence of the room. The stalker collapsed and disappeared, its body nothing but air.

"Rose!" Nix shouted. "Help!" The girl was kneeling next to Valduin, who had collapsed, unmoving, in a communal pool of vomit and blood next to his father. Her hands glowed with dark green energy as she poured her magic into healing her friend.

"How close were you to dying?" Amelia asked.

"*Really* close," Logan replied, shaking his head slowly in disbelief. "We were still poisoned, and the poison damage meant we had a failed death save every round. One more round could have been the end of the entire Yesfiel family."

"Amazing job, Amelia," Madison said. "I liked your finishing move, too. You're a scary little life cleric," she added with a laugh.

Amelia grinned. "Nix made all the difference. That Faerie Fire spell was amazing, even if it's spelled weird. I can't believe it's only first-level. Why didn't any of us ever get it?"

Logan shrugged. "Well, we will have it when I take over playing Nix. Valduin is officially useless. We will leave him here with his dad, and the three women will go defeat the Voidbringer."

Amelia waved a finger at her brother. "Nope. We are fixing Valduin. You have magic in your blood. You just need to unlock it. All we need to do is hunt down your mom's magic friends."

"Actually, I'd vote that we go deal with Beulah next," Madison cut in. "We can't keep getting attacked by her minions. I think she is going to come after us until we go talk to her. We can't be hunting for the Voidbringer and fighting off invisible stalkers and evil trees all at the same time. We didn't kill The Gnarled. It could show up again somewhere."

"As much as I want to find the Circle of the Silver Thread, I think Madison is right," Logan said to Amelia, wincing apologetically. "We need to get Beulah off our backs. Especially now that we came to my dad's house. She could kidnap him or something to keep us under her control. We need to end this once and for all."

Amelia giggled. "That's fine. We can go see Beulah, as long as you promise not to say, 'once and for all' ever again."

Madison laughed along with her little sister.

Logan glared at them.

34

Valduin groaned as he sat up. He leaned his back against the remains of a bookcase and took in the state of the sitting room. Books, decorations, furniture, paintings, and papers littered the floor. Blood, both red and blue, stained the carpets and the furniture and even the ceiling in places. Adelaide and Rose had collapsed on a sofa. Nix was fiddling with something near a bookcase by the window.

Rose had healed his wounds, and Nix had cured the poison that had filled his body, but Valduin was still hesitant to stand up and bring on another bout of lightheadedness. His father was moving again as well, though he had not yet managed to sit up.

"Valduin," Eamon mumbled, "what happened?"

"Remember that evil hag that I said had tried to kill us? This was her trying again," Valduin replied.

"Are we safe?" He asked. He began the arduous process of pushing himself to a sitting position.

"Relatively," Valduin answered. "That thing is dead and gone. When the next one will come is anyone's guess. I am so sorry to have brought this danger to you."

Eamon swung his legs around and placed his back against the wall next to Valduin. He put his arm around his son's shoulders. "Wait until you hear of all the times your mother's work put all three of us in danger." He chuckled and shook his head. "I am not surprised that you followed in her footsteps of sowing outrage amongst the powerful."

Valduin turned toward his father, his head cocked in curiosity. "What do you mean?"

Eamon smiled. "Not tonight. One day, when these dangers that haunt you have been put to rest, we will talk. For now, I need to sleep." He scanned the carnage within the sitting room. "And tomorrow, we will need to clean up."

"I am afraid you will have to do that yourself," Valduin said. "I cannot justify putting you in any more danger than I already have." He looked at Adelaide, who had perked up at his words. "We leave tonight. We head for the Virdes Forest. We will confront Beulah. We are ending this one way or another."

Eamon sighed. "Just like your mother," he muttered. He shook Valduin lightly by the shoulders. "My offer stands. Once you've wrapped all this business up, you come home and I will tell you everything. Until then, please stay safe."

"We will certainly try," Valduin replied. He hauled himself to his feet, and then he helped his father stand up.

Adelaide and Rose got to their feet as well. They gathered their gear from around the room. Adelaide made a half-hearted effort to shift the chair she had kicked back to its original position.

Eamon waved her off. "Don't worry about that stuff," he said. "I've needed to redecorate this room for a while." As he scanned the destruction, he noticed Nix, who was still making herself busy near the bookcase she had thrown the stalker into. "What are you up to over there?" he asked as he stepped over a toppled table toward her.

Nix stood back. She turned toward Eamon as she replaced a pair of tools into their pockets on her leather vest. "I was fixing it. I'm really sorry that I broke your stuff." Behind her, the bookcase was repaired, its shelves replaced in their positions. Neither crack nor seam nor fastener could be seen.

"This is some impressive handiwork," Eamon said after inspecting the repairs. He narrowed his eyes at Nix. "You are a talented young lady. Thank you for keeping my son safe."

Nix blushed and looked at her feet.

Eamon turned back to Valduin. "Well, I guess you should be heading off. It sounds like the storm has passed. I would recommend sleeping at some point. You do look tired. Do you need anything before you leave?"

Valduin looked to Rose. She answered for the group, "We have what we came for. It was a pleasure to meet you, Mr. Yesfiel. Hopefully, the next time we come here will be a longer, and calmer, visit."

The storm had indeed passed. The city was silent in the early hours of the morning. The party of four made their way out of the labyrinthine city, following Valduin around twists and turns. Adelaide and Rose were certain that the route they took away from the Yesfiel house was different from the route that they had taken to it, but they could not be sure. The streetlamps burned on, but every building was now dark.

Valduin marched forward, his head down, unspeaking. Nix staggered along like a zombie, exhausted by the late night. After they made their exit through the city gate, Adelaide broke the silence.

"What's the plan? We going all the way to Beulah's house tonight?" she asked.

"Yes, are you coming home tonight?" a different voice asked Valduin. A hoarse, grating voice. A voice he wished he would never have to hear again. Valduin froze; Adelaide jerked to a halt next to him. "I'll put the kettle on. I can't wait to see you. Then we can settle our little disagreement."

"There is no disagreement," Valduin hissed. "We did what you asked. You lied to me. You tricked me. You broke the deal." He closed his eyes, waiting for the lightning to strike his brain.

Adelaide cried out and clutched her temples. She staggered to the side, but she kept her balance.

"What's happening?" Nix asked, fear in her voice. She backed away from Adelaide as the human fought to stay on her feet.

Rose screamed and collapsed, pitching forward onto her face on the packed earth of the road.

Nix jumped and redirected her retreat away from Rose's body. She began to whimper, looking around the dark road and planning her escape.

Valduin waited, but the pain did not come. He reached out to help Adelaide steady herself.

"I'm so sorry," he whispered.

Adelaide, eyes still squeezed closed, growled, "I know it's not you." She shook her head and looked toward Nix. "It's okay, Nix. That was the witch we have been talking about. The one that told The Gnarled to attack us. She likes to pop in and hurt us from time to time."

Nix did not look convinced, but she stopped backing away. "Is she okay?" she asked, pointing at Rose's prone form.

As if on cue, Rose groaned and rolled over onto her back. "Yes, I'm okay. Some days it hits harder than others," she mumbled, rubbing the back of her head. She put her hands in the air like a toddler. Adelaide helped her to her feet.

"Well, what's the plan?" Adelaide asked Valduin, continuing their conversation as if the events of the last minute had not transpired. "It's late. Or early, depending. We're all tired. And we all had better be well-rested before we run up to Beulah's hut. There's no telling what will happen when we get there."

"How far away is the next town?" Rose asked. "The one where we passed the caravan?"

"Triroad is several hours from here," Valduin said. "We won't make it there tonight."

"Let's just stop and camp," Adelaide said. She stopped walking to emphasize her commitment to this plan. "We've been going all day. And all night. We need to sleep. Tomorrow we can make all sorts of plans."

Valduin stepped to the side of the road and let his pack fall to the ground. He collapsed next to it, not even taking the time to lay out his bedroll. He put his head on his bag and passed out. Rose was not far behind. She did not take off her armor; she did not take out her blanket. She fell asleep with her head on her rolled-up bedroll.

Nix used her magic to start a fire. Without asking permission, she crawled into Adelaide's bedroll and fell asleep. Adelaide took watch, stroking knots out of Nix's tangled hair with one hand as she listened to the sounds of the night around them.

Valduin ran.

Corridors of gray stone stretched in every direction, fading into darkness at the edge of his vision.

He ran, turned, ran. Corner after corner whizzed past. Sometimes he turned left. Other times right. Always running.

In that darkness, just beyond the range of his vision, skittering movement followed him. He could never make out what was lurking there, but each turn he took brought him farther from it and closer to it. In every direction, down every passageway, around every corner, someone followed him. *Something* hunted him.

He was sweating. His legs and lungs burned. He ran on through endless hallways.

His heart pounded in his chest and his ears, louder than his footsteps, louder than the hunter's movement.

Tears streamed down his face.

He ran.

Straight. Turn. Straight. Don't turn, don't turn, turn.

Stop.

Valduin doubled over, hands on his knees at the end of the corridor. It was not a dead end.

It was a pit. A chasm in all directions. The hallway ended roughly as if it had been shattered by the arrival of this unthinkable expanse of darkness.

Valduin looked down. No bottom in sight. Left, right, and up were all the same.

Darkness.

The hunter's movement grew louder, drowning out the sound of Valduin's heartbeat. The hunter slowed. The scratching, skittering movement approached the last corner before it would turn and catch him.

"I'm coming."

The voice came from the pit.

Valduin leapt.

He fell into blackness.

Silence.

By morning, the sky had cleared. The party continued north, back toward the Virdes Forest. They passed through Triroad and turned west onto the Seawalk Road that led to Tarsam and then on to Westray in the Sandgate Mountains.

"How are we going to find Beulah's clearing?" Adelaide asked. They were walking down the middle of the wide road, which was paved with broad, flat stones. They had left the outskirts of Triroad; the last farmhouse was miles behind them.

"We have never really had trouble finding it before," Valduin said. "Anywhere in the forest, if we want to find her, we find her. Even that first time, you were the one that wanted to find her." He gave Adelaide a sidelong glance.

"Don't you start on about this being my fault," Adelaide grumbled. "Taranath would have killed all of us if she hadn't been there after the fight with Kano and Tristan. Things have been complicated for a while. We are going to be shedding some baggage today. Or tomorrow. Or whenever we find her."

"I could ask Selaia to help me find the way," Rose piped up. "Like I did when we were stuck in the desert. But I had another idea first." Her voice trailed away, and she glanced from one of her friends to the other nervously.

"Well, what is it?" Valduin asked. With the stress of the looming conversation with Beulah and the whispers of his nightmare from the previous night, he did not have patience for Rose's reticence.

"I was thinking that we could stop back at my home. I'm pretty sure if we go off the road here and head directly for the forest, our path will go right through the Mossy Hills. It might give us a safe place to get ready for meeting Beulah," she glanced at Nix as she explained her reasoning.

Adelaide picked up on her insinuation. "That's a great idea," she said. "It would be nice to finally meet your friend Halfred!"

"Do we really have time for another stop?" Valduin asked. He could hear his footsteps echoing down endless stone corridors. "What if Beulah sends another monster to attack us?"

"Beulah knows that we are coming to see her," Adelaide retorted. "Her last two assassins failed. Why would she attack us again?"

Valduin scanned their surroundings. Meadows dotted with small clusters of trees lined the road. A family of deer grazed near the horizon. A few lonely clouds drifted through the sky. "Because she is evil," he replied, "and she does not like being wrong."

"Beulah!" Adelaide shouted at the empty fields. "Just leave us alone for one day! We will see you—"

"Shush!" Valduin cried, slapping a hand over Adelaide's mouth.

Adelaide pushed him away. "What? She seems to be able to see and hear everything we do, anyway. What's the difference?"

Valduin chewed on the inside of his lower lip. He glanced around again, suspicious of every rock and blade of grass now, before answering, "I guess nothing. Yes, Rose, going to your temple would be fine for tonight. But we definitely need to go to Beulah tomorrow."

"Great!" Rose said, smiling more broadly than she had in days, or maybe weeks. "This is lovely! I can't wait to see Halfred again." Her eyes went to the horizon as she continued, "Halfred! It's Rose! I'm coming home! Just for tonight, we'll have to leave tomorrow, but I'll see you soon!"

"That's wonderful," Rose heard Halfred's reply. "Travel safe. I'll have dinner ready." She could hear the smile in his voice.

She skipped ahead of the party, veering off the right side of the road to head northwest, across the open fields toward her home.

"We are really going to stop at your house before we go to Beulah's?" Logan asked. He was shaking his head, staring down at the table.

"Yes, we are," Amelia replied. "For lots of reasons. You'll see. It's for the best."

"Well, Valduin tags along, sulking about not having magic anymore, about his failures almost leading to his father's death, and about missing the chance to learn about his mother's magic," Logan said. He stood up from the table. "I'll go get some more snacks. How long are you going to be? Am I making popcorn or like a batch of brownies?" He headed to the kitchen without waiting for a reply.

"That's it. Make it all about you," Amelia said. She stuck her tongue out at him as he walked away.

"And about Nix doing more damage to the Invisible Stalker than Valduin could," he called from the other room.

"Did everything go okay?" Madison asked in a lowered voice, her tone turning serious.

"With what?"

"You know with what," Madison said. "At school. With those boys."

Amelia sat back in her chair. "Yeah, I guess." She sighed. "I don't really want to talk about it."

Madison stiffened. "What did they do?"

"Oh! Nothing," Amelia said. "I just didn't want to admit that you were right about everything. I didn't talk to them directly. I talked to Mom, and she talked to Dad, and then they sent an email to the school counselor. I still had to go talk to her, but she didn't make me confront those boys."

Madison relaxed and breathed a sigh of her own. "Have they left you alone now?"

Amelia nodded.

"Good." Madison nodded with finality.

"Thanks," Amelia said. She leaned over and hugged her sister. She paused, her head on Madison's shoulder. "Thanks a lot."

"What is happening?" Logan asked. He stood in the doorway with a bowl of chips in his hands, looking at his hugging sisters with curiosity. "What did I miss?"

"Brownies," Amelia shouted, not letting go of Madison. "We need brownies."

35

"Rose Fairfoot, welcome home!" Halfred said. He stood in front of the altar in the main chapel of the temple. He held his arms up, and Rose ran forward and hugged him. Adelaide and Valduin emerged from the entrance hallway, where they had needed to stoop under the low ceiling, into the chapel, where they could stand up straight again. Nix had had no such trouble, and she giggled at Valduin as he held his lower back and stretched.

"Hello, Halfred," Rose said once she had released him. "How have you been?"

"Just fine. Better now that you are home safe. These must be Valdoonan and Adelaide, yes? And who is the little one?" Halfred smiled at the rest of the new arrivals.

"My name is Valduin Yesfiel," Valduin stepped forward and introduced himself. He bowed. "This is Adelaide Bellamie." He indicated the taller human. "And this is Nix." He patted the young human on the top of her head.

"Well, it is so nice to meet you all," Halfred said. "Rose has told me so much about you. Well, about you two at least. Nix, you must be new to the party." He smiled at the girl.

Nix nodded. "They rescued me a few days ago."

"They would do something like that, wouldn't they?" Halfred replied.

"That's something I was hoping to ask you about, Halfred," Rose interrupted him, her tone cautious.

Halfred held up his hands. "Not yet. No questions. You all need food. Come, sit, eat." He turned and walked out of the chapel without hesitation. He led the adventurers to the kitchen, the taps of his staff on the stone floor echoing through the subterranean halls of the old temple.

The table where Rose and Halfred used to eat their meals was stacked with food. Fruits and vegetables of all sorts were arranged in overflowing bowls and baskets. An entire wheel of hard cheese lay on a cutting board with a knife sticking out of it ominously. Sacks of jerky and uncut salami surrounded the cheese.

"Halfred!" Rose gasped when she saw the spread. "This is too much food!"

"You come home after months of adventuring, fighting devils and giants and hags, rescuing youngsters across the land, and I'm not allowed to throw a feast? You're lucky I didn't invite the rest of the Fairfoots!" He looked up at Rose from his seat at the head of the table. The corner of his mouth twisted up into a wry grin. "I didn't break out the nice plates, and we aren't in the banquet hall. Be thankful."

Halfred took a bite of a pickled beet the size of his fist. With his mouth full he waved to the other seats at the table. "Sit! Eat!" he invited the adventurers. "Then we can talk, and you can ask your questions. And then it will be off to bed with the lot of you. It's too late for old men and young children to be up partying." He took another slurping bite of the beet.

Nix giggled.

Halfred acted startled, whipping his head around toward the child. He gasped, pretending to see her for the first time. "And we have a *baby* here too!" He turned back to Rose and waved an accusatory finger at her. "Children should not be up past their bedtime."

Nix laughed. Rose stared at Halfred, bewildered. He had always been nice to her, but he was usually on the edge of cranky. She had never seen him this jovial. "Are you okay, Halfred?" she asked, lowering her voice. "You're acting a little strange."

Halfred waved a dismissive hand at her. "I'm just excited to see you and hear about your journey! It has been so long since I heard a good story of adventure."

"I've told you most of the stories already," Rose said.

"Only in little snippets with your magic messages," Halfred pointed out. "And clearly, I need an update, since I had not yet heard about you rescuing Nix. I need the *whole* story." He reached for a jar of pickles.

Rose watched him for another moment before shrugging and digging in. The group sat at the table late into the night, eating and drinking and sharing their stories. Halfred listened, laughing and crying along with the adventurers as they relived their last few months on the road.

Adelaide sat back in her chair and rubbed her stomach. "Thank you, Halfred. That was amazing." The party had eaten most of the fruit and vegetables that Halfred had served, and half of the wheel of cheese was gone. "Rose, we are going to have to come back here a lot more often."

"I've been thinking about that," Rose replied. "And I think I could make it happen."

Adelaide cocked her head and asked, "What do you mean?"

"More on that in a second. First, Halfred, I have a question for you."

Halfred shifted in his chair to face Rose. He nodded for her to continue.

"Who has been tending the garden in my absence?"

Halfred grimaced. "I've convinced a few of the kids in the village to come out and weed once in a while. And a couple of other people have helped with the harvesting now that most of the fruit is ready. But it has not been easy. Everyone is busy this time of year."

Rose grinned. "What would you think about taking Nix on as your new gardener?"

Halfred sat back in his chair and inspected the young girl, whose head had shot up at the mention of her name.

"She looks feral," he said with a sly wink to Rose. "Is she safe to keep around?"

Nix's mouth, still full of cheese, fell open.

Rose played along, "Well, she does bite. Especially when she turns into a mouse."

Nix gave an ornery squeak.

Halfred raised his eyebrows. "I hope the mouse won't eat all of my cheese. Well, she isn't too tall for the temple yet. Does she know anything about gardening? Those tools don't look like those of a gardener." He gestured toward Nix's vest.

"You know, I'm not sure," Rose said, struggling to conceal her smile. "Let's see." She picked up a peach pit from the side of her plate and tossed it to Nix. "Do you know what that is?" she asked.

Nix caught the pit. She turned it over a couple of times in her hands. "Yes, I know what this is," she said. She brought the pit up to her lips and whispered a few breathy, breezy words to it that made the hair stand up on the back of Valduin's neck. It was the language that they had heard The Gnarled speaking.

As they watched, the pit split open, and a green leaf emerged from the crack.

Halfred gasped. The leaf pushed upward from Nix's hands on a stem that sprouted a dozen more leaves as it grew.

"I can fix things, too," she said. She looked up at Halfred. "I can be useful. I promise."

Halfred clapped his hands and laughed. "You're hired! We'll pick out a room for you in the morning. When can you start?"

"Really? I can stay here? Forever?" Nix's eyes glistened with tears.

Halfred cleared his throat. "No, not forever. You will be too tall to stay in the temple at some point, and you will have your own adventures to go on. But you are welcome to stay as long as you like. Welcome home."

Nix wiped her eyes on her sleeve. She placed the pit, with the seedling peach tree sticking out of it, on the table.

"Great!" Adelaide broke in. "Now, Rose, what were you saying about coming back here?"

Rose grinned. "Let me try something new," she said. She took her amulet in her hands and closed her eyes. *"Selaia, when my path takes me through darkness and danger, your love leads me home,"* she prayed in Halfling.

The amulet glowed with golden light, shining through Rose's fingers, as Valduin and Adelaide had grown accustomed to, but this time the shine grew brighter. And brighter. And brighter. The light filled the kitchen, illuminating the dark corners far from the table and the candles of the chandelier.

The light receded. Rose opened her eyes. Her friends were blinking and rubbing their eyes, trying to clear the spots of residual light from their vision. She looked around the room. Everything was outlined in a golden glow that was slowly fading. She nodded her head, satisfied that the spell had worked.

"Yup, I can bring us back here if I ever need to," she said.

Halfred stared at Rose, his mouth hanging open. "Did you just mark this room as your target for a word of recall spell?" he asked, his voice hushed.

Rose shrugged. "Is that what other people call this one? I've not used it before, but it felt right."

"You have learned a lot during your time away," Halfred said, speaking with awed reverence. "That is magic far beyond what I have ever been capable of using. I have only read about clerics that could perform such magics."

Rose leaned forward. "You have read about them? Do you know about any other magic I might be able to do?" She paused for a moment, and then she narrowed her eyes at the old halfling. "And where were you keeping these books? I read every book in the library at least once."

Halfred grinned. "Not every book is appropriate for the library. I have a few old books that contain descriptions of magic done in the name of Selaia, or other gods. Would you like to see them?"

"Yes!" Rose exclaimed. "That would be so helpful. There are a couple of other things that we need to do, and I am sure that I could get Selaia to help, but I'm not sure how to ask for it."

"Walk with me," Halfred said. To the rest of the party, who were listening with varying levels of interest, he said, "You are welcome to come with us, but if you would rather retire for the night, we can show you to your rooms."

"I think I'll go to bed," Adelaide said, "and Nix should too." Adelaide chuckled as the girl yawned and nodded.

"I'd like to listen," Valduin said.

"Great," Rose said, looking at Valduin, "because one of the things we are going to try to figure out is how to help you with those nightmares."

"Rose, you can get your friends set up in the guest chambers. I'll go grab what books I have that might help. Meet me in my sitting room."

With Adelaide and Nix tucked in, Valduin and Rose sat down on the sofa in Halfred's sitting room. The same sofa that Rose had sat on the day she had met Valduin and Adelaide, discovered her magic, and set off on her adventures. It had only been a couple of months, but this room felt smaller now. It was still cozy, and it was still home, but Rose had seen so much in the meantime. This windowless room, with its comfortable sofa and chairs and its wall of old books, was a cocoon of warm memories in a cold, dangerous world.

Halfred shuffled in from his bedroom. He had a stack of books in his hands and his staff under his arm. Rose hopped off the sofa to help him, taking the books with the care of someone picking up a sleeping infant.

Halfred sat down in a chair as Rose laid out the books on the low table. Valduin watched with fascination. His interest in, and love of, magic had only increased with the loss of his own. These old books held his focus as Halfred and Rose talked. He kept his hands squeezed together in his lap and leaned over the table to inspect the covers.

"These are all of the books that I have that talk about divine magic," Halfred said. "A few are diaries or journals of clerics from long before my time." He pointed to three smaller books with unadorned leather covers and bindings. He pointed to the next couple of books in the row. "Those two were given to me by Fulbert, who you met, when I decided to settle down in the Mossy Hills. One is a tale of a cleric of Selaia from a few centuries ago, and the other is actually about the exploits of an elf that served one of the gods the elves worship, I can't remember which. And that last one," he said, pointing to the largest book on the table, "was here when I took over this temple."

Valduin's eyes looked like they might fall out of his head as he stared at the book with the Elvish script on the front. He kept his hands in his lap, though this took all of his self-control to accomplish.

Rose picked up one of the small journals. "So, there are two things we need to do. One is to travel to another plane. The other is to stop Valduin's nightmares." She flipped through a few pages, read a line or two, and then flipped forward again.

Halfred, noticing Valduin's interest, gestured toward the book written in Elvish. "Feel free to take a look. My Elvish is not very good; I did not get very far in that book. I think it might have the answer to one of your questions, though. I remember there being talk of moving between planes. Maybe you can get more information for us there."

He turned back to Rose. "As for the nightmares, tell me a little more, please. Then I might be able to direct you."

Rose glanced at Valduin before she explained, "Remember the hag I told you about? Beulah? Well, she has been sending Valduin nightmares. They are usually nightmares that are related to the monsters that she is sending to hunt us. Right, Valduin?"

Valduin nodded, but he did not look up from his book. "Yes. There is always something terrible happening to me. Then there is a monster. I hear Beulah's voice. And I die. Every night."

"Well, if the hag is sending the dreams, a magic circle might protect you," Halfred said. His eyes scanned across the books for a moment, and then he picked up the oldest volume, the one that had been at the temple before him. He flipped through to the middle of the book, read for a moment, and turned the book to Rose.

Rose read the paragraphs that Halfred pointed to, a smile spreading across her face as she put together what she needed to do for the spell. "Valduin, I think this will work!" she whispered, her voice brimming with excitement.

"And I think you will be able to do this, too," Valduin replied. "To travel to another plane, all you need is one of those tuning forks. The three of us hold hands while you have the tuning fork. You focus on a location on the plane that the tuning fork is connected to, and we will all shift there. It looks like you do not always end up *exactly* where you aim for, but you should get close."

"Well, we have a bunch of tuning forks," Rose said, "but I only know the linked plane for one of them. Does it say anything about what happens if you don't know which plane you are going to?"

Valduin read to the bottom of the page, turned to the next page, and then turned back. "Not really. It might be random, like your banishing spell." He grimaced.

"Well, let's hope we never get to that point," Rose said. "Come on. You need to sleep. Let's put you in a magic circle and see if it helps tonight. Then I'll do some reading." She gave Valduin a sly look out of the corner of her eye as she turned to Halfred and said, "Halfred, there's another book I have a question about, while we are on the subject. Remind me to ask you about it after we perform the ritual for the magic circle."

"Magic Circle!" Amelia exclaimed. She read the spell description again. "Wait, this says the spell only lasts for one hour. Does that mean she'll be able to get to you after that?"

"I don't know," Logan replied. "Plus, the description of my nightmares sounded more like the Dream spell than the Night Hag's nightmare ability."

"Well, as long as it works, we won't ask questions," Amelia said. She scanned down her spell list again. "Well, I guess that's that. Big day tomorrow."

"This is it, then? In the morning we go to Beulah's hut?" Madison asked. "I can't wait to take the old witch down."

"Whoa, whoa, whoa," Logan said, holding up both hands. "We are not *fighting* Beulah. She will destroy you two. And me, obviously."

Amelia patted Logan on the shoulder. "You're gonna do great tomorrow," she said. "Alright, you need to leave."

"What?" Logan asked in surprise.

"Rose needs to do something. Actually, Rose needs Halfred to do something. Either way, Valduin is asleep, so he doesn't know about it. Goodbye!" She smiled.

"No! I need to hear it! I won't let Valduin know, I promise!"

Amelia's smile grew with the volume of Logan's complaints. "Sorry, but not this time. No eavesdropping either. Go outside, just for a few minutes. It won't take long."

"Well, what about Madison?"

Amelia looked at her sister. Madison shrugged.

"She can stay."

Logan erupted. "That's not fair! Why does she get to stay?"

Amelia waved at Logan as if he was already halfway out the door. "Because it doesn't affect her one way or the other. Now, take a lap around the block. When you get back, we'll be ready."

36

Rose opened her eyes. She lay in her own bed, her head on her own pillow. She breathed in the smell of the sheets; they smelled the same as they had the day she had moved into the temple. That felt like ages ago, before Valduin and Adelaide. Before Moire and Azereth and Luvrolen. Before Kano and Tristan and Tor. Before Taranath had sent her to the afterlife and before Beulah had brought her back. Before she had traveled to other planes, walked through a desert, and teleported across the continent.

Footsteps came from the corridor, reverberating down the stone tunnels of the temple, echoing through her closed door.

She rolled toward the window. Warm sunlight shone in. A familiar vase sat on the windowsill. A single pink rose in full bloom sat in the vase.

Rose sat up with a start.

There had been no flower in the vase last night.

The footsteps stopped outside her door.

She looked around. She was wearing her robe, not her armor. Her pack was gone. Her shield was gone.

She leapt from the bed when the knock came.

A muffled voice followed the knock. "Rose? Rose, are you—"

She threw open the door. The figure standing hunched in the hallway was not Halfred, nor was it Adelaide nor Valduin nor Nix.

"Hello, Halamar," she greeted the elderly elf. "I wasn't expecting you."

"Who else would visit you here?" he asked with a sly grin.

"Well, we went home to my temple yesterday. I was sleeping in this very bed for the first time since we began having these meetings, so I didn't know it was a dream right away."

"Ah. Well, yes, that makes sense. Shall we return to the chapel? This hallway is a little cramped for me."

Rose giggled. "Certainly." She closed the door behind her and led the way back to the main chapel.

"Did you have your meeting with the council?" Rose asked. "Did they listen to you?"

"They allowed me to speak," he began, his words slow and measured, "but they did not listen. I voiced my concerns about someone having left the city and the risks that such actions would pose. I also brought up the chance that we had been betrayed by our benefactor. This statement was not received well. They demanded evidence, which I could not produce."

"Is there anything I could do to help?" Rose asked.

"I do not know," Halamar admitted. They had reached the main chapel of the dream temple. Rose sat in the front row of pews while Halamar paced back and forth in front of the altar. "I know you are important, Rose Fairfoot. I *saw* it. You are the most important person to the future of Eydon. You will save our city. I just don't know how."

"Well, let's do some brainstorming," Rose said. "What do we know?"

"We know that an elf left the demiplane that currently contains the city of Eydon and all of its residents," Halamar replied. "This elf claimed to have been betrayed by someone he considered a friend, or at least someone that was supposed to protect him. The elf was held captive on your plane, during which time his foot was removed and used to create tuning forks linked to our demiplane." He paused to turn toward Rose. "Everything right so far?"

Rose nodded. She continued the story while Halamar resumed his pacing. "My friends and I rescued him. He was very rude to us, and then he grabbed the Eydon tuning forks and disappeared, presumably using them to jump back to Eydon. He probably used a plane shift spell," Rose said, recalling what Valduin had told her during their research the previous evening. "Which means he might have shown up in a weird place. So, anyone that was suddenly in a location that they should not have been in would be a suspect."

Halamar froze. He pivoted toward Rose. "Why didn't I think of that earlier?"

"What?" Rose asked, sitting forward on the bench with excitement. "What did I say?"

"Plane shift," Halamar answered. "You can't plane shift to the city. That was one of the protections that was built into the demiplane when it was created for us."

Rose pursed her lips. "I'm pretty sure that's how he left, though. And he only took some of the tuning forks for Eydon, not any of the other ones, so he couldn't have gone anywhere else."

"Oh, he could plane shift to our demiplane. He just couldn't come straight to the city. He would have landed *below.*" A grin spread across Halamar's face. "Which means the Dreamweaver would have seen him! That's all the proof I'll need."

He raised a hand as if to end the dream, but he paused. His smile faltered. "Did you say he only took *some* of the tuning—"

Rose opened her eyes. She lay in her own bed, her head on her own pillow. She breathed in the smell of the sheets; they smelled the same as they had the day she had moved into the temple.

She rolled toward the window. Warm sunlight shone in. A familiar vase sat on the windowsill, empty.

Another loud knock sounded on her door.

She sat up with a start, the conversation with Halamar rushing back to her mind.

"Rose! It's time to get up! We have work to do!"

Rose dragged herself out of bed. She stepped over the pile of chainmail and past her pack, which had spilled most of its contents into the corner of the room. She opened the door to find Adelaide in the hallway, hunched in the same position that Halamar had been in.

"What's the rush? Beulah isn't going anywhere," Rose said.

"Val's anxious. He's been up since before dawn. He wants to get going."

"Fine." Rose sighed. "Help me get back into my armor. Then breakfast. Then we can go."

"Sure," Adelaide said, ducking into Rose's bedroom.

"Did Valduin have another nightmare last night?" Rose asked.

"He didn't mention one," Adelaide said.

"Good. The magic circle must have worked. Thank goodness Halfred had plenty of holy water. I did not have enough left to cast that spell."

"Did you find out about any other helpful magic that you can do?" Adelaide asked.

"Yes, a few things. Some of them require expensive components, though."

"Like how much? We have some money. We can buy whatever you need."

"How about one thousand gold pieces to set a trap? Or to eat a fancy feast?" Rose said with a chuckle.

Adelaide's eyes went wide. "Okay, you're right. We can't afford that."

They finished suiting Rose up, and they headed for the kitchen. They found Valduin sitting and staring at the empty table, a cup of coffee in his hands. Nix was standing next to Halfred at the stove while the old man cooked.

"You see how the white of the egg is clouding up now?" he asked the girl.

Nix nodded.

"That's when you flip it. And the second side is shorter, only long enough to cook the top of the white, otherwise, the yolk won't be runny."

Nix nodded again.

"Putting her to work already?" Rose asked. She sat down at the table. "Feeling alright? More nightmares?" she muttered to Valduin.

"Nervous. But no nightmares. Thanks to you." He tried to smile, but it was not convincing.

"I've got a chance to teach this one early," Halfred said from the stove. "You were too old to learn properly by the time you got here." He grinned at Rose.

Rose's mouth fell open in shock. "I was the one that taught *you* how to cook!" she cried.

Halfred laughed. He moved the fried egg to a plate with toast and potatoes. "Alright," he said to Nix, "you're up. I want to see runny yolks!" He brought the plate to the table and sat down across from Rose. His smile faded and his tone turned serious. "Are you ready for today?"

Rose glanced at Valduin. He did not look up, did not reply. Rose answered, "Yes, we are. We know what we need to do."

Halfred nodded. "Good. I have a little magic in me that might be able to help you if things get, uh, *exciting*," he said. "A bit of protection, a sort of last line of defense against death."

Rose smiled. "Yes, we know about death wards."

"Well, I could grant this to one of you. That would use most of my energy, but it might help."

Adelaide and Rose exchanged a look. They nodded in silent agreement.

"Give it to Valduin," Rose said. "Until he can get his own magic back, he needs it more than we do."

Valduin's head popped up. He opened his mouth as if to argue, but he said nothing. His shoulders slumped in resignation. He turned to Halfred. "Yes. I agree. If you do not mind," he said.

"Of course not," Halfred said. "We can do that just before you leave. To make sure it lasts as long as possible. Now, you all need a good breakfast. Nix!" he called over his shoulder. "How are we doing with those eggs?"

The party stood at the mouth of the cave that held the temple's front door. The same spot where they had first met, hiding from a pack of angry kobolds. They did not dwell or reminisce.

"Thanks, Halfred," Rose said. "We'll see you again soon."

"I hope," Valduin muttered. Adelaide elbowed him in the ribs.

Halfred pretended not to have heard him. "I am sure of it," he said. "Let me see what I can do to help you all on your way." He took his staff in both hands and prayed in Halfling, *"Selaia, grant these adventurers your aid. Protect them on their journey to this witch, Beulah. Watch over them as they work to free themselves from Beulah's grasp."* The rising sun emblem of Selaia that was affixed to the top of the staff pulsed with golden light.

Halfred continued. *"And protect this young man, Valduin Yesfiel, even at the brink of death."* He leaned the staff forward and touched the glowing emblem to Valduin's chest. He watched the light seep off the golden sun and into his body.

"Thank you," Valduin said. He bowed his head out of respect for the old halfling.

Halfred nodded. "Be safe. All of you."

The adventurers set out, walking around the base of the hill that held the temple, heading toward the Virdes Forest.

For hours they walked, heading north and west toward the Virdes River and the deep parts of the forest.

Adelaide's head never stopped moving, pivoting back and forth, looking over her shoulder, around trees and rocks, down ravines, and over streams. "I'm never going to feel safe in a forest again," she muttered. "Not after The Gnarled."

"Me neither," Rose agreed. "I'm waiting for one of these trees to take a swipe at us."

"How much farther do you think?" Valduin asked. "It's already after noon."

Adelaide shrugged. "Beats me. I have no idea how her hut works. I'm not following any kind of path. We are just walking. It could be anywhere."

"Could you get your snake friend to fly us over the trees for a bit?" Valduin asked Rose. "It might make it easier to find where we need to go."

"It definitely would," Rose said, "but that would use up a lot of my strongest magic. I'll do it, but only if you are absolutely sure that it is the only way to get there."

Valduin sighed and put his head down. He marched forward. "No, don't do that," he said. "Let's just keep walking."

"So much for Aid and Death Ward," Logan grumbled. "We're almost eight hours into this trek and no sign of the hut."

"I'm not worried," Amelia said. "I have plenty of magic. If it makes you feel better, I'll give you a Death Ward as soon as we find those dead trees that are all around Beulah's clearing."

"That would be great," Logan said. "Otherwise, I'll be a sitting duck if we fight."

"What if she's watching?" Madison asked.

"What do you mean?" Logan asked.

"Like, the day before, she spoke to you right after I asked when we were going to visit her, right?"

Logan nodded.

"Well, what if she saw Halfred cast those spells? What if she is keeping herself hidden until the spells wear off? She could probably do that."

Logan's eyes drifted to his character sheet while he considered this possible complication. "She could probably do that," he repeated. "Yeah, okay, no more buff spells. We let Halfred's spells wear off, and then we see where we are."

"Are you sure?" Amelia asked, sounding concerned. "You are really weak without magic. What if we have to fight her?"

"If we start a fight with her," Logan said. "You are going to Word of Recall us right back to your temple as fast as you can. Magic or no magic, she is an enemy we can't kill." He paused. "And if you could stop calling me weak, I'd appreciate it."

37

The afternoon faded into evening. The adventurers walked. And walked. And walked.

After what felt like two days of travel crammed into one, Adelaide stopped walking. She peered between the trees to their right. Her body was tense, and her hands rested on her handaxes, though she did not take them from her belt.

"What do you see?" Rose whispered, picking up on the change in Adelaide's demeanor.

"Look over there," Adelaide whispered back as she pointed into the gloomy darkness of the twilight. "I think there are a few of those blackened trees."

"Let's go, then," Valduin said, not lowering his voice. "It's not like we are going to surprise her." He walked past the women, heading in the direction that Adelaide had indicated.

Adelaide and Rose followed him, their eyes darting from side to side, inspecting every rustle of sound, every shiver of movement in the forest. As the ambient noises of the living forest were left behind, their footsteps seemed painfully loud as each step cracked another twig or crunched through more dried leaves. In the cursed, disease-stricken land surrounding Beulah's hut, the only noise was the occasional scratching of tree branches when a cold breeze blew through.

Valduin kept his eyes forward. He had one task, one goal.

The party emerged from the trees into the clearing. The hut stood in the middle, its front door facing their approach, as it always did. A faint, orange glow flickered through the singular window next to the door.

Rose glanced toward the chicken coop, ever suspicious of Beulah's animals. The yard was empty; the door to the coop was closed. Beulah's familiar, the raven that usually sat atop the coop, was nowhere to be seen.

Halfway across the clearing, Valduin stopped.

"Beulah!" he called out. "We need to talk."

The door flew open. Beulah's cackling laughter echoed out from the hut. The hag appeared in the doorway, a shadow against the firelight within.

Adelaide stepped off to Valduin's left side. She remained vigilant, her eyes scanning the tree line around the clearing, the roof ridge, and the corners of the hut. Her hands ran along the handles of her handaxes, but she still did not take them up. She did not want to be the one to initiate the hostilities that she felt were coming.

Rose did the same to the half-elf's right, flanking him with Adelaide. The halfling kept her gaze fixed on Beulah, watching like a hawk for some sign of trouble.

"Welcome home," the hag croaked. "Ready for your next task? You still have debts to settle."

Valduin froze. He stared at Beulah.

"Nothing to say? No apologies for your behavior?" She glared at Valduin.

Valduin opened his mouth, but no words came out. A creaking, moaning, uncertain sound squeaked from his throat. He closed his mouth without saying a word.

Beulah's eyes flicked to Rose and then to Adelaide. "And what do you two want? Looking for work?" Her lips pulled back in a malicious grin.

Rose looked at Valduin out of the corner of her eye. He stared at Beulah, but he still said nothing.

Rose took a step forward. "We want you out of our heads. We ran your errands, just like you said we had to. We figured out what Stela, Tabitha, and Anise were up to. We settled your contract with Mr. Hancock. And we made the exchange with Misery." She counted off the tasks on her fingers. "Three errands as debt for three crimes. Our agreement is complete. You have to remove whatever it is you did to us that lets you see us and hear us and hurt us."

Beulah raised her eyebrows and cocked her head at the halfling. "Well, well, well. Someone has been paying attention. However, there was a problem with that last one. The information acquired from Misery is not reliable. I sought real information about the Voidbringer."

"That's not our fault!" Adelaide roared.

Rose's head whipped around. "Let me handle this," she hissed at her friend. Turning back to Beulah, she leveled her voice and continued, "The usefulness of the information was not part of the assignment. You only said we needed to trade the souls for the object. We did that. And in case that wasn't enough," she said as she reached into a side pocket of her backpack. She pulled out a cloth sack, its contents clinking as she held it up. "We will return the souls that you sent as payment, too. So, you gained the information that Misery is working for the Voidbringer, and you lost nothing." She took another step forward, placed the sack on the ground, and stepped back to Valduin's side.

Beulah narrowed her eyes at Rose and held out her hand. The sack took to the air and floated toward her. The top of the sack opened itself, and Beulah glanced inside. She nodded, and the sack closed itself again and floated over her shoulder, disappearing into the hut.

"Satisfied?" Rose asked. "We did our part. Remove whatever bond or curse you placed on us."

"Very well," Beulah said. She waved her hand at the three adventurers. Each one became aware of a cold knot in their chest. A knot that they had forgotten was there, that they had been living with ever since the first day they met Beulah. That knot warmed, untangled, and melted away. Three curses lifted and met with three sighs of relief.

"Thank you," Rose said, remaining polite. She was still conscious of the danger of making deals with the hag. She took a step backward. "Well, I think that's about it," she said, more to her friends than to Beulah. "We really should be moving along."

Beulah burst out in wicked, sarcastic cackling.

"Not yet!" she screeched, cutting off her own laughter. "This one still has a debt to settle," she pointed a long, crooked finger at Valduin. "You were given tools in exchange for a book. Where is it?"

Valduin held up his hands. "We couldn't get the book!" he cried in panic. "There was a machine in the tower, and it attacked us. We barely escaped!"

"Ah, you woke up the Inexorable? Well, that was your own fault. You were given a task and you *failed*."

Valduin winced.

"Because you are a *failure*."

Valduin winced again.

"And you are *still* in my debt. I don't even know what to do with something so *pathetic*."

Valduin looked like he might cry.

Rose spoke up again. "Maybe if you had warned him about the machine, we would have been able to deal with it. We still got *this*." She pulled the shimmering, iridescent cloak from her bag.

Beulah cocked her head to the side a degree. Her eyes devoured the cloak.

Rose continued, "Take the cloak. Take back your wicked wand. Take back your magic backpack. Release Valduin and leave us alone." Rose threw the cloak to the ground. She tugged on the backpack on Valduin's back.

He looked down at her with panic in his eyes.

Rose smiled at him. "It's fine," she whispered. "Just put it down."

"But—" Valduin tried to protest before Rose cut him off.

"*Stop*. It's fine," her tone took on an edge that was unusual for the halfling. It caught Valduin's attention.

"Okay," he muttered. He let the bag slide off his back, and he dropped it next to the cloak.

Beulah pursed her lips. She stroked her chin as she considered Rose's offer. After a minute of painful silence, she nodded. "Hold out your arm," she commanded Valduin.

He held up his right hand. He could not stop it from trembling; he hoped that Beulah could not see the tremor this far away in the low light. He did not have much hope.

Beulah rolled her eyes. "The one with the wand, *worm*," she hissed.

Valduin winced, but he did as he was told. He held up his left hand and pulled back the sleeve of his cloak. The bramblewood wand dropped from his wrist, the thorns tearing his skin one last time as the bond broke. Valduin gasped, pulling the arm back and cradling it against his chest.

The wand, the bag, and the cloak floated across the clearing to Beulah. She shifted to the side of the doorway to allow them to pass. They disappeared behind her.

"That's it," Rose said. "That's everything."

Beulah said nothing. She was still stroking her chin, looking from one adventurer to the next.

Rose glanced at Valduin and Adelaide. "Are we good? Are we done?" she whispered, though she was sure Beulah could hear her.

Adelaide was pulling at the straps that held her handaxes to her belt. She glanced around the clearing for the thousandth time since they had arrived before replying to Rose. "Yeah, let's go. Val?"

Valduin was staring at Beulah. He nodded and whispered, "Please."

Rose straightened up and prepared to use her magic to whisk them away.

Beulah interrupted her. "Almost," she said. The word hung in the air, not echoing around the clearing, but lingering in the adventurers' minds. "You will settle one more debt for me. And then I will be done with you."

Adelaide cracked. She stepped forward, her face flush with anger. "We are *done*. No more chores. No more jobs. No more missions or quests or heists. No more spying, disfiguring, or murdering. Done."

Beulah smiled at Adelaide's outburst. "Dearie, I did not say that you had to complete another task. I said you would settle another debt. A debt of my own."

She raised her hand toward an open space in the clearing. When she spoke again, her voice was louder, larger.

"*Zilgannuug Yrrdrixzadrosth Agmoxxamnor Muzrumon'grag! Your presence is required,*" she shouted in Abyssal, though only Valduin understood the grating, grinding, screeching words.

These words echoed through the clearing. They sounded like they were echoing off the walls that held the planes apart, somehow increasing in intensity with each reverberation. Louder and louder, the words overlapping in painful dissonance until they had combined into a single, harsh scream. That scream crescendoed into a tear, a rip through the fabric of the multiverse.

The tearing sound was familiar to the adventurers. They stumbled backward from a whirling planar gate as a monstrous creature, over fifteen feet tall, came hurtling through the portal. It landed with an impact that shook the clearing. The grass at its feet erupted into flames; an aura of fire enshrouded the monster, shimmering heat obscuring the air around it.

It lifted its horned head and snorted smoke from its snout. It looked around the clearing, ignoring the three terrified adventurers. Its gaze fell on Beulah.

"*Witch,*" it growled, "*why have you summoned me?*"

"Oh, don't be grouchy, Zilgan," Beulah replied. "Be happy. I am paying another part of my debt to you." She waved a hand at the party. "Some nice, strong souls for your collection."

The demon turned and leaned forward toward Valduin, Adelaide, and Rose. It sniffed the air, and a deep, rolling sound rumbled out of it.

It took Rose a moment to identify the sound. The monster was laughing.

"Time to go, guys," Rose muttered. She grabbed her amulet. *"Halfred, we're coming ho—"*

"Not so fast!" screeched Beulah. Her piercing voice made Rose wince, interrupting her spell. The hag cackled, a sound Rose had now heard far too many times. "You no longer belong to me. You belong to Lord Zilgan now. Don't be rude to your master." Her laughter redoubled.

Zilgan pulled a coil off its belt. The coil unfurled into a whip, forty feet long. The whip burst into flames at the demon's touch. Zilgan stepped toward them.

"We'll leave those bodies here," they felt Zilgan's words coalesce in their minds. *"You won't need them where we're going."*

"Balor? *Balor*? Why? Whyyyy?" Logan moaned. He crossed his arms on the table and buried his face into them.

"What are you complaining about?" Amelia asked. "I'm the one that just lost one of my biggest spells to Beulah's Counterspell!"

"Get your head in the game," Madison said, shaking her brother's shoulder. "What's the range on Counterspell? We need to get out of here."

"Sixty feet," Logan replied, his voice muffled. He picked his head up to elaborate, "but we can't risk her having Metamagic like the other hags did. As long as we can see her, we probably aren't safe. If we can't see her, we definitely aren't safe." He dropped his head back onto the table.

"We can't bamf out," Amelia mused, "and we probably can't outrun it." She let her voice trail away. She raised an eyebrow at Madison.

A grin crept across Madison's face. "We might as well go down swinging," she finished Amelia's thought. "Oh boy, this is gonna be a good one. Book boy, is this a fiend? Like, good for Fiend's Lament?"

"I guess this is as good a time as any to end the campaign," Logan grumbled, sitting up again. "Yes, it's a fiend. Yes, use Fiend's Lament. Rose, you may have guessed already, but don't use Flame Strike or Fire Storm. It's immune to fire damage."

Amelia nodded.

"I'll just try to stay as far away as possible and shoot it with this crossbow. Woo. Hoo," he concluded with a notable absence of enthusiasm.

38

Adelaide reached back and pulled Fiend's Lament off her pack. She swung the enchanted axe into her hands and prepared to charge the monster. Before she could take a step, however, Zilgan flicked its wrist. The flaming whip lashed out and wrapped around her, locking her arms to her sides.

Adelaide gasped as the scorching-hot leather seared her arms. She fought to break free, but before she could, the balor wrenched the whip to pull her spinning across the space between them. She stumbled on unsteady feet in front of the demon. The shimmering heat of its presence enveloped her. It felt like diving into a pool of lava. The tip of her braid smoldered; loose threads that hung from her clothes curled and burned away.

Before she caught her balance enough to attack the monster, it drew a gargantuan longsword with its other hand. Instead of bursting into flames, however, the blade crackled with infernal lightning, white arcs jumping over the crossguard to the balor's hand and arm. It slashed the sword across Adelaide. The lightning from the accursed blade coursed through her, locking her jaw and muffling her scream.

The balor's rumbling chuckle returned.

Rose watched with wide eyes as the demon laid into Adelaide. She sidestepped away from the hut, trying to get some more distance between herself and Beulah, and prayed, "*Selaia, banish this monster—*"

"*Stop!*" Beulah shrieked. Again, Rose winced, her spell interrupted and lost. She turned her head toward Beulah, preparing to shout at the old witch, but she held her tongue. There was something different in Beulah's tone that time. And there was something different in the way the hag looked at the balor now. Rose could not put her finger on it in the moment, distracted by other matters, but she knew there was more going on here than she had initially thought.

Adelaide's scream of pain warped into a scream of rage. Her eyes burned with the heat of the balor and the heat of her fury. She could not reach the monster's head, its chest, or even its abdomen. She started on its knee with two strikes of her magic battleaxe, the impossibly sharp blade carving through the demon's hardened skin like she was cutting a fat salami.

Zilgan jerked its leg away from her like someone who was bitten by their pet cat. Its laughter stopped. It snorted through its bovine nose and raised its weapons for another round of attacks.

Valduin seized the opportunity to put some distance between himself and the balor. He ran straight away from the monster, across the clearing, toward the chicken coop. As he retreated, he pulled out his crossbow and loaded a bolt into it.

He glanced over his shoulder in time to watch the balor raise its wings wide and high above its head. It bent its knees. In one motion, it gave those expansive wings one hard flap down as it jumped up. The force of its wings blasted heat out around it; Adelaide held up one arm to shield her eyes as the flames on the grass below her flared up.

The balor vanished the moment its feet left the ground as if it had leapt right off this plane of existence.

It reappeared five feet in front of Valduin.

It was the heat as much as the leg that stopped Valduin's run short. The half-elf gasped as the ground burned his feet through his boots. The tattered hem of his cloak began to smoke.

"*There is no escape,*" Zilgan's words pierced Valduin's mind.

It raised the crackling longsword, but before it could strike, a beam of golden energy arced from Rose's outstretched finger and seared into the balor's stomach.

Zilgan grunted, its eyes flicking over toward the halfling. If it could have shot fire from those eyes, it looked like it would have.

Adelaide had been left farther from the action than she liked. She took off at a run, trying to close the distance to the demon. She switched Fiend's Lament to her left hand and pulled a handaxe off her belt with her right. As she pulled back her arm she shouted, "You're next!" to mark Zilgan as her quarry. The handaxe whirled across the clearing, flying over Valduin's head and planting itself into the glowing, golden target that Rose had burned into the balor's red skin.

The wooden handle of the axe burst into flames. With a swipe of its whip, Zilgan knocked the blade from its abdomen. It snorted again and narrowed its eyes. It looked from one adventurer to the next, infernal calculations running behind its inscrutable eyes.

Valduin did not wait. He ran again, heading for the trees at the edge of the clearing. Zilgan swiped the longsword across the half-elf's back. Valduin grunted and stumbled, but he kept running. Zilgan flapped its wings again, lifting itself into the air. It flew toward Rose and brought the sword down on her petite form as it landed.

Rose raised her shield, but she could not hold back the incredible power of the balor's attack. The sword crushed the shield against her and drove her onto her back with a cry of pain. The balor glared down at her. Without looking over, it flicked the whip out to wrap around Valduin. A strong tug brought him skipping back across the smoking grass of the clearing to the balor's feet.

"This is hardly a gift," Zilgan rumbled. *"Next time, witch, have your payment ready for me."*

Rose scrambled to her feet. She looked up at the monstrous demon. When she opened her mouth to speak, she spoke with two voices, her own joined by another, deeper, larger voice. A voice that Valduin and Adelaide had heard the first time they met the cleric. The voice of the Watchful Mother, the goddess Selaia, coming from the mouth of Rose Fairfoot. "Flee, you wretch!" she commanded the demon.

The balor's stance faltered. It took a step back, wincing as that voice rang out, drowning out the crackling of burning grass and the ever-present hum of the portal.

Adelaide saw the opening and took it, slashing into Zilgan's calf with Fiend's Lament and spilling steaming-hot, maroon blood to quench the flames beneath the demon's feet. Zilgan staggered. It stuck the sword into the ground like a cane to keep its balance.

Valduin did not notice. He stood in the shadow of the balor, his arms over his head, whimpering and waiting for the next blow from the monster's terrible weapons. He did not look up until he felt the blast of heat as the balor flapped its wings and teleported back to the portal. It took one step into the swirling blue gate before it stopped, blinking and shaking its head.

Beulah erupted into malicious laughter. "What's wrong, Zilgan? Afraid of a few mortals?"

Zilgan stepped out of the portal again. It glared at Beulah and snorted, but it made no reply to the hag's ridicule.

Rose opened her eyes, which she had clenched closed against the heat of the balor's presence. Her friends stood near her, each charred and bleeding from the balor's weapons. *"Selaia, hold us together,"* she prayed, summoning a swarm of golden lights out of her amulet. The motes swirled around her and divided themselves between Valduin and Adelaide, soothing burns and closing wounds.

Adelaide sighed as the warmth of Rose's healing washed over her. "Thanks, Rose," she said. "I think we can take this thing." She turned to Valduin and said, "You pull yourself together! We need you in this. Stop crying and *fight!*"

Pep talk completed, Adelaide turned and charged across the clearing toward Zilgan. With each step, she grew a foot taller until she had reached her enlarged size, now coming up to the balor's chest. She roared at the balor across the remaining space, clenching Fiend's Lament and waiting to meet the monster's attacks.

"I can't," Valduin whined to Rose while staring at the enraged demon across the clearing from them. "What can I do? This crossbow can't hurt that thing. I have nothing!"

Rose grabbed the front of his armor and shook him. "Hey! What did we just hear from your dad?" she asked.

Valduin looked down at the halfling. He shrugged.

"The magic is *inside* you. It's in your blood. Your mother's magic. You have the power; now find the strength. We *need* it."

Valduin stared at her, his mind racing. He said nothing.

Before Rose could continue, Beulah's hysterical cackling pulled their attention back toward the balor.

Zilgan had lashed out with the whip at Adelaide, but instead of being pulled toward it, Adelaide had held her ground.

She grabbed the end of the whip and yanked. Not prepared for this, the balor stumbled forward. Adelaide met it at a full run with a mighty swing of her axe. Zilgan grunted and tried to turn away from the blade, but it managed only to prevent the axe from becoming lodged into its shoulder. A spray of hot blood covered Adelaide's face and torso, burning into her skin. She howled in pain, but it did not stop her from hitting Zilgan with the axe again. Again, the burst of heat scorched the human. This time it was too much. Adelaide collapsed, shrinking down to her normal size, tendrils of smoke rising all across her body.

"We need to help!" Rose shouted at Valduin. "*She* needs your help!" Rose gave him a final shake before turning and running toward Adelaide. As she approached, she raised her hand and blasted the swaying monster with another guiding bolt, the golden beam streaking over Adelaide's unmoving body.

Valduin stood where Rose had left him. He looked at the crossbow in his hand, and he looked at the demon locked in battle with his friend. Smoke filled the clearing; everything the balor touched, and everything that touched it, was set ablaze. He thought about what Rose had said, about what his father had said, about everything he had done to get here, about what he had done for magic in the past. About what he might do for it in the future. About what he would do to help his friends.

"I can't do it!" he cried. "I need my power. I need help. I need magic."

Zilgan regained its footing. It lowered its head and took a deep breath. It roared a deafening, terrifying, soul-shaking roar. Rose's chainmail rattled with the ferocity of that sound. She winced under its power. She winced just long enough to not see the whip coming at her.

It wrapped around her, its flames heating her armor and burning her skin. She began to scream, but the air was pulled from her lungs when Zilgan jerked the whip and pulled the halfling across the intervening space. She slammed into Adelaide's body at the foot of the balor. Before she could catch her balance the sword hit her, its lightning coursing through her armor and into the ground. She could only whimper as her back arched and her jaw clenched with uncontrollable spasms.

The balor composed itself. It glanced toward Beulah again. *"Watch your tone, witch. Or next time, I'll collect you,"* it growled.

Rose lay on the ground, muscles aching from the balor's attacks. She could smell Adelaide's charred body next to her. She groaned and pushed herself to her feet. She wavered, squinting against the unbearable heat of the balor's proximity.

"Adelaide, you can't quit now," she muttered, nudging her friend with her foot. It was enough to transfer her healing magic; Adelaide's eyes opened. The human gasped and coughed and spat out soot-blackened sputum onto the scorched earth beneath her.

Rose turned toward Valduin, who still stood frozen in fear. "You don't need help," she said, no longer shouting. Her voice was sad, desperate. "It's inside you. We just need *you*. And we need you now." She turned back to face down the monstrous demon that towered over her.

Adelaide staggered to her feet. With Fiend's Lament in her hands, she dove back into the balor's fiery aura, slashing into its legs again. Zilgan growled and raised its weapons. *"This is the end of you,"* its voice rumbled through the adventurers' minds.

Valduin stepped forward. He closed his eyes, replaying the feeling of using magic. How it would spread from his mind to his hands and out into the world. He thought about the first spell he ever cast. He thought about every magic he had learned, the powerful and the mundane.

He thought about his mother, who had died on a quest to help him unlock his inner power.

He thought about his family lineage, descended from the Fey, linked forever to the Inner Plane of Light.

He thought about the Circle of the Silver Thread and their mission to protect this plane from extraplanar threats. Threats just like this demon that was threatening his friends.

When he opened them again, tongues of fire burst forth from his eyes. He could feel the warmth on his face, but there was no pain. The warmth was familiar. It was the feeling of magic.

While his eyes burned, his hands poured black smoke.

He stepped forward again, raising his hands toward the balor.

"Death comes for all," he said in Abyssal.

Zilgan, weapons raised, hesitated. It turned its head toward the half-elf.

"*And now it comes for you!*" Valduin screamed. The black smoke swirled out toward Zilgan, enveloping the monster in an asphyxiating cloud.

"You did it!" Amelia shouted, jumping up and down and shaking Logan's shoulder. "I told you we would fix you!"

Logan grinned and tolerated Amelia's excitement.

"The fire coming from your eyes? That *was* pretty awesome," Madison agreed. "You got everything back now?"

Logan nodded. He consulted his character sheet. "And more," he answered. "I've got all twelve levels of Warlock powers back, and I get a whole new set of things for my first level in Sorcerer."

"Multi-classing *is* pretty cool," Madison agreed with a knowing smirk. "I told you that you should have done it earlier."

"It didn't make sense earlier," Logan countered. "It had to make sense with the story. Yours did when you became a barbarian. Mine had to, too."

"Tutu," Amelia muttered, snickering as she returned to her seat.

Logan rolled his eyes. "*Anyway*, we still need to get out of this. Lord Zilganarshmertz Hoozywhatsit is not dead. Both of you are close to dying."

"First of all, I'm glad there's finally a name you can't pronounce," Madison said, "and secondly, it has got to be close. I've done over a hundred and fifty damage myself, and Rose did some too."

"Yeah, but every time you hit, you take almost the same back in fire damage," Logan pointed out. "You'll knock yourself out if you hit it again."

"Maybe Beulah will help," Amelia suggested. "She's acting a little strange."

"You're kidding right?" Madison asked. "She's the one giving us to the demon as payment! She's not going to help us escape from it."

"I think she likes to see the demon suffer as much as she likes to see anyone suffer," Logan said. "She was just laughing at him. I doubt it goes much further than that."

39

Zilgan gasped, struggling for breath against the penetrating decay of Valduin's magic. When the arcane smoke cleared, the demon's red skin had faded to an ashy gray in patches across its chest and abdomen. The gray areas were crisscrossed with cracks that oozed dark blood as the balor moved.

Zilgan did not howl. It did not scream. It did not growl. It glared at Valduin, its eyes burning figuratively while Valduin's burned literally. Without looking down, the balor slammed the handle of the whip into the top of Adelaide's head, sending her sprawling to the ground. It slashed the sword into Rose, who spun around and fell prone. Neither woman made a move to get up.

"One more for the collection," it rumbled. It stepped over the women's bodies toward the half-elf.

With its back to Rose and Adelaide, Zilgan did not see the flash of white light from Rose's crown. It did not see the halfling open her eyes, nor did it see her whisper into the human's ear. It did not see Adelaide open her eyes and use her magic to soothe her scorched skin and bleeding wounds. It did not notice Adelaide getting to her feet and bringing Fiend's Lament up into her hands.

Valduin smirked up at the oncoming monster. *"Hold it right there,"* he commanded in Abyssal.

Zilgan's eyes went wide. It froze mid-stride, its wings extended behind it. Only the dancing flames and crackling lightning of its weapons moved. The rest of the terrible demon was held in place.

Valduin flinched and threw an arm in front of his face as a bolt of lightning blasted across the clearing. The blinding-white beam of energy coursed through Zilgan, squeezing an extended groan through its locked teeth. The blood that ran from its dry, cracked skin sizzled and steamed with the power of the lightning bolt. Zilgan tried to find the source of its pain, but only its eyes could move.

When the magic had passed, Valduin peered through the smoke-filled air of the clearing.

Beulah stood in the charred grass, fifteen feet outside the door to her hut. She held the bramblewood wand that Valduin had returned to her ten minutes prior, arm outstretched, pointing at the balor.

Her eyes were wide. Her breaths were rapid, panicked. Her black and broken teeth were gritted and bared. Her eyes flicked from the balor to Valduin. Back to the balor. Over to the swirling gate.

The portal disappeared without a sound. The wand trembled in her hand. Her gaze darted to Adelaide.

"Do it now!" she cried. "You must use the accursed axe. Taranath's blade. Finish it. *Lock it away,"* she hissed.

"She's right," Rose moaned. She still sat on the ground next to Adelaide. "You need to kill it." Rose put her hand on Adelaide's ankle and prayed, *"Selaia, protect her from these abyssal flames."*

Rose's protective magic spread through her, cooling her skin. Adelaide let the axehead slide to the ground so that she was holding the end of the handle. She broke into a run, charging the balor from behind.

Frozen in place, Zilgan could not see her approach; it could only hear her footsteps. It could feel her leap onto its back. It felt the cold metal of Fiend's Lament hook around its wing as Adelaide used the weapon to aid her climb. It felt her perch atop its wing joints, behind the shoulders, a hand holding one of its horns for balance.

For the shortest of moments, the balor Zilgannuug Yrrdrixzadrosth Agmoxxamnor Muzrumon'grag, Hunter of Secrets, Shredder of Minds, and Breaker of Souls, Four Hundred Forty Second Lord of the Abyss, felt the keen edge of Fiend's Lament enter the top of its skull.

A pulse of purple energy flared from the battleaxe as Zilgan's essence was absorbed into it.

Then, at the moment of its death, its seventh and final death, the balor detonated.

Valduin lifted Rose's head and poured the healing potion into her mouth. The shimmering liquid disappeared, and the halfling shuddered back to life. She groaned and rolled onto her side. Valduin collapsed next to the halfling, panting, sore, and relieved that they were all alive.

Adelaide lay in the crater left behind after the balor's dramatic departure. She had survived the blast, thanks to Rose's protective magic.

Beulah looked little worse for wear. She still held the bramblewood wand as she paced in front of her hut. She was mumbling to herself, words pouring from her mouth in a frantic chatter that none of the adventurers could understand.

She stopped walking and turned her face toward the sky.

She smiled. She gave a sigh of relief. She looked at Valduin.

"You did it. She did it. Taranath did it when he cursed that wicked axe." She turned to Adelaide. She reached a hand toward the axe, her arm and fingers stretching thirty feet across the smoking crater. She ran one finger across the face of Fiend's Lament's blade, feeling the grooves of the roots engraved upon it.

Adelaide jerked the weapon away, terrified by the sight of Beulah's outstretched finger. The stretching was even more disconcerting out in the open than it was inside the hut.

Beulah giggled and pulled her hand back.

Valduin dragged himself to his feet. He swayed, his head hanging forward, his eyes trained on the hag. He wanted to scream at her, to berate her, to punish her, but he knew there was no point. Not today, at least. Not in this state.

Instead, he spoke to her. "We are even." It was not a question. It was not a request.

"We have cleared whatever debt you owed that thing," he continued, "and in doing so we have cleared whatever debt you might think we still owe you."

Beulah narrowed her eyes at Valduin for a moment, and then she broke out in the childish, maniacal giggling again.

Valduin preferred her cackle to this unhinged laughter.

"Yes, even," she agreed. "Even, even, even. We are *even.*" The laughter cut off. Her face hardened. She raised a finger to point at Valduin. "But if I ever see you again, I will take your soul and take it to the deepest layers of the abyss. With everything you've done, I'm sure the auction houses would be fighting over the chance to sell your soul."

Her words cut through Valduin. He felt a chill in his chest. He did not reply.

"Can you take us away from here?" he asked Rose.

The halfling, now on her feet, nodded. She beckoned to Adelaide.

The human dragged herself to Rose's side. Rose took her hand. Valduin stepped next to his friends, though his gaze never left Beulah.

Beulah spun around and headed toward the hut.

"Let's go home," Rose said.

Her amulet flashed. The adventurers clenched their eyes closed against the light as they folded into the symbol of the rising sun, now a gateway back to the temple in the Mossy Hills. For a moment, after their bodies had been stretched thin and tucked through the tiny doorway, the amulet alone hovered in the smoky air of Beulah's clearing. Its divine light pushed back the deepening evening of the Virdes Forest, and then it folded in on itself and disappeared.

Valduin, Adelaide, and Rose tumbled out of the tiny, arched doorway onto the floor of the temple's kitchen. They could smell and hear onions and garlic sautéing. Nix stood at the stove, sliding sausages into a pan with a satisfying sizzle. She jumped at the crash of bodies hitting the kitchen's stone floor.

"Oh my goodness!" she cried when she saw the state of the party. She glanced at the pan in front of her before hurrying to Rose's side. She pulled the charred and bloodied halfling from the pile.

"Ow, ow, ow!" Rose whined.

Nix released her arm. "Oh! I'm sorry!" Nix cried, wincing with sympathetic pain at the sight of Rose's wounds. "Here, take this." Her hands glowed with the same dark green energy that Adelaide's did when she used her healing magic. Nix placed her hands on Rose, and the light soaked into Rose's skin and cleared away the burns on her arm. It did not fix everything, but it helped.

Adelaide and Valduin pulled themselves to their feet and collapsed into the chairs at the table where they had feasted the night before. They sat across from each other, slumped, out of breath, but smiling.

"We did it," Valduin said. "We are free."

"You did it," Adelaide countered. "You were amazing."

"We believed in you the whole time," Rose said. She patted Valduin on the shoulder and sat down next to him.

Adelaide grimaced. "Well..." she mumbled.

Rose sighed. "Okay, *I* believed in you the whole time. Adelaide does now, *right*?" She glared at the human.

Adelaide chuckled. "Yeah. I definitely do now."

"Well, well. You made it back," Halfred said from the doorway. He shuffled into the kitchen and sat down at the head of the table. "Mind those sausages," he muttered to Nix.

The girl spun around and skipped back to the stove. Her eyes went very wide when she glanced into the pan; she hastily stirred its contents while glancing over at Halfred to see if he had noticed her panic.

"Everything went according to plan, I assume," Halfred continued, ignoring Nix.

The adventurers exchanged glances. "Pretty much," Adelaide replied.

"So, you'll be wanting this back?" the old halfling asked. He placed a book on the table. An old, brown leather book held closed with a leather strap. An ominous skull looked up at them from the wings of a moth embossed on the cover.

Valduin sat forward with a jolt. "How'd you get that?" he asked. "I thought we gave it to Beulah."

"We never said that," Rose replied with a smirk. "I told Beulah exactly what we were giving her. She knows nothing of the book."

"That's a good thing, too," Halfred said. "There is some mighty powerful magic in here."

"You read it?" Valduin's jaw dropped.

"I may have taken a peek," Halfred replied, reveling in Valduin's shock. "*I* can't use any of this magic, but I could understand what some of it does. Just from how complicated those spells are, I know they must be incredibly strong. And dangerous in the hands of a hag."

Valduin sat back, the pieces coming together in his mind. "That must be Misery's spellbook," he said. "One of them at least. I am sure he keeps one with him as well. I bet there is some spell in there that Beulah does not know. That is why she wanted it."

"Well, I certainly don't want it to stay here," Halfred said, pushing it forward with one finger.

"I'd take it," Valduin said, "but I don't have a bag anymore." He gave a weak laugh and reached into the pockets of his cloak. "I've got a wand and a dagger." He placed his remaining magic items on the table. "That's it."

"Well, if I'm not mistaken, we do have a small selection of things in the armory that would work for you," Halfred said. "We don't keep much gear in your size, but we should have a bag and a bedroll at the very least."

"Really? That would be great."

"I could use some new armor, while we are at it," Rose said. She looked down at the gaping holes the balor's sword had left in her chainmail, though the skin beneath was intact.

Something crashed from the other side of the kitchen. The party spun toward the sound to see Nix struggling with a large pot of water. A wooden bowl lay broken on the floor. Carrots were scattered across the kitchen.

Halfred chuckled. "You okay over there?" He did not wait for an answer. "We are going to resupply our friends. When we return, we'll eat. Do you need help? Or can you manage on your own?" The last sentence sounded more like a test than a question.

"I'll manage," Nix replied, not looking up at him. She grabbed the carrots in one hand and the bowl in the other. She whispered in that breathy, windy, scratchy language again, and the wood of the bowl came to life, sealing itself back into its original shape. She placed the mended bowl on the counter and replaced the carrots before moving on to her next task.

Halfred nodded from his seat. To Rose, he whispered, "She's going to do great. I'll be sending her out on an adventure in no time at all I expect." His eyes misted over as he spoke. He blinked back the tears and pulled himself to his feet. He forced down the knot in his throat. "To the armory, then," he said, and he shuffled out of the room.

Rose opened her eyes. She lay in her bed in the temple. Warm sunlight streamed in through the window.

"What a day," she muttered, still astonished that they had survived the battle with the balor. And that Valduin had gotten his magic back. And that Beulah had seemingly freed them from her service for real this time.

She thought about the fight. How close it had been. How the balor's sword had burned her whole body when it hit her, the lightning coursing through her chainmail, heating it in a flash to char her skin.

She moved her legs under the sheets, testing them. They felt amazing, not sore at all. She poked herself in the side, where the sword had run her through. She felt no pain. In fact, the more she surveyed her body, the more she realized how great she felt.

She sat up with a jolt and looked toward the window.

There was a single pink rose in the vase.

Rose leapt from her bed and sprinted to the central chapel of the temple.

Halamar was waiting for her.

"I was wondering if I was going to have to go get you again," he said. His voice was stern.

"Sorry," Rose said. "I'm still staying at my temple, so it took a minute to realize I wasn't just waking up the regular way."

"Well, that's nice that you've had some time at home," Halamar said.

Rose cocked her head. "I haven't had that much time. We've only been there two days."

Halamar returned her look of confusion. "Didn't you say you had just arrived at your home the last time we met?"

Rose nodded. "That was yesterday."

Halamar stiffened. His eyes grew wide. His voice was a tense whisper when he asked, "What do you mean?"

"What do you mean, 'What do you mean?'" Rose asked. "We arrived two days ago. We talked last night. Today we did some, uh, errands, and now we are back at the temple."

"That can't be. The time, our time, your time..." Halamar's voice trailed away. He shook his head in disbelief at what Rose had told him.

Rose did not know what to say. She sat in silence and let Halamar process this information. The old elf leaned against the wall and let himself slide down until he was crouched with his knees to his chest.

"Eydon is broken," Halamar whispered. He had tears in his eyes. "Something is breaking Eydon. That is the only way this could have happened."

He looked at Rose. "We need you to get here," he said, conviction displacing the shock from his voice. "You are the key to saving Eydon. I know this to be true."

Rose nodded slowly. "I'm not sure what you mean by 'broken,' but if we can help, we will. We'll come right away."

"But how to get you here?" Halamar asked himself. "I do not know of any rifts, gates, or portals that connect from the Astral Plane to where you are. Well, no safe ones anyhow. The ones within Eydon were closed before we left. Could you get yourself to the Astral Plane? It would not be easy, but I could come get you from there, maybe." He grimaced as he ran through options in his head for getting the adventurers to Eydon.

Rose smiled. She leaned forward and said in a conspiratorial whisper, "I still have one of the mean elf's bones!" She laughed. "We'll come to you the way he went home. I can plane shift us. See you soon!"

"Wait! You can't—" Halamar tried to interrupt her, but it was too late.

The dream ended.

Rose opened her eyes.

"Finally, the plane-hopping part of the campaign," Madison said, rubbing her hands together in excitement. "We have gotten to level thirteen by *walking* around! Except for when Beulah Plane Shifted us, but that's beside the point. We are in control now. It's time to travel in *style*."

"All we have to do is hold hands," Amelia said as she reviewed the spell description in the rulebook again. "And we'll bamf right out of this universe and into another."

"I haven't read the spell," Madison said. "Is it an issue that it's a demiplane and not a full plane? Do you need like a Demiplane Shift spell to get there?"

Amelia shrugged. "This is clearly where the story is headed. I'm sure it will work, even if it isn't *exactly* how the rules are written."

Madison nodded. "Makes sense."

Logan looked back and forth between his sisters, aghast. "Was neither of you paying attention?" he asked.

Madison and Amelia looked back at him. "What?" they asked in unison.

Logan groaned. "Halamar was about to tell you something important! He already said that no one can Plane Shift to the city of Eydon. Something about going 'below' instead." He flipped through his notebook to the section bookmarked with a sticky note labeled 'Halamar.'

"And then he mentioned someone, or something, called the Dreamweaver," he continued. "And his last words to you before you woke up were 'You can't.'" He slapped his notebook closed in exasperation. "This is not going to go well."

"Well, it'll be fun either way," Amelia said. "Have you leveled up yet? You get a bunch of cool new stuff now, don't you?"

Logan could not help but smile as he glanced down at

his character sheet, pushing his concern for Halamar out of his mind. "Yes, another level of Sorcerer, so I'm starting to get Metamagic. And I have *so many cantrips.*" He heaved a satisfied sigh and sat back in his chair. "I love this game."

Letter from the Author

Thank you so much for choosing to read *Beulah's Grasp*. If you enjoyed this story of Logan, Madison, and Amelia's adventures playing as Valduin, Adelaide, and Rose, and you would like to keep up-to-date with more of their exploits, check out my website:

www.VoidbringerCampaign.com

I would be very grateful if you could take a moment to rate *Beulah's Grasp*, or even post a short review, wherever you found this book. These ratings and reviews will help new readers discover the Voidbringer Campaign.

If you would like to get in touch, or are looking for other family-friendly content for your tabletop roleplaying games, you can find me on Twitter, Instagram, and Facebook.

Thanks again,
M. Allen Hall
@M_Allen_Hall

OPEN GAME LICENSE Version 1.0a

The following text is the property of Wizards of the Coast, Inc. and is Copyright 2000 Wizards of the Coast, Inc ("Wizards"). All Rights Reserved.

1. Definitions: (a)"Contributors" means the copyright and/or trademark owners who have contributed Open Game Content; (b)"Derivative Material" means copyrighted material including derivative works and translations (including into other computer languages), potation, modification, correction, addition, extension, upgrade, improvement, compilation, abridgment or other form in which an existing work may be recast, transformed or adapted; (c) "Distribute" means to reproduce, license, rent, lease, sell, broadcast, publicly display, transmit or otherwise distribute; (d)"Open Game Content" means the game mechanic and includes the methods, procedures, processes and routines to the extent such content does not embody the Product Identity and is an enhancement over the prior art and any additional content clearly identified as Open Game Content by the Contributor, and means any work covered by this License, including translations and derivative works under copyright law, but specifically excludes Product Identity. (e) "Product Identity" means product and product line names, logos and identifying marks including trade dress; artifacts; creatures characters; stories, storylines, plots, thematic elements, dialogue, incidents, language, artwork, symbols, designs, depictions, likenesses, formats, poses, concepts, themes and graphic, photographic and other visual or audio representations; names and descriptions of characters, spells, enchantments, personalities, teams, personas, likenesses and special abilities; places, locations, environments, creatures, equipment, magical or supernatural abilities or effects, logos, symbols, or graphic designs; and any other trademark or registered trademark clearly identified as Product identity by the owner of the Product Identity, and which specifically excludes the Open Game Content; (f) "Trademark" means the logos, names, mark, sign, motto, designs that are used by a Contributor to identify itself or its products or the associated products contributed to the Open Game License by the Contributor (g) "Use", "Used" or "Using" means to use, Distribute, copy, edit, format, modify, translate and otherwise create Derivative Material of Open Game Content. (h) "You" Not for resale. Permission granted to print or photocopy this document for personal use only. System Reference Document 5.1 2 or "Your" means the licensee in terms of this agreement.

2. The License: This License applies to any Open Game Content that contains a notice indicating that the Open Game Content may only be Used under and in terms of this License. You must affix such a notice to any Open Game Content that you Use. No terms may be added to or subtracted from this License except as described by the License itself. No other terms or conditions may be applied to any Open Game Content distributed using this License.

3. Offer and Acceptance: By Using the Open Game Content You indicate Your acceptance of the terms of this License.

4. Grant and Consideration: In consideration for agreeing to use this License, the Contributors grant You a perpetual, worldwide, royalty-free, nonexclusive license with the exact terms of this License to Use, the Open Game Content.

5. Representation of Authority to Contribute: If You are contributing original material as Open Game Content, You represent that Your Contributions are Your original creation and/or You have sufficient rights to grant the rights conveyed by this License.

6. Notice of License Copyright: You must update the COPYRIGHT NOTICE portion of this License to include the exact text of the COPYRIGHT NOTICE of any Open Game Content You are copying, modifying or distributing, and You must add the title, the copyright date, and the copyright holder's name to the COPYRIGHT NOTICE of any original Open Game Content you Distribute.

7. Use of Product Identity: You agree not to Use any Product Identity, including as an indication as to compatibility, except as expressly licensed in another, independent Agreement with the owner of each element of that Product Identity. You agree not to indicate compatibility or co-adaptability with any Trademark or Registered Trademark in conjunction with a work containing Open Game Content except as expressly licensed in another, independent Agreement with the owner of such Trademark or Registered Trademark. The use of any Product Identity in Open Game Content does not constitute a challenge to the ownership of that Product Identity. The owner of any Product Identity used in Open Game Content shall retain all rights, title and interest in and to that Product Identity.

8. Identification: If you distribute Open Game Content You must clearly indicate which portions of the work that you are distributing are Open Game Content.

9. Updating the License: Wizards or its designated Agents may publish updated versions of this License. You may use any authorized version of this License to copy, modify and distribute any Open Game Content originally distributed under any version of this License.

10. Copy of this License: You MUST include a copy of this License with every copy of the Open Game Content You Distribute.

11. Use of Contributor Credits: You may not market or advertise the Open Game Content using the name of any Contributor unless You have written permission from the Contributor to do so.

12. Inability to Comply: If it is impossible for You to comply with any of the terms of this License with respect to some or all of the Open Game Content due to statute, judicial order, or governmental regulation then You may not Use any Open Game Material so affected.

13. Termination: This License will terminate automatically if You fail to comply with all terms herein and fail to cure such breach within 30 days of becoming aware of the breach. All sublicenses shall survive the termination of this License.

14. Reformation: If any provision of this License is held to be unenforceable, such provision shall be reformed only to the extent necessary to make it enforceable.

Made in the USA
Middletown, DE
17 February 2023

25078547R00239